THE LOST STEPS

ALEJO CARPENTIER (1904–1980) was one of the major Latin American writers of the twentieth century, as well as a classically trained pianist and musicologist. His best-known novels are *The Lost Steps*, *Explosion in a Cathedral*, and *The Kingdom of This World*. Born in Lausanne, Switzerland, and raised in Havana, Cuba, Carpentier lived for many years in France and Venezuela before returning to Cuba after the 1959 revolution. A few years later he returned to France, where he lived until his death.

ADRIAN NATHAN WEST has translated more than thirty books from Spanish, Catalan, and German, including Benjamin Labatut's *When We Cease to Understand the World*, a finalist for both the National Book Award for Translated Literature and the International Booker Prize. He is the author of *The Aesthetics of Degradation* and the novel *My Father's Diet*, and his essays and literary criticism have appeared in *The New York Review of Books*, *London Review of Books*, *The Times Literary Supplement*, and *The Baffler*. He lives in Philadelphia.

LEONARDO PADURA is the most internationally successful contemporary Cuban novelist, as well as a journalist and critic. His novels featuring the detective Mario Conde have been translated into many languages and have won literary prizes around the world. Padura lives in Havana.

ALEJO CARPENTIER

The Lost Steps

Translated by
ADRIAN NATHAN WEST

Introduction by
LEONARDO PADURA

PENGUIN BOOKS

PENGUIN BOOKS

An imprint of Penguin Random House LLC
penguinrandomhouse.com

The Lost Steps was originally published in Spanish as *Los pasos perdidos*
by E.D.I.A.P.S.A., Mexico City.

The introduction was originally published in Spanish as
"*Los pasos perdidos*: La gran batalla en la guerra del tiempo"
in *Los pasos perdidos* by Vintage Español, New York.

LIBRARY OF CONGRESS CATALOGING-IN-PUBLICATION DATA
Names: Carpentier, Alejo, 1904–1980, author. |
West, Adrian Nathan, translator. | Padura, Leonardo, writer of introduction.
Title: The lost steps / Alejo Carpentier ; translated by Adrian Nathan West ;
introduction by Leonardo Padura.
Other titles: Pasos perdidos. English
Description: New York : Penguin Books, 2023.
Identifiers: LCCN 2022057112 (print) | LCCN 2022057113 (ebook) |
ISBN 9780143133896 (paperback) | ISBN 9780525505686 (ebook)
Subjects: LCSH: Composers—Fiction. | South America—Fiction. | LCGFT: Novels.
Classification: LCC PQ7389.C263 P313 2023 (print) |
LCC PQ7389.C263 (ebook) | DDC 863/.64—dc23/eng/20230210
LC record available at https://lccn.loc.gov/2022057112
LC ebook record available at https://lccn.loc.gov/2022057113

Printed in the United States of America
1st Printing

Set in Sabon LT Pro

Contents

Introduction

The Great Battle in the War of Time

Once more, I've retraced my steps. I've made my way back to the familiar, and being forewarned, I do so with the confidence of the adept. And yet, no sooner have I begun my task than I question myself in a way I never did when I set forth on my several prior journeys down this path. I tread not like a discoverer, nor can I (nor should I) pretend to expertise, because, on this occasion, I am here to orient those from elsewhere, and more than to reveal, my mission is to guide. For this reason, on commencing, I have asked myself for what reason others would wish to trace and retrace this path, follow my footsteps, glimpse the marvelous, see what is known to me even if it remains forever mysterious and impossible to plumb.

In other words: I've asked myself why a reader of the twenty-first century, a user of social media, surely, a fanatic or fanatical repudiator of the cinema of Quentin Tarantino, an aloof consumer of "ephemeral" art (a real banana taped to a real wall, sold—just the banana—for $120,000 and immediately replaced by another banana that will be sold in turn), a devourer of Yuval Noah Harari's unsettling *21 Lessons for the 21st Century*, which speaks abundantly of artificial intelligence and future uncertainty . . . why this reader, I repeat, would be interested in reading a novel titled *The Lost Steps*, which speaks of possible voyages in real time (not virtual, not future) and was published in the for-many remote year of 1953. Why? What might one hope to get out of it?

In this—my ninth or tenth reading of this novel by Alejo Carpentier—convinced that I will still encounter new surprises, that its congenial story will take me in once more, I think of the values and qualities that transform great works of art into permanent revelations, polysemic, defined by their privileged resistance to the blows of time in a war that levels so many walls and pedestals, an unceasing chronological struggle that, in our day, a day of *influencers* who feign to possess "the truth," has taken on the proportions of a massacre at speeds so vertiginous they make obsolete by night what was the height of novelty in the morning.

Art entails a kind of knowledge that is undoubtedly transcendent in character. And yet art must be, *is*, something more. Aesthetic creation possesses the faculty of showing from within to humanity, as a universal entity beyond time, the reality that surrounds it, and of reflecting through it and within it the doubts, uncertainties, and even the revelations and learning that characterize us. Only in this way is it possible to make sense of the fact that today we read, and beyond that are moved by, the classics of the Greek tragedians (poor Oedipus, Prometheus forever bound), that the outrages of Lady Macbeth still horrify us, that the absurd adventures of Don Quixote provoke laughter and compassion in similar degrees. This is why George Orwell's *1984*, written in the middle of the foregoing century with reference to a future that is already past, remains so disturbing and revealing in our present place and time.

True art speaks of circumstance, but also of the eternal, being rooted in the investigation of the human condition, taking as its protagonist the immortal man (you, me, us) we have been and will be until we are replaced (or not) by those artificial intelligences that produce such dread in me. Its great mission, as Flaubert wrote, is no more and no less than to "reach the soul of things."

But let us make these affirmations a bit clearer. In the final pages of *The Lost Steps*, the narrator and protagonist of the novel, apprised of the enormity of the error that led him to take a decision, reflects:

You dwell in ignorance as you embark upon new roads, and do not recognize marvels as you live them: stepping out past the familiar, beyond what man has cordoned off, you grow vain in the privilege of discovery, and think yourself the owner of unknown paths, and you tell yourself you can repeat this feat whenever you wish. And one day, you are foolish enough to retrace your steps, thinking that the exceptional can be exceptional again, but when you return, you find the landscape changed, the reference points erased, the informants' faces different.

Written in 1953, in principle for the men and women of 1953, this reflection on the impossibility of reliving the exceptional, on the fleeting nature of the contingency or hazard ("concurrent chance," the writer José Lezama Lima called it) that flares up one time in our existence and is virtually never repeated, was valid for the generations that came before the characters of *The Lost Steps* and naturally remained so for those living at the time. In essence, the novel's hero has confronted the eternal drama of decision involved in the exercise of free will, the trial that free will as put into practice implies . . . The singular value of its artistry lies in the enduring pertinence of this conclusion of crossroads for those of us who read the novel today and might ourselves know or be forced to reckon with an ordeal that will take us down one of those "exceptional" paths that luck may (or may not) bring us and that force us to take a decision.

Alejo Carpentier wields two grand, universal, eternal principles in the conception and shaping of this, one of his finest works, which for many readers is the most alluring of his novels thanks to its plot, characters, uncertainties, and exotic locales. One is the real possibility of traveling through time and history, and the other, dramatically counterposed, is the simultaneous impossibility of avoiding the historical moment one has been shaped by and for. These seemingly contrary principles are valid for people in all places and times. They are a wellspring of art, and it is because of them that today it is possible to read and enjoy *The Lost Steps*, a novel published seventy years ago.

Alejo Carpentier (1904–1980), one of the foremost figures in twentieth-century Spanish American literature, focused in his work on the urgent need to define and delineate in literary and conceptual terms the singularities of the Latin American continent often subsumed by the explanations of it that emerged from the centrist gaze of a Europe anchored in the times of the "discovery of America" and the conquistadors.

A member of an intellectual generation born at the dawn of the twentieth century and preoccupied above all with the intricacies of identity and the need to cordon off, define, and reveal what belonged to them, Carpentier drew on the breakthroughs of the European avant-garde of the first decades of the past century, especially the experiments of Surrealism, which he took part in during his eleven years in France. He likewise possessed a comprehensive grasp of the history and culture of the Americas that allowed him to coin a sociohistorical, literary, and above all ontological theory he would first formulate in 1948 in the concept of "the American marvelous real."* As a theoretical proposal, Carpentier's idea was to distinguish and define in concrete terms a reality the singular expressions of which were extremely complex to capture and assimilate. A reality permeated even by manifestations of magic, but consistently presumed to emanate from a context in which certain temporal slippages, natural conditions and geographies, and ethnic and cultural confluences, viewed against the backdrop of devastating historical traumas, had produced a definite, multiple, and unique identity that expressed itself in myriad ways.

This principle, which was fed by firsthand experiences in certain regions of Latin America and expressed in theoretical articles and reportage, would find mature expression in the Cuban author's work with the noteworthy publication in 1949 of the novel *The Kingdom of This World*, set in Haiti in the run-up to and the aftermath of the revolution that gave the

---

* The article "On the Marvelous Real in America" was first published in 1948. An expanded version would become the famous prologue to the 1949 first edition of *The Kingdom of This World*.

country its independence. This would be followed by one of his masterpieces, *The Lost Steps*.

In these two novels, which represent the most orthodox expression in literary terms of his theory of "the marvelous real,"* Carpentier delves deeply into several of the obsessions that would pursue him throughout his career, presenting them as aspects of American reality that attain the level of the marvelous (or singular, or strange) as a result of the particular conditions and legacies that circumscribe their appearance and determine their development.

If Carpentier in *The Kingdom of This World* investigates the presence of magical performance in American reality through Black Haitians and their cosmology, seeking the causes of the revolution's failure and the consequent foundering of its social utopia, what sustains his narrative in *The Lost Steps* are Latin America's temporal discordances and the consequent possibility of traveling in time.

A Cuban composer, residing in a large Western capital, suffers all the burdens of alienation that his surroundings, his civilization, his era give rise to. When the opportunity presents itself to travel to a Latin American country on a mission to locate prehistoric musical instruments and explain their ancestral function, which predates all aesthetic intentions, this twentieth-century intellectual undertakes a geographical, cultural, physical, and sentimental journey across time that brings him to the very origins of humanity and music and even further, to the fourth day of the book of Genesis, to the biblical origins of creation. With this real journey through chronology inverted, he confronts an aspiration many have dreamed of: evading one's own time, overcoming one's era, and thereby escaping alienation and finding one's own human essence.

The emblems of this adventure begin to reveal themselves from the moment he arrives in the Latin American capital that

---

* I expand at length upon this subject in *Un camino de medio siglo: Alejo Carpentier y la narrativa de lo real maravilloso* (Havana: Editorial Letras Cubanas, 1994).

is the first stop on his voyage. For him, the city represents a return to belonging in terms of both physical realities (the architecture, the outbreak of revolution) and his memories and sensibility (flavors, scents, heat). From there, he proceeds to a provincial city where he finds himself returned to the years of nineteenth-century Romanticism, then further backward to the colonial era with his arrival in Santiago de los Aguinaldos, a village of rubber tappers and miners, before finally, on the threshold of the uncharted forest, reaching the days of the discovery of America, and even managing to glimpse the time that preceded it.

> Yesterday it had amused me to imagine us as Conquistadors searching for Manoa. But it baffles me now to recognize no difference exists between this Mass and the Masses heard in these climes by the Conquistadors of El Dorado. Time has stepped back four centuries . . . We are, perhaps, in the year 1540. A tempest lashed our ships, and now the monk is telling us in the language of Scripture how a great shifting of the seas battered the ship with waves; He was asleep, and when His disciples arrived they woke Him, saying: *Lord, save us, lest we perish*, and He said to them, *Why fear ye, ye of little faith?* and then He rose and restrained the wind and sea, and the weather turned clement and fine. It is, perhaps, the year 1540. But no. The years decrease, dilute, desist in the vertiginous process of time. We have not yet entered the sixteenth century. We are living long before. We are in the Middle Ages.

In the lost world of Grandes Mesetas, essentially unseen by Western man, where the Pathfinder has founded the city of Santa Mónica de los Venados, the temporal reversal extends to the Neolithic and Paleolithic eras. The narrator finds a sort of Arcadia or utopia in which the only social order that exists is the imperative to ensure survival, just as at civilization's origins. This is a time that precedes writing, and therefore history, where the hero seems to have found justification for his flight and paradise on earth.

All around me were people devoted to their vocations in the tranquil concert of the errands of a life subject to primordial rhythms. I had always seen the Indians through fantastical stories, as beings on the margins of man's true existence, but in their medium, their environment, they were absolute masters of their culture. Nothing was more alien to their reality than the absurd concept of the *savage*. The fact that they were unaware of things that for me were essential and necessary in no way relegated them to the primitive . . . Here there were no useless occupations, as mine had been for so many years.

Faithful to the author's patented method, each of the incidents and revelations the narrator and hero experience—this twentieth-century intellectual transported to an increasingly remote past—is noted down in the novel with geographic, natural, and historical precision. These necessary references validate the possibility that all historical time past, every culture that has developed, may converge on the Americas, making possible the realization of a marvelous reality the confirmation of which is expressed in the novel on the wealth of occasions when the narrator is "surprised," "impressed," "amazed," "astonished," "stunned." "I wondered," he remarks, "if the purpose of these lands in human history might not be to make possible, for the very first time, certain symbioses of culture," of civilizations and people who, for dozens of centuries, lived unconnected before finally creating in America a reality at once mestizo and absolutely unique.

Here, Carpentier hits on an essential point that manages to reveal America's singularities beyond the undoubtedly important geographical peculiarities that the novel nonetheless emphasizes. The marvelous, the bizarre, the extraordinary can manifest themselves only through contrast and comparison. In none of his other works—not even in his most celebrated and substantive novel, 1962's *Explosion in a Cathedral*, concerned with the failure of revolution and the perversion of the ideals of social utopia in a story that crisscrosses the Caribbean and Europe—does Carpentier so explicitly oppose a Latin American *here* to a European *there* as a method of validating his theoretical proposals regarding the singularities of the so-called New World.

In disclosing the mythical and extraordinary nature of this *here*, Carpentier utilizes comparisons themselves typical of the twentieth-century intellectual, but their implications, including their philosophical ones, go further.

Upon arriving in the almost feudal village of Santiago de los Aguinaldos, the narrator notes that "the sight of that ghostly city was more mysterious, more pregnant with marvels, than the finest inventions of the modern painters she esteemed most highly. The subjects of fantastic art were three-dimensional here," while characterizing the vanguardist art of his time as simple diversions of an imagination exhausted by the decadence and alienation that reign back *there*.

Later, in prehistoric Santa Mónica de los Venados, the city recently founded in the middle of the jungle, he adds: "'Gold,' the Pathfinder says, 'is for people who go back there.' And this *back there* echoes with contempt—as if the preoccupations and commitments of the people from *back there* were a mark of inferiority."

Shortly after undertaking his journey through geography and time, Carpentier's protagonist issues his verdict on the civilized world. The intellectual charged with the mission of traveling south is the inhabitant of a world freshly emerged from the barbarism of the final bloody years of World War II. Already he has tried to evade his time.

> Tired of . . . hearing talk of new exoduses, imminent terrors, of bodies piled in the streets, I took shelter, like a refugee, in the solace of shadowy museums, embarking on long journeys across time. But when I left the paintings behind me, things had gone from bad to worse. The papers were calling for beheadings. Believers shivered under the pulpits when the bishops screamed. Rabbis hid the Torah . . . At night, in public squares, the students of illustrious universities burned books on great bonfires.

And he concludes: "The age wearied me. And horribly, the imaginary was the only possible escape in that world without hiding places, its nature tamed for centuries."

Hence the enthusiasm he finds for the *here* of a world distant from the rites and horrors of his day, a society that—in line with thinkers like Oswald Spengler—he deems decadent. *Here* the universe is ebullient, the rare is quotidian, the marvelous is real, palpable. And it is here that he presumes to have found his utopia and the real possibility of escaping from his time.

By entering the world of civilization's origins in Santa Mónica de los Venados, the narrator seems to have found the keys to a possible, perhaps even practicable evasion. When he decides to stay *here*, to escape his time and space, his epoch, he begins to experience the marvelous. From that moment forward, the novel's subchapters, previously marked by precise dates, are no longer so distinguished. The hero has entered into unmeasured time. He has distanced himself from the age of the motor, crossing long centuries of navigation to arrive in the Lands of the Horse, the Lands of the Dog, and the virgin Lands of the Bird. There he has found, to his great intellectual profit, evidence of the magical origin of music and physical plenitude, potency, the highest degree of freedom and humanity. Even love. What else can one aspire to?

Nonetheless, even there, he is obsessed by the need to fulfill his mission of bringing back those instruments he was sent to the jungle to collect (he will find a solution to this problem) as well as by the idea of confirming his thesis about the origin of the practices that would evolve toward the birth of musical art (he will learn to live without this). Then, like a call from the most uncorruptible part of his conscience, the notion of composing a threnody (a funeral song that conforms perfectly to the origin of music he believes he has discovered) strikes him, and he can think of nothing better than a piece inspired by Shelley's *Prometheus Unbound*, because "the chained god's liberation, which I associate with my escape from *back there*, implies resurrection, return from the shadows, and responds to the original conception of the threnody, a magical chant intended to bring the dead back to life." And he commits himself to the deed only to discover that "it exasperates me, this evidence of an unconscious desire *to see my work performed*" in the world *back there*.

The hero's social and moral atavism reveals itself most consummately in the judgment of the leper Nicasio, who has committed a blood offense. With the rifle that justice demands in his hands, he recognizes that "inwardly, I resisted, as if once I pulled the trigger, *something would change forever*. There are acts that raise walls, milestones, boundaries in an existence. And I feared what time would be for me the second after I became Executioner."

The man transplanted in time, who has almost everything, who nonetheless hesitates at certain ethical limits, also requires certain things from his time, essentials for his profession—his calling, his need, which is inalienable. He needs books, he needs paper. And suddenly there appears in the sky of Santa Mónica de los Venados an airplane sent to rescue him.

All at once, the "150,000 years" that separate "the Indian Chief . . . hand clutching his bow" and "the flying machine" have vanished. What returns to him with the airplane is his era. He knows that just three hours' flight time separates Santa Mónica de los Venados from the capital: "the fifty-eight centuries between the fourth book of Genesis and the current year *back there* are traversable in 180 minutes, and with that, one can return to the era some identify with the present—as if here, one weren't also in the *present*—traveling past cities from the Middle Ages, the Conquests, the Colonial and Romantic periods, that survive to this day."

And the moment to take a decision, to exercise his will, arrives.

The man of the twentieth century decides to return, thinking he won't be gone long. His profession demands it, and he cannot avoid it. In his time is everything he needs to fulfill his mission in the kingdom of this world. "I've managed to do without all that I once thought essential . . . But paper and ink I cannot do without: the things expressed or begging to be expressed with paper and ink."

   In the sixth and last chapter of the novel, the dates reappear.
The hero returns to the big city, to his time, and everything
falls to pieces. He is back in the world where people live in fear
("Fear of some reprimand, fear of the hour . . ."). It is also the
world of the Apocalypse ("Everything foretells it: the covers
of the magazines in the shop windows, the titles, the letters over
the cornices, the phrases shot up into space"). He is trapped by
the city, its time and its laws, which he wants to escape but
can't, the same way so many in this age, our age, can't . . . And
yet, he does manage to break away to attempt to recover the
abandoned earthly paradise, retracing his own steps.

> Here, a more pressing question arises as regards my wanderings
> through the Kingdom of this World—the only question, in the
> end, that admits no dilemmas: whether I or others will be the
> master of my time, whether I am prepared to live rather than
> row alongside the galley slaves. So long as my eyes are open, my
> hours are mine in Santa Mónica de los Venados. My steps are
> mine, and I shall leave them where I choose.

And here, the theme of the work, the motif that makes eternally contemporary this novel from the 1950s, overtakes him.
He has made his decision, and he understands, as we've already quoted, that:

> One day, you are foolish enough to retrace your steps, thinking
> that the exceptional can be exceptional again, but when you re-
> turn, you find the landscape changed, the reference points
> erased, the informants' faces different.

The road back to the ideal world outside time has closed; for
the hero, it is closed forever, and he will realize it. As the novelist hints at one point, the vacation of Sisyphus is over and he
must go back to pushing the rock that defines him. His grand
decision has led him into error. Or was it always futile, the pretense that one could sidestep one's human and historical time?
The war of time knows no truces. It is constant, eternal combat,
revocable, perhaps, for a while, but ultimately invulnerable to

human resistance. To the people of yesterday and those of today. Perhaps even to those of tomorrow.

It is of those battles and of our decisions in the midst of a world both marvelous and real that this beautiful and stirring novel speaks, this book of voyages through space and time, which Carpentier wrote in 1953 and which has been celebrated and canonized ever since. And with that, I leave it in your hands.

LEONARDO PADURA
Translated by Adrian Nathan West

A Note on the Translation

Translations shouldn't be confused with their source texts: the criteria of a translation's success are not the same as those of an original, and there are questions that occur to readers, and particularly scholars, to which only the original can provide answers. There's a famous, probably too-good-to-be-true, but still-illustrative story about a lecture by George Steiner on the use of the definite article in Dostoevsky, in which a student points out to him that the Russian language doesn't employ definite articles. If you want to dive deep into questions about the bones of a text, its points of intersection with other works by the same author, or its place in a given literary tradition, you need to look at the original.

Retranslations—of which the present book is one—have numerous justifications. Sometimes the old version is too fusty, as many (though not I) feel about Constance Garnett's versions of the nineteenth-century Russians. Sometimes it's just bad: I have read a translation of a poem by Peter Handke in which Bayreuth was replaced with Beirut—it's probably best to go back to the drawing board on that one. But the usual thing is that readers' tastes and demands evolve. For a long time, the names of fictional characters and even historical figures were changed to accommodate the target language (my Spanish father-in-law has several books in his library by a certain Carlos Marx). Nowadays, there is more of a call for fidelity, even if no one can agree on what fidelity is or whether it's possible. For this reason, many books translated in the twentieth century, when it was felt the foreign needed to be eased for readers and approachability was favored over particularity, are now appearing in new versions. Such is the case for *The Lost Steps.*

Harriet de Onís first translated *The Lost Steps* into English in 1956. As an editorial adviser to Alfred A. Knopf, she was responsible not only for bringing a significant number of Latin American writers into English in the years before the so-called Boom, but also for helping spread awareness of the region through her translations of historical and sociological works. At the time, Latin American literature was already abundant, but not well known abroad, even among the well-read, and granting it a foothold in the English-speaking world must have taken priority over presenting readers with a faithful view of writers' idiosyncrasies.

The dilemmas that Spanish confronted Onís with would have been particularly acute with regard to Carpentier, whose style at times is baroque to the point of impenetrability. Had every distended metaphor, every obscure word been respected, the original translation of *The Lost Steps* would doubtless have proved a critical and commercial failure. Onís thus chose to ease matters for readers, in her way. Long paragraphs and long sentences are broken up; difficult passages are sometimes smoothed out; and the tone is jauntier and more welcoming than in the original. This isn't a criticism: Onís was a talented writer, capable of turning out beautiful phrases with ease, and her ability to decipher the more cryptic parts of the text half a century before Google is deeply to be admired.

Still, tastes have changed, and there is a greater tolerance now than before for difference, as well as a greater desire on the part of readers to know how writers distinguish themselves stylistically, at the level of paragraph, sentence, and word. In this translation, I've tried to present readers with a Carpentier who is more Carpentier than the one they might have encountered before. I have left intact the ornateness of his vocabulary, have sought, when reasonable, not to dismember his complex sentences, with their long chains of subordinate clauses, and have respected the text's original layout. In a broader sense, I've tried to restore the book's lushness, and approximate its narrator's ecstatic, abstruse lyricism.

This approach has its limits, limits that perhaps have more to do with irreducible differences between literary Spanish and English than with Carpentier's style per se. I recall attending a conference once in Sweden and hearing a speaker, a German, refer to "close reading in the Anglo-American sense." It sounded odd to me at the time, but having translated, conservatively, thirty or forty thousand pages of Spanish prose, including tourist brochures, business proposals, contracts, self-help books, and hundreds of chapters of books, I must conclude that in general—in general!—the criteria for good English prose that many of us picked up in high school (no superfluous words, no excessive adverbs, clarity, "show don't tell," and suchlike proscriptions) simply do not have an analogue in Spanish, and an insistence upon them can seem parochial when not impertinent. Even today, after nearly a decade in Spain, I notice this when I write emails: what my American brain produces instinctively feels skeletal and gruff, and demands a bit of stuffing, some expansiveness, not to come across as off-putting. In the same way, high style in Spanish, rendered word for word in English, can feel like an exercise in obfuscating substance beneath digression. And so, when translating a writer from Spanish, literality can mean betrayal. What you have to ask yourself is what the effects of a given book are in the minds of those approaching it in the original, and figure out how to reproduce them in the minds of those accustomed to reading in your language.

A trifling but not irrelevant example is the word *very*, which more than one guide to good writing has recommended expunging from the English language. Its Spanish equivalent, *muy*, appears as many as five times per page in Carpentier's novel. In part, this can be chalked up to the copious selection of adjectives and adverbs in English, with distinctions between them so fine that a word like *very* is rarely necessary, but in part, it has to do with the rhythm of reading in the different languages; in English, we snag on words like *very*, and if they appear in excess, they derail us. In Spanish, we more or less glide past words like *muy*, as it should be, and a text completely lacking in them can give the feeling of driving on a bumpy road.

An exasperated editor asked me once, with reference to

another Cuban novelist, "Why is he constantly telling us when somebody isn't talking?" There probably is no real answer, but it's a fixture of writing in Spanish in general to mark silences, whereas in English we must take for granted that if a character isn't speaking, she is keeping silent. I would argue that servility to such peculiarities of a language is often the opposite of fidelity, and with those I've mentioned, and many others I haven't, I've attempted in this translation to follow Michael Hofmann's advice of trying to do the kinds of things the author does in the original while working at the same time to produce a version of Carpentier's prose that is credible and, I hope, at times beautiful.

ADRIAN NATHAN WEST

The Lost Steps

CHAPTER ONE

And thy heaven that is over thy head shall be
brass, and the earth that is under thee shall
be iron. . . . And thou shalt grope at noon-
day, as the blind gropeth in darkness.

DEUTERONOMY 28: 23–29

I

It had been four years and seven months since I'd seen the house
with the white columns, its facade with the scowling pediments
that gave it a severe appearance like a courthouse, and now,
standing before the never-shifting furnishings and rubbish, I
had the almost mournful sensation that time had turned backward. Near the lantern, the curtain the color of wine; where the
rosebush climbed, the empty cage. Some way off were the elms
I had helped to plant in those early enthusiastic days when each
did his part in our common enterprise; next to a scaly tree
trunk, the stone bench that gave off a wooden echo when I
kicked it. In the back, the river path with its dwarf magnolias
and the fence with its scribbly filigree, done in the New Orleans
style. I walked beneath the portico, as I had my first night there,
hearing that same hollow resonance beneath my steps, then
crossed the yard to sooner reach the place they were moving in
groups: slaves scarred by branding irons, horsewomen with
skirts drawn up and draped over their arms, and wounded soldiers in rags, badly bandaged, all waiting their turn in shadows
stinking of mastic, old felt, sweat seeping into frock coats already redolent of the sweat of before. After a time, I stepped
into the light, when the hunter fired his shot and a bird fell onto
the stage from the drapes. My wife's crinoline flew past my
head, as I was standing right where she was meant to enter,
crowding the already narrow passage. To keep from bothering,

I went to her dressing room, where time and date once more converged, and the objects there made evident that four years and seven months could not pass without breakage, taint, degeneration. The laces for the finale were grayish; the black satin of the dance scenes had lost the pleasant suppleness that made it rustle like a whirl of dry leaves at every curtsey. Even the walls had wilted, always touched in the same places, bearing traces of a long acquaintance with makeup, haggard flowers, with disguises. Taking a seat on the divan, which had faded from sea green to moss green, I fretted at how bitter this prison of stage timbers, flying bridges, ropy webs, and fake trees had become for Ruth. When this Civil War tragedy had just debuted, and we were helping the young playwright with his company, which had just quit an experimental theater, we imagined this folly might last twenty nights at most. Now we were just shy of fifteen hundred performances, and the actors, tied down by contracts that could be extended indefinitely, were no longer able to pull out; what had once been an altruistic, juvenile exercise was now big business, part of a professional portfolio. And for Ruth this theater, far from an escape hatch—an open door to the vast world of Drama—had become a Devil's Island. The occasional brief hiatus under Portia's wig or Iphigenia's toga was permitted as a charitable contribution in kind, but brought scant relief to Ruth, as the spectators sought the same crinoline beneath these novel costumes, and when she tried to channel Antigone through her voice, what they heard were the contralto inflections of the Arabella now onstage, being taught by a certain Booth—in a scene the critics held to be tremendously intelligent—the correct pronunciation of Latin through repetitions of the phrase *Sic semper tyrannis*. She'd have needed a peerless tragedienne's genius to rid herself of that parasite that had taken up residence in her bloodstream, that guest in her body that clung to her flesh like an interminable illness. She was more than happy to break her contract. But rebellion had a price in this profession, namely long periods without work, and Ruth, who first uttered these lines at thirty years of age, found herself entering thirty-five repeating the same gestures, the same words, every weeknight and every afternoon on Sundays, Saturdays, and holidays—apart from the summer performances, when they went on tour. The play's success annihilated the actors bit by bit; they were aging before the public's eyes in their immutable attire, and when one of them had died of a heart attack one evening, not long after the curtain fell, the company had gathered the next morning in the cemetery, flaunting their mourning clothes, perhaps without realizing it, the way people used to do in daguerreotypes. Growing rancorous, losing faith that she might make a proper career of this art she loved deeply despite herself, my wife let the automatism of the job assigned to her bear her along, and I, too, was borne along by the automatism of my profession. There had been a time when she'd tried to stay hopeful, cataloging the great roles she aspired one day to play: Norah, Judith, Medea, Tessa, each promising renewal; but the sorrow of monologues uttered before the mirror eventually snuffed out the feeling of anticipation. Finding no normal way to make our lives coincide—an actress doesn't keep regular hours—we ended up sleeping apart. On Sundays, in late morning, I'd spend a bit of time in her bed, performing what I took to be my marital duty, but unsure whether my actions responded to any real desire on Ruth's part. She, in turn, may have supposed this weekly physical procedure was an obligation incurred by placing her signature at the foot of our marriage contract. What drove me to it was the notion that it wasn't right for me to ignore an urge I might be able to satisfy, thereby quieting, for a week, certain scruples of conscience. At any rate, that embrace, though it grew increasingly insipid, tightened the bonds weakened by the decoupling of our activities. Bodily heat reestablished an intimacy that was like a brief return to the early days of home. We watered the geranium forgotten since last Sunday; we moved a painting; we dealt with the household expenses. But soon a carillon of bells close by reminded us that the hour of captivity was near. And when I left my wife onstage at the start of the afternoon function, I had the impression of returning her to a prison where she was meant to serve a life sentence. The shot rang out, the fake bird fell from the second of three drop curtains, and with that, the Seventh-Day Intimacy was ended.

Today, though, the Sunday rule was broken, and the fault lay with the tranquilizer swallowed at the crack of dawn to fall asleep quickly—because covering my eyes with the black bandage Mouche had recommended no longer worked. When I woke, my wife was gone, and the disordered clothing half torn from the chest of drawers, the tubes of theater makeup thrown in the corners, the powder boxes and perfume bottles left all around suggested an unforeseen voyage. Ruth stepped back offstage, followed by a roar of applause, and quickly opened the clasps of her bodice. She kicked the door shut as she had so many times, the print of her heel was worn into the wood, and when she pulled off her hoop skirt over her head, it flared across the carpet from one wall to the other. Her lace garments stripped off, her body was bright and new and pleasing, and I was readying to caress her nudity when velvet was drawn over it, smelling of the fabric swatches my mother kept when I was a child in the very back of her mahogany wardrobe. I had a sudden hatred for her stupid profession and pretense that came between us like the angel's sword of the hagiographies; for the theater, which had divided our house, casting me out into another—one with walls adorned with star charts—where my desire found a spirit always ready to embrace. And because I had looked kindly on that career's unlucky beginnings, because I'd wished to see the woman I loved so much happy, my destiny had turned astray, and I'd sought material security in a job that kept me no less a prisoner than she! Now, her back turned, Ruth spoke to me in the mirror, smirching her unquiet face with the greasy colors of her makeup: she told me once the performance was over, the company was setting off on tour, and would leave immediately for the country's other coast. That was why she'd brought her suitcases with her to the theater. She asked me vaguely about last night's film. I was going to tell her it had been a success, to remind her my vacation was beginning now that it was done, but then a knock came at the door. Ruth stood, and I found myself faced with someone who ceased again to be my wife in order to become the protagonist of a play; she slipped an artificial rose into her waistband, excused herself softly, and walked toward the stage, where the Italianate curtain had just opened, shifting an air redolent of dust and old wood. She looked back at me, waving goodbye, and set off on the path of the dwarf magnolias . . . I didn't feel like waiting for the intermission, when the velvet would be switched out for satin, and new makeup spread thickly over old. I went home, where the disorder of a hasty departure was palpable, like the presence of her absence. The weight of her head was still molded in the pillow; a glass of water stood half drunk on the nightstand, with a precipitate of green droplets and a book opened to a chapter's end. My hand found a spot of spilled lotion, still damp. A sheet from a datebook, which I'd overlooked when I entered, informed me of the unannounced trip: *Love, Ruth. P.S.: There's a bottle of sherry on the desk.* I felt terribly abandoned. It was the first time in eleven months that I found myself alone, other than when I slept, with nothing pressing to do, nowhere to run to, frantic, not wanting to show up late. I was far from the madness and confusion of the studios, in a silence neither mechanical music nor voices piped through speakers interrupted. Nothing plagued me, and for that very reason I felt myself subject to a nebulous menace. In this room deserted by the person whose perfume still lingered, I rankled at the possibility of dialogue with myself. I was surprised to find myself talking to myself in hushed tones. Lying back again, looking at the smooth ceiling, I replayed the past few years, saw them run from autumn to Easter, from cold winds to soft asphalt, without having the time to live them—marking their passage by the restaurants' offerings in the evening: the return of wild duck, the opening of oyster season, or the reappearance of chestnuts on the menu. At other times, I was informed of the passing of the seasons by the red paper bells unveiled in shop windows, or the arrival of trucks loaded with pines whose perfume left the street transfigured for a few seconds. In the chronicle of my existence, there were voids of weeks and weeks; seasons that left me without a single valid recollection, the impress of some strange sensation or lasting feeling; days when with every gesture, I was obsessed by the thought that I'd already made it in identical circumstances—that I'd sat in the same corner, told the same story, looking at the sailboat imprisoned in a glass paperweight. Celebrating my birthday amid the same faces, in the same places, with the same song repeated in chorus, the idea assailed me that the lone difference from its predecessor was the appearance of another candle on the cake whose flavor was identical to the one before. Ascending and descending the hill of days, with the same stone on my shoulder, I was sustained by momentum, the product of fits and starts—and sooner or later, this momentum would give out, on a day that might fall even this year. In the world I'd been born into, trying to evade this fate was as pointless as trying to relive the deeds of heroes and saints of yore. We had sunken to the era of the Wasp Man, the Nobody Man, with souls sold not to the Devil, but to the Bookkeeper or the Slave Driver. Realizing it was vain to rebel, after an uprootedness that had forced me to live two adolescences—one on the other end of the sea and one here—I saw no freedom apart from my disordered nights, when anything was a pretext for endlessly repeated excesses. The Accountant had bought my daytime soul—I thought, detesting myself—but the Accountant had no notion that at night I undertook strange voyages through the meanders of a city he couldn't see, a city within the city, with abodes where you could forget the day, like the *Venusberg* and the House of Constellations, unless a vicious craving, fired by liquor, took me to those covert apartments where your last name is forgotten upon entering. Chained to technology, amid clocks, chronographs, metronomes, in windowless rooms lined with felt and insulation, surrounded by artifice, every evening instinct drove me to the street after sundown in search of those pleasures that made me forget the passing hours. I drank and I idled with my back turned to the clocks, until drink and idleness threw me at the feet of an alarm clock in a stupor I tried to deepen by placing a black mask over my eyes, giving my sleeping self the air of a Fantômas in repose . . . This churlish image put me in a good mood. I drank a tall glass of sherry, resolved to put a stop to this surfeit of reflections in my cranium, and with the alcohol of the night before stoked by the wine of the present one, I peeked out Ruth's bedroom window, and by then her perfume had begun to disintegrate into the lingering aroma of acetone. After the grays glimpsed on waking, the summer had arrived, announced by the horns of ships answering each other across the buildings between two rivers. Above were the summits of the city, amid the warm, evanescent mist: the dull needles of the Christian temples, the cupola of the Orthodox church, the big clinics where White Eminences held court beneath entablatures too classical, too ungainly in the heights, made by architects from the beginning of the century who had lost their judgment in thrall to verticality. Solid and silent, the funeral home with its infinite corridors seemed a replica in gray of the immense maternity hospital a synagogue and concert hall away whose facade, stripped of all ornamentation, had a row of uniform windows I liked to count from my wife's bed when we ran out of things to talk about on Sundays. From the asphalt of the streets rose a bluish swelter of gasoline, cut through with chemical vapors, that lingered in courtyards with their stench of rotting food, where a panting dog stretched out like a flayed rabbit searching for cool patches on the hot ground. The carillon hammered an Ave Maria. Strangely, I was curious to know what saint was being praised today: *June 4. Saint Francis Caracciolo*, said the Vatican-issued volume in which I used to study the Gregorian chants. The name meant nothing to me. I looked for the volume of the lives of the saints, printed in Madrid, which my mother had read to me often in the bliss of those minor sick spells that had kept me out of school. It made no mention of Francis Caracciolo. But still, I glanced at a few pages with pious headings: *Rose receives visits from Heaven. Rose wrestles with the Devil. The miracle of the sweating portrait.* And at a festooned border interwoven with Latin phrases: *Sanctae Rosae Limanae, Virginis. Patronae principalis totius Americae Latinae.* And at these versicles of the saint, passionately addressed to her Husband:

> *Alas! Who causes*
> *My beloved thus to tarry?*
> *He is late, midday looms,*
> *And yet he hasn't come.*

A bitter ache swelled my throat as I remembered, in the language of my youth, too many things all at once. There was no denying it—my time off was making me soft. I drank what was left of the sherry and looked out the window again. The children playing beneath the dusty firs in Model Park left behind their castles of gray sand to gawk at the rascals in the municipal fountain swimming among shreds of newspaper and cigarette butts. This made me think of going to the pool for a bit of exercise. I shouldn't stay home just with myself. Looking in the closet for a swimsuit, which I didn't manage to find, I thought it might be wiser to take a train to some wooded area where I could breathe the clean air. And I was already walking to the rail station when I stopped in front of the Museum where a large exhibition of abstract art was opening, announced by mobiles hanging from poles whose wooden mushrooms, stars, and loops twisted in the varnish-scented air. I was about to climb the stairs when I saw the bus to the Planetarium stopping close by, and I thought a visit would be just the thing to give me ideas for Mouche, who was redecorating her studio. But the bus just wouldn't leave, so I wound up walking like an idiot, dazzled by all the prospects, stopping at the first corner to examine the drawings a cripple with many military medals pinned to his chest was tracing on the sidewalk in colored chalk. The mad rhythm of my days was broken, I was free for three weeks from the business that fed me in exchange for several years of my life, and I didn't know what to do with my leisure. I was as though sickened by sudden rest, bewildered on familiar streets, wavering in the face of desires that wouldn't take shape as desires. I was tempted to buy the *Odyssey*, or the latest crime novels, or the American Comedies of Lope de Vega advertised in the window at Brentano's, to be intimate again with Spanish, a language I never used, though it was the only one I could multiply in and I used the phrase *llevo tanto* to add. But *Prometheus Unbound* was there, too, and it pulled me away from the other books, its title evocative of an old project for a composition that, after a prelude ending in a grand chorus of brass, had made it no further than the sovereign cry of rebellion in the initial recitative: *Regard this Earth / made multitudinous with thy slaves, whom thou / requitest for knee-worship, prayer, and praise, / and toil, and hecatombs of broken hearts, / with fear and self-contempt and barren hope.* The shops called to me too loudly after months when I'd neglected them. Here there was a map of islands circled by galleons and wind roses; there, a treatise on oceanography; farther away, a portrait of Ruth in an advertisement for a jeweler, gleaming in borrowed diamonds. I was irate when I remembered her departure; it was she I was pursuing in that moment, the one person I wished to have at my side on this suffocating, hazy afternoon, the sky of which was turning gloomy behind the monotonous shivers of the first neon signs to light up. But once more, a text, a stage, a distance had come between our bodies, which no longer found on their Seventh-Day Intimacy the joy of their early couplings. It was too early to go to Mouche's. Weary of cutting a path between all those people walking the wrong way, tearing silver wrappers or digging their fingers into orange peels, I wanted to go where there were trees. And soon I got free of the people on their way back from the stadiums, gesturing in the midst of discussions, mimicking the movements of the athletes, and just then, a few cold droplets fell on the back of my hand. After a time I wouldn't quite know how to measure—failing to grasp the brevity in which this process of dilations and recurrences might take place—I remember the sensation of those drops touching my skin had something exquisite about it, like the prick of needles: the first, and for me unintelligible forewarning of an encounter—a trivial encounter, in a way, in the nature of those encounters that only reveal their true import later, in the weft of their implications . . . We must search for where it all started in the cloud that burst into rain that afternoon with a violence so unexpected that its thunder seemed the thunder of other latitudes.

2

The cloud began pouring rain as I was walking behind the great concert hall on a long sidewalk that offered the pedestrian no cover whatsoever. I remembered an iron stairway led to the musicians' entrance, and as some of those going in just then were acquaintances of mine, I had no trouble reaching the stage, where the members of a famous choir were grouping by voice parts before mounting the risers. A kettledrummer rapped his fingers on the skins, which were pitched high on account of the heat. With a violin beneath his chin, the conductor told a pianist to play *la* while the French horns, bassoons, and clarinets blew a mingled fervor of scales and trills, tuning up, until the notes coalesced. Seeing the instruments of a symphony lined up behind music stands, I felt, as always, an acute anticipation of that instant when the noise would shed its disorder to be framed, organized, bent to a human will that had preceded it and was embodied now in the gestures of a Mediator of Passing Time who in turn was subject to canons put in place a century, two centuries ago. Printed in signs between the covers of the partiturs were mandates of men deceased, laid in florid mausoleums if their bones hadn't gone missing in the sordid disorder of a common grave, but who nevertheless retained proprietorship of time, and could impose lapses of attention or fits of zeal upon men of the future. I thought how at times those postmortem powers suffered diminution, or grew, in accordance with the demands of generations. Taking account of the performances of a given year, you might prove that in a certain period, Bach or Wagner had been the greatest consumer of time, while Telemann or Cherubini had lagged behind. It had been at least three years since I'd visited the symphony; when I left the studios, gorged with bad music, or good music put to contemptible ends, it felt pointless to then set foot into a time made a sort of object by its surrender to the strains of the fugue or the sonata. And so I found an unaccustomed pleasure, a surprise, almost, in being there in a dark corner beside the double basses, which gave a view of the stage on that rainy afternoon, its tranquil thunder rumbling over the puddles in the nearby road. And after a silence cut through by a gesture, a light fifth blew from the horns, exalted into triplets by the second violins and cellos, and two descending notes overwhelmed it, plummeting in a way from the first line of strings and the violas with a reluctance turned to anguish, quavering at the horror of a suddenly unchained force . . . I stood up with disgust. After forgoing music so long, and finally recovering the desire to listen to it, *this* had to appear, this thing swelling in a crescendo at my back. I should have known when I saw the choir take the stage. But I'd thought it might be a classical oratory. Had I known the Ninth Symphony was the score in the stands, I would have happily stayed outside under the downpour. If I scorned all that music bound up with the memory of the infirmities of my youth, even less could I tolerate *Freude, schöner Götterfunken, Tochter aus Elysium*! I had avoided it since *then* like a person who spends years averting his eyes from certain objects evocative of a death. Besides, like many men of my generation, I hated everything that smacked of the *sublime*. Schiller's "Ode" was as abhorrent to me as the Supper at Montsalvat and the Elevation of the Graal . . . Now I'm back outside looking for a bar. If I walk too long to find a glass of liquor, that long-familiar depression will invade me, making me feel like a prisoner with no exit in sight, despairing at my inability to change one single thing about my existence, overruled by the will of others who barely leave me the freedom to choose which meat or grain I will have for breakfast each morning. I start running as the rain falls harder. Turning the corner, I careen into an open umbrella: the wind strips it from its owner's hand and the wheels of a car crush it, so absurdly that I let fly a cackle. Instead of the insult I expect in reply, a cordial voice calls me by name: "I was looking for you," it says, "but I've lost your address." And the Curator, whom I haven't seen in more than two years, tells me he has a gift for me—an extraordinary gift—in that old house from the turn of the century with the dirty windows and the gravel beds that stick out like an anachronism in his neighborhood.

   The springs of the not quite entirely sunken armchair eat into my flesh like the bristles of a hair shirt, forcing me to feign an aplomb that is the furthest thing from my nature. I see myself stiff as a child on a family visit in the glass of the old mirror in its thick rococo frame, enclosed by the Esterházy family crest. Complaining of his asthma, the Curator of the

Organographical Museum snuffs out a tobacco cigarette that
makes him wheeze and lights another, rolled with jimson-
weed, that makes him cough; taking short steps through a little room packed with cymbals and Asian tambourines, he
prepares cups of tea, thankfully accompanied by Martinican
rum. An Incan flute hangs between two shelves; on the work
table, not yet cataloged, lies a sackbut from the Conquest of
Mexico, a highly precious instrument, its bell an ornamented
serpent's head with silvery scales and enamel eyes, with open
jaws that reveal two rows of copper teeth. "That belonged to
Juan de San Pedro, a trumpeter in Charles the Fifth's court and
one of Hernán Cortés's most famous cavalrymen," the Curator
tells me, tasting the tea to see if it's properly steeped. Then he
pours the liquor in the cups with the excuse—comical, if he'd
stopped to think of his listener—that the body demands a little
alcohol now and again, for atavistic reasons, as man in all ages
and latitudes has never failed to procure for himself some intoxicating beverage. When he informs me my gift isn't here, on
the ground floor, but wherever it is, his deaf servant is shuffling
around in search of it, I glance at my watch, ready to feign distress at some unavoidable commitment. It has stopped at three
twenty, and I remember I didn't wind it last night, imagining
in that way I might get used to the idea that my vacation was
beginning. In a frantic voice, I ask the time, but he tells me it
doesn't matter; that the rain has already darkened this June
afternoon, one of the longest of the year. Taking me from a
"Pange Lingua" of the monks of Saint Gall to the editio prin-
ceps of a cipher for vihuela by way of a rare printing of Saint
John Damascene's *Octoechos*, the Curator tries to quell my
impatience, which has turned now to exasperation since I've
let myself be dragged to another floor, where there is nothing
for me to do amid the endless Jew's harps, rebecs, dulzainas,
loose tuning pegs, splinted violin necks, and barrel organs
with burst bellows scattered in dark corners. I am about to ap-
prise him, in an acid tone, that I'll return for my gift another
day when the servant comes back in, taking off her rubber
boots. She hands me an unlabeled, half-cut record, which the
Curator lays on a gramophone, carefully choosing a soft-tone

needle. At least, I think, the nuisance will be brief: two minutes or so, to judge by the breadth of the grooves. I turn to refill my glass when I hear a bird chirping behind me. I look at the old man with surprise, and he smiles with a gently paternal air, as if he had just given me a priceless gift. I want to ask him something, but he bids me be silent, pointing with an index finger at the spinning disc. Something else must be coming. But no. It's not even especially musical, this birdsong; there's no trill, no glissando, just three notes repeated over and over, their timbre no more sonorous than Morse code tapped out in a telegraphist's cabin. As the record nears its end, I am left to wonder where this gift my erstwhile teacher touted is to be found, and asking myself what relevance this document, which could only interest an ornithologist—if at all—might have for me. The absurd performance ends, and the Curator, transfigured by inexplicable delight, asks me, "Don't you get it? Don't you get it?" Then he declares the chirping comes not from a bird, but from a baked clay instrument the most primitive Indians on the continent use in order to mimic the sound of a bird before hunting it, taking ritual possession of its voice to make their hunt propitious. "It's the first confirmation of your theory," the old man says, nearly embracing me amid a fit of coughing. Seeing his intentions all too clearly, I am invaded, as the record plays a second time, by a growing irritation that my two drinks, gulped down quickly, only inflame. The bird that isn't a bird, its song that is a magical parody and not a song, reverberates unbearably in my chest, reminding me of my writings from so long ago—it wasn't the years that alarmed me, but the pointless haste of their passing—about the origins of music and primitive organography. That was back when the war had interrupted the composition of my ambitious cantata, *Prometheus Unbound.* When I returned, I *felt* so different that I left the finished prelude and the scripts for the opening scene boxed up in an armoire, and drifted off into the techniques and stopgaps of cinema and radio. Defending this century's arts with contrived passion, swearing that they opened up infinite possibilities for composers, I must have been seeking relief from the complex sense of guilt I felt at abandoning my work, and a justification for my participation in a commercial enterprise after Ruth and I had run away and destroyed the life of a perfectly good man. At the end of our period of amorous anarchy, I quickly grew convinced that my wife's vocation was incompatible with life together as I yearned for it. For the same reason, I tried to make her absences less unpleasant, looking for a task that could be undertaken on Sundays and holidays, without the continuity of purpose that artistic creation demanded. And so I began visiting the home of the Curator, whose Organographic Museum was the pride of a venerable university. Under this same roof, I gained knowledge of elementary percussion instruments, hollowed trunks, lithophones, animal jawbones, bull-roarers, and ankle rattlers that man had used to make sound in the long days of his emergence on a planet still teeming with gigantic skeletons, setting out on a road that would end in the *Missa Papae Marcelli* and *The Art of the Fugue.* Driven by that peculiar form of sloth that consists of vigorous devotion to tasks that are not precisely befitting, I grew passionate about classification methods and the morphological study of those pieces wrought in wood, baked clay, copper plate, hollow cane, gut, and goatskin—the mothers of sound-making techniques that endure across millennia in the rich varnishes of Cremona craftsmen or in the sumptuous theological piping of organs. At odds with accepted opinion about the origins of music, I had arrived at a clever theory that explained the birth of early rhythmical expression as the desire to imitate the stomping of animals or the chanting of birds. As hunting magic underlay the first images of reindeer and bison painted on the walls of caverns—dominating one's prey by taking ownership of its image—it wasn't so wrong for me to assume the elementary rhythms were those of trotting, galloping, leaping, chirping, and trilling, sought out by the hand on a resonant body or by the breath in the hollows of a reed.

Now the spinning record incensed me, as I realized my clever—perhaps even true—theory had been relegated, like so much, to an attic of dreams that this era with its workaday tyrannies would never allow me to fulfill. A hand raises the diaphragm from the groove. The clay bird stops singing. And the thing I feared most happens: the Curator corrals me affectionately in a corner, asks how my work is going, reassures me that he has more than enough time to listen and talk. He asks what I've been digging up, what my latest research methods are, considers my conclusions about the origins of music—which I sought once on the basis of the theory of *magico-rhythmic mimetism*. Seeing there's no escape, I start to lie, alleging hurdles that delayed the completion of my work. But I'm no longer fluent in the jargon, and make ludicrous terminological blunders, muddling classifications, leaving out essential information, even though I know it quite well. I grasp for bibliographical references, only to find out—when my listener corrects me sardonically—that specialists have already refuted them. And when it strikes me that I might defer to the need to access certain primitive chants recently recorded by explorers, the copper gongs seem to fill my voice's echoes with resonant falsehood, making me pause mid-phrase, unforgivably unaware of the proper organographical vocabulary. In the mirror I see the miserable face of a swindler pinched with marked cards up his sleeve, and at that second, this face is my own. Finding myself so ugly, my shame turns to rage and I rain obscenities on the Curator, asking how he expects people to make a living studying primitive instruments in this day and age. He knew I'd been uprooted as a teenager, inflamed by false notions, convinced to study an art that fed none but the worst hawkers on Tin Pan Alley, shuffled across a world in ruins for months as a military interpreter, then thrown back on the asphalt of that city where poverty was hardest to bear. Ah! I had lived, I knew the terrible path of those who wash their one shirt at night, walk through snow with holes in their shoes, smoke the castoff butts of cast-off butts, cook in closets until hunger so besets them that the mere idea of eating is all their intellect can handle. It was that, or the comparable sterility of selling the finest hours of one's existence from sunup to sundown. "Anyway," I shouted, "I'm empty! Empty! Empty . . . !" To my surprise, the Curator, impassible and distant, gives me a cool stare, as if he expected this outburst. I speak again, but muffled and hastily, as though a somber exaltation sustained me. And like the

sinner at the confessional who pours out the black sack of his
iniquities and lusts—driven by a mania for speaking ill of himself that ends in a longing for execration—I paint for my
teacher a picture in the grimiest colors and darkest of blacks of
the futility of my existence, its numbness by day, its stupor by
night. I sink as deeply in my words as if they were uttered by
another, by a judge I carry unawares inside me, who uses me
to express himself, and when I hear myself, I am horrified by
how difficult it is to be a man when one has ceased to be a
man. Between the present me and the me I had once aspired to
be lay the pitchdark of the pit of lost years. I had the feeling I
was silent, and the judge was speaking through my lips. We
shared a single body, he and I, sustained by a hidden architecture that was the presence of our death in our lives, in our
flesh. Performing in the figure in the mirror's baroque frame
were Libertine and Preacher, the protagonists in every moral-
ity play, in every exemplary tale. To escape the looking glass,
my eyes fled to the library. But there, stamped on a calfskin
spine, in the corner of the Renaissance musicians, alongside
the several volumes of the *Penitential Psalms*, stood a title
placed there as though purposely, *Rappresentazione di animo
e di corpo*. A curtain seemed to fall, the lights to go out, when
the silence returned, and the Curator, in his bitterness, let it
stretch on a long while. Then he did something strange that
bespoke an impossible power of absolution. He got up slowly
and lifted the telephone, calling the rector of the university,
whose office shared a building with the Organographical Museum. With growing surprise, not daring to look up from the
floor, I heard myself praised to high heaven. I was portrayed as
the ideal collector to locate certain pieces missing from the gallery of American aboriginal instruments, which remained in-
complete, even as its abundant documentation made it the only
one of its kind in the world. Leaving aside my expertise, my
teacher stressed that my physical endurance, which had already been tested in war, would allow me to search through
regions too arduous for older specialists. Moreover, Spanish
had been the language of my childhood. Every reason he laid
out must have raised my status in the mind of his unseen

hearer, conferring upon me the stature of a young von Horn-
bostel. I noted with trepidation that he was certain I would
find, among any number of singular ideophones, a hybrid
drum and sounding stick André Schaeffner and Curt Sachs
were unfamiliar with, as well as the storied pitcher with two
mouthpieces of cane that the Indians used in the funeral rites
Fray Servando de Castillejos had described in 1561 in his treatise *De barbarorum Novi Mundi moribus*; though absent from
all the organographical holdings, the continued existence of
the people the friar claimed had blown it in their rituals suggested it might still be in use, especially as more recent explorers and traders seemed to have seen it. "The Rector is waiting
for us," my teacher said. The very notion struck me as so absurd that I wanted to laugh. I looked for a friendly way out,
invoking my ignorance, my distance now from all intellectual
labors. I knew nothing, I said, of the most recent methods of
classification, which were based on the morphological evolution of instruments and not their sound or the manner of playing them. But the Curator was so determined to send me to a
place I did not care to go that he resorted to an argument I
couldn't reasonably oppose: the task he was proposing could
be easily carried out while I was on vacation. The question was
simply whether I was so committed to the sawdust of bars that
I would deprive myself of the chance of traveling up a mighty
river. I had no valid reason to refuse. Deceived by a silence he
took as acquiescence, the Curator went to the adjoining room
to retrieve his coat, for the rain was now pounding against the
windows. I used this moment to flee. I was craving a drink. All
that interested me, in that moment, was to reach a nearby bar
with walls adorned with photographs of racehorses.

3

Mouche had left a note on the piano telling me to wait for her.
To busy myself, I tinkled the keys, making inane combinations
of chords, my glass set on the edge of the last octave. It smelled
of fresh paint. Past the sound box, on the back wall, sketched

figures were beginning to take shape, of the Hydra, the Argo
Navis, Sagittarius, and the Coma Berenices, and soon they
would give a unique flair to my friend's studio. Though I'd often
made fun of her astrological proficiency, I'd had to take a bow
when I saw what the horoscope business brought in. She conducted her transactions by mail, was mistress of her time, and
adopted a delightful gravity in her personal consultations, which
she received more than a few requests for. With her water-
colors and ink pots and her doctrines from outlandish treatises,
Mouche painted Maps of the Fates, from Jupiter in Cancer to
Saturn in Libra, to send off to remote parts of the country
adorned with Zodiac signs I helped solemnize with *De Coeleste
Fisonomiea*, *Prognosticum Supercoeleste*, and other attractive
Latin inscriptions. I often thought men must be terrified of their
times to turn to astrologists, to feverishly contemplate the lines
on their hands, the quirks of their penmanship, fret over the
black portents in tea leaves, dusting off ancient techniques of
divination, since they couldn't read the entrails of sacrificed
beasts or observe the flight of birds holding the crook of the
auspices. My friend, with her bottomless faith in seers with
veiled faces and her intellectual schooling in the Surrealists'
rubbish bazaar, found pleasure as well as profit in contemplating the sky through the mirror of books, mulling over the
lovely names of the constellations. It was her way of making
poetry, because when the initial exaltation from the fumes of
the printer's ink had passed, her attempts to do so in words—
memorialized in a plaquette illustrated with photomontages of
monsters and statues—had disappointed her, and she considered them insufficiently inspired. I'd met her two years before,
during one of Ruth's many professional absences, and though
my nights began or ended in her bed, we spoke few tender
words to each other. Our quarrels were dreadful, and we embraced in fury, our faces so close they couldn't see each other
while they exchanged insults that bodily reconciliation would
transform into crude praises of pleasures received. Mouche,
who was measured and even parsimonious with words, adopted in those moments a whorish idiom, and I had to respond
in kind so that from these dregs of language, a sharper delight

would emerge. It was hard to know if what bound me to her
was true love. She exasperated me often, with her dogmatic attachment to ideas and attitudes drawn from the beer halls of
Saint-Germain-des-Prés, sterile talk of which drove me from
her home with a desire never to return. But the next night, the
mere thought of her insolence made me weak, and I would retreat to that flesh that I needed, because I found in its folds a
demanding and self-serving animality that could alter my perennial fatigue, shifting it from the nervous plane to the physical. When I was done, I might come to know a sleep so rare
and longed for, like shutting my eyes after returning from a
day in the country—one of those few days of the year when the
scent of the trees swelled my entire being and intoxicated me.
Tired of waiting, I attacked the first chords of a great Romantic concerto, but then the doors opened and people filled the
apartment. Mouche, whose face blushed the way it did when
she was drinking, was back from her dinner with the painter
of her studio, two of my assistants, whom I hadn't expected to
see, the decorator from the first floor, who always pried into
other women's lives, and a dancer who just then was preparing
a ballet based on the rhythm of clapping hands. "We've got a
surprise," my friend announced, laughing. And soon they had
set up the projector with a copy of the film shown the night before, which was received so warmly I'd been allowed to start
my vacation right afterward. With the lights out, the images
were reborn before my eyes: the tuna fishing, with the splendid
rhythm of the nets and the maddened roiling of the fish
hemmed in by black boats; the lampreys poking out from the
holes in their stone towers; the encircling sweep of the octopus;
the coming of the eels; the vast coppery vineyard of the Sar-
gasso Sea. And then, the still lives of snails and fishhooks, the
coral forest and the hallucinatory warring of the crustaceans,
so clearly magnified that the lobsters appeared before my eyes
like armored dragons. We had done our work well. Again, I
heard the high points of the score, the liquid arpeggios of the
celesta, the fluid portamenti of the ondes Martenot, the waves
of the harp, and the abandon of xylophone, piano, and percussion during the combat sequence. It had taken three months of

arguing, perplexity, experiments, and exasperation, but the result was astonishing. Even the text, written by a young poetess and an oceanographer under the vigilant eyes of our company's specialists, deserved a place in an anthology of the genre. Nor could I find cause for self-criticism in the montage and the musical direction. "A masterpiece," Mouche said in the darkness. "A masterpiece," the rest repeated in unison. When the lights came up, they congratulated me, asking to see the film again. And because guests were still arriving, after the second screening they called for a third. But each time I saw what we had done, each time the florid *FIN* made of algae, our work's colophon, appeared, I found myself less and less proud. A truth poisoned my initial satisfaction: this excruciating labor, the shows of good taste, my mastery of my profession, my choice and coordination of collaborators and assistants, had yielded, when all was said and done, an advertisement commissioned by the Fisheries' Consortium in its ferocious struggle with a network of cooperatives. A team of technicians and artists had slaved away in darkrooms for weeks on end to complete this work in celluloid, whose purpose was to draw the attention of a certain public to the profitability of an industry capable, day in, day out, of stimulating the reenactment of the feeding of the multitudes, with fish if not with loaves. It was as if I heard my father's voice, in the gray days of his widowerhood, when he used to cite the Scriptures: "That which is crooked cannot be made straight: and that which is wanting cannot be numbered." He always walked around with that phrase on his lips, applying it to whatever struck him as opportune. And the words of Ecclesiastes were bitter to me then, and I thought of how the Curator, among others, would have shrugged his shoulders at that labor of mine, deeming it, perhaps, tantamount to tracing out letters in the sky with smoke, or provoking, with a tour de force of draftsmanship, the midday salivation of a person looking at an ad for an especially crunchy puff pastry. For him, I'd be an accomplice of those people who mar the landscape, pasting posters on walls, hawking snake oil. But then, I mused, the Curator was a man from a generation burdened by the *sublime*, who fell in love in the stands at Bayreuth, in the shadows smelling of old red velvet . . . People kept coming in, their heads passing through the light of the projector. "Advertising is where new techniques evolve!" shouted the Russian painter beside me, who had recently abandoned oils for ceramic, as if he had read my mind. "The mosaics of Ravenna were nothing more than advertising," said an architect enamored of the abstract. And new voices emerged from the shadows: "All painting is advertising." "Like some of Bach's cantatas." "*Gott der Herr ist Sonne und Schild* is a regular slogan." "Cinema means working collaboratively; the art of the future will be an art of collaboration." As more people showed up bearing bottles, the conversations grew disjointed. The painter showed a series of drawings of crippled and flayed figures he was considering transferring to his trays and dishes, to make *anatomical plates with volume* that would symbolize the spirit of the age. "True music is mere speculation with frequencies," said my assistant sound engineer, throwing Chinese dice on the piano to reveal how chance could yield a musical theme. We were all talking in shouts when an energetic "Halt!" coming from the entryway immobilized us, like wax figures on the verge of gestures, our words half-pronounced, half-drawn clouds of smoke now streaming from our lips. Some stopped in the arsis of a step; others held their glass in the air halfway between table and lips. (*I am I. I am sitting on a divan. I was about to scrape a match against the sandpaper strip on the box. Hugo's dice had reminded me of that verse by Mallarmé. But my hands were striking the match unbidden by my consciousness. So I was asleep. Asleep like everyone around me.*) The new arrival uttered another command, and everyone finished the phrases, gestures, and steps that had been trapped in suspension. This was one of the many exercises XTH—we never called him by anything but his initials, which frequent pronunciation had compressed into *Extyaich*—liked to submit us to in order, as he said, *to rouse* us and induce a conscious and analytical perspective on our acts at any given moment, irrespective of how trivial they were. Inverting for his own ends a philosophical formula we all knew well, he repeated that the person who acted automatically was "an *essence* without *existence*."

From professional weakness, Mouche would rhapsodize about the astrological aspects of his teachings, the principles of which were highly seductive, but got lost too soon for my tastes in Oriental mysticism, Pythagoreanism, Tibetan tantras, and who knows what all else. Extyaich had foisted on us a series of practices related to yogic asanas, making us breathe in a certain way, using mantras to calculate the length of our inhalations and exhalations. Mouche and her friends hoped doing all this would allow them greater self-mastery and an acquisition of powers that struck me as problematic, particularly in people who drank every day to ward off despair, the grief of failure, self-hatred, the fear of a rejected manuscript, or just the hardness of that eternally bustling city where no one ever had a name, eyes crossed only by chance, and a smile from a stranger always concealed a proposition. Extyaich proceeded to cure the ballerina of a sudden migraine by laying his hands on her. Addled by the crisscrossing conversations, which went from *Dasein* to boxing, from Marxism to Hugo's attempts to modify the piano's sounds by sticking shards of glass, pencils, silk paper, flower stems between the strings, I stepped out onto the balcony, where the evening rain had cleansed Mouche's dwarf lindens of the inevitable summer soot from the factory whose chimneys rose up on the river's opposite bank. At gatherings like the present one, I'd always found amusing the mad pinwheel of ideas, whirling from the Kabbalah to Angst via some man's scheme to start a farm in the West that would vouchsafe a number of artists' work through the raising of purebred hens, leghorns or Rhode Island Reds. I loved those leaps from transcendental to perverse, from Elizabethan theater to gnosis, from Platonism to acupuncture. I even meant once to record those conversations on a tape deck beneath the furnishings, to document the vertigo of those elliptical processes of thought and language. I found in those mental gymnastics, that high-wire acrobatics of culture, a justification for sundry moral disorders that in other people would have struck me as odious. But humanity didn't offer much to choose from. There were the merchants and businessmen whom I worked for during the day, who spent all they made on such absurd, unimaginative diversions that I couldn't help but think I was cut from a different cloth; then there were those present here, people happy to be given a few bottles of liquor, allured by the Powers Extyaich promised, bubbling over constantly with grandiose plans. In the implacable order of the modern city, they had submitted to a sort of asceticism, renouncing material goods, suffering hunger and penury, just to find themselves elusively in a finished work of art. That night, however, they tired me no less than the men of wealth and profit. The scene at the Curator's home had shaken me deep inside, and I couldn't allow these people's keenness for the advertising film I'd slogged away at to beguile me. The ludicrous words spoken about publicity and artistic collaboration were just a manner of reshuffling the past to try to justify the work's meager ambitions. With its irrisory ending, it was so far from gratifying that when Mouche approached to offer words of praise, I changed the subject, telling her about my adventure that afternoon. To my surprise, she embraced me, shouting that the news was *très formidable*, corroborating a prophecy she'd formulated in a recent dream in which she'd flown alongside big birds with saffron feathers. The meaning, without a shadow of a doubt, was: *travel, success, a change of scene*. Before I had time to rectify her error, she turned to timeworn clichés about the yearning for escape, the call of the unknown, and serendipity in a tone that owed something to the arrow-pierced *haleurs* and dazzling Floridas of "The Drunken Boat." In due time, I disappointed her, saying I'd escaped the Curator's home without taking him up on his offer. "But that's the height of foolishness!" she exclaimed. "You might have thought about me!" I told her I lacked the funds to pay her way through remote regions, and that the University had agreed to underwrite only a single traveler's expenses. After a distasteful silence, a nasty sheen of spite overtaking her eyes, Mouche burst into laughter: "And to think we just had the painter of Cranach's Venus here . . . !" My friend then explained to me what she had in mind: to reach the land of the peoples who beat sounding sticks and blew into funeral jugs, we would have to stop first in a large tropical city, famed for its beautiful beaches and local color; we could stay there, with the odd foray into the jungle that apparently lay nearby, living at our ease for as long as the money held out. No one would know whether I was following the itinerary my duties as a collector imposed. And to preserve my honor, I would hand in, upon my return, *archaic* instruments—faithful, genuine, accurate—painstakingly assembled following my sketches and measurements by the friendly painter, a true aficionado of the primitive arts, so devilishly crafty at copies and reproductions that he paid his bills counterfeiting the works of the masters: he'd carved fourteenth-century Catalan virgins complete with flaking gold leaf, wormholes, and cracks; his crowning achievement had been selling the Glasgow Museum a Venus by Cranach that he completed and *aged* in just a few weeks. This scheme was so rotten, so denigrating, that I rejected it with disgust. In my mind, I saw the University majestic as a temple, and I was being told to hurl rubbish at its pristine white columns. I went on talking a long time, but Mouche didn't listen. She returned to the studio and announced the news of our journey, and the guests responded with cries of jubilation. And off she went, without paying me mind, making a gleeful racket in one room and the next, dragging out suitcases, folding and unfolding clothes, taking stock of all we'd have to buy. This jauntiness cut me deeper than any mockery, and I left, slamming the door behind me. But the street was especially sad on this Sunday night, timid before the anguishes of Monday, its cafés deserted by people already dreading the morning hour and digging out house keys beneath streetlamps that spilt the molten tin of light over the rain-drenched asphalt. I stopped, irresolute. What awaited me at home was the disorder Ruth had left behind on her departure, the imprint of her head on the pillow, the scents of the theater. And when the alarm sounded, waking up would be pointless, and I would cower before that character abstracted from myself whom I met again each year at the start of my vacation—a man teeming with reproaches and bitter justifications, the same man who'd appeared a few hours before in the Curator's mirror to rake me over the coals. The demands of maintaining the synchronization equipment, of finding new locations with soundproofed walls, abetted this encounter, in which I changed out one burden for another, throwing down the stone of Sisyphus only to feel another laid over my chafed shoulder, and there were times when I wondered if the weight of the basalt was not preferable to that of my judge. A mist coming from the nearby docks rose over the sidewalks, wreathing the streetlights in prismatic light run through with the needles of raindrops falling from the low clouds. The grilles of the cinemas were locked over the broad vestibules, their floors scattered with torn tickets. I would soon have to cross the coldly lit, deserted street, taking the sidewalk uphill toward the Oratory in shadows, where I would stroke the fence with my fingers, counting its fifty-two bars. I leaned against a post, thinking of the void of those three insubstantial weeks, too short to really do anything, but still destined to be soured, as the days dragged on, by the feeling of possibilities disdained. I hadn't sought out this proposed mission. It had come to me, and I wasn't responsible for any exaggeration of my abilities. It wouldn't cost the Curator himself a cent, and the University's scholars, grown old among their books, unacquainted with the artisans of the jungle, would be hard-pressed to recognize the deception. The instruments that Fray Servando de Castillejos had described weren't artworks, but objects made by primitive techniques still in use. If museums housed more than one spurious Stradivarius, then where was the blame in falsifying a savage's drum? The instruments they were seeking could be ancient or contemporary, it didn't matter . . . "This journey was already written on the wall," Mouche said to me when she saw me return, pointing to the figures of Sagittarius, the Argo Navis, and the Coma Berenices, their ocher lines brighter now that the lights had been dimmed.

In the morning, while my friend dealt with formalities at the consulate, I went to the University, where the Curator, who had gotten up early, was restoring a viola d'amore with a luthier in a blue apron. He was unsurprised to see me there, and peered at me over the edge of his glasses. "Congratulations!" he said, and I wasn't sure whether he was commending my decision or whether he sensed I could string two thoughts together thanks only to a drug Mouche had administered to me upon waking. I was taken to the Rector's office, made to sign a contract, and given money for my journey along with a document that outlined the task assigned to me. Taken aback by the swiftness of these preliminaries, still not knowing what they expected of me, I found myself just afterward in a long, empty room, where the Curator told me to wait while he went to the Library to speak with the Dean of Philosophy, just back from the Amsterdam Conference. I was happy to find myself in what was in effect a museum of photographic reproductions and plaster casts for the Art History students' use. There were images there that formed part of our universal heritage—an impressionist Nymph, a family by Manet, the mysterious gaze of Madame Rivière—and they took me back to the distant days when I'd tried to allay my sorrow—the sorrow of the disillusioned traveler, of the pilgrim repelled by the profanation of Sacred Grounds—in the almost windowless world of museums. Those were months when I visited artisans' shops, opera stalls, gardens and cemeteries from Romantic prints, going with Goya to the battles on May 2 or following him to the Burial of the Sardine, where the sinister masks of the crowd looked less like revelers' disguises than like the faces of drunk penitents or devils in a passion play. After reposing with Le Nain's peasants, I plunged into the Renaissance in a portrait of a condottiero straddling a horse more marble than flesh between columns adorned with banderoles. At times I liked to while away the hours quaffing spiced wine with medieval burghers who'd had themselves painted beside a Virgin they'd donated, to authenticate the donors' identity—men who carved suckling pigs with charred teats, threw Flemish fighting cocks into the pit, cupped the breasts of waxen-faced ribalds who less resembled whores than beaming girls on a Sunday afternoon, off to sin again after their confessor had absolved them. An iron buckle, a savage crown bristling with hammered thorns, later brought me to the Merovingian Europe of deep forests, terrains without roads, migrating rats, wild, rabid beasts foaming at the mouth, that had famously arrived on a feast day in a city's town square. Then came the stones of Mycenae, the sepulchral finery, the compact stoneware of a gruff and venturesome, pre-classical Greece, redolent of cattle roasted over flames, of carding combs and dung, of the sweat of stud beasts in rut. And in this way, step by step, I reached the display cases of scrapers, axes, silex knives, and I stood there staring at them, fascinated by the nights of the Magdalenian, the Solutrean, the Pre-Chellean, feeling I had arrived at the edge of man's compass, at that limit of the possible that for certain primitive cosmologists had been the edge of the *terra plana*, where the head peeked out into the starry vertigo of the infinite, and the sky was visible *below as well as above* . . . Goya's *Saturn* returned me to the present, in a row of spacious kitchens ennobled in still lifes. The banker lit his pipe with an ember, the maid scalded a hare in the roiling water of a cauldron, and chatty seamstresses seen through a window broke the silence of a courtyard beneath an elm's shadows. With these familiar images before me, I asked myself if men in ages past had also longed for ages past, as I yearned on this summer morning—as if I myself had known them—for ways of life man had lost for all time.

CHAPTER TWO

Ha! I scent life!

SHELLEY

4

(June 7)

From the feeling in our ears, we'd known for several minutes now that we were descending. All at once the clouds were above us, and the plane started to shake, as though wary of the unstable air that dropped it, lifted it back up, left one wing to fend for itself, then commended it to the rhythm of unseen waves. To the right rose a chain of moss-green mountains blurred by rain. There lay the city, bathed in sunlight. The journalist sitting next to me—Mouche was stretched out asleep on the seat behind us—spoke with a blend of affection and scorn of that diffuse capital with its anarchic topography, which lacked an overarching style, as the first of its streets appeared below. To go on growing along that strip of sand beside the sea, bordered by hills capped with fortifications built by Philip II, the populace had waged a centuries-long war against the marshes, yellow fever, insects, and the antipathy of black crags of scattered rock, unscalable, solitary, gleaming like aeroliths hurled by a celestial hand. Those unwieldy eminences, rising between buildings, church towers, antennas, old belfries, fin de siècle cupolas, displaced one's perception of scale, substituting for it one inhuman, as though these stones were structures destined to an unknown end in an inconceivable civilization that had vanished into the remoteness of night. For hundreds of years, these people had struggled against the roots that lifted flagstones and cracked the walls; and still, when a rich landlord went to Paris for a few months, leaving his home in the hands of indolent servants,

these roots would wait for idle stretches when the help was singing or had dozed off to arch their backs and lay waste in twenty
days to Le Corbusier's finest utilitarian inspirations. The eminent city planners had ordered the palms uprooted in the suburbs, but they reappeared in the yards of the colonial homes,
like columns fencing off the avenues of downtown—which
followed the first streets the founders of the old city had traced
out on the best terrains with the tips of their swords. Over the
swarm of streets lined with stock exchanges and newspaper
offices, overshadowing the marble Banks, the sumptuous Bro-
kerages, the pale public offices, a world of scales, caducei,
crosses, winged genies, flags, trumpets of Fame, cogwheels,
hammers, and victories rose under a perpetually canicular sun
to proclaim, in bronze and stone, the lavish prosperity of a
town governed in accordance with exemplary statutes. But
when the rains came in April, the drains never sufficed, and the
main squares would flood, disorienting the drivers; the cars
that wound up in unknown neighborhoods would knock down
statues, stray onto dead-end streets, sometimes crashing in hollows that strangers and eminent visitors were never allowed to
set eyes on, where the inhabitants spent their lives half naked,
tuning their guitars, pounding drums, and drinking tin jugs of
rum. Electric light glowed everywhere, and machines hummed
under leaky roofs. The people here embraced technology with
ease, and what those from the old country, mired in history,
still handled with caution was already part of their everyday
routine. Progress was evident in the smooth lawns, the splendid embassies, the multiplication of bread and wine, the happy
merchants whose forebears had lived through the horrific days
of marsh mosquitoes. Nonetheless, there was something like a
malignant pollen in the air—fairy dust, unseen rot, hovering
mold—that worked with haste and mysterious designs to open
what was closed and close what was open, to mangle calculations, misreckon weights, corrupt all guarantees. One morning,
ampules of serum at a hospital were found full of fungus; the
precision instruments erred; liquors bubbled in their bottles;
an unknown parasite immune to acids gnawed at the Rubens
in the National Museum; people stormed the tellers' windows

at a bank without justification, made hysterical by the words
of an old black woman the police were searching for in vain.
When these things happened, those who knew the city's secrets
gave credence to just one explanation: "It's the Worm!" No
one had ever seen the Worm. But the Worm existed, and it
lived to sow confusion, appearing where least expected and
shocking even the most jaded. Apart from that, there were frequent dry thunderstorms in these parts, and every ten years, a
cyclone somewhere far off in the Ocean would begin its circular dance, demolishing hundreds of homes when it struck land.
We were flying low now, with the runway ahead of us, and I
asked my companion about a huge building, very pleasing to
the eye, surrounded by terraced gardens with statues and foun-
tains stretching down to the shore. He told me it was the home
of the new President of the Republic, and that if I'd been here
a few days earlier, I could have seen the celebrations, with parades of Moors and Romans, that accompanied his solemn in-
vestiture. Now the sumptuous residence disappeared beneath
the plane's left wing. We return gently to earth, roll over solid
ground, and file dully to the stamping office, where every question gets a guilty face in reply. Faint in the unfamiliar air, waiting out the leisurely inspection of our suitcases, I think of how
I have yet to properly realize how far I am from my customary
rambles. At the same time, there is something recognizable in
the light, in the scent of warm esparto or of seawater that the
sky seems to pierce to the depths, reaching its profoundest
greens—and a change in the breeze that brings the fetor of rotten crustaceans from some cavern on the coast. At dawn, in
flight among filthy clouds, I regretted my departure; I hoped
to use my first layover to book a return flight as soon as possible; the money I'd give back to the University. I felt imprisoned, kidnapped, accomplice to some vile deed, sealed up in
this airplane oscillating in three-quarter time, a robust body
in internecine struggle against adverse winds that now and
then threw tenuous rain across the aluminum wings. But then
a strange luxuriance stilled my scruples. A force penetrated my
ears, my pores: the language. This was the language I had spoken in childhood; the language I learned to write and hum in;

a language gone mossy in my mind from underuse, thrown aside like a useless tool in a country where it was of little use to me. *Estos, Fabio, ¡ay, dolor! que ves agora* . . . These fields, Fabio . . . Long forgotten, that verse returns to my mind, an example of an interjection from a tiny grammar book that must be stored somewhere along with a portrait of my mother and a lock of my blond hair cut off when I was six years old. The language of those verses is printed on the signs of the shops I see through the window of the waiting room; cackled and deformed in the black porters' dialect; ridiculed in a *¡Biva el Precidente!* whose misspelling I point out to Mouche with pride, and from this instant forward, I will be her guide and interpreter in this unknown city. With this sudden feeling of superiority over her, the last of my scruples disappears. I am no longer upset that I've come here. And something occurs to me that I hadn't imagined before: the instruments I've been asked to collect must be on sale somewhere in this city. It's impossible to imagine that no one—no seller of curios, no explorer weary of adventure—has thought of making a profit from these objects so prized by foreigners. I would find that someone and silence the spoilsport I carried around inside me. This prospect so pleased me that even as we strolled over the rundown neighborhood streets on our way to the hotel, I had to stop at a facade that might well have promised the good fortune I was seeking. It was a house with twisted railings, an old cat in every window, dusty-looking parrots dozing on the balconies with stiff feathers, resembling a mossy vegetation spreading on the greenish outer walls. The antiquarian—or better, junk seller—knew nothing about the instruments I was seeking, but to keep me there, he showed me a large music box with golden butterflies on hammers that played waltzes and redowas on a kind of psaltery. On tables covered with glasses held by carnelian hands stood portraits of professed nuns crowned with flowers. A Saint Rose of Lima, emerging from a rose's calyx in a busy whirl of cherubs, shared a wall with several bullfighting scenes. A hippocamp in the middle of cameos and coral pendants caught Mouche's eye, but I told her that she could find one like it anywhere. "It's Rimbaud's black hippocamp!" she replied, paying for this dusty literary artifact. I wanted to buy a colonial filigree rosary in a vitrine, but it cost too much, because the cross was inlaid with real precious stones. As we walked out beneath the mysterious banner reading *Zoroaster's Market*, my hand grazed a basil plant in a flowerpot. I stopped, deeply moved while inhaling that perfume I knew from the skin of a girl—María del Carmen, the gardener's daughter—in the days when we used to play husband and wife in the backyard of the house overshadowed by a thick tamarind tree, while my mother practiced a recent habanera on the piano.

5

(June 8)

Addled, my hand searches the marble of the nightstand for an alarm clock ringing, if at all, thousands of miles away, high up on the map. Taking a long look at the town square through the blinds, I reflect awhile before I realize that I've been duped into resuming my habit from every morning back home by the chiming triangle of a street peddler. This is followed by the piping of the scissor sharpener, which enters into strange harmony with the melismatic hawking of a giant black man with a basket of squids on his head. Shaken by an early breeze, the trees shed white wisps over a statue of a founding father who resembles Lord Byron with his windblown bronze cravat, and Lamartine in the way he waves his flag for the invisible rioters. In the distance, the bells of a church toll with a parochial rhythm made by tugging ropes, a far cry from the electric bells of the fake Gothic towers in my country. Sleeping, Mouche has spread out across the bed, and now there's no room left for me. Unused to the heat, she tries now and then to pull off the sheet, but only manages to tangle her legs up worse. I look at her, somewhat embittered by the disappointment of the night before: that allergy attack occasioned by the scent of a nearby orange tree that reached us on the fourth floor and cut short the feast of physical euphoria I had promised myself I would share with her on that first night in a new climate. I gave her a sleeping pill to calm her down, and resorted to the black blindfold to submerge my spite in dreams as quickly as I could. I look through the blinds again. Past the Palace of Governors, its classical columns sustaining a baroque cornice, I recognize the Second Empire facade of the theater where the night before, for lack of spectacles with more local color, the marmoreal drapery of the Muses enveloped us beneath chandeliers of crystal surrounded by busts of Meyerbeer, Donizetti, Rossini, and Hérold. A curving stairway with rococo foliage on the handrail led us to the hall with its fleshy velvets and gilded dentils trimming the balcony, where the ebullient talk of the crowd drowned out the orchestra tuning its instruments. Everyone seemed to know each other. Laughter rose and spread through the stands, and from the warm penumbra rose naked arms, hands grasping objects held on to from other centuries, like nacre cufflinks, lorgnettes, and feather fans. The flesh around the necklines, the cleft between the breasts, the shoulders had a soft and powdery abundance about them that evoked cameos or lace camisoles. I thought I might amuse myself with a ridiculous opera flaunting the traditions of bravura, coloratura, fioritura. But the curtain soon rose over the garden of the Castle of Lammermoor and the outmoded set with its false perspectives, its gossip mills, its gimmickry disarmed my sense of irony. Instead, what overcame me was an indefinable charm, wrought from vague and remote recollections and tattered longings. That grand velvet rotunda with its generous necklines, lace handkerchiefs warmed between breasts, towering hairstyles, the sometimes excessive perfume; that stage where the actors sang their airs with their hands held to their hearts against a vast vegetation of hanging cloth; that complex of traditions, behaviors, ways of being, impossible to bring back to life in a modern capital, was the magic world of theater as my passionate and pallid great-grandmother would have known it, the woman with the eyes both sensual and veiled, dressed all in white satin in an oil portrait by Madrazo that used to make me dream of childhood, until my father fell on hard times and had to sell it off. One afternoon, at home alone, I found a book with ivory covers and a silver clasp in the bottom of a trunk, the girlhood diary of the woman in the portrait. On one page, beneath rose petals that time had turned the color of tobacco, I found the charmed description of a *Gemma di Vergy* sung in a Havana theater that must have been identical to what I was witnessing that night. There were no more coachmen waiting outside in high boots and top hats with rosettes; the lanterns of the corvettes no longer swayed in the harbor, and no one sang old songs when parties reached their end. But in the public were the same faces, red with pleasure at this romantic performance; the same disdain for the crooning of the bit actors, already familiar from the librettos, which was a mere melodious backdrop to the vast mechanism of pregnant gazes, vigilant looks, whispers behind fans, muffled laughter, circulating rumors, discretions, dismissals, and feints, a game whose rules were unknown to me, but that I observed with the envy of a boy left out of a costume ball.

At intermission, Mouche declared she couldn't take it anymore, and said it was just like "the *Lucia* that Madame Bovary saw in Rouen." The observation was not entirely unjust, but her habitual smugness grated on me; she turned hostile no sooner than she'd come into contact with anything unbeholden to the codes and shibboleths of the artistic environments she frequented in Europe. She was now dismissive of opera not because it clashed with her paltry musical sensibility, but because contempt for the opera was a mark of her generation. Even invoking the Opera of Parma in Stendhal's day would not get her to return to her seat, so I left the theater, deeply annoyed. I felt the urge to quarrel with her, to cut short a reaction that might ruin the finest pleasures of this trip. I wanted to neutralize those criticisms foreseeable for one like me, who knew the inevitably dogmatic intellectual conversations that took place at her home. Soon we found ourselves in a night darker than the night of the theater; a night that pressed down on us with shades of silence, a solemn presence freighted with stars. The stridency of the traffic might tear it at any moment. But then it would grow whole again, slipping down hallways and through

gates, gathering in abandoned-looking houses with open windows, weighing on deserted streets with grand archways of
stone. A noise made us stop, dumbfounded, and we started
walking and stopped again several times until we were sure of
it: our steps were audible on the sidewalk across from us. In a
square, facing a drab church of shadows and stucco, stood a
fountain of Tritons with a shaggy dog on hind legs dipping its
tongue in and splashing with delight. The hands of the clocks
were sluggish, marking the hours at their whim, on the ancient
belfries and municipal facades. Downhill, near the sea, were
hints of bustling modern neighborhoods, but despite the twinkling in luminous characters of the nocturnal establishments'
unavoidable street signs, it was clear that the truth of the town,
its genius and its figure, was expressed here, in habits and
stone. At the end of the street, we found a large house with a
broad portico and a mossy roof, its windows opening into a
salon with old paintings in gilded frames. We pressed our faces
to the bars, and saw a magnificent general in a kepi and gold
braids, an exquisite painting of three ladies traveling in a
carriage, and next to them, a portrait of Taglioni with little
dragonfly wings on her narrow torso. The cut-glass lamps were
glowing, but it was impossible to distinguish any human presence in the hallways leading to the other lighted rooms. It was
as if, a century ago, everything had been arranged for a dance
that no one had attended. From a piano whose tones the trop-
ics had transposed to those of a spinet, four hands played the
bombastic prelude to a waltz. Then the breeze shook the curtains and the salon seemed to vanish in a whirl of tulle and
lace. The spell broken, Mouche said she was tired. Just as the
enchantment of that night that revealed to me the significance
of certain vague memories was about to carry me further away,
my friend shattered a timeless peace that I might have dwelt in
until dawn without fatigue. Over the roof, the stars revealed,
perhaps, the vertices of the Hydra, the Argo Navis, the Sagittarius, and the Coma Berenices, the same figures that adorned
Mouche's studio. But there was no point in asking her, as she
knew no better than I—apart from Ursa Major and Minor—
the constellations' exact positions. Realizing how preposterous

such ignorance was in a woman who made her living from the stars, I turned to her and started laughing. She opened her eyes without waking, looked at me without seeing, sighed, and turned to the wall. I wanted to lie down again, but thought it best to do as I'd intended the night before and look for the indigenous instruments while she slept—they had come to obsess me. I knew if she saw me so determined to find them, she would regard me at the very least as a buffoon. And so I dressed quickly and left without waking her.

The Sun filled the streets, reflecting in the windowpanes, wove unquiet threads across the water of the ponds, and it was so strange, so new, that to stand before it, I had to buy spectacles with dark lenses. I tried to find my way back to the neighborhood where I'd seen the colonial home, thinking there must be flea markets and curiosity shops nearby. Climbing a street with narrow sidewalks, I stopped at times to contemplate the signs of the small business, handsome in a way that evoked workshops of times past: the florid letters of the *Tutilimundi*, *The Golden Boot*, *King Midas*, and *The Melodious Harp* next door to the hanging Planisphere of a secondhand bookstore twisting wildly in the breeze. On a corner, a man fanned the fire of a grill, roasting a veal shank studded with garlic, its fat turning to acrid smoke under a drizzling of oregano, lemon, and pepper. Some way off, they were selling sangrias and garapiñas, and I smelled the oozing oil of fried fish. A warmth of pastry, of recently baked dough, emerged from the vent shaft of a basement where men were singing and sweating away in the shadows, coated in white dust from their hair to their clogs. I stopped in delighted surprise. I'd long forgotten that presence of flour in the mornings, *back there* where the bread was kneaded who knew where and shipped at night in sealed trucks, like contraband; this was not the bread broken by hands, the bread the father hands out after blessing it, the bread that must be received with a deferential gesture before tearing its crust over a broad bowl of leek soup or sprinkling it with oil and salt to rediscover that savor which is less that of bread and salt than of the great Mediterranean that clung to the palate of Ulysses and his men. My reunion with

flour, my discovery of a shop window showing prints of
mestizos—children of blacks and Indians—dancing the mari-
nera, distracted me from my objective on those unknown
streets. I stopped at one place before an execution of Maximil-
ian; at another I leafed through an old edition of Marmontel's
The Incas, whose illustrations recalled the Masonic aesthetics
of *The Magic Flute*. I listened to a *Mambrú* sung by children
playing in a courtyard that smelled of custard. Drawn by the
morning cool of an old cemetery, I walked in the shadows of
cypresses between neglected graves overgrown with grass and
bellflowers. Panes of glass clouded by fungus boasted now and
then a daguerreotype of the person lying beneath the marble: a
student with feverish eyes, a veteran of the Frontier War, a poetess crowned with laurel. I was staring at the monument to
those lost on a foundered riverboat when the air ripped like
wax paper struck by fire from machine guns. Probably the students of the military academy were practicing their marksman-
ship. Doves cooed through the ensuing silence, puffing their
necks beside the Roman vases.

> These fields—oh misery!—you see now, Fabio,
> Fields of solitude, withered hill,
> Were once the famed Italica.

Over and over I recited these verses, snippets of which had
risen into my mind since my arrival until the poem at last re-
constituted itself entire in my memory, just as I heard again,
stronger now, the clatter of the machine guns. A child ran past,
followed by a horrified, barefoot woman carrying a tray of wet
clothes, seeming to flee grave peril. A voice shouted somewhere, behind a wall, "It's starting! It's starting!" Ill at ease, I
left the cemetery for the modern quarter. The streets were
empty, and there was something ominous in the speed with
which the shops had locked their doors and closed their metal
grates. I reached for my passport, as if the stamps between
its covers might somehow protect me; I was frightened now,
and the shouting made me freeze behind the shelter of a column. A vociferous, horrified multitude poured onto an avenue,

toppling everything in their path to escape the relentless rifle fire. It rained broken glass. The bullets struck the metal lamp-posts, making them quiver like the pipes of an organ pounded by stones. A high-tension cable whipped across the street, and the asphalt started to burn in patches. An orange seller next to me fell on his stomach, his fruits rolling off to all sides and flying in the air when the bullets fired near the ground struck them. I ran to the nearest corner to take shelter under an arcade where a departed vendor had left his garlands of lottery tickets hanging unattended. Only a bird market lay between me and the hotel. When a bullet hummed past my shoulder and punched through the window of a pharmacy, I decided to take off running. Jumping over the cages, hurtling past canaries, kicking hummingbirds, knocking down frightened parrots' perches, I reached the service doors, which were still open. A toucan skipped behind me dragging a broken wing, as though bidding me to protect it. Behind me, posted on the handlebars of an abandoned velocipede, a dauntless macaw remained alone in the middle of the deserted plaza, warming itself in the sun. I went up to our room. Mouche was hugging a pillow, still asleep, her nightgown bunched at her hips and her feet twined in the sheets. Relieved to see her, I went back to the vestibule in search of answers. People said it was a revolution. But this meant little to a person like me, whose knowledge of the country extended no further than the Discovery, the Conquest, and the voyages of a few priests who had left behind descriptions of its primitive peoples' musical instruments. So I directed my questions to those who were talking at length and gesturing heatedly, assuming they were the best informed. And yet it became clear soon enough that each had his own version of the events, and they kept repeating the names of persons who meant absolutely nothing to me. I tried to get some sense of the beliefs and demands of the warring parties, but still, nothing was clear. For a moment, I seemed to grasp that the socialists were taking on the conservatives or radicals, or else the communists were warring with the Catholics, but then the tables turned, the positions were inverted, and the same names from before were invoked, as if all this were a personal rather than

a partisan dispute. Over and over, I had to admit my ignorance
of the chronicles of events revealed to me, which, like the tales
of the Guelfs and Ghibellines, resembled a family quarrel,
strife among brothers, a struggle between people who just yesterday were united. In the midst of what I would ordinarily
have considered a conflict typical of the time, I found it more
like a war of religion. In the rivalry between those I took to
represent the progressive and conservative positions, the ideals
in question seemed so antiquated, it was as though a battle
were being fought beyond time between inhabitants of different centuries. "Right you are," a lawyer in a frock coat answered me, a man of the old school who viewed the events
with surprising aplomb. "Remember, we've traditionally been
accustomed to living with both Rousseau and the Holy Office
of the Inquisition, with banners sewn with the figure of the
Virgin and *Das Kapital* . . ." Mouche appeared then, shaken
after being roused by the sirens of passing ambulances, which
were pulling in to the bird market in great numbers and
screeching to a stop at the apparent obstacle of the piles of
cages, crushing the last of the remaining mockingbirds and
troupials. Facing a forced confinement, my friend began to rail
against the events that had upset her plans. In the bar, the ill-
humored foreigners were playing cards and shooting dice,
drinking and carping about the mestizo countries that were
always mired in some kind of chaos. Word came that several of
the hotel's waiters had disappeared. We saw them pass, soon
afterward, beneath the arches out front, armed with Mausers,
with bandoliers slung over their shoulders. Seeing their white
blazers, we joked about their martial bearing. But when they
reached the nearest corner, the two marching in front turned
back, struck in the stomach by a volley of machine gun fire.
Mouche shouted in horror, bringing her hands to her belly.
We retreated silently to the rear of the foyer, eyes pinned to the
carnage lying on the asphalt stained red, insensible now to
the bullets that continued to pelt it, leaving bloodstains on the
bright khaki. Our jokes of a moment before depressed me. If
people in these countries died for passions I couldn't grasp, that

did not make their death any less death. At the feet of ruins looked upon with no sense of pride in triumph, I had treaded more than once on the bodies of men who died defending convictions probably no worse than those they were proclaiming here. Now armored cars passed—hand-me-downs from *our own* war—and when their gears stopped whining, it seemed the fighting in the street grew more intense. In the vicinity of Philip II's fortress, the gunfire merged briefly into a compact clamor that drowned out the individual explosions, jarring the air with a ceaseless deflagration that came or went, depending on the wind, in time with the crashing waves behind it. Now and then, there was a sudden pause, and everything seemed to be over. A sick baby cried in a nearby house, a rooster crowed, someone knocked on a door. But then, a machine gun would rattle, and the commotion returned, along with the dreadful ululation of the ambulances. A mortar opened fire near the old Cathedral, where the bells rang sonorously when struck by stray bullets. "*Eh bien, c'est gai!*" a woman next to us exclaimed in a deep but cloying, somewhat affected voice. She introduced herself as a Canadian painter, ex-wife of a Central American diplomat. I left Mouche in conversation with her and downed a strong drink of alcohol to forget the nearness of the cadavers stiffening on the sidewalk. After a lunch of cold cuts that boded ill for future banquets, the afternoon hours passed quickly in disorderly readings, games of cards, conversations in which the mind was elsewhere—none of them assuaging the general anxiety. At nightfall, Mouche and I drank heavily in our room to keep from thinking of what was happening; eventually we felt sufficiently at ease to turn to the play of bodies, finding a rare, acute voluptuousness in embracing while others around us were playing with death. Our yearning to pull close to each other—to be absorbed into impossible depths— while bullets beyond the blinds whizzed past or lodged in the dome that crowned the building, cracking the stucco, was like the frenzy that exalts the lovers in a danse macabre. Later, we fell asleep on the white carpet. And that was the first night in a long time we could sleep without masks or drugs.

6

(June 9)

The next day, unable to leave, we tried to accustom ourselves
to the reality imposed on us by fate: that of a village under siege,
of a quarantined ship. Far from inducing apathy, the tragic situation on the streets drove the people behind these walls keeping
them safe from the outside to do something, anything. Profes-
sionals tried to set up workshops or offices, as though to convince the others that in extraordinary circumstances, one's
vocation remained, and could even provide a shelter from the
madness. In the dining room, on the orchestra's stage, a pianist
played the trills and mordents of a classical rondo, trying to
make the stiff keys sound like a harpsichord. A corps de ballet
warmed up along the bar while the principal danced slow arabesques across the polished floor, between tables pushed against
the walls. Typewriters clacked throughout the building. In the
writing room, businessmen rummaged through their big brief-
cases of lambskin leather. The Austrian Kapellmeister, a guest
of the city's Philharmonic, conducted Brahms's *Requiem* with
sweeping gestures in the mirror of his room, signaling the
fugal entrances to a vast imaginary chorus. The kiosk was sold
out of magazines, crime novels, and leisure reading of all sorts.
Mouche went for her bathing suit, because they'd opened the
patio, and idlers were sunbathing there beside the mosaic fountain, arecas in planters, and green ceramic frogs. I was alarmed
to find that the cannier guests had stocked up on tobacco, and
not a single cigarette was left in the hotel gift shop. Outside the
foyer, the bronze gate was still closed. But the shooting had diminished. Small bands, guerrillas, must have been fighting farther off, in brief but relentless battles, to judge by the sudden
volleys. Isolated shots reverberated from roofs and balconies.
A blaze had broken out in the north of the city—some said the
army's barracks were on fire. But I had stopped asking questions, since the names of the principals remained meaningless
to me, and instead devoted myself to reading old newspapers,
amused by the stories of faraway lands with their abundant

storms, stranded cetaceans, and episodes of witchcraft. The clock struck eleven—the hour I was waiting for impatiently—and I noticed the bar tables remained shoved against the walls. This meant that the last of the faithful servants had departed before dawn to join the revolution. Nothing about this alarmed me in particular, but it caused panic to spread among the other guests. Leaving aside their diversions, they huddled in the foyer, where the manager tried to calm their nerves. When she heard there would be no bread that day, a woman burst into tears. A faucet emitted a rusty gargle, then exhaled a kind of yodel that echoed through all the pipes in the building. When the spurt that arced from the Triton's mouth ran dry, we realized we were left with what little water there was in storage. People talked of epidemics, which the tropical climate would make worse. Some rang their Consulate, but the telephones were out of service, and without sound they were useless, a puny limb hanging from the switch hook; in exasperation, people shook them and banged them against the tables, trying to make them talk back. "It's the Worm," the manager said, repeating the old joke that explained any and all catastrophes in the capital. "It's the Worm." I thought of how it frustrated man when his machines disobeyed him as I looked for a ladder to reach a bathroom window on the fourth floor that offered a protected view outside. The prospect of the roofs was dismal, but something startling was happening under the soles of my feet. It was as if subterranean life were suddenly revealing itself, sending forth a multitude of weird little beasts from the shadows. The dry pipes, hiccuping somewhere, produced strange nits, gray wafers with feet, wood lice with mottled shells, and short centipedes with what seemed to be a craving for soap; when frightened, they curled into tiny copper spirals and lay there immobile on the floor. Leery, inquisitive antennae poked from the faucets, while the bodies that moved them stayed behind. The cabinets were full of almost imperceptible noises, of gnawed paper or scratched wood, and any door opened would free a storm of insects inept at walking over waxed wood, slipping and landing with their legs in the air, playing dead. A bottle of syrup left on a nightstand drew the red ants upward. Vermin teemed under the rugs, and spiders peeked through the keyholes. In this city, a few disordered hours, a moment's neglect on the part of man for his creations, sufficed for the creatures of the humus to climb through the parched plumbing and invade the embattled square. An explosion close by made me forget the insects. I returned to the foyer, where the tension had reached a fever pitch. The Kapellmeister, baton in hand, appeared at the top of the stairs, drawn by the shouts of those arguing. His hairless head, his severe stare beneath bushy brows, imposed silence. We stared at him in hopeful anticipation, as if he'd been vested with the power to ease our worries. Professionally habituated to the exercise of authority, the maestro stepped forward to condemn the cowardice of the alarmists, demanding the swift nomination of a commission of guests to get a clear picture of the provisions on hand, and said he would resort to rationing if needed. He invoked the Heiligenstadt Testament to stiffen our resolve. A corpse, a dead animal, was rotting in the sun near the hotel, and a stench of carrion crept through the sky- lights in the bar, the only windows on that floor that could be left open without danger, because they sat higher than the cor- bels above the mahogany paneling. Since midmorning, the flies seemed to have multiplied, and buzzed around our heads with irritating resolve. Bored of the patio, Mouche came into the foyer, tying the belt of her terry-cloth bathrobe, to complain she'd gotten no more than a half bucket of water to bathe with after tanning in the sun. With her was the Canadian painter who'd introduced herself the night before, a somewhat ugly yet still alluring woman with a deep but singsongy voice. She knew the country and took a blithe approach to the events, saying the situation would soon resolve itself, and this eased my friend's agitation. I left Mouche with her new friend and fol- lowed the summons of the Kapellmeister, going to the base- ment with the commission to take inventory of the foodstuffs. We'd evidently be able to endure the siege for several weeks, so long as we made judicious use of our supplies. The manager declared that he and the hotel's foreign staff would prepare a simple stew for each meal, and we could serve ourselves in the kitchen. We walked underground over the damp, cool sawdust, and there was comfort in the shadows reigning there and the pleasant scents of the larder. Relieved, we inspected the liquor stocks, finding enough bottles and barrels to hold out a long time . . . When the others noticed we hadn't hurried back, they, too, came down to the basement, roaming the hallways till they found us tapping barrels and drinking from any receptacle that lay close to hand. The joy was contagious when we told them our findings. Liquor was decanted into bottles and taken from the basement to the first floor, where gramophones soon replaced the typewriters. The past few hours' nervous tension was transformed into a bottomless thirst for drink, even as the stench of the carrion wafted in stronger and the insects crawled all round. Only the Kapellmeister remained in a foul mood, imprecating against the agitators whose revolution had spoiled the rehearsals of Brahms's *Requiem*. Rabid, he recalled that letter in which Goethe praises tamed nature, *forever freed from its mad and febrile commotions*. He roared, "Here, jungle!" stretching out his long arms as though demanding a *fortissimo* from his orchestra. The word *jungle* made me look out at the patio with the arecas in planters, and from that angle, in the shadows, they looked like enormous palm trees surrounded by quaking walls, while above, a flight of vultures drawn by the carnage cut furrows across the cloudy sky. I had supposed I'd find Mouche back in her deck chair; when I didn't see her, I assumed she was dressing. But she wasn't in our room, either. I waited for her a moment, but under the spell of several glasses of strong liquor drunk early, I soon went looking for her, leaving the bar like a man on a mission, climbing the stairs of the foyer between two caryatids with solemn marmoreal miens. My face was numb after the local brandy with its savor of honey, in addition to more familiar spirits, and drunk, I flailed like a blind man in the darkness between the handrails and the wall. Reaching narrower steps of a sort of yellow scagliola, I realized I'd walked a long way, more than four floors, and still had no idea where my friend had gone. And yet I carried on, sweaty, obstinate, my tenacity unaffected by the mocking stares of those who stepped aside to let me through. I traversed endless hallways on carmine

carpets wide as streets, past numbered doors—excruciatingly
numbered—which I counted as I passed, as though doing so
were another part of my quest. A recognizable shape made me
stop and tremble, with the strange sense I'd gone nowhere, that
I had been *back there* the whole time, led by one of my daily
walks into some impersonal, démodé mansion. I recognized
the red metal fire extinguisher, with its instructions on a metal
plate; I recognized from long ago the carpet I was treading, the
modillions of the smooth ceiling, the bronze digits on doors
enclosing familiar furnishings, appurtenances, objects laid out
as they always were beside a print of the Jungfrau, Niagara
Falls, or the Leaning Tower of Pisa. At the thought that I'd
never departed, the tremors descended from my face to my
body. The image of the hive recurred to me, and I felt smoth-
ered, crushed between these parallel walls where the staff's
abandoned brooms recalled the discarded oars of absconded
galley slaves. I felt I'd been condemned to wander eternally
among numbers, among the dates of a gargantuan calendar en-
crusted in the walls—a chronology in maze form, perhaps the
maze of my existence, with my inevitable obsession with the
hour, walking in a haste that could do nothing but return me
each morning to my departure point of the night before. In
that row of rooms where men left no mark of their passing, I
no longer remembered who I was looking for. I despaired at
the number of steps still to climb until I reached the floor where
the building shed its plaster and acanthus leaves and stood
bare save for the gray concrete with paper glued to the windows to protect the servants from bad weather. I thought again
of the Theory of the Worm as I walked through these superimposed paths; nothing else explained this Sisyphean labor I
was engaged in, bearing the stone of a woman on my shoulder.
I giggled at this image, and stopped worrying about finding
Mouche. When she drank, I knew, she was vulnerable to all
kinds of sensual seductions, not from a penchant for vice as
such, but from a dubious curiosity. But I didn't care now that
the drink had made my legs too heavy to drag. I returned to
our room and collapsed into bed on my stomach, falling asleep,

soon tormented by nightmares rife with the idea of hunger and thirst.

And my mouth was dry when I heard someone calling me, and found Mouche standing there with the Canadian painter we'd met the day before. For the third time, I was there with that woman with the slightly angular body, whose face, with its straight nose beneath a stubborn forehead, had a statuary poise that contrasted with her somewhat formless and gluttonous girlish mouth. I asked my friend where she had been all afternoon. "The revolution's over," she said by way of an answer. The radio stations were announcing the winning party's triumph and the imprisonment of former government officials. Here, they said, it was never a long trip from the halls of power to a jail cell. Before I could celebrate the end of our confinement, Mouche informed me that a six p.m. curfew had been extended indefinitely, with severe penalties for anyone found outside after that hour. Frustrated, seeing our last chances for amusement cut short, I vowed to return home immediately and to go to the Curator empty-handed. Fate had excused me from needing to pay back what I'd thus far spent on this vain enterprise. But Mouche had been informed that in light of many similar demands, the airlines couldn't guarantee us tickets for a week or more. She didn't seem especially angry, and I imagined her acceptance of the circumstances was due to the relief at seeing the chaotic situation resolved. When she was done speaking, the painter invited us to spend a few days at her home in Los Altos, a calm summer village well-liked by foreigners for its climate and its silver workshops, where the police were lax in enforcing regulations. She kept a studio there in a seventeenth-century house she'd bought for a song; its courtyard was a replica of the patio of the Posada de la Sangre in Toledo. Mouche had accepted her invitation without consulting me, and spoke now of paths lined with wild hortensia and a convent with high baroque altars, elaborate coffered ceilings, and a room where the sisters flogged themselves at the foot of a black Christ facing the grotesque relic of a bishop's tongue kept in alcohol as a testament to his eloquence. I was doubtful, and didn't answer, not

so much from reluctance as from rancor at my friend's insouci-
ance, and since the danger was past, I opened a window to reveal an evening that was already becoming night. I noticed the
two women had put on their flashiest dresses to wear to the
dining room. I was on the verge of making a joke about it when
I saw something outside far more interesting to me in that moment: *Faith in God*, an oddly named grocer's shop with strands
of garlic hanging from its beams, which opened a small door
to admit a man who walked over, dragging his finger against
the wall, with a basket hanging from one of his arms. He left
just afterward carrying bread and bottles and smoking a freshly
lit cheroot. I had awakened craving a cigarette and there was
no tobacco in the hotel, and I pointed him out to Mouche, who
was already reduced to collecting butts. Afraid the shop would
soon close, I walked downstairs and jogged across the square.
I had twenty packs of cigarettes in my hand when heavy fire
opened on the next street over, and snipers posted along a sloping roof shot their rifles and pistols over the cornice in response. The store owner hurried to close the door, sliding a
thick crossbar behind it. I sat on a stool, defeated, seeing the
foolishness of trusting my friend's words. Maybe the revolution was over, in the sense that the important points in town
had been taken, but they would go on hunting down the rebel
groups. Women were humming a rosary in the back of the shop.
A scent of brined pollock stung my throat. I picked up a deck of
cards on the counter, recognizing the long-forgotten clubs,
cups, coins, and swords of the Spanish deck. Then the shooting
grew more diffuse. The clerk, smoking a cigar, looked at me in
silence beneath a poster of the miserable shopkeeper who sold
his goods on credit and the happy, prosperous one who sold his
wares for cash. The prevailing atmosphere of calm, the scent of
jasmines growing under a pomegranate tree in the courtyard,
the dripping water filtering from a *tinajero,* sank me into a
kind of lethargy: a sleepless sleep, nodding off and returning to
my surroundings every few seconds. The clock on the wall
struck eight. The gunfire had ended. I cracked the door and
looked toward the hotel. Its glow brightened the surrounding
shadows through the skylights in the bar and the foyer's chan-

deliers, which were visible through the bars of the door beneath the awning. I heard applause, then the first bars of *Les barricades mystérieuses*: the pianist was playing the pieces he'd practiced that morning in the dining room, most likely after a good number of drinks, since his fingers stumbled over the ornaments and appoggiaturas. On the mezzanine, behind the metal blinds, people were dancing. The entire building was celebrating. I shook hands with the shopkeeper and took off at a trot, and there was a shot—just one—and a bullet hummed past a few feet away at the height of my chest. I ran back in dread. I had been in war, it was true, but as an interpreter in the State's employ, and that was something different—the risks were shared among many, and no one person could choose to retreat. Whereas here, if death caught me out, it was no one's fault but my own. Ten minutes or more passed without a report rending the night. But another explosion came just as I was wondering whether to go back out. A lone watchman posted somewhere seemed to be firing occasional shots from an old weapon, most likely a breechloader, to keep people off the road. To reach the next sidewalk would take just a few seconds, but a few seconds were enough in that horrible game of chance. A chain of thoughts took me back to Buffon's gambler, who throws a rod down on a floor and bets it won't cross any parallel lines. But here, the parallels were bullets fired aimlessly, indifferent to my designs, slicing through space when least expected, and it petrified me that I might be the gambler's rod, and that the angle of incidence might place my flesh in the projectile's path. Nor did fate enter into my calculations, because the risk was mine alone, and even venturing everything, I would gain nothing. I had to admit, it wasn't the wish to be back in the hotel that fed my frustrations on the far side of the street. It was a repetition of what had driven me to stumble drunk through the building's many hallways hours before. I was impatient because I mistrusted Mouche. From here, on this side of the abyss, of the despicable game board of possibilities, I saw her as capable of the worst carnal treachery, though as long as we'd known each other, I had no concrete grounds for reproaching her. My suspicions, my ineluctable misgivings, lacked foundation, but I knew perfectly well that her intellectual pedigree was rich with ideas, with pretexts, that could justify anything, convincing her to give in to whatever rare experiences the peculiar setting of that evening offered up to her. For that very reason, I told myself, it was stupid to risk death to clear up my doubts. And yet I couldn't bear the thought that she was in that building full of drunkards without me there to watch over her. Anything was possible in that labyrinth of dark cellars and endless rooms long used for couplings that left behind no trace. The idea wormed its way into my mind—I don't know why—that this street, this pit, this gulf, wider and more impassable with each shot, was like a warning, a foretaste of events to come. Just then, something strange happened in the hotel. The music, the laughter broke off all at once. Shouts, moans, bellows echoed through the building. Some lights went out, others turned on in a sort of dull commotion, a panic without flight. More shots flew by from the nearest corner. Then a few infantry patrols appeared with rifles and machine guns. The soldiers scattered slowly behind the pillars of the buildings until they'd reached the store. The snipers were gone from the roof, and troops stood all around on the stretch of road I had to cross. A sergeant escorted me to the hotel. They opened the grate and I entered the foyer, where I stopped, stunned: on a large walnut table that served as bier lay the Kapellmeister with a crucifix between the lapels of his smoking jacket. For lack of anything better, the funeral candles stood flickering in four silver candlesticks with a motif of twisting vines; a stray bullet had struck the maestro in the temple when he dared stand too close to the window in his room. I looked at the faces around him: unshaved, filthy, sagging from a debauch that death had interrupted. The insects were still crawling in the pipes, and the onlookers' bodies smelled of acrid sweat. The entire building stank like a latrine. Skinny, haggard, the ballerinas resembled ghosts. Two of them, still dressed in the tulles and mesh of an adagio danced moments before, sank sobbing into the shadows of the grand marble staircase. There were flies everywhere, buzzing around the lights, crawling over the walls, hovering around the women's

hair. Outside, the carnage was growing. I found Mouche collapsed on the bed of our room in a nervous fit. "We'll take her
to Los Altos at dawn," the painter said. Already, the cocks
were crowing in the courtyards. Downstairs, men in black on
the granite sidewalk were unloading candles from a black-and-
silver hearse.

7

(June 10)

We reached Los Altos shortly after midday in a little narrow-
gauge train that resembled a choo-choo ride at an amusement
park. I liked it there so much that, for the third time that
afternoon, I leaned on my elbows on the short bridge that
spanned the stream to stare at that place I'd already walked
every inch of, peeking indiscreetly into the houses. The eye
never settled on anything monumental or illustrious, fit for a
picture postcard or encomiums in a tourist guide. And yet, in
this part of the provinces, where every corner and every studded door bespoke a particular mode of life, I found a charm
absent from other museum towns, where the stones had been
touched and photographed all too many times. At night, the
town had the glory of a city carved into the side of a mountain,
and the lampposts lifted buildings from the shadows and illuminated scenes from Hell. Those fifteen lamps, haloed by flying insects, drew out and isolated whatever they shone on, like
altar lamps or floodlights in a theater, brightening the stations
of a winding road to Calvary. Since the wicked are always
roasting at the bottom of every allegory of temperance and dissipation, the first lamp brightened the drovers' tavern, a seedy
gambling den serving pisco, charanda, and watercress and
blackberry brandies, with drunks asleep on barrels in the entryway. The second light hovered over Lola's place, where Carmen, Ninfa, and Esperanza sat waiting in white, pink, and
blue under Chinese lanterns on a threadbare velvet divan that
had once belonged to a Magistrate of the Appellate Courts.

Near the third lamp spun the camels, lions, and ostriches of a carousel, and a Ferris wheel whose cabins rose into the shadows and returned—because the light reached only so high—in the time it took the cardboard disc of "The Skater's Waltz" to end. As though descended from the firmament of Fame, the fourth lamp cast pale light upon the statue of the Poet, a favorite son of the city, author of an esteemed "Hymn to Agriculture," shown versifying in his marble notebook with a pen that dripped verdigris, guided by the index finger of a muse who was missing her other arm. Under the fifth lamp, nothing was noteworthy apart from two sleeping donkeys. The sixth revealed the Grotto of Lourdes, a laborious structure of concrete and stones brought from far away, an edifice all the more striking if one kept in mind that to build it, they'd had to fill in the real grotto that had stood there before. The seventh lamp stood in thrall to the greenish-black pine and a rosebush climbing a portico sealed off for eternity. The eighth lamp drew the cathedral with the shadowy buttresses from the murk; its post being particularly high, it shone on the face of the clock, whose hands were dormant and had been for forty years, marking, according to the smug and snooty church ladies, the hour of seven thirty on an approaching day of judgment when the fallen women of the neighborhood would be brought to account. The ninth lamp presided over the Athenaeum, where cultural events and patriotic commemorations were held, and its little museum whose holdings included a ring from the hammock of the hero of the Hillside Campaign, several passages from the Quixote copied out on a grain of rice, a portrait of Napoleon made with the X key of a typewriter, and a complete collection of the region's venomous snakes preserved in jars. Impassable, mysterious, framed by two grayish-black Solomonic columns supporting an open compass that spanned their capitals, the Lodge filled the entirety of the tenth lamp's reflections. Then came the Cloister of the Recollect Nuns, its arbor badly lit by the eleventh lamp, its bulb full of dead insects. Nearer by stood the barracks, sharing the glare of the next lamp with a Doric gazebo whose dome had been split by a lightning bolt, but which was still used for open-air concerts in summer, with the boys dancing on one side, the girls on the other. A green horse reared in the cone of the thirteenth lamp, mounted by a rain-washed bronze rider whose brandished sword cut the mist into two slowly moving currents. Next was a black strip quivering with candles and camp stoves: the Indian lands with their scenes of births and vigils. The penultimate lamp's radiance overlooked a concrete pedestal waiting for the Sagittarian pose of the Brave Archer, slayer of Conquistadors, which the free-masons and communists had ordered from a stonecutter to the exasperation of the clergy. After that, the night closed, and the blackness persisted save for on high, where a light burned so lofty it seemed part of another world and the wind lashed hardest over three wooden crosses rising from gravel mounds. With that, the urban hallelujah ended against a backdrop of stars and clouds and a speckling of hardly noticeable lesser lights. The rest was roofs of clay, which merged in the darkness with the clay of the hillsides.

Beaten by the cold sweeping down from the summits, I returned through tortuous streets to the painter's home. I admit that this character, whom I had ignored over the foregoing days—accepting the fact of our living together as I would any other coincidence—had begun to irritate me since we left the capital, just as Mouche's esteem for her had grown. She had struck me as a colorless figure at first, but her contrariness was growing by the hour. A studied lentitude, which gave weight to her words, conferred on her an authority with regard to even the most minor decisions affecting us, despite her apparent humility, so much so that my friend invariably gave in with a tameness quite unusual for her. Mouche, who was used to making a law of her whims, never lost her chance to tell our hostess she was right, even when she had agreed with me moments before and sworn off practices she now returned to with gusto. When I wished to stay, we had to leave, we had to rest when what tempted me was to climb the mountain's misty summit, in an interminable quest to placate this other woman, to anticipate and praise her reactions. Mouche clearly found something important in her new friend that hinted at how much she missed—after just a few days—the realities we had left behind. While in me, the change of altitude, the clean air, the interruption of my habits, the rediscovery of the language of my childhood were contributing to a still inchoate but palpable feeling of return, the restoration of a long-lost equilibrium, for her the signs of boredom were evident, even if she still refused to admit it. Nothing we had seen so far must have been the kind of thing she'd hoped to find on this adventure, if indeed she'd hoped to find anything at all. Mouche used to talk intelligently of her travels through Italy before we'd met, and for that same reason, noticing how erratic or misguided were her reactions to this country where we'd unexpectedly found ourselves—naive, knowing nothing of its past, without having read a word about it—I asked myself whether her sharp observations about the strange sensuality of Palazzo Barberini's windows, the obsessive cherubim on the ceiling of Saint John Lateran, the almost feminine intimacy of San Carlo alle Quattro Fontane, with its shady, curving cloister, were not just opportune citations, suited to the spirit of the times, things read, heard, drunk from the sources of general opinion. Her judgments responded to the aesthetic fashions of the moment. She went for the mossy and shadowy when it was thought novel to speak of moss and shadows, but if placed before something unfamiliar that aroused no clear associations, say, a school of architecture unknown to her from books, she turned disconcerted, hesitant, incapable of formulating a valid opinion—buying a dusty hippocamp for literary reasons when she could have had a crude figurine of Saint Rose with her flowering palm. The Canadian painter had been the lover of a poet well known for his essays on Matthew Lewis and Ann Radcliffe, and this permitted Mouche the pleasure of returning to the terrain of surrealism, astrology, and dream interpretation, with everything that implied. Whenever—and this wasn't infrequent—she came across some woman who, in her words, *spoke her same language*, she would commit herself to this new friendship with endless hours, a luxuriance of expectations, a restlessness that maddened me. These crises of effusion were short-lived, and would end as suddenly as they'd begun, on the day you least expected. But while they lasted, they aroused in me the most intolerable suspicions. As always, what I had now was a hunch, a doubt, an agitation, with no evidence of guilt. This fixation had overtaken me the evening before, after the Kapellmeister's funeral. When I returned from the cemetery, where I'd gone with a group of guests, I found petals from the mortuary flowers—so aromatic in this country—scattered on the floor of the foyer. The street sweepers proceeded to carry off the dead creatures that had stunk so abominably throughout our confinement, and when the feet of a horse gnawed to bits by the vultures wouldn't fit in the carriage, they hacked them off with machetes, sending the hooves flying with bones and horseshoes into the swarms of flies whirling over the asphalt. Back from the revolution as from a weekend jaunt, the servants rearranged the furniture and burnished the doorknobs with chamois. Mouche seemed to have left with her friend. When they reappeared after curfew, saying they'd gone out to walk the streets and mingle with the multitude celebrating the victors' triumph, I had the feeling they were up to something strange. They both had a sort of cold indifference to everything, a self-sufficiency—like people returning from travels to forbidden realms—that struck me as out of character. I observed them, doggedly trying to catch some pregnant gaze; I looked for the hidden meaning in each phrase they uttered; I tried to trick them with unnerving, contradictory questions, but all of it was for nothing. I had been around, I was jaded, and I knew there was something bizarre going on. But what I suffered from was far worse than jealousy—it was the unbearable feeling I'd been left out of a game, and this exclusion lay at the root of my vehemence. I couldn't bear the underhandedness, the fakery, the image in my mind of a secret, delightful *something* being done behind my back by two women in cahoots. My imagination made tangible the most contemptible physical arrangements, and despite having repeated to myself a thousand times that what tied me to Mouche was sensuality and habit and not love, I was tempted to behave like a husband in a melodrama. I knew that when the storm had passed and I confessed these torments to my friend, she would shrug, saying I was too silly to ever anger her, and would attribute the *animal nature* of my reactions to my Hispano-American upbringing. And now, in the stillness of those deserted streets, suspicions were assailing me again. I hurried home, at once dreading and yearning for proof. What I found there was unexpected: there was a tumult in the studio, with abundant drinks poured into glasses. A moment earlier, three young artists had arrived from the capital, fleeing the same curfew we had, not wishing to be shut up in their homes at nightfall. The musician was so white, the poet so Indian, the painter so black that I inevitably thought of the three wise men when I saw them standing around the hammock where Mouche lay lazily replying to their questions as though lending herself to a kind of adoration. There was only one subject: Paris. And I watched these young men interrogate my friend as medieval Christians would question a pilgrim returned from the Holy Land. They tirelessly asked for more details about the appearance of the leader of a school of artists Mouche flaunted her acquaintance with; they wondered if this or that writer still frequented this or that café, or if another two had ever settled their row over Kierkegaard, or if the same people were still championing nonfigurative art. When their French and English were too poor to grasp my friend's replies, they gazed imploringly at the painter, begging her to translate the anecdote, the phrase whose precious essence they might have lost. After interrupting the conversation with the malign purpose of stealing the floor from Mouche, I questioned the young men about their country's history, the first stutterings of its colonial literature, its folk traditions, and I could see it displeased them deeply that the conversation had taken this turn. Then, to keep my friend from speaking further, I asked whether they'd been to the jungle. The Indian poet shrugged, saying there was nothing to see there, no matter how far you went, and that forays into the wild were best left to foreigners collecting bows and quivers. There was no culture in the jungle, the black painter affirmed. The musician told me today's artist must reside where thought and creation had attained the greatest vigor, mentioning again that city whose intellectual topography was imprinted on the minds of his mates, all of whom fell into waking reveries, as he himself confessed, looking at a

Carte Taride with the *métro* stations drawn in thick blue circles: *Solférino, Oberkampf, Corvisart, Mouton-Duvernet*. The train lines connected these circles, superimposed on the streets, cutting several times across the Seine, woven together like cords in a net. That net would soon sweep up the young Three Kings, who were following a star shining over the grand manger of Saint-Germain-des-Prés. Depending on the day's weather, someone would talk to them about the yearning for escape, the advantages of suicide, the importance of slapping corpses, or the need to shoot the first passerby. Some delirious teacher would cajole them into embracing the worship of Dionysus, *god of ecstasy and fear, of savagery and liberation, a mad god whose mere appearance throws living beings into frenzy*, but omitting how Officer Nietzsche, the great summoner of Dionysus, had posed for a portrait once wearing the uniform of the Prussian Army, with a saber in hand and a helmet resting on a Munich-style console, like the grim prefiguration of the god of fear who would be unleashed upon the Europe of the Ninth Symphony. I could see them growing pale and haggard in their unlit studios—the Indian olivaceous, the Negro unsmiling, the white gone utterly to seed—gradually forgetting the sun they'd left behind, trying desperately to do whatever it was they were supposed to do trapped in that net. At the end of a few years, they would return to their homeland with vacant eyes, their youth lost in the undertaking, their courage broken, too enervated to perform the only task that struck me as worthwhile in this place that was now beginning to reveal to me its colors: Adam's task of putting names to things. Observing them that night, I saw how I'd been harmed by a premature expulsion from an environment that had been my own until my adolescent years; how I'd been led astray by the facile ardor of men of my generation, drawn by theories into intellectual mazes only to be devoured by Minotaurs. Certain ideas were tiresome to me because I'd held them for so long, and I wanted darkly to say something other than the things said all over every day by those who thought themselves *up-to-date* for their acquaintance with notions that would be discredited, even abhorred in fifteen years. Here again, I was party to the same debates that had occasionally amused me in Mouche's home. But leaning on the balcony, with the torrent gurgling softly at the bottom of the gorge, inhaling a biting air that smelled of wet hay, so close to the creatures of the earth that slithered with death in their fangs over the red and green alfalfa—now, when the night was singularly tangible to me—these *modern* topics were becoming excruciating. I wished I could hush the voices speaking behind me so I could hear the diapason of the frogs, the high tones of the crickets, the rhythm of a cart creaking at the axles past the Calvary of Fog. Vexed at Mouche, at everyone, with the desire to write, to compose, I left the house for the edge of the stream, once more to contemplate the panels of the urban tableau. Someone essayed a few chords on the painter's piano. Then, the young musician—from his self-assured manner, I could tell he was a composer, too—began to play. I counted twelve notes, not a single one repeated, that preceded the initial flat of that tense andante. I could have guessed as much: atonality had arrived in the country, where its prescriptions were already finding followers. I continued downward till I reached the tavern, where I drank a few blackberry brandies. Bundled in their ponchos, the drovers spoke of trees that bled when the axes wounded them on Good Friday, of nettles that would spring from the bellies of dead wasps in the smoke of woods from the mountains. Night had fallen, and a harpist approached the bar. Shoeless, hat in hand, his instrument slung over his back, he asked permission to play a bit of music. He'd come from far away, from a village in the Tembladeras District, where he'd gone, as he had for years now, to keep a promise to play at the Church of the Invention of the Cross. Now all he wanted was to wet his whistle, to trade a bit of his art for their fine agave liquor. Amid silence, with the gravity of an officiant at a rite, the harpist laid his hands on the strings, and his inspired prelude, intended to loosen his fingers, filled me with admiration. His scales, in his solemn recitatives, interrupted by dense, majestic chords, evoked somehow the festive grandeur of the organ preambles of the Middle Ages. At the same time, because his rustic instrument was crudely tuned, the musician had to keep to a limited range of notes, giving the

impression that his playing represented a thorough acquaintance with ancient modes and ecclesiastical tones, attaining
with its unfeigned primitivism the ambitions of many present-
day composers. His improvisation brought to mind the organ,
the vihuela, and the lute, whose traditions throbbed with life
in the conical sound box he held steady between his scaly ankles. Afterward, there was dancing: dances of vertiginous
movements, with binary rhythms gliding in three-quarter
time, in a modal system never before rehearsed in such a way.
I was tempted to go back to the house and drag the young composer over by his ear to make him pay due attention to what
was happening here. But then the patrolmen showed up with
their lanterns and oilcloth capes and ordered the tavern closed.
Here, too, they said, there was a curfew after nightfall. Seeing
now that our—for me unpleasant—stay with the Canadian
would find us sharing a great deal of time in close quarters, I
made a decision, the culmination of a long series of thoughts
and reconsiderations. There were buses leaving Los Altos that
stopped in the port, which gave access by river to the great
Southern Forest. We would give up the scheme my friend had
proposed, which circumstance was thwarting at every turn.
Thanks to the revolution, my money had risen dramatically
against the local currency. The easiest, most honest, most interesting thing was to use what was left of my vacation to do
the work the Curator and the University had asked of me. To
avoid backtracking on my resolution, I bought two bus tickets
for the next morning from the tavern keeper. I didn't care what
Mouche thought: for the first time, I felt I could impose my will.

CHAPTER THREE

It will be the time in which he chooses a
path, adorns his face and speaks and vomits
what he swallowed and releases his burden.

BOOK OF CHILAM BALAM

8

(June 11)

We argued till past midnight. Mouche alleged she had a sudden cold; she asked me to feel her forehead, which was in fact
rather cool, then told me she was getting chills; she coughed so
much, her throat became irritated, and then she couldn't stop
herself. I packed the suitcases without paying her mind, and it
wasn't yet dawn when we took our seats on the bus full of people wrapped in blankets, with plush towels around their necks
like scarves. To the very end, my friend went on talking with
the Canadian, arranging meetings in the capital when we returned from a journey that would last some two weeks at most.
Soon we were rolling over a road on a gulley through mountains so thick with mist that their black poplars were hardly
even shadows in the rising sun. Mouche was the type who
passed easily from pretending to believe to believing her pre-
tenses, and I knew she would go on feigning illness for some
time, so I turned away, closed up in myself, determined to
enjoy in solitude all that could be seen, forgetting her, even if
she was sleeping on my shoulder and sighing mournfully. Our
travels from the capital to Los Altos had permitted me to step
back in time to the years of my childhood—to return to the
morning of adolescence—finding again ways of living, flavors,
words, things, that had marked me deeper than I might have
believed. The pomegranate tree, the *tinajero*, the coins and

clubs, the courtyard with basil, and the door with the blue
wings had begun to speak to me again. But now I saw what lay
beyond the images that offered themselves to my eyes when I
ceased to know the world by touch alone. When we cut through
the opalescent mist that the sunrise turned green, there began
for me a kind of Discovery. The bus whined at the axles,
throwing dust to the wind, swaying over the precipices, climbing arduously, as if every hill imposed wretched sufferings on
its run-down shell. It was a sorry thing with a red roof, rising,
wheels clinging, hugging the stones between the almost vertical slopes of a ravine; a thing shrinking in the midst of towering mountains. Because the mountains were growing. With the
sun illuminating the summits, those summits multiplied, from
end to end, crude, extensive, like immense black axes, their
blades slicing a wind that blew through the gorges with a never-
ending roar. Everything dilated in a crushing affirmation of
new proportions. At the end of that climb of a hundred turns
and returns, when we thought we had reached the peak, another, more abrupt, less accessible bank would appear between
frozen crests that soared above the crests we'd seen before. The
tenacious vehicle shrank to nothing deep in the defiles, pushing
itself upward with its round back feet, kindred more to the insects than the rocks. It was day now, and between sullen summits, like rough-hewn silex, the clouds twisted in the sky,
shaped by the breath from the gullies. When the black axes
that sliced the wind and the terraces overlooking them gave
way to the volcanoes, our human prerogatives ended, just as
the prerogatives of the vegetation had been annulled some time
before. We were measly creatures, mute with rigid faces, in a
wasteland where the lone foliaceous presence was a cactus of
gray felt that hung like lichen, like a flower of ash, on the ground
stripped bare of soil. Behind us, far below, lay the clouds that
had shaded the valleys, and other clouds presided over them
forever hidden by clouds familiar to those men who dwelled in
a world of things of human scale. We were on the backbone of
the storied Indies, on a vertebra where the Andean crests,
buckling between summits, like the mouth of a fish surfacing
to sip the snow, decimated the winds trying to blow from

ocean to ocean. We reached the edge of the craters packed
with geological rubble, dreadfully black or spiny with forlorn
crags that resembled petrified animals. Mute dread overtook
me in that affluence of vales and vertices. The enigmas of fog
to either side of the spectral road made me wonder if, beneath
its fleeting substance, a void lay as deep as the distance between us and home. Because from here, land with its beasts, its
trees and breezes, seemed different from, alien to the resolute
ice that whitened the peaks: a world made for man free of the
nocturnal bellows of storms piping through gorges and abysses.
A transit of clouds divided this wasteland of black rubble from
our soil. Unsettled by the mute telluric menace every form suggested in these skirts of lava, this scree cast down from the
summits, I noticed with immense relief that our miserable con-
veyance was agonized a bit less as it turned onto the first downhill slope I had seen in several hours. On the opposite face, we
braked suddenly in the center of a stone bridge over a torrent
so far below we couldn't see its waters, despite their deafening
roar. A woman in a blue poncho was sitting on a stone wall,
her bundle and umbrella on the ground. She didn't respond
when spoken to, and seemed stunned, her gaze misted over and
her lips quivering; she shook her head softly beneath a red kerchief that had come untied beneath her chin. A fellow traveler
walked over and placed a square of molasses in her mouth,
squeezing her jaw to force her to swallow. Seeming to understand, the woman began slowly to chew, and her eyes became
once more expressive, as though she were returning from far
away, rediscovering the world with surprise. She looked at
me as if she recognized me, and struggled to stand up, still
leaning on the barrier. Just then, a distant avalanche echoed
overhead, stirring the still-emerging mists that rose like vale-
dictions from the heart of a crater. Jolting into awareness, the
woman screamed and grabbed me, begging in a voice that
cracked in the thin air that we not leave her there to die. She'd
been brought there by people from elsewhere who thought she
knew that drowsiness was dangerous in these altitudes, and
only now did she realize she'd barely survived. Stumbling, she
allowed us to bring her into the bus, where she swallowed the

last bits of the molasses. When we'd descended farther and the air was better, she took a sip of brandy, and soon enough, her fear had dissolved into laughter. All over the bus, people told stories about death from cold, about others who'd lost their lives on this very road, but with relish, as though discussing the ordinary vicissitudes of life. Someone said that half a century ago, eight members of a scientific expedition who had fallen ill were found frozen in the ice, like curios in a vitrine, near the mouth of a volcano hidden by the nearby hills. Sitting in a circle, frozen in mid-gesture, just as death had come upon them, they stared out through the transparent crystal that covered their faces like a death mask. Now we were descending quickly, the clouds that once were below us were again above us, and the mist was decaying in fringes, offering a view of the still distant valleys. We returned to the land of men, and our breath recovered its accustomed rhythm after having known the bite of cold needles. A village appeared on a round plateau surrounded by a river. It looked oddly Castilian to me, despite its baroque church, because of the tiled roofs on tortuous, crowded streets clustered around the square. A braying ass reminded me of the illustration of a donkey in the foreground of a view of El Toboso in my third-grade reading textbook—not unlike the vista I was contemplating now. *Somewhere in La Mancha, in a place whose name I'd rather not recall, there lived, not long ago, a nobleman of the sort that keeps a lance in its perch, an old leather buckler, a skinny nag and a greyhound* . . . I was proud to still remember what we'd been taught so gruelingly to recite, all twenty of us kids, by the schoolteacher. And yet, I had once known the whole paragraph by heart, and now I could get no farther than the greyhound. The lapse annoyed me, and I kept returning to the words *somewhere in La Mancha* to see if I could call up the next phrase, when the woman we'd rescued from the mist pointed to a broad curve on the flank of the mountain before us and said this place was known as *La Hoya*. Instantly I recollected the *olla*, the *pot of rather more beef than mutton, peppered leftovers on most nights, pork and eggs on Saturdays, lentils on Fridays, and an occasional squab on Sundays consumed three*

fourths of his avails . . . That was as far as I could get. But now
my attention was fixed on the woman who had so opportunely
uttered the word *Hoya*, and I looked at her with sympathy.
From where I sat, I could see a little less than half her face, its
cheekbone prominent beneath an eye that stretched toward the
temple, sinking into deep shadows under her willfully arched
brow. Her profile was stern, from forehead to nose; but beneath those proud, redoubtable traits, her mouth was thick
and sensual beside narrow cheeks that seemed to flee toward
her ears, emphasizing the vigor of that face framed with thick
black hair, pulled back, here and there, with celluloid combs.
Several races clearly found themselves mingled in this woman,
with her Indian hair and cheekbones, her Mediterranean forehead and nose, her Negress's round, firm shoulders and unusu-
ally broad hips, which I had noticed when I saw her stand to
tuck her bundle of clothing and her umbrella behind the mesh
that held the baggage in place. A living fusion of pedigrees, she
was also evidently a woman of pedigree. When I saw her startling eyes, which had not a single trace of blackness, I recalled
those figures from archaic frescoes that gaze out from the front
and side with such alarming persistence from circles of ink
drawn on their temples. That in turn reminded me of *La Pa-
risienne*, and I had to admit that the blood of this voyager from
the wilderness and mist was no more mixed than that of the
races that had mingled for centuries in the Mediterranean basin.
I even asked myself if certain amalgams of the minor races, their
roots left intact, were not preferable to the more vigorous couplings between Celts, Negroes, Latins, Indians, and even *New
Christians* in the early days on the meeting ground of the Americas. Because what had mingled here were not consanguineous
peoples, like those that history had malaxated on crossings of
the sea of Ulysses, but rather the great races of the world, the
farthest flung, the most distinct, those that for millennia had
known nothing of the others with whom they shared the
planet.

The rain started falling with monotonous intensity, and the
windows misted over. The return to an almost normal atmosphere sank the travelers into a sort of torpor. After eating a

piece of fruit, I tried to nap, and realized in passing that a week
into this journey, I could fall asleep irrespective of the hour,
just as I'd been able to do in my adolescence. When I woke, and
night was falling, we were in a village of whitewashed houses
built into the mountainside beneath a dark vegetation of cool
forests where the clearings carved out by farmworkers seemed
imprisoned by the underbrush. Thick vines hung from the tree-
tops, swaying over the roads and scattering across them con-
densed droplets of fog. The night, carried in by the long
shadows of the mountains, now enveloped the summits. Exhausted, Mouche grabbed me by the arm, saying the changes
in altitude had done her in. Her head ached, she was feverish,
and she wanted to take some medicine and lie down. I left her
in a whitewashed room with no more luxuries than a pitcher
and basin, and went to the dining room, a meager extension of
the kitchen with a wood fire burning in a large hearth. After
eating corn soup and rustic mountain cheese that smelled of
goat, I felt lazy and happy in the glow of the fire. I was contemplating the dance of the flames when a silhouette cast a shadow
in front of me from the other end of the table. It was the woman
rescued that morning, but rested and groomed, and I amused
myself by cataloging her droll formal attire. She wasn't well or
badly dressed. Her garments were not of this time, not of any
time whatsoever, with their intricate combination of lace,
pleats, and ribbons, some undyed and some blue, everything
clean and starched, stiff as playing cards, looking partly drawn
from the closets of some whimsical tailor and partly from a
magician's box of tricks. A dark blue velvet ribbon cinched her
bodice. She ordered dishes I had never heard of and ate slowly,
without talking, her eyes staring at the tablecloth, as though
tragic worry overwhelmed her. After a while, I dared to address her, and found out she would be traveling with us for
some time, as she had a pious duty to attend to. She had come
from the other end of the country, crossing deserts and waste-
lands and island-studded lakes, passing through jungles and
plains to bring her ill father a picture of the Fourteen Holy
Helpers, who had answered her family's prayers with authentic
miracles. It had been left with an aunt who kept it on display

on more brightly lit altars. We were now alone in the dining room, and I walked over to the corner, where a chest of drawers aroused my curiosity, and smelled the sweet perfume of wild herbs emanating from it. Beside flasks of tinctures and infusions were drawers labeled with the names of plants. The young woman followed me, and removed some dry leaves, moss, and sprigs of broom, squeezing them in her palm and singing the praises of their properties, identifying each by its aroma. This was aloe vera, good for inflammation of the lungs, and here was pink liana, which added body to your hair; then bishop's wort for coughs, basil to ward off bad luck, and bear grass, Angelonia, pitaya, and Russian rosebud for ills I no longer recall. She referred to the herbs as if they were beings ever vigilant in a proximate but nonetheless mysterious domain guarded over by nervous dignitaries. The plants spoke through her mouth and boasted of their powers. The forest had a lord, a spirit who hopped on one foot, and nothing that grew in the shadows of the trees should be taken without payment. If you entered the woodlands looking for curative shoots, mushrooms, or vines, you had to give a greeting and leave coins between the roots of an ancient tree as a way of asking permission. And upon leaving, you were to turn deferentially and utter a word of goodbye, for millions of eyes watched our every movement from the bark and leaves. I don't know why that woman seemed so beautiful to me suddenly as she threw a handful of bitter aromatic couch grass into the fire, which carved her traits from the shadows in high relief. I was about to utter some trivial compliment when she told me good night brusquely, turning her back to the flames. I stayed there observing the fire alone. It had been a long time since I'd done so.

9

(Later)

Not long after she left, I heard soft voices in one of the corners. Someone had left on a radio, a very old one sitting on a kitchen

table nestled between corn ears and cucumbers. I was going to
turn it off when the battered box projected a fifth of French
horns I knew very well: the same one that drove me from a
concert hall not so many days before. But tonight, beside the
firewood breaking into embers, with the crickets chirping between the brown roof beams, that remote performance possessed a mysterious force. The unknown, invisible, faceless
players were like the abstract expositors of the written score,
which had landed at the foot of these mountains after soaring
over the summits, arriving from who knew where with sounds
that weren't notes, but echoes in myself. Leaning toward it, I
listened. And a light fifth blew from the horns, exalted into triplets by the second violins and cellos, and two descending notes
overwhelmed it, plummeting in a way from the first line of
strings and the violas with a reluctance turned to anguish, quavering at the horror of a suddenly unchained force. It was, in
an eruption of storm and shadow, the first movement of the
Ninth Symphony. I thought I might sigh with relief as the tones
took shape, but the rapid extinction of the strings, the spectral
collapse of the entire edifice, returned me to the disquiet of the
phrase being gestated. After so long wanting to hear nothing
of it, the musical ode returned with the flood of memories I
tried in vain to separate from the inchoate crescendo, still wavering, as though unsure of its footing. Every time the metallic
sound of a horn underlay a chord, I thought I saw my father
with his trim little beard bending forward to read the music
with that peculiar attitude of the horn player, who seems unaware, while he plays, that his lips are affixed to the mouthpiece
of a great copper volute that gives his entire body the appearance of a Corinthian capital. With that mimetism that makes
oboists thin and haggard, trombonists jocose and chubby
cheeked, my father wound up possessing a brassy voice that
throbbed from his nose when I used to sit beside him in his
wicker chair and he would show me engravings of the ancestors of his noble instrument: oliphants from Byzantium, Roman
buccinas, Saracen busines, and the silver tubas of Frederick
Barbarossa. According to him, only a blast from a horn—he
pronounced this word, heavy like bronze on his lips, with a

rolled *r*—could have toppled the walls of Jericho. Educated in
the conservatories of German Switzerland, he deemed superior the horn of a fine metallic timbre, descendant of the hunting horns that had echoed throughout the Black Forest, over
what he dubbed pejoratively, in French, *le cor*, believing the
techniques taught in Paris brought his masculine instrument
too close to the feminine woodwinds. To illustrate his words,
he would raise the bell of his instrument and blow the Siegfried
motif over the low walls of the patio with the force of a herald
of the Last Judgment. I owed my birth on this side of the ocean
to a hunting scene from Glazunov's *Raymonda*. The assassina-
tion in Sarajevo had caught my father in the high point of Wagner season at the Teatro Real in Madrid and, shocked by the
unexpected bellicosity of the German and French socialists, he
turned his back on the rotten old continent, taking the post
of first horn on Anna Pavlova's tour of the Antilles. There followed a marriage whose sentimental foundations were far from
clear to me, then there I was making my first forays on all
fours in the courtyard beneath the shadows of a tall tamarind
tree while my mother, helping the Negro cook, sang the story
of a certain Sir Cat who sits on a golden throne and is asked
if he wants to marry a wildcat, niece of the ocelot. The war
dragged on, and there was little work for an instrument only
needed during opera season, when the wintry north winds blew,
and so my father opened a small music shop. Now and then,
nostalgic for the symphonic orchestras he'd once played in, he
would take a baton from the display case, open the pages of
the Ninth Symphony, and conduct an imaginary orchestra,
mimicking the gestures of Nikisch or Mahler, singing the work
in its entirety with tremendous onomatopoeias of percussion,
bass, and brass. My mother would run and close the windows
so no one would think him mad, while nonetheless accepting,
with traditional Hispanic forbearance, that as long as her husband didn't drink or gamble, even his worst extravagances were
beyond reproach. The coda was beginning now, over chro-
matic tremolos in the lower ranges, a coda whose ascending
movement—plaintive, funereal, and triumphant all at once—it
had so pleased my father to intone in noble phrases rising

toward baritone. Two quick scales conjoined in an exordium drawn from the orchestra by an almost physical violence. And then there was silence. A silence soon pervaded by singing crickets and crackling coals. I waited impatiently for the sudden opening of the scherzo, and let the haunted arabesques of the second violins envelop me and bear me away, and for a moment I knew nothing but music, and then the peculiar doubling of the horns Wagner had inserted, to correct a transcription error, into Beethoven's score sent me back to my father's side in the days when *she* was no longer with us—the woman with the blue velvet sewing kit who sang to me so many times the tale of Sir Cat, the romance of Mambrú, and Alfonso XII's lamentation upon Mercedes's death: *Four dukes bore her / through the streets of Aldaví.* Our vigils were now devoted to the reading of an old Lutheran Bible hidden for years in the back of a closet, on account of my mother's Catholicism. Grave in his widowerhood, embittered by unrelieved solitude, my father broke his every bond to the warm and bustling city of my birth, leaving for North America, where he opened another store with little success. Rumination over Ecclesiastes and the Psalms became linked in his mind with sudden longings. Around this time, he began telling me about the workers who used to listen to the Ninth Symphony. The fiasco in North America transformed gradually into a yearning for Europe characterized by its peaks and summits, apotheoses and feasts. This New World, as they called it, was for him a hemisphere without history, alien to the great traditions of the Mediterranean, a land of Indians and blacks, peopled by the castoffs of the great European nations—and here he would not fail to mention the storied whores shipped to New Orleans by gendarmes in tricornes, sent off with a piping of fifes, a detail I always supposed he'd gleaned from some repertory opera. He would evoke with devotion his fatherland on the Old Continent, describing before my marveling eyes a University of Heidelberg that I imagined green with venerable ivy. In my imagination, I used to voyage from the theorbos of the angelic concert to the illustrious slates of the Gewandhaus, from the contests of the minnesingers to the concerts of Potsdam, learning the names of cities the mere

spellings of which inspired mirages of ocher, white, and bronze—
like Bonn—or the dander of swans, like Siena. But my father,
for whom the affirmation of certain principles constituted the
supreme legacy of civilization, appreciated, above all, the respect for the sanctity of human life back home. He told me of
authors who, from the ease of their writing rooms, had made
monarchs tremble, and no one had dared to reproof them. His
discussions of *J'accuse*, of the struggles of Rathenau, the fruits
of Louis XVI's capitulation before Mirabeau, led inevitably
into considerations of the relentlessness of progress, the spread
of socialism, and collective culture, and ended with tributes to
those enlightened workers in the city of his birth, with its
seventeenth-century cathedral, who spent their leisure hours in
public libraries and took their families to hear the Ninth Symphony on Sundays instead of dulling their wits at Mass—this
was a country where science was gaining ground on superstition. Since my adolescence, the eyes of my imagination had
gazed toward these workers in blue smocks and corduroy pants,
nobly moved by the breath of genius in the work of Beethoven,
perhaps listening to this very same triad whose warm, intricate
phrasing was rising now in the voices of cellos and violas. This
vision cast such a spell on me that when my father died, I devoted the little money left over after auctioning the sonatas
and partitas that formed his meager bequest to getting acquainted with my roots. I crossed the Ocean one fine day, convinced I would never return. But at the end of an apprenticeship
in bewilderment I would later refer to jokingly as *the adoration
of the facades*, I met with realities that contradicted my father's teachings. Far from taking inspiration from the Ninth
Symphony, the minds there were eager to make their mark
with parades below newly built triumphal arches and totem
poles with the icons of sun worshippers of old. The transposi-
tion of the marble and bronze of the sects of old into gigantic
pinewood monstrosities erected for a single day, of cardboard
emblems painted gold, should have deepened the distrust of
the crowds there listening to words amplified over speakers.
And yet that wasn't what happened. Everyone there felt pro-
foundly invested in these undertakings, and many were pleased

to sit at the right hand of God and judge people from the past
for the crime of not seeing the future. I saw a metaphysician
from Heidelberg play drum major to a gang of young philoso-
phers who marched—rather, strode—to vote for men who
scorned any and all things one might call intellectual. I saw
couples climb the Witches' Mountain on solstice nights to light
old votive fires now stripped of all meaning. But nothing left
such an impression on me as the call to judgment, the postmortem trial, the profanation of the tomb of a man who ended a
symphony with a chorale of the Augsburg Confession, or another who shouted in the purest of voices before the verdigris
waves of the great North: *I love the sea like my soul!* Tired of
reciting the intermezzo *sotto voce* and of hearing talk of new
exoduses, imminent terrors, of bodies piled in the streets, I took
shelter, like a refugee, in the solace of shadowy museums, em-
barking on long journeys across time. But when I left the paintings behind me, things had gone from bad to worse. The papers
were calling for beheadings. Believers shivered under the pul-
pits when the bishops screamed. Rabbis hid the Torah, preach-
ers were cast out from their chapels. Rites were dissolved, the
Word was shattered. At night, in public squares, the students of
illustrious universities burned books on great bonfires. Wherever you stepped on the continent, you saw photos of children
killed in bombings on open cities, heard tales of scholars imprisoned in salt mines, unexplained abductions, harassment
and summary dismissals, field hands shot to death in bull
rings. I was shocked—bitter, wounded to the quick—by the
cleft between the world my father had yearned for and the one I
had found. I had looked for Erasmus's smile, the *Discourse on
Method*, the spirit of humanism, Faustian yearning and the
Apollonian soul; I had found autos-da-fé, Inquisition courts,
political trials that reenacted the ordeals of the Middle Ages. No
more could you simply contemplate a beautiful tympanum, a
campanile, a gargoyle, or a smiling angel without telling yourself they foretold the strife of the present and that the figures in
the Adoration were paying homage to something far different
from what was represented in the manger. The age wearied
me. And horribly, the imaginary was the only possible escape

in that world without hiding places, its nature tamed for centuries, where the almost total synchronization of human life had reduced disputes to two or three problems to be fought out on the fields of slaughter. Discourse stood in for myth; slogans had taken the place of dogma. Tired of ironbound commonplaces, of bowdlerized texts and empty academic chairs, I returned to the Atlantic with a yearning to cross, but this time in the opposite direction. And, two days before I left, I stood there musing over the motifs of a forgotten danse macabre on the beams of the ossuary of Saint-Symphorien-des-Bois. I was in a country courtyard invaded by weeds and centenary sorrow, and over its pillars was again displayed the timeless theme of the vanity of pomp, the skeleton beneath the luxuriating flesh, the rotten rib under the prelate's chasuble, the drum pounded with two tibias amid a xylophone composed of bones. And this shabby barn architecture around the eternal Parable, the roiling, muddy river nearby, the outlying farms and factories, the pigs grunting like Saint Anthony's Swine, all this at the feet of the skeletons carved in timbers gone gray from centuries of rain gave a singular urgency to this reredos of dust, ash, nothingness, bringing it forward to the present. And the kettledrums resounding in Beethoven's scherzo took on a fateful resonance now, associated in my mind with the vision of the boneyard in Bois, by the door to which the evening papers surprised me with news of war.

The firewood had turned to cinders. On a hillside past the roof and pines, a dog was barking in the mist. The music itself had estranged me from the music, and I returned to it through the crickets, waiting for the B-flat already chirping in my ear. Following a muffled invitation from the bassoon and clarinet, the admirable adagio was born, profound in its meek lyricism. This was the one passage of the Symphony that my mother— more used to habaneras and excerpts from the opera—managed to play sometimes, thanks to its easy rhythms, from a transcription for piano that she used to take from one of the drawers in the shop. On the sixth beat, rounded off with a placid echo of woodwinds, I arrive home from school at a jog, slipping on the little fruits of the poplars covering the sidewalk.

Our house has a wide porch of whitewashed columns, and looks like a stairstep between the neighboring porches, the one higher, the other lower, all traversed by the incline plane of the sidewalk sloping toward the Church of Jesús del Monte, which looks down on the roofs amid a stand of trees on a hill enclosed by railings. The house had once belonged to aristocrats, and still has the old furnishings of thick, dark wood, deep closets, and a cut glass chandelier whose pendants fill with little rainbows when the last ray of the sun pierces the panes of the transom window—blue, white, and red—that fills the arch of the vestibule like a great glass fan. I sit stiff-legged deep in a rocking chair too tall and wide for a little boy and open the Royal Spanish Academy's *Epitome of Grammar*, which I have to study that evening. *These fields, oh misery! you see now, Fabio* . . . begins the example I recalled only recently. *These fields, oh misery! you see now, Fabio* . . . The black woman busy with her sooty pots and pans sings something about colonial days and the Civil Guard and its officers with mustaches. My mother's finger strikes the F key on her piano, as usual holding it a little long. At the other end of the house is a room with a pumpkin vine climbing the bars of the window. I call María del Carmen, who is playing surrounded by arecas in planters, rosebushes in pots, and beds of carnations, calla lilies, and sunflowers in the backyard of her father, the gardener. She crawls through a gap in the holly hedge and lies beside me in the laundry basket that is shaped like a ship and is the ship of our travels. It swaths us, this basket brought every week by a sweating giant who eats huge plates of beans and goes by the name of Baudilio, in aromas of esparto, fiber, hay. I never tire of squeezing the girl in my arms. Her heat suffuses me with a luxuriant torpor I wish would stretch on forever. When she gets bored of staying there immobile, I ease her mind by telling her we are still at sea, but that it won't be long before we reach the quay; that the ship will moor at that trunk with the beveled top covered in polychrome tin. In school, I heard boys and girls did filthy things with each other. Indignant, I refused to believe; those were dirty tales the big children invented to make fun of the little ones. The day I was first told all that, I didn't dare look my mother in the eyes. I ask María del Carmen now if she would like to be my wife, and since she says yes, I squeeze her tighter, and to keep her from pulling away, my voice mimics the sound of the siren on a ship. I can barely breathe, I'm throbbing all over, and this unease is so pleasant and I don't know why, when the black woman catches us like this, she gets angry, jerks us from the basket, throws it over a wardrobe, and shouts that I'm too big for these kinds of games. Still, she tells my mother nothing. Eventually, I complain to her, and she says it's time to study. I turn back to the *Epitome of Grammar*, but the odor of fiber, of wicker, of esparto pursues me. The memory of this scent at times transpires from the past so palpably that I shake all over. It's the same scent I've found again tonight by the cabinet with the wild herbs, as the adagio concludes with four chords—pianissimo, the first broken in an arpeggio—and a ripple, perceptible through the broadcast, moves the chorus just before it makes its entrance. I envision the sweeping hands of the invisible conductor making dramatic preparations for the advent of Schiller's Ode. The untrammeled tempest of brass and kettledrums will soon hear itself echoed, framing a repetition of themes from before, but broken now, lacerated, tattered, chaotically gestating a future, rising up, asserting themselves, returning to their prior essence. A symphony of this kind, in ruins (and for me, that was the nature of the symphony as a whole), would form a dramatic accompaniment, I think—hazards of the trade—to a documentary on the roads I traveled as a military interpreter at the end of the war. Those roads were of the Apocalypse, winding between shattered walls looking like the characters of an unknown alphabet, pitted, filled with chunks of statues, crossing roofless abbeys marked with decapitated angels, turning before a Last Supper the howitzers had exposed, ending in the dust and ash of what for centuries had been the greatest archive of Ambrosian chant. But the horrors of war are the work of man, not God. Every age has left its versions engraved in copper or etched and stamped with ink. What was new, unprecedented, modern, was that lair of horror, the chancellery of dread, the forbidden ground of terror we came to know as we

advanced: a House of Tremors where everything was a testament to torture, mass extermination, cremations in walls
splashed with blood and excrement, piled bones, human den-
tures shoveled in mounds, and the worse deaths wrought coldly
by rubber-gloved hands in the antiseptic white light of operating
rooms. Two steps away, a sensitive and cultivated group of
humans—ignoring the abject smoke of chimneys from which
prayers howled in Yiddish had bellowed not long ago—went on
collecting stamps, studying the glories of the race, playing Mo-
zart's *kleine Nachtmusik*, reading Andersen's "The Little Mer-
maid" to their children. This, too, was new, grimly modern,
wretchedly unprecedented. Something collapsed in me that
afternoon, when I emerged from that fairground of iniquity I
had forced myself to visit, despite its repulsiveness, to be certain
it was really possible, and my mouth was dry as though I'd swallowed powdered plaster. Never could I have imagined such an
absolute rupture of Occidental man as the one depicted in
these horrific residues. As a child, I was terrified by the stories
going around then about atrocities committed by Pancho Villa,
whose name I associated with the hairy nocturnal shadow of
Mandinga. "Culture obliges," my father used to say, looking at
photos of executions in the newspapers, and this motto represented a new chivalry of the mind and a faith that the spread
of literacy would spell the end of infamy. A Manichaean in his
way, he saw the world as a battlefield between the light of the
printing press and the darkness of a primordial animality that
propagated endless cruelties among people oblivious to profes-
sorships, music, and laboratories. Evil for him was personified
in the man who lined up his enemies against the wall, emulat-
ing after centuries that Assyrian prince who blinded his captives with a lance, or the bloodthirsty crusader who immured
the Cathars in the cave of Montségur. Beethoven's Europe had
freed itself from Evil, which had its last redoubt in the Continent with Little History . . . But after standing in the House of
Tremors, in a camp dreamed up, built, and organized by people so steeped in nobility, the *dorado* gunslingers, the doggedly
besieged cities, the trains derailed among cactuses, and the
shoot-outs on drunken nights were like spirited scenes from an

adventure novel with sunny cavalcades, manly deeds, dignified deaths on sweaty saddle leather or over the shawl of a sutler woman who'd given birth by the roadside. Still worse was the night of my encounter with history's cruelest barbarians, the assassins and guards and those who carried bloody garments in buckets, those who made notes in their journals bound in black oilcloth, all of them imprisoned in a hangar—and how they started singing after their communal meal. Sitting up on my cot, startled awake, I heard them sing the same words as that chorus spurred on by the gestures of some distant conductor:

> *Freude, schöner Götterfunken,*
> *Tochter aus Elysium,*
> *Wir betreten feuertrunken,*
> *Himmlische, dein Heiligtum!*

At last I was listening to the Ninth Symphony, cause of my prior departure, and certainly not where my father would have imagined. *Joy! Lovely sparks divine, daughter of Elysium. Drunk on fire, heavenly one, we enter your sanctuary . . . all men shall be brothers when you gently take flight.* The irony of Schiller's verses was cutting. They were the culmination of centuries of progress, a ceaseless march toward tolerance, kindness, and understanding of the other. The Ninth Symphony was the warm pastry of Montaigne, the azure of *Utopia*, the essence of Elzevir, the voice of Voltaire in the Calas trial. And now *Alle Menschen werden Brüder, wo dein sanfter Flügel weilt* swelled joyously as it had that night when I lost my faith in those who spoke mendaciously of principles, drawing on texts whose deeper meaning they'd forgotten. To think less of the danse macabre around me, I adopted a mercenary's mentality, letting my comrades in arms drag me off to their taverns and brothels. I drank like them, sinking into a fitting oblivion that allowed me to finish the campaign without losing my head over words or deeds. Our victory left me defeated. Even the prop room of the theater at Bayreuth failed to impress me beneath its Wagnerian zoology of swans and horses hanging from the ceiling, next to a moth-eaten Fafnir whose head seemed to wish to hide beneath

my invader's cot. It was a man without hope who returned to
the big city and walked into the first bar he could find to arm
himself against all idealism. A man who tried to feel strong
when stealing another man's wife, but returned, when all was
said and done, to the solitude of an unshared bed. A man called
Man who, just the morning before, was still ready to pawn off
flea market instruments on another who had trusted him . . . All
at once, I grow bored of this Ninth Symphony with its unkept
promises, its messianic yearnings, capped off by the shooting
gallery of *Turkish music* running riot in a nod to the masses in
the *prestissimo* finale. I don't wait for the maestoso *Tochter aus
Elysium! Freude schöner Götterfunken* of the exordium. I turn
off the radio, wondering how I could listen to the piece almost
in its entirety, lost to myself when not subdued by the memories
it called forth. With one hand, I reach for the cool skin of a cu-
cumber, with the other I grasp a green pepper, pressing my
thumb into it to free the juice my mouth drinks in with delight.
I open the apothecary's cabinet plants, take out a handful of
dried leaves, and sit there inhaling their scent. The last ember
is still throbbing as though alive in the fireplace. I look out the
window: even the trees closest by are lost in the mist. The
goose in the backyard untucks its head from its wing and
opens its beak slightly without waking. A fruit falls somewhere
in the night.

10

(June 12)

When Mouche left the room, a little past dawn, she seemed
wearier than the night before. The discomfort of a day riding
over arduous roads, rising early, ceding to discipline, had diluted her personality. This woman, so wily and vivacious in
our disordered lives *back there*, was here the very image of list-
lessness. Her bright complexion had clouded, and her kerchief
sat askance over hair that ranged untidily in greenish blond.
Her peevish expression disfigured her, lifting the unsightly

slack in the corners of her thin lips, which she'd been unable to make up properly in the bad mirrors and scanty light. To distract her over breakfast, I told her of the traveler I'd spoken with the night before, who arrived as I did so, laughing and shivering all over after washing at a nearby spring with the ladies of the house. Her hair, twisted into braids around her head, was still dripping over her matte face. She addressed Mouche familiarly, as if she'd known her a long time, asking questions that I translated for her. By the time we got into the bus, the two women had established a language based on gestures and the odd word that allowed them to understand each other. My companion, still tired, rested her head on the other woman's shoulder and complained to her about the sorrows of that unpleasant voyage, while Rosario—as we'd learned she was called—heard her out with a maternal solicitude in which I detected a trace of irony. Happily relieved of Mouche, at least in part, I traveled comfortably, alone in a broad seat. That afternoon, we would arrive at the river port where boats left for the borders of the Southern Forest. From bend to bend, always descending along the hillsides, we moved toward sunnier hours. We stopped in peaceful villages with few open windows surrounded by increasingly tropical vegetation. Flowery creepers appeared, cactuses, bamboo; a palm tree blossomed in a courtyard, opening over the roof of a house where seamstresses worked out in the open. The rain that came at midday was so dense, so constant, that I saw nothing through the gray windows until late in the afternoon. Mouche took a book from her suitcase, and Rosario followed suit, rooting around in her bundle. She withdrew a chafed volume printed on cheap paper, with a trichrome cover of a woman in bearskins or a pelt of some kind embracing a stately knight at the mouth of a cave beneath the elated gaze of a slender-necked doe: *The Tale of Geneviève of Brabant*. There was an amusing contrast between it and the modern novel in Mouche's hands, a famous one I had put aside by the third chapter, embarrassed at the deluge of obscenities it contained. I detested sexual modesty and carnal hypocrisy of all kinds, but I still found dispiriting any literature or language that coarsened physical love with

jokes, sarcasm, or vulgarity. In intercourse, I believed one
should reserve the simplicity of the impulse, the spirit of play
appropriate to animals in heat, submitting with joy to this pleasure in the awareness that isolation behind closed doors, an absence of witnesses, involvement with another in the search for
delight, excluded anything motivated by irony or mockery—of
the discrepancies between the bodies or the animal nature of
certain acts—in that bond between two people who couldn't
see themselves with the eyes of strangers. For the same reason,
I could no more tolerate pornography than I could those lewd
stories, nasty phrasings, the metaphorical application of certain words to sexual activity, and I detested that literature,
very fashionable at present, that seemed determined to degrade
and uglify whatever might make a man in his moments of desperation and discouragement seek compensation for his fail-
ures in the affirmation of his virility, feeling it consummated in
the flesh he clove. I read over the two women's shoulders, con-
trasting the black and purple prose, but this game became impossible, because Mouche turned the pages too quickly, while
Rosario took her time, her eyes moving languidly from the beginning to the end of each line, lips spelling out the words,
stirred by their succession, which didn't always follow the order
she would have liked. She stopped sometimes, with an indignant look, when some infamy was inflicted upon poor Geneviève; then she would start the paragraph over, not believing
such wickedness was possible. Again she would pass through
the grievous episode, consternated at her impotence before
events. Her face showed profound anxiety now that Golo's
foul designs were made clear. "Those are stories from another
era," I said, to get her to talk. She turned to me, startled to realize I'd been reading over her shoulder. "What they say in
books is true," she responded. I looked over at Mouche's book,
wondering if it, too, was true, that prose showing multiple am-
putation scars from the hand of some scandalized editor,
which had done nothing to help it achieve—despite its laborious ostentation—that obscenity the Hindu sculptors or the
rustic Inca potters had elevated to a plane of authentic grandeur. Now Rosario closed her eyes. "What they say in the

books is true." For her, the story of Geneviève was most likely something current: something happening, while she read, in a country of the present day. For those unacquainted with the wardrobe, decor, and props of the past, the past itself is inconceivable. She must have imagined the castles of Brabant like the lavish haciendas with crenellated walls in her part of the world. Here men still hunted and rode on horseback, and deer and peccaries were harried by packs of hounds. Rosario would have imagined the attire in her novel as painters of the Renaissance saw the Gospel, draping figures from the Passion in their day's fashionable dress, casting head-down into Hell a Pilate draped in the garb of Florentine magistrates . . . Night fell, the light grew scarce, and everyone looked inward. We rolled on a long time in the darkness before turning at an outcropping and emerging into the illuminated vastness of the Valley of Flames.

I had already heard on this journey of the town built in a few weeks when petroleum gushed from the swampy terrain. But that didn't prepare me for the prodigious spectacle that spread out now at every bend in the road. Across a stripped plain, flickers danced and crackled in the wind like banners in some divine devastation. They swayed and shook with the seeping gases from the wells, twisting around themselves, whirling, both free and prisoner to the stacks—fire masts, fire trees, swarming yet pinned to the soil, flying in place, whistling in exasperated purple. The air transformed them into exterminating lights, raging firebrands, then gathered them in a sheaf of torches, a single blackish-red trunk that buckled like a human torso; just afterward, this unity was sundered, and the ardent body, wracked with yellow convulsions, twisted into a burning bush, lashed by sparks, bellowing audibly before stretching in a thousand hissing lashes toward the city, as though to punish the sinful populace. Along those chains of pyres lay the mechanisms of their extraction, tireless, regular, obsessive machines in the shape of great black birds, beaks digging isochronally at the earth like a woodpecker hollowing a tree trunk. There was something impassive, obstinate, maleficent in those silhouettes that dipped and rose without burning, like salamanders born from the flux and reflux of bonfires thrown high by the wind and stretching on in waves toward the horizon. They seemed to demand the names of demons, and I was amusing myself dubbing them Crowling, Ferrovulturus, Eviltooth, and the like when we stopped at a courtyard where black pigs, painted red by the splendor of the flames, were splashing in puddles whose waters were crusty with congealed grease and gleaming with oil. Men shouted all over the dining room at the inn, looking blackened by the smoke of grills. Still in their work clothes, gas masks strapped under their chins, they seemed to live forever stained, smudged, and dusted by the darkest exudations of the earth. They drank insatiably from bottles they grasped by the neck, with cards and chips scattered across their tables. Then the games stopped, and the players turned toward the courtyard in jubilation. Theatrically, delivered by who knows what vehicle, women showed up in ball gowns, with high-heeled shoes and sparkles all in their hair and on their necks, and their presence in that muddy corral lined with feed troughs seemed to me like a hallucination. The bead necklaces and the pearls and stones on their dresses caught the light in flickers, and every change in the wind revealed novel splendors. The women glowed red as they ran past the dark men, clamoring, carrying bundles and suitcases, and the commotion frightened the donkeys, which stood there paralyzed, and woke the hens sleeping on the beams of the lean-tos. I was told then that tomorrow was the festival of the town's patron saint, and the women were prostitutes who traveled from place to place throughout the year, from fairground to parade, from mine to procession, to make hay when the men were feeling generous. They followed an itinerary of bell towers, fornicating for Saint Christopher or Saint Lucy, for the pious Dead or the Holy Innocents, on roadsides, by cemetery walls, on the shores of great rivers, or in narrow hired rooms in the back of taverns furnished with washbasins set out on the dirt floor. What astonished me was the good humor of the better sort in taking these women in: the honest women of the house—the wife and young daughter of the innkeeper—disdained them not in the least. They seemed to show them the clemency due imbeciles,

or gypsies or amusing lunatics, and the kitchen servants laughed
as they watched them caper in their ball gowns past the pigs and
puddles, trailed by miners who helped them with their bundles,
already hankering after the first fruits. Those peripatetic prostitutes transported to our era struck me as cousins of the Medieval ribalds who traveled on feast days from Bremen to
Hamburg, from Antwerp to Ghent, to restore the flagging spirits of master and apprentice, relieving some pilgrim to Com-
postela along the way for a chance to kiss the scallop shell he'd
brought from so far. Their things put away, the women made
a boisterous entrance into the dining room. Dazzled, Mouche
told me to follow them to get a good look at their garments
and hairstyles. Sleepy and indifferent just before, she was now
thoroughly transfixed. There are creatures whose eyes light up
when they sense the proximity of sex. Oblivious, plaintive
since the night before, my friend revived once she found herself
in a seedy atmosphere. She made her way toward the prostitutes, declaring them *très formidables*, unique, of a kind no
longer to be met with. Watching her sit on a bench in the back
beside a table now occupied by the new arrivals, waving her
hands showily to get the women to talk, Rosario looked at me
anxiously, as though she had something to tell me. To forgo an
explanation she probably wouldn't understand, I took our
things and went to find our room. The ecstasy of fires danced
over the courtyard walls. I was tallying our recent expenses
when I thought I heard Mouche shouting for me in distress. In
the mirror on the wardrobe I saw her run to the other end of
the hall, seeming to flee some man who was pursuing her.
When I reached them, he had grabbed her around the waist
and was shoving her into a room. I punched him, and he turned
brusquely, sending me flying over a table covered with empty
bottles that crashed to the floor. I clung to my adversary and
we rolled on the ground, the glass jabbing our hands and arms.
My strength failed me in our brief struggle, and he pinned me
on my back between his knees, raising his fat fists like mallets
and pounding me in the face. Just then, Rosario entered, followed by the innkeeper. "Yannes!" he shouted. "Yannes!" The

innkeeper grabbed the man by the wrists, and Yannes got up slowly, seeming ashamed of what he'd done. The innkeeper spoke to him, but in my nervous excitation I couldn't hear his words. My adversary was humbled, and spoke to me remorsefully: "I didn't know ... Mistake ... She should have said she had husband." Rosario washed my face with a rum-soaked rag: "It was her fault. She was there with the others." Worst of all, I was angry not with the man who struck me, but with Mouche, who had sat with the prostitutes with her customary flamboyance. "It's nothing ... it's nothing," the innkeeper told the onlookers filling the hallway. Blithely, Rosario had me shake hands with the man, who was now blubbering excuses. To ease my mind, she told me she'd known him a long time, not here, but in Puerto Anunciación, the village close to the Southern Forest where her sick father was waiting for her to cure him with the miraculous picture. Hearing his nickname— the Diamond Hunter—I took a sudden interest in my former assailant. Soon we were in the cantina, our stupid quarrel forgotten after a half bottle of spirits. Broad-chested and thin-waisted, with a wisp of beard and the gaze of a bird of prey, the miner was so stern and resolute in profile, he might have stepped down from a triumphal arch. Discovering that he was Greek—which explained his omission of all articles when he spoke—I thought to ask jokingly if he was one of the Seven Against Thebes. But then Mouche appeared, looking indifferent, as if she knew nothing of the fight that had left our hands bloodied and scabbed. I reproached her, but in words too meek to express my irritation. Paying me no mind, she sat on the other end of the table, eyeing up the Greek—who had turned courteous, and pushed his stool away to avoid close contact with my friend—with an interest I found gallingly defiant. When the Diamond Hunter excused himself, saying he was a *stupid damn idiot*, she replied that the whole episode was forgotten. I turned back to Rosario, who was looking at me from the corner of her eye with an ironic gravity there was no way of interpreting. I wanted just to talk and forget everything that had happened, but no words came to my lips. Mouche edged over toward the Greek with a smile so provocative and flustered that rage flooded my temples. No sooner had we emerged from a potential disaster than she was amusing herself by arousing the same miner who had treated her like a whore just thirty minutes before. Her attitude was so literary, so indebted to a contemporary frame of mind that had glorified seamen's taverns and docks cloaked in mist, and I was disgusted at her attachment to her generation's clichés, even when they bore no relation to the reality before her. She simply had to pick a hippocamp, in memory of Rimbaud, in a shop selling rustic colonial handicrafts; had to ridicule the Romantic opera at the theater that had evoked the true fragrance of the garden of Lammermoor; and fixated on an idea of them derived from her Escapist novels, she failed to see that the prostitutes here were one part fairground hawker, one part Mary of Egypt, but without the halo of sanctity. I looked at her, baffled and jealous, and Rosario, thinking I might start a fight, placated me with an obscure phrase that was both proverb and verdict: "When a man fights, it should be to defend his home." I don't know what Rosario thought *my home* was. But she was right if she meant what I hoped she meant: that Mouche wasn't *my home*. To the contrary, she was that loud and stubborn woman of the Scriptures whose feet abide not in her house. Those words threw a bridge between Rosario and me that spanned the long table, and I felt borne up by her sympathy, realizing that it might have wounded her to see me defeated again. With the passing hours, Rosario grew more substantial before my eyes as she blended into the environment, whereas Mouche was tremendously strange here, and more and more, the disparity between her person and her surroundings was impossible to overlook. An aura of exoticism encircled her, making her distant from the others, her customs jarring when viewed against those that obtained in these parts. Bit by bit, she turned into something strange, misplaced, like the turbaned heads of ambassadors of the Sublime Porte in a Christian court. There was no comparing her to Rosario, who was like a Cecilia or Lucy restored to her leaden frame when a stained-glass window is repaired. From morning to evening and evening to night, she grew more authentic, truer, embedded deeper in a country that revealed its essence the closer we came to the river. A kinship was established between her flesh and the ground we treaded, written on skin made darker by light, in similar tones of hair, an affinity of silhouettes, the preferred shape of shoulders and thighs, the maker's marks of forms perfected by the same lathe. I felt closer and closer to Rosario, and she grew more beautiful by the hour, while Mouche blurred in the distance. Her every word sounded right to me, and yet, when I saw her as a woman, I felt awkward, inhibited, too aware of my exoticism before her intrinsic dignity, which seemed to rebuff easy conquest. It wasn't just the bottles we were raising, the glass barrier that kept curious hands occupied; it was the thousand books I'd read that she didn't know, and her beliefs, customs, superstitions, notions, which I in turn didn't know, but which furnished her with reasons to live no less valid than my own. My education, her prejudices, all that she'd learned, all that had happened to her—just then, there seemed to be no reconciling them. I kept telling myself none of that should hinder our bodies' coupling, but I knew an entire culture's mores and obligations stood between me and that head that likely harbored only the vaguest notion of the roundness of the earth or where the different countries stood on the map. This occurred to me as I remembered her beliefs about the monopod spirit of the forests. And when I saw the little golden cross around her neck, it struck me that the conviction we might have shared, a faith in Christ, had been abandoned by my people on my father's side a long, long time ago, when the revocation of the Edict of Nantes had forced the Huguenots from the Savoy; thanks to my greatgrandfather, a friend of Baron d'Holbach's, they had relinquished the Bible for the Encyclopedia, though they kept the Scriptures in the family even when they'd ceased to believe, saying they weren't lacking in a certain poetry . . . Miners done with the late shift now filed into the tavern. The red women returned from the rooms in the courtyard, tucking away the money from their first transactions. To put an end to the farce that kept us lingering hopelessly at the table, I proposed we take a walk to the river. Mouche's conniving deference had turned the Diamond Hunter diffident; she'd asked him to re-count to her his adventures in the jungle, but hadn't listened as he stammered in a French so meager he never found the words to finish his phrases. Relieved at my suggestion, he bought bottles of cold beer and guided us down a straight road that vanished into the night, away from the fires in the valley. Soon we were at the banks of a shadowy river that flowed noisily, with the deep, continuous sonority of a mass of water cleaving the very earth. This wasn't the agitation of slender currents or splashing rapids or cool waves lapping calmly over shallow beds, of the kind I'd heard on the edge of many other rivers before; it was a sustained onslaught, the genesiacal rhythm of a descent begun hundreds of leagues higher up, where other rivers come from still further afar, united with the weight of their cataracts and springs. In the darkness, the water, perennial mover of the water, seemed bordered only by noise, which would now proceed to the edges of the earth. Walking in silence, we reached an inlet—a backwater, really—with a cemetery of old abandoned ships, helms rotting and orlops full of frogs. Among them, lodged in silt, was an old sailboat of noble profile, with a figurehead of an Amphitrite carved in wood on the prow, her nude breasts swelling from veils that stretched back like wings to the hawseholes. We stopped next to the hull, almost at the feet of the figure that seemed to fly above us now, reddened by a writhing flame from one of the flares. Numbed by the cool of the night and the unceasing noise of the rushing river, we stretched out on the gravel. Rosario let down her hair and combed it slowly with movements so absorbed, so somnolent, that I didn't dare address a word to her. Mouche went on talking nonsense, questioning the Greek and laughing at his answers in a near screech, seemingly unaware that we were in an unforgettable setting of a kind a man sees few times in his life. The figurehead, the flames, the river, the derelict ships, the constellations: nothing seemed to move her. That must have been the moment in which her presence began to weigh on me like a bundle made heavier each day by new burdens.

I I

(June 13)

Silence is my watchword. A musician, I've used it more than
men from other professions. I know how to speculate with silence, how to measure and frame it. But now, sitting on a
stone, I live the silence, a silence come from so far, enriched by
so many distant silences that a word uttered in it would rever-
berate like creation itself. If I spoke, even to myself, as I often
do, it would frighten me. The sailors are down below on the
banks, cutting grass for the stud bulls traveling with us. Ignoring them, I observe the immensity of the plain, its frontiers dissolving in a slight circular darkening of the sky. My vantage
point is that of the pebble, of couch grass, and I take in, in its
totality, almost, a circumference that is pure, and one of my
planet's perfections. I no longer have to look up to find a cloud;
those immobile cirrus bodies seem to rest there forever at the
height of the hand that is sheltering my eyes. Solitary trees
with billowing tops stand isolated in the distances beside cactuses like long candlesticks of green stone with sparrow hawks
perched atop them, impassible and heavy as heraldic birds.
Nothing else makes a sound, touches, rolls, or quivers. When
a fly strikes a spiderweb in flight, its terrified hums ring out
like thunder. Then the air is calm again, with nothing audible
from horizon to horizon. I've been here more than an hour
without moving; there's no point in walking to remain always
at the center of one's contemplations. Far off, a deer peeks
through the rushes beside a stream. Then it stops, head nobly
raised, so stationary against the flatland that its figure is monumental, emblematic like a totem, like the mythical ancestor of
men yet to be born, the founder of a clan whose blazon, an-
them, banner, will be its horns hung from a pole. Catching my
scent in the breeze, it departs with measured steps, not rushing, leaving me alone with the world. I turn to the river. Its bed
is so vast that the torrents, whirlpools, and eddies that quake
in its timeless descent merge into a pulse that has throbbed
from summer to the rainy season with the same jolting and

repose since before the creation of man. Today we set forth at dawn, and I've spent long hours observing the banks, looking up now and again from the tale of Fray Servando de Castillejos, who came here with his sandals three centuries ago. His old words remain true. Where he writes of a stone with a saurian profile rising on the right bank, I see a stone with a saurian profile rising on the right bank. Where he marveled at gigantic trees, I have seen gigantic trees, their offspring, born in the same soil, inhabited by the same birds, felled by the same bolts of lightning. The river enters my field of vision through a rent, a tear in the horizon where the sun sets; it swells until its opposite bank vanishes vaguely in a tree-greened mist, and leaves as it came, penetrating the eastern horizon and spilling over its edge, where countless islands proliferate a hundred leagues from the sea. It is granary, wellspring, and road, and human worries are meaningless beside it, and private haste a matter of no account. Railway and thoroughfare lie behind us. You navigate against the current or with it. Either way, you move in a time that is immutable. Here, the Code of Rains arbitrates man's journeys. Manic measurer of instants, professional observer of metronomes and chronographs, I have gone for days now without thinking of the hour, letting the sun's altitude guide my appetites and sleep. I laugh to myself boisterously on this timeless plane when I realize my watch has stopped. Around me, quails stir; with shouts like shanties, raising squawks from the foul, the captain of the *Manatee* calls me onboard. I lie back on the bundles of fodder beneath the broad canvas tent, with the stud beasts to one side and the black cooks to the other. They sweat and sing as they mash peppers, and their scent and the ruttish bulls and the acrid aroma of alfalfa combine in a sort of perfume that intoxicates me. Nothing about it could be called pleasant, and yet it invigorates me, as if it answered a secret need of my organism. It is like the peasant who returns to his parents' farm after passing some years in the city, and cries with emotion at the smell of manure in the breeze. I realize now there is an invocation of the backyard of my childhood, where another black woman sweated mashing peppers and, farther off, the cattle grazed. And above all—above all!—there was that esparto basket, ship of my voyages with María del Carmen, and it smelled like this alfalfa I sink my face into with almost painful disquiet. Mouche, whose hammock hangs where the breeze is strongest, is chatting with the Greek miner, ignorant of my perch, my hideaway. Rosario, though, climbs on this pile of bales often, unbothered by the rainwater that filters through the fabric and cools the freshly cut fodder. She lies back a few feet away from me and smiles, biting into a piece of fruit. Her bravery surprises me: without hesitation or fear, she's embarked on a journey the Museum directors employing me considered a risky enterprise. This solid disposition of women seems a common thing in these parts. On deck, a mulatta with an adolescent body is bathing, dumping buckets of water over her flowery gown, before meeting with her lover, a gold prospector, at the mouth of a nearly unexplored tributary. Another, in mourning clothes, is going to try her luck as a prostitute in hopes of ascending from whore to *kept woman* in a one-horse town near the jungle that still has famines in the months when the river floods. More and more, I regret bringing Mouche along. I would have liked to mingle with the crew, to eat food from the ship's mess alleged to be too coarse for refined palates, to live alongside those firm, resolute women, and have them all tell me their stories. Most of all, I'd have liked the freedom to get close to Rosario, whose depths elude me, especially as the women I'd known before then had all more or less resembled one another. I'm constantly afraid of offending her, irritating her, being overly familiar, lavishing her with attentions she might find absurd or unmanly. At times I think our solitude between the narrow pens of the beasts is an invitation to pull her down brutally; everything invites me to do so, and yet I don't dare, however much the slightly ironic crudity and ease of the men on board appears to please the women. For I am ignorant of these people's rules, codes, idioms. Yesterday, looking at my finely woven shirt, which I'd bought in one of the world's best-known shops, Rosario burst out laughing, saying it was a garment better suited to a woman. Alongside her, I never cease to worry I'm falling into ridicule, a ridicule too powerful to console myself with the thought that

these people *have no idea*, because here, in their world, they
do. Mouche doesn't realize that my show of jealousy, my
feigned agitation at her banter with the Greek, is a response to
what I presume Rosario feels, that I should watch over the
woman sharing the hazards of this voyage with me. Rosario's
ambiguous looks, gestures, words seem to me at times to imply
an assignation. I climb over the bundles and I wait. But I wait
in vain. The lusty bulls roar, the Negresses sing to rile up the
sailors, I grow drunk on the scent of the alfalfa. With a throbbing in my temples and my genitals, I close my eyes and fall
into the tiresome absurdity of erotic dreams.

At sundown we moored at a rudimentary dock of pylons
sunken into mud. Entering a village where all the talk is of
bucking animals and lassos, I realized we had come to the
Lands of the Horse. All round was the scent of circus tracks, of
sweaty flanks that had wandered the world for ages, proclaiming the culture of the neigh. A dull hammering announced the
blacksmith nearby, busy in the darkness with his anvils and
bellows, in his leather apron before the fires of the forge. Red
irons hissed when quenched in cold water, and the nails sank
into the hooves like song. The courser trotted nervously in its
new shoes, afraid of slipping on stones, and a steed reared and
bucked in its bridle before a young woman at her window with
a ribbon in her hair. With the horse came the saddler's shop
perfumed with leather, cool with cordovan, its employees hec-
tic amid saddle straps, stirrups for cowhands, embossed leather
saddle trees, and Sunday tackle with silver studs in the head-
stalls. In the Lands of the Horse, man was something more
than man. He was once more master of millenary methods
that put his hands in contact with iron and pelt, learning the
arts of taming and riding, developing prowess to be boasted of
on feast days in front of women who admired men who knew
how to squeeze with their legs and use their arms. Reborn here
were those manly games of breaking the grunting stallion and
grabbing the bull—the sun beast—by the tail, shoving its ar-
rogance into the dust. A strange solidarity existed between the
animal with the well-hung testicles that penetrated its females
deeper than any other and man, who had taken it as a symbol

for universal courage, cast in bronze or carved in marble by
the sculptors of equestrian statues determined to make the
courser no less handsome than the hero mounted upon it, so
that both could give shade to lovers who met in city parks.
Men gathered in great groups in homes with many horses nodding under the colonnades; but where a single horse waited in
the night, half hidden in the weeds, its master would have removed his spurs to sneak into a house where a shadow was
waiting to receive him. It was odd how this former highest
treasure of the man of Europe, his war machine, vehicle, mes-
senger, pedestal of heroes, adornment of metopes and triumphal arches, prolonged its proud history in America, and only
in the New World had the horse carried out its centuries-old
duties with such grandeur. Omitted from maps, like the medieval terra incognita, the Lands of the Horse would whiten the
fourth part of the hemisphere, attesting to the preponderance
of the Horseshoe in a place where the Cross of Christ made its
entrance on horseback, not dragged, but held aloft, borne up
by men thought to be centaurs.

12

(June 14)

We embarked again with the full moon, as the captain had to
pick up a Capuchin monk in the port of Santiago de los Aguinaldos on the opposite bank of the river, and there were particularly rough rapids he hoped to pass by morning, freeing the
afternoon for trading. Gripping the helm, guiding the bow
skillfully past the rocks, he arrived, and I found myself by midday in a prodigious city in ruins. The streets were long and deserted, with empty houses with rotten doors reduced to jambs
or the dangling chains of locks and mossy roofs that sagged in
the center where the beam had crumbled, eaten by termites or
blackened by mold. Porch columns stood freighted with the remains of a cornice broken by the roots of a fig tree. There were

stairways without beginning or end, suspended in the void, and balconies with mullions hanging from a window frame open to the sky. Lily of the valley shone pale through the curtains in vast salons with scratched tiles, and in the corners were the burnished gold of acacias and the flesh-pink of poinsettias, and cactuses like candelabra, arms trembling through cross breezes in the hallways as though held by invisible sacristans' hands. Fungus grew on the thresholds and cardoons in the fireplaces. Trees climbed along the facades, sinking claws into the cracks in the stonework; of a charred church, there remained a few counterforts and archivolts and a monumental arch on the verge of collapse, and in its tympanum, in blurry relief, were the figures of a celestial concert, with angels playing bassoon, theorbo, organ, viola, and maracas. I so admired it that I wished to go back to the ship for pencil and paper, to sketch this rare organographical reference and share it with the Curator. But then came a banging of drums and a piping of shrill flutes, and devils appeared in a corner of the plaza, striding toward a miserable brick-and-plaster church in front of the burnt cathedral. The dancers' faces were hidden by black cloth, like the penitents of Christian fraternities; they advanced slowly, skipping, behind a leader or conductor who could have played Beelzebub at the Mystery of the Passion, or Tarasque, or the King of the Mad, with his three-horned demon mask and his pig's snout. I was frightened before those faceless men, their features veiled like parricides, their masks emerged from the enigmas of time to feed mankind's eternal penchant for False Visages, disguises, the avatars of animal, monster, or wraith. The dancers reached the church's door and pounded with the knocker, then stood there a long time, crying and wailing. The wings opened with a rattle and the Apostle James, son of Zebedee and Salome, appeared in a cloud of incense, mounted on a white horse the worshippers carried on their shoulders. The devils retreated before his crown of gold in what looked like spasms of horror, stumbling, falling, rolling on the ground. Behind the icon, a hymn was played on clarinet and trombone, which had the old echoes of sackbut and shawm:

Primus ex apostolis
Martir Jerosolimis
Jacobus egregio
Sacer est martirio

Children straddling the gable kicked the bell back and forth
above us, sending tocsins echoing downward. The procession
wove around the church, led by the pastor's nasal falsetto, and
the devils, drawing out the torments of their exorcism, stepped
back en masse, howling beneath the aspersions of the aspergil-
lum. When it was over, the Apostle James, he of the *Campus
Stellae*, draped in a ragged velvet pallium, was engulfed again
by the church, the doors of which closed with a rude clash and
a rippling of lamps and tapers. Then the devils took off running, laughing and skipping, no longer demons but buffoons,
and they vanished in the ruins of the city, shouting crudely
through the windows to ask if the women here were still of
birthing age. The faithful dispersed. I stood alone in the middle of the sad plaza, its flagstones ousted and cracked by the
roots of trees. Rosario, who had gone to light a candle for her
father's recovery, appeared soon after with the bearded Capuchin who would depart with us, and he introduced himself as
Father Pedro de Henestrosa. Sparing with his words, the friar
told me with slow assertiveness that here, the tradition was to
bring out Saint James for Corpus Christi, and had been since
that icon of the saint arrived here, not long after the village
was founded. Soon two Negro pickers joined us with bandolas
over their backs, complaining that the festival this year was
nothing more than a few salvos and processions, and swearing
they would never return. In this way, I discovered that this had
once been a bustling town with full coffers, with rich families
and wardrobes filled with Holland sheets; but it had been
sacked repeatedly in a long-running war, and its palaces and
estates were ruined, and now ivy clung from the blazons on the
facades. Whoever could do so emigrated, selling off their ancestral homes for crumbs. Then, from the rice fields, abandoned and turned back to swampland, the scourge of plagues
brought death to the palaces, leaving them empty save for

Bermuda grass and thornbushes and letting the arches, roofs, and dentils go to ruin. Now it was a village of shadows, was itself a shadow of the once-rich town of Santiago de los Aguinaldos. Intrigued by the missionary's tale, I thought of the cities ruined by Barons' Wars, ravaged by the plague, while Rosario asked the pickers to entertain us with whatever song they pleased, and they began to strum their their the bandolas. Their music took my musings to further reaches of history. The two black jongleurs' verses spoke of Charlemagne, of Roland, of Bishop Turpin, of Ganelon's treachery, and of the sword that felled the Moors at Roncesvalles. When we reached the wharf, they told the tale of the Lara Princes, and though I knew nothing of them, they must have been ancient, and that moved me there beneath those crumbling facades covered with lichen, resembling abandoned castles from days of yore. We departed just as twilight was dilating the shadows of the ruins. Leaning on the gunwale, Mouche said justly that the sight of that ghostly city was more mysterious, more pregnant with marvels, than the finest inventions of the modern painters she esteemed most highly. The subjects of fantastic art were three-dimensional here, felt and lived. These weren't imaginary architectures or tawdry poetic props: you could walk in their labyrinths, climb their stairs with shattered landings, with the railing from a vanished balustrade sinking into the night of a tree. They weren't stupid, these observations of Mouche's, but with her, I had reached that saturation point at which a man is so tired of a woman that even her intelligent comments bore him. With its cargo of bellowing bulls, caged hens, pigs loose on deck, running under the Capuchin's hammock and knotting themselves up in his rosary of seeds; with the black cooks' singing, the laugh of the diamond hunter Greek, the whore in her mourning gown washing up on the prow, the racket of the pickers making the seamen dance, our vessel put me in mind of Bosch's *Ship of Fools*: a ship of fools taking off now from a riverbank I could situate nowhere, for if the roots of this place drew from canons, concepts, myths I could easily identify, this expression of them, the tree that grew from this soil, disconcerted me no less than the enormous trees now clustering on

the banks and at the mouths of the tributaries, tall against the
setting sun, their trunks bent backbones and their crowns like
a dog's muzzle—like councils of giant cynocephali. The geography as such I could identify, of course. But in this humid
world, the ruins were more ruins, vines upset the stones differ-
ently, the insects were capricious, the devils more devilish,
with dancing Negroes moaning beneath their horns. An angel,
a maraca were familiar to me. But an angel playing maracas
carved into the tympanum of a burned-down church was something I had never seen elsewhere. I wondered if the purpose
of these lands in human history might not be to make possible,
for the very first time, certain symbioses of culture, but then I
was distracted by something that sounded at once quite close
and quite distant. At my side, Father Pedro de Henestrosa was
commemorating Corpus Christi with a soft Gregorian chant
printed in neumes on the yellow, moth-eaten pages of a very
old *Liber usualis*:

> *Sumite psalmum, et date tympanum:*
> *Psalterium jucundum cum cithara.*
> *Buccinate in Neomenia tuba*
> *In insigni dei solemnitatis vestrae.*

13

(Friday, June 15)

When we reached Puerto Anunciación—a humid city waging
a pointless, centuries-long war against creeping vegetation—I
realized we had left the Lands of the Horse to enter the Lands
of the Dog. Past the last of its roofs rose the first trees of the
still-distant jungle, its vain sentinels, more obelisks than trees,
scattered sparsely over the riotous vastness of the underbrush
of viny wetlands whose squirming fecundity could erase the
roads in a single night. There was no use for a horse in a world
without trails. Past the green mass bordering the paths leading
south, the trails and footpaths sank between interlocking

branches that wouldn't allow a rider through. But the Dog, whose eyes were at the height of men's knees, saw everything hidden in the treacherous malangas, in the hollow of fallen trunks, in the rotten leaves; with its tense muzzle, its acute sense of smell, its back that warned of danger with bristling hair, the Dog had honored the terms of its early alliance with Man throughout history. It was a pact that linked the Dog with Man: complementary powers that made them work as brothers. The Dog possessed the senses that had atrophied in his fellow hunter: he saw with his nose, walked on four feet, approached animals as kin; while man brought initiative, weapons, oars, verticality. The Dog was the only creature that shared with Man the benefits of fire, and in his nearness to Prometheus, he pledged to take Man's side in any war waged against the Animal. This was the City of the Bark. In hallways, behind bar tops, under tables, dogs stretched their legs, sniffed, dug, yapped. They sat on the prows of the boats, ran on the roofs, watched the meat on the grills, attended meetings and re-unions, went to church—this last so often that an old colonial order, never observed because nobody cared for it, created the post of dogcatcher to throw these animals from the temple *on all Saturdays and on the eve of feast days*. When the moon rose at night, the dogs adored it with a chorus of howls that custom no longer saw as a bad omen; instead, the resulting sleeplessness was accepted with resignation, as one tolerates the tedious rituals of a kinsman who practices a strange religion.

The so-called inn at Puerto Anunciación was an old bar-racks with cracking walls. Its rooms opened onto a muddy courtyard where big turtles dragged themselves about, captive there with an eye to days of penury. The only furnishings were two canvas cots and a wooden bench, with a shard of mirror held to the back of the door by three rusty nails. The moon had just risen over the river, and with it, shortly afterward, the antiphonic ululation of the canines, from the giant silvery trees of the Franciscan mission to the islands enveloped in black, with startling responses from the opposite bank. Mouche was in a foul mood, unable to accept that we'd left electricity be-hind, that we were in the era of oil lamp and candle here, that there wasn't even a pharmacy to buy toiletries and makeup. She knew enough to moderate the attention she lavished on her face and body, so the foreigners would think her above such feminine vanities as were unsuited to an intellectual, at the same time making plain that her youth and natural beauty were attractive enough on their own. Knowing all this, I had amused myself spying on her from atop the bundles of esparto, watching with malign irony as she examined herself over and over in a mirror, furrowing her brow spitefully. The skin of her face seemed to have withered since she'd awakened that morning. The hard water had reddened her complexion, accenting the large pores on her nose and temples. Her hair resembled a greenish blond tow, unequally shaded, and I saw now how much its dazzling copper owed to the intelligent application of dye. Her bust looked less firm beneath that blouse stained by strange resins from the sailcloth, and her nails were chipped from always having to grab hold of something on the deck stacked with buckets and barrels on the floating storehouse of our ship. Her eyes, of a brown slightly mottled with green and yellow, reflected a mixture of boredom, weariness, all-consuming disgust, and latent rage at her inability to scream how she detested this journey she had undertaken willingly, praising it in the pompous language of literature. The night before our departure—I now remembered—she had spoken clichés about the *longing for escape*, used the grandiose word *Adventure* in the sense of a *chance to travel*, to escape the quotidian, with fortuitous encounters and hallucinatory, poetic visions of dazzling Floridas. Before now—for a woman estranged from the feelings that delighted me each day, restoring sensations forgotten since childhood—the word *Adventure* had meant forced enclosure in a downtown hotel, panoramas of monotonous, reiterated grandeur, movement without surprises, the plodding fatigue of nights without a bedside lamp, falling asleep only to be wakened by the rooster's crowing. Hugging her knees, unconcerned by the view her disordered skirts offered, she swayed gently on her cot, taking little sips of brandy from a tin jug. She referred to Mexican pyramids and Inca fortresses—which she knew only from images—to the stairs of Monte Albán and the Hopis' baked-clay villages, complaining that in this country, the Indians had failed to erect such marvels. In the categorical jargon of the person *in the know*, abounding in technical terms—*economists' cant*, I liked to call this idiom so beloved of many of our generation—she lambasted the locals' way of life, their prejudices and superstitions, their antiquated farming methods, their mismanaged mines, and naturally, all this led to a discussion of surplus value and the exploitation of man by man. Playing devil's advocate, I told her that if anything had amazed me on this voyage, it was the realization that there were still large parts of the world whose inhabitants were oblivious to the manias of the day and that even if a thatched roof, a pitcher, a clay oven, a hammock, and a guitar were enough for many people here, they still possessed a certain animism, an awareness of ancient traditions, a living memory of myth that attested to a culture likely more honest and valid than the one we'd left *back there*. For them, it mattered more to preserve the *Chanson de Roland* than to have hot water at home; and I was thankful that there still existed men unwilling to sell their souls for an electrical appliance that, by relieving the washerwoman of her duties, took away her songs as well, abolishing a thousand years of folklore thereby. Pretending she hadn't heard me, or that my words didn't matter to her, Mouche insisted there was nothing here worth seeing or studying, that this country had no history or character. Deeming the matter concluded, she said she would leave tomorrow at dawn, as our ship, traveling with the current, could have her back in little more than a day. But I didn't care what she wanted. This was unusual for me, and when I told her dryly I would perhaps keep my commitment to the University, going onward to look for the musical instruments they'd asked me to locate, she flew into a rage. *Bourgeois*, she called me, and that insult—how well I knew it!—was the relic of a time when many women of her upbringing had declared themselves revolutionaries because militancy had allowed them intimacy with more than a few interesting intellectuals, and its philosophical and social principles had justified their libertine excesses, just as the aesthetic ideals of certain literary creeds had done before. Ever attentive to her own desires, putting her pleasures and whims above all else, Mouche was the archetypical *bourgeoise*. And yet for her, *bourgeois* was the supreme affront, and she applied the term to whatever opposed her own appetites in the name of principles and duties—to anything that rejected licentiousness, called for order, or honored the preoccupations of religion. My commitment to do right by the Curator and in this way assuage my conscience was a hindrance to her, and she couldn't fail to denounce it as *bourgeois*. She got up from her pallet, tangled hair in her face, and raised her little fists up to my temples in a vehement gesture I was now seeing for the first time. She wanted to be back in Los Altos as soon as possible, she shouted; she couldn't recover without the cool of the highlands; we were going there, and that was where we would spend what remained of my vacation. The very words *Los Altos* infuriated me, reminding me of the Canadian painter and the suspicious indulgence she'd shown to Mouche. Normally I was careful not to say too much when we argued, but that night, relishing her wretched appearance in the light of the oil lamp, I needed to wound her, to break her, to lay down that burden of accumulated malice I carried in the deepest parts of myself. I began by insulting the Canadian, calling her a name that made Mouche flinch as though jabbed with a hot needle. She stepped back and threw a bottle of brandy at my head, missing me by barely an inch. Frightened at her own actions, she waved her hands penitently, but this outburst permitted me to speak uninhibited, and I shouted that I no longer loved her, that her very presence was intolerable, that even her body repelled me. She had never known me like this—my words astonished me as well—and she ran off to the courtyard, as if such invective necessitated some punishment. But she forgot about the mud, and slipped and fell into the turtle pond. Feeling the wet shells beneath her, shifting like helmeted warriors swallowed by a bog, she howled in terror, rousing the packs of dogs that had long since fallen quiet. In the middle of concerted barking, I brought Mouche back to our room, took off her clothing with its stench of the swamp, and scrubbed her from head to toe with a coarse red cloth. I had her take a long

swig of brandy, then tucked her into bed and went outside, ignoring her shouts and sobs. I wanted—I needed—to forget her
for a few hours.

In a nearby tavern, I found the Greek drinking avidly with a
little man with matted eyebrows whom he introduced as the
Pathfinder. The yellow dog beside him lapping beer from a bowl
was a noble being, he said, who answered to the name Sparrowhawk. The miner said I was lucky to have met so quickly a man
rarely to be seen in Puerto Anunciación. He told me the jungle
covered vast expanses, with mountains, abysses, treasures,
wandering peoples, vestiges of disappeared civilizations; it was
a world unto itself, self-sufficient, with food for its fauna and
men; it shaped its own clouds, engendered its own climate, provoked its own rains; it was a hidden nation, mapped in code, a
vegetal country with few ways in. "Like Noah's Ark, which
could hold all the animals of the earth, though it only had one
little door," the diminutive gentleman said. To make his way
there, the Pathfinder had learned the keys to secret inroads; he
alone knew a certain path between two trees, the only one of
its kind in fifty leagues, which led to a narrow stairway of stone
slabs that plunged into the mystery of the great telluric baroque. He alone knew the footbridge of lianas that passed beneath the waterfall, the egress of fallen leaves, the trail through
the cave of petroglyphs, the hidden inlet that led to navigable
tributaries. He had broken the code of bent branches, of incisions in the bark, of boughs that looked fallen but had been
placed there purposely. He disappeared for months at a time,
and would emerge when least expected through a wall of
vegetation, bearing merchandise: a load of butterflies or lizard
skins or sacks full of heron feathers, live birds that cheeped
strangely, or bits of pottery shaped like men, quaint household
items, peculiar baskets that might interest some foreigner. One
time he'd shown up after a long absence followed by twenty
Indians bearing orchids. The dog had got the name Sparrowhawk thanks to his ability to catch birds and bring them to his
master to see if they were worth anything without even tearing
a single one of their feathers. When someone outside called for
the Pathfinder, and he left to greet the Tuna Fisherman, who

was working with some of his forty-two legitimate children, the Greek told me softly that, according to general opinion, that extraordinary character had stumbled on a prodigious vein of gold, the location of which he kept secret. No one could say why, when he sent off his porters, they would reappear with more goods than needed to sustain so few men, along with one or two stud pigs, bolts of cloth, combs, sugar, and other effects useless for navigating on remote waterways. He dodged all questions related to his affairs and would shout at his Indians to hurry off into the woods, forbidding them to wander through town. People said he was mining with the help of fugitives from justice, or using captives purchased from an enemy tribe, or that he'd made himself king of a settlement of Maroons who had fled to the mountains three hundred years before, whose village was surrounded by stockades and echoed at all hours with pounding drums. The Pathfinder soon returned, and the miner changed the subject to the purpose of my trip. No stranger to foreigners seeking unusual objects—among them, a friend he praised highly, an herbalist named Montsalvatje—the Pathfinder said I could find the instruments in question in the settlements of a tribe that lived three days away by river on the banks of a tributary known as El Pintado for the constantly shifting color of its murky waters. I asked him about their primitive rites, and he described every musical contrivance he could remember—from drums made of tree trunks to bone flutes and horns, cranial trumpets, vases to blow in at funerals, and medicine men's tambourines—mimicking their sounds in brandy-addled warbles and imitating the movements of those who played them. At that moment, Father Pedro de Henestrosa appeared to tell us Rosario's father had just died. The news struck me with its suddenness, and I had a longing to see her, as I knew nothing about her whereabouts since our arrival; and with the Greek, the Capuchin, and the Pathfinder, followed by Sparrowhawk, who never missed a wake, I headed off to find the deceased along streets with turbid runnels in their center. I savored the hazelnut aftertaste of the agave liquor I had drunk down thirstily in that dive with the florid sign displaying its absurdly affected name: *Memories of the Future.*

14

(Friday night)

In a ramshackle house of eight barred windows, death was still at work, diligent, solicitous, in all places at once, overseeing ceremonies, coordinating cries, lighting candles, making certain the entire village would fit in the broad rooms with deep benches and wide doorways that gave pride of place to its labors. The coffin lay on a pile of mildewy velvet, still resonant with hammer blows, with the thick silver nails knocked in not long before by the Carpenter, who never failed to build to the exact measures of the deceased, and who conserved in his scrupulous memory the dimensions of every person in the village. The flowers plucked from the courtyards at night, from boxes, from gardens overrun by the jungle—thick-petaled spikenards and jasmines, wild flax, waxy magnolias—were pungent in their bouquets, tied with ribbons that yesterday adorned the hair of dancing girls. In the alcove, in the hall, men stood and spoke gravely, while the women in the bedrooms prayed in antiphon, obsessively repeating *Hail Mary, Full of Grace, the Lord is with thee. Blessed art thou amongst women,* the murmur of which echoed in dark corners between images of saints and rosaries hanging from tacks, rising and falling with the invariable tempo of soft tossing gravel over a reef. The mirrors, which had harbored death in their depths, were veiled with crepe and canvas. Several notables—the Whitewater Ace, the Mayor, the Teacher, the Tuna Fisherman, and the Hide Tanner—were bent over the cadaver after dropping their cigarette butts into their hats. A bony girl in black shrieked and fell to the floor, shaking with what looked like convulsions, and people from the crowd picked her up and carried her out. Now Rosario approached the bier. Dressed in mourning, lips pallid, lustrous hair pulled tight to her head, she struck me as a thing of overwhelming beauty. She looked at all those present with eyes swollen from grief, brought her stiff hands to her mouth, as though wounded within, and released the long, unhuman howl of a beast struck by an arrow, or birthing, or possessed by a demon, throwing her arms around the casket. In a hoarse voice interspersed with heaves, she said she would shred all her garments, tear out her eyes, that she didn't want to live, that she would throw herself into the grave and wait for the earth to cover her. When others tried to pull her away, she turned her wrath on them, threatening all who tried to tear her fingers from the black velvet, speaking a mysterious, horrifying tongue that seemed to have emerged from the shadow realms of prophecy and clairvoyance. Her throat rent by sobs, she evoked great disgraces, the end of the world, the Last Judgment, plagues and expiations. Finally, they dragged her faint body from the room, her legs hanging inert, her hair bedraggled. Her black stockings were torn, her polished shoes with their worn heels slid across the floor with the tips pointing inward. All this made my heart ache. And now another sister was hugging the casket . . . Their violent grief put me in mind of ancient tragedy. Death was commonplace in those large, extended families, where everyone kept mourning clothes folded in their trunks. Any mother who gave birth was aware of its presence. But these women who divvied up their duties around deathbeds, who knew from childhood how to dress the deceased, cover the mirrors, speak the right prayers, *were protesting* death in rites come down to them from prior ages. I was observing a desperate, menacing, almost magic remonstration at Death's presence in the house. Those peasant women chanted before the corpse, in chorus like Libation Bearers, their thick hair dangling in black veils over their fierce faces, like those of the daughters of kings: howling Trojans, sublime dogs cast out of their burning palaces. This obstinate despair, the nine sisters' admirable sense of drama as they filed through the doors on the right and left, preparing the portentous Hecuba of their mother, who cursed her solitude, sobbed over the ruins of her home, shouted that she had no God, made me suspect that there was a good deal of theater in all this. Next to me, one of their mourners observed in admiration that it was a pleasure to watch these women weeping over their dead. And yet I felt stifled, dragged away, awakened by it all to dark remembrances of funeral rites as observed by the men who came before me into the kingdom

of this world. And from some fold in my memory arose now
that verse of Shelley's that reverberated as though in the shell
of its own meaning:

> *. . . How canst thou hear*
> *Who knowest not the language of the dead?*

The men in the cities I'd lived in no longer knew the meaning
of these voices, and had forgotten the language of those who
know how to speak to the dead—of those familiar with the
final horror of being left alone, who know the anguish of those
who beg not to be left alone on their last, uncertain road.
Shouting that they would throw themselves into their father's
grave, the nine sisters were following one of the noblest customs of a thousand-year-old rite in which things are given to
the dead, impossible promises made to them, assuaging their
solitude with coins placed between their lips, surrounding
them with the figures of servants, of women, of musicians, giving them code words, credentials, safe conducts for the Ferry-
men and Lords of the Other Shore, whose tariffs and demands
are not even known. I remembered just then how despicable
and mediocre death had become for the men of my Shore—my
people—with their cold funeral homes, bronze, pomp, and ad-
dresses that concealed poorly behind the wreaths and beds of
ice the dissimulations of the guild of mourners with its per-
functory solemnities, rented furnishings, and hands stretched
over the corpse in expectation of recompense. Some might
laugh at the tragedy being performed here. But it offered a perspective onto mankind's first rituals. I was considering this
when the Diamond Hunter approached with a singularly malicious expression, telling me to go to the kitchen, where Rosario was alone, brewing coffee for the women. Bothered by his
sarcasm, I replied that this struck me as an ill-timed moment
to distract her from her grief. "Go inside, be bold, do not fear,"
the Greek said, as though reciting a lesson, "for the bold man
is ever fortunate in his undertakings, no matter that he come
from distant shores." I intended to reply that I had no need of
such dreadful advice, when he declaimed unexpectedly, "The

queen is the first one you will encounter in the halls; her name is Arete and she comes from the same stock that birthed our King Alcinous." Seeing me stupefied, he stared into my face with his bird eyes and concluded with a laugh, "Homer, *Odyssey*," before shoving me into the kitchen. Amid pots and tureens, clay vessels and wood fires, Rosario was pouring boiling water into a large cloth cone stained from years of grime. Her violent attack seemed to have eased her pain. Calmly, she told me the prayer to the Fourteen Holy Helpers had come too late to save her father. She spoke to me of his illness in mystical terms that revealed her spiritual conception of human physiology. It all started with a disagreement with a mate, aggravated by sunstroke when the old man crossed the river, which led the humors to rise in his brain, where an air current congealed them, leaving half his body without blood, inflaming his thighs and genitals and inducing, after forty days' fever, a hardening of the walls of the heart. While Rosario spoke, I came closer to her, attracted by the heat of her body, which reached my skin through our clothes. Next to her on the floor was an enormous clay tub, and when she leaned her elbows on the edge of it, her body arched toward me. The fire of the oven glowed on her forehead, shifting remote flickers in her somber eyes. Ashamed of myself, I lusted for her with an ardor I hadn't known since adolescence. I don't know if I'd fallen prey to that abominable yearning—the subject of so many fables—that live flesh feels for live flesh in the presence of flesh that will never live again, but my gaze, stripping her of her mourning clothes, must have looked ravenous, because she walked around the tub with measured steps, placing it between us, as though walking around a well to prop her elbows on its other side, staring back at me across that pit full of black water that made our voices echo like the nave of a cathedral. She left me alone a few times, going to the room with the body, then returning, drying her tears, while I waited for her with a lover's impatience. We didn't say much to each other. She allowed me to contemplate her over the water in the basin with a flattered, somehow docile passivity. The clocks marked the hour of sunrise, but the sun didn't rise. Unnerved, we all went out to the courtyard.

Where the sun should have risen, the sky was coated by a strange reddish cloud of smoke, burning ashes, dun pollen that shot upward from horizon to horizon. When it was above us, butterflies started raining over the roofs, the urns, our shoulders. They were small, of a deep, amaranth pink streaked with violet, and had taken off in hordes from some unknown part of the continent beyond the immensity of the jungle, frightened, scattered perhaps, after their vertiginous multiplication, by some cataclysm, some horror without witnesses or history. The Pathfinder told me such transits of butterflies were far from rare in the region, and when they happened, you might not see the sun for an entire day. And so they would bury Rosario's father by candlelight, on a diurnal, wing-reddened night. In this corner of the world, they were still familiar with such migrations as chronicled in the Dark Ages, when the Danube flowed black with rats and wolf packs invaded market towns. The week before, they told me, the neighbors had killed a huge jaguar in the atrium of the church.

15

(Saturday, June 16)

The cemetery where they buried Rosario's father, invaded by weeds that have overgrown its walls, is a kind of dependency of the church, divided from it by a rough door and a row of flagstones that form the base of a heavy cross with short arms in which are chiseled the Arma Christi. The church is squat with thick walls, its heavy stones striking for their deep niches and stubborn buttresses that seem more like the counterforts of a castle. Its arches are low and rustic; the wooden roof, with beams laid over spare corbels, evokes the primitive Romanesque churches. After midmorning, a red night pervades the interior from the exodus of butterflies still crossing between earth and sun. Surrounded by tapers and lamps, like figures from an altarpiece or objects of praise, the old saints labor away, as though the church were formerly a workshop: Isidore, hoe in hand, works his pedestal of couch grass and cornstalks; Peter holds an enormous ring of keys, to which a new one is hung every day; George lances the dragon with such fury that his weapon resembles a javelin; Christopher, clutching a palm tree, is so huge that the Christ Child hardly stretches from his shoulder to his ear; real hair has been glued to the dogs of Lazarus, and they seem to be licking real wounds. Burdened by pleas, attributed many powers, paid in the hard currency of ex-votos, these saints, borne in processions at any and all hours, possessed, in the locals' daily life, the status of divine functionaries, piecemeal intercessors, celestial bureaucrats, ever on call in Heaven's Ministry of Requests and Complaints. Each day, they received gifts and candles of a sort normally offered for forgiveness of a major blasphemy. People asked them questions, pleaded with them to cure their arthritis, still the hailstorms, bring the runaway beasts back to the manger. Gamblers called to them when playing a card and prostitutes lit a candle for them when business was good. All this—which the Pathfinder told me amid laughter—reconciled me with a divine world that had shed all vitality in the cities I knew, where the golden legends dwindled in metal chapels under the plastic pomposity of new stained glass windows. Before a Christ of black wood that seemed to bleed on the high altar, I found the atmosphere of sacrament, of mystery, of hagiography that had awed me once in a very old Byzantine chapel at the sight of martyrs with cutlasses sunken in their skulls from ear to ear and warrior bishops whose horses dug their bloody shoes into the heads of the pagans. I would have lingered a bit longer in the rustic church had the penumbra of butterflies surrounding us not begun to enervate me like an eclipse prolonged beyond the possible. This, and my weariness from the night before, brought me back to the inn where Mouche, who thought the sun hadn't yet risen, was still sleeping, clutching a pillow. When I awoke after a few hours, she was no longer in the room, and the sun had reappeared after the great ashen exodus. Happy to have escaped a possible quarrel, I went to Rosario's, hoping she was awake. There, the rhythms of the day-to-day had returned. The women in mourning were pleasantly lost in their chores—life remain-

ing for the living after the inevitable event of death. In the yard
full of sleeping dogs, the Pathfinder was conferring with Father
Pedro about an imminent journey to the forest. Soon Mouche
appeared, followed by the Greek. She seemed to have forgotten
the desire to return that she had given vent to furiously the
night before. Indeed: she wore an expression of malign, defiant
relish that Rosario, busy sewing mourning clothes, noticed at
the same time as I. Mouche felt obliged to tell us she'd bumped
into Yannes in the port, near the dugout boat of a group of
rubber tappers setting off upriver, bypassing the rapids of Piedras Negras on a narrow tributary navigable at this time of
year. She had asked the miner to take her to see this granite
barrier, which had bedeviled boatmen since the first discoverers cried bitterly before its foamy whirlpools and jostling waters full of tree trunks wedged across roaring falls. Already she
was making literature of the sight, showing us strange flowers,
wild lilies of some kind, that she claimed she had picked beside
the roaring gullies, when the Pathfinder, who never paid attention to what women said, and who couldn't understand her
anyway, waved impatiently for her to hush. In his view, we'd be
wise to use the rubber prospectors' vessel to continue on in rela-
tive comfort. Yannes assured us we could reach his brothers'
diamond mine that very night. Against all expectation, when
she heard the words *diamond mine*—dazzled, I suppose, by
the vision of a grotto twinkling with gems—Mouche accepted
the idea with delight. She threw herself around Rosario's neck,
begging her to accompany us on this tranquil stage of our journey. Tomorrow we would stop at the mine, and she would wait
there for our return while we traveled on. I imagine Mouche
was curious to see what inconveniences lay ahead and saw a
short journey as no risk, being certain she'd have company for
her return to Puerto Anunciación if she chose to abandon us.
But still, I was happy Rosario was coming. I looked at her and
found her tense over her sewing, as though waiting to know
my desires. I nodded, and she rushed off to see her sisters, who
flew into a rage in the bedrooms and washrooms, protesting
that such a journey was madness. But she paid them no mind,
and reappeared soon with a bindle of clothes and a coarse

shawl. While Mouche walked ahead of us on her way to the
inn, Rosario told me, as if revealing a grave secret, that the
flowers she had brought didn't grow in Piedras Negras, but on
a leafy island, site of an abandoned mission, which she pointed
out to me just then. I wanted to ask her to tell me more, but she
was careful not to be alone with me from then until we found
ourselves standing where the rubber prospectors had docked.
After a short stretch where they needed the pole, the boat advanced upriver, listing slightly against the powerful rush of the
current. Over a triangular sail from an old galley, the lights of
the setting sun glowed. In the forest's anteroom, the landscape
looked both solemn and somber. On the left bank were slaty,
damp-streaked black hills, looking prey to an overwhelming
sorrow. At their feet lay blocks of granite shaped like saurians,
tapirs, petrified beasts. Three bulks were piled in the quietude
of an estuary, a barbarous cenotaph capped off by an ovoid for-
mation like a gigantic frog preparing to leap. Everything in that
mineral, almost treeless landscape breathed mystery. Basaltic
piles, rectangular monoliths appeared at intervals, collapsed in
the scarce and scattered brush, menhirs and dolmens—remains
of a lost necropolis in a place where everything was silence and
immobility. It was as if a strange civilization of unknown men
had flourished there, leaving the vestiges of an architecture created for unknown ends lost in the night of the ages. A blind
geometry governed the dispersion of these arrect or fallen slabs
that descended in angular, flat, and mingled series to the river,
bridged paths of tiles marked with shattered obelisks. The islands in the current were like piles of misshapen blocks, like
fistfuls of inconceivable pebbles thrown around by a fantastical dismantler of mountains. Each island made throb in me
again a fixed idea suggested by Rosario's enigmatic words.
Finally I asked blithely about the island with the abandoned
mission. "Santa Prisca," Father Pedro said, reddening slightly.
"They ought to call it Saint Priapus," the Pathfinder chimed in,
cackling, and the rubber tappers laughed as well. For years, they
informed me, the ruined walls of the old Franciscan settlement
accommodated lovers who had nowhere to curl up in the village. Fornication was so rampant there, the helmsman told us,

that the mere scent of the humidity, the fungus, the wild lily that grew there sufficed to arouse the most virginal of men, even a Capuchin friar. I walked to the prow, standing next to Rosario, who was reading the story of Geneviève de Brabant. Sitting on a sack of tonka beans, with no idea what anyone was saying, Mouche failed to grasp the harm that had been done to our relationship. I wasn't angry, and I had no desire just then to punish her for what she'd done. On the contrary: in that nightfall with frogs croaking in all the reedbeds, the humming of the insects swarming around us as their diurnal counterparts withdrew, I felt light, at ease, relieved by her betrayal, like a man setting down a burden too long borne. Magnolia flowers grew on the bank. I thought of my wife and her daily travels. But her face wasn't clear in my mind, and it drifted apart in vague, diffuse forms. The boat's hollow bottom reminded me of the basket from my childhood that had been my true ship on portentous journeys. Rosario's arm, next to mine, radiated a heat my own arm accepted with a strange and delightful stinging sensation.

16

(Saturday night)

In the manufacture of his dwellings, man reveals his lineage. The Greeks here have made their homes from the same materials as the Indians their huts, and the consistencies of fiber, palm fronds, and adobe have dictated their proportions, as in every architecture in the world. But the softer slope of the eaves, the thicker beams suffice to give their gables the character of an architrave crowning a facade. They have chosen trunks wider at the base for columns, following an instinctive desire to imitate the Doric. The surrounding landscape of stones contributes to the strangely Hellenic ambience. And Yannes's three brothers, whom I've now met, reproduce in slightly younger or older faces bas-relief profiles fit for a triumphal arch. I've been told that Dr. Montsalvatje—whom the

Pathfinder spoke to me of the night before—is in a nearby hut
that serves as a goat pen at night, ordering and adding to his
collection of strange plants. Now he is coming toward us, waving his arms and talking in his pompous accent, this scientific
adventurer, collector of curare, of yopo, peyote, and other toxins and stupefacients of the jungle, their mechanisms still
poorly understood, which form the basis of his studies and experiments. Taking little interest in who we are, he erupts in a
flow of Latin terminology for never-before-seen fungi, grind-
ing a sample between his fingers and telling us why the name
he's chosen is the correct one. When he realizes we aren't bota-
nists, he laughs, declares himself the Lord of the Venoms, and
asks for news of the world we have come from. I venture a
reply, but I can see from the people's inattention that nothing I
have to say holds any interest for those here. Dr. Montsalvatje's
interest is the life of the river itself. He asks for a quinine pill
from Father Pedro de Henestrosa and swallows it as soon as he
receives it. On Monday he will take his herbaria to Puerto Anunciación, but will return soon afterward, because he's discovered an unknown *Clavaria* the mere scent of which produces
visual hallucinations, and a crucifer that causes condensation
to appear on metals when it's brought close to them. The
Greeks bring their index fingers to their temples, as if pointing
toward the stone of folly. The Pathfinder mocks the odd sound
the indigenous vowels take on in his mouth. But the rubber
tappers call him a great doctor, and tell how he relieved an ab-
scess with the tip of a chipped knife. Rosario knows him, and
says he always carries on like this after spending long periods
in silence. Mouche dubs him Señor Macbeth and speaks to him
in French, but wearies quickly of his stories about plants and
asks Yannes to hang her hammock in the house. Father Pedro
tells me the herbalist, imaginative but not a madman in the
least, relieved his months of solitude in the brush concocting a
fanciful lineage of alchemists and heretics, declaring himself a
direct descendant of Raymond Lully—whom he insists on calling Ramon Llull, doing honor to the Catalan form of his name.
Even in the *Ars Magna*, the Doctor Illuminatus's obsession
with the tree suggested a certain kinship between the two of

them. The uproar of our arrival and introductions subsides at
the sight of the rough trays the miners bring out, with cheese
from their goats' milk, radishes and tomatoes from their tiny
garden, and cassava bread, salt, and liquor, which they pass
around first—perhaps to commemorate the ancient rite of salt,
bread, and wine. We take a seat now around the bonfire,
united by the primeval urge to see live fire in the night. Some
lean on their elbows; others tuck their chin into their hands;
the Capuchin bundles up in his habit; the women lie on a blanket; Sparrowhawk lets his tongue loll out next to Polyphemus,
the Greeks' one-eyed mastiff: we watch the flames grow in
leaps between damp branches, dying in yellow here, reborn in
blue over a dry splinter, while the logs beneath crumble slowly
into cinders. The great still slabs on the slaty gradient resemble
steles, milestones, monoliths posed along a staircase whose uppermost steps vanish in the night. It was an exhausting day. But
no one goes to sleep. We stay here bewitched by the fire, drunk
on its heat, closed up in ourselves, thinking without thinking,
complicit in our tranquility, the atavistic solace we share. A
cold clarity soon overtakes the horizon of irregular rocks, and
the moon rises over a tree with vines running through its crown,
and the crickets rise up in chorus. Two white birds fly past, caw-
ing as they descend. As the fire blazes, words come easier: one
of the Greeks complains that the mine might be exhausted. But
Montsalvatje shrugs and tells him that farther on, up toward
Grandes Mesetas, the very riverbeds abound with diamonds.
His words stoke my imagination, and the Herbalist—in his
thick-framed glasses, bald head burnt by the sun, stubby hands
dotted with freckles, fleshy fingers reminiscent of a starfish—
becomes for me a sort of household deity, a gnome who
watches over the grottoes. When he speaks of Gold, everyone
falls silent, because all men like to talk of Treasures. The
narrator—telling stories by the fireside, as it should be—has
studied all that pertains to gold in far-flung libraries across the
world. And now, remote and glazed by the moon, we see it: El
Dorado. Father Pedro smiles scornfully; the Pathfinder listens
with a phlegmatic mien, tossing twigs on the fire. For the botanist, the myth reflects reality. In the highlands, in the lowlands,

across the vast phantasmal province where men sought the city of Manoa, diamonds lie in the mud of the riverbanks and gold abides in the water's depths. "Alluvium," Yannes objects. "Which means," Montsalvatje replies, "there's a central massif we're unacquainted with, a laboratory of telluric alchemy in those immense, strangely shaped mountains and waterfalls that abound in the region—the least explored on the planet—that stands immediately before us. Walter Raleigh calls it 'the mother lode,' the matrix, and it gives birth to an inexhaustible sediment of precious metals and stones, casting them down into rivers by the hundreds." That name—*Serguaterale*, they call him in Spanish—begins a recitation of other testimonies of daring adventurers who emerge from the shadows to heat their chain mail and ichcahuipilli by our fire's flames. Here are Federmann, Belalcázar, Espira, Orellana, along with their chaplains, drummers, and sackbuts, and a necromancer company of algebraists, herbalists, and tenders to the dead. We see blond Germans with curly beards and thin Extremadurans with goatees, their standards flapping in the wind, riding coursers like those of Gonzalo Pizarro, which donned shoes of hammered gold no sooner than they sank their hooves into the shifting soils of El Dorado. Prominent among them was Philipp von Hutten, *de Utre* to the Spanish, who stood mute with stupor amid his men atop a hill one memorable afternoon, astonished at the sight of the great city of Manoa and its splendid fortresses. Word spread of it ever after, and there followed a century of doomed wanderings through the jungle, failed expeditions, strayings, circling aimlessly, eating saddle leather, drinking horses' blood, reiterated deaths in the manner of Saint Sebastian, pierced by arrows. And these were the expeditions we knew of: the chronicles have forgotten the names of those smaller bands burnt up in the fire of myth, whose skeletons lie in their armor at the foot of an insurmountable wall of rocks. A tall shadow before the flames, the Pathfinder produced an axe the unusual shape of which had caught my eye that evening: it was Castilian, with a handle of olive wood now blackened but still wedged inside the metal. Some peasant soldier had scratched a date into it with a knife—a date from the time of the Conquistadors. We handed it around in silent reverence, not really sure what we felt, and the Pathfinder told us he had found it in the darkest heart of the forest, in the midst of human remains, beside a motley pile of helmets, swords, and harquebuses trapped in the roots of a tree, with one halberd standing at man height, seemingly held by absent hands. We were dazzled as our fingertips touched the cold blade of the axe. And we allowed the fantastical to embrace us, and longed for greater portents. Montsalvatje evoked medicine men who closed wounds reciting the Spell of Bogotá, the Giant Queen Cicañocohora, the amphibian men who slept at the bottom of the lakes, and others who nourished themselves on nothing but the scent of flowers. We believed his tales of the Ruby Dogs with a gleaming stone between their eyes, the Hydra that Federmann's people had seen, the miraculous properties of the bezoar found in the entrails of deer, the *tatunachas* whose ears could give shelter to five people, the savages with ostrich claws instead of feet, attested to in the true account of a devout prior. For two centuries, the blind on the Camino de Santiago had sung of the wonders of an American Harpy displayed in Constantinople, who died there bellowing in rage . . . When these stories appeared earnest, and had been transmitted by men of the cloth, Father Pedro de Henestrosa felt obliged to dismiss them as the work of the Devil; when soldiers had recounted them, he cursed their mania for tall tales. But Montsalvatje played the Prodigals' Advocate, and swore that the missionaries accepted the truth of the Kingdom of Manoa and set off in search of it even in the Age of Reason. Seventy years before, a famed geographer affirmed in a scientific treatise that in the vicinity of Grandes Mesetas he had glimpsed what might have been the phantom city espied by Utre. The Amazons had existed; they were the wives of the men the Caribs killed when they migrated to the Empire of Maize. In the Mayas' jungles, stairways, quays, monuments, and temples arose, covered with ominous images of the rites of fish priests and lobster priests. Enormous heads appeared behind felled trees, and stared at their discoverers with sunken lids more terrible than two fixed pupils, because they had contemplated Death from within. All over stretched out long Avenues of Gods, rows of them facing each other, their names forever unknown—gods defunct, defeated, who for centuries and centuries had been the image of that immortality denied to men. On the shores of the Pacific lay gigantic tracings of a piece with the landscape that people had trod upon forever, not noticing them beneath their steps, seemingly meant to be seen from another planet, laid out by people who wrote with knots and punished the use of alphabets with death. In the jungle, each day, new stones were hewn; the Plumed Serpent was painted on remote cliffsides, and no one had deciphered the thousands of petroglyphs speaking in animal forms, constellations, enigmas on the banks of the Great Rivers. By the fire, Dr. Montsalvatje pointed to the distant deep blue plateaus rising toward the moon: "No one knows what lies behind those Forms," he said in a tone that brought back to us a feeling forgotten since childhood: we felt the urge to stop there, to take off on foot, to reach the door to the prodigies before dawn. Again the waters of Lake Parime glimmered. Again the strongholds of Manoa rose inside us. They were real to us again when we saw the way the myth of them lived on in the imaginations of so many forest dwellers—so many denizens of the Unknown. I saw the Pathfinder, the Greek miners, the rubber tappers, and all those who blazed trails into the Undergrowth when the rains ended as seekers of El Dorado like those who had sought it long before, entranced by its name. The doctor uncorked a glass vial of tiny dark rocks that yellowed in our hands by the firelight. We touched the Gold. We brought it close to our eyes, to convince ourselves of its truth. We weighed it like alchemists. Mouche licked it, to see its flavor. And when the grains were poured back, it seemed that the fire glowed dimmer and that the night was colder than before. In the river, immense frogs croaked. Father Pedro threw his cane into the fire, and the cane became the rod of Moses when he lifted the serpent he had just slain.

17

(Sunday, June 17)

I return from the mine, gleefully anticipating Mouche's dis-
pleasure when she realizes the marvelous, gem-crusted cavern,
the treasury of Agamemnon that she's surely expecting, is a
dug-out streambed, tilled, torn apart, a mud pit hacked top to
bottom and side to side by shovels that have returned twenty
times to the place they found fortune in hopes their hands had
missed by millimeters a startling Stone of Affluence buried in
the grime. Along the way, the youngest diamond hunter describes to me the profession's miseries, the daily desperation
and the rare stroke of luck that makes the finder of a precious
gem, now poor and indebted, return to the place where fortune
shone on him. But every time a splendid diamond emerges
from the earth, the myth is reborn, and the thought of its even-
tual luster, even before it's been cut, leaps past jungles and
mountains, and hearts skip a beat among those men who end
their pointless days peeling crusts of mud from their bodies. I
ask where the women are, and he says they're bathing in a
nearby creek where no dangerous creatures lurk in the eddies.
But then we hear their voices. As they come closer, these voices
make me hurry from the cabin, alarmed at the violence in their
tone and incapable of imagining what has frightened them. We
wonder whether someone's gone to spy on their nudity from
the banks or with some vile purpose in mind. Now Mouche is
here, her clothing soaked, asking for help, perhaps in flight from
some terror. Before I can take a step, I see Rosario, her thick
underskirt thrown on hastily, and when she reaches us, she
shoves Mouche to the ground and pounds at her with a stake.
Her hair loose around her shoulders, hurling insults, kicking,
bludgeoning, punching with her free hand, she looks ferocious,
and we struggle to restrain her. She writhes, kicks, bites the
people clutching her with a rage expressed in growls and snorts,
because she can find no suitable words. When I lift Mouche up,
she can hardly stand. One of the blows has chipped two of her

teeth, and she has a nosebleed. Bumps and scratches cover her body. Dr. Montsalvatje takes her to the herbarium—a simple hut—to treat her. In the meanwhile, we gather around Rosario, trying to find out what's happened. She is obstinately silent, unwilling to respond. She sits on a stone, bows her head, repeatedly shaking it, and her black hair whips from side to side, concealing her irate face. I go to the Doctor's hut, where Mouche, patched with gauze and stinking like a pharmacy, is lying in a hammock and moaning. When I ask her, she tells me she has no idea what's happened, that Rosario seemed to have lost her mind, and without another word, she starts crying, saying she wants to go back now, she can't take it anymore, this journey is exhausting her, she'll go crazy if she stays any longer. She begs, and it strikes me that not so long ago, a plea from her—the rarest of rarities—would have convinced me to do anything. But beside her now, watching her body shake with sobs of apparently real desperation, I am cold, protected by an armor of inflexibility that impresses me, as I might be impressed by a man's strength of will when times turn hard. I could never have guessed that Mouche, whom I'd shared so much life with, could come to feel so distant, so irrelevant. Whatever love I'd felt was snuffed out—I even doubted it was ever there—but one might have expected a gentleness, the bond of friendship, to remain. And yet, the twists and turns, the changes, the reconsiderations of the past two weeks—in reality, not even that—left me numb to her entreaties. Letting her cry, I returned to the Greeks' house, where Rosario, now calm, was balled up, silent, arms over her face in a hammock. Uneasy, the men furrowed their brows, but their minds seemed to be elsewhere. With nervous movements, the Greeks garnished an enormous clay pot of boiling fish soup, arguing about oil, chilies, and garlic in what sounded like falsetto. The rubber tappers were mending their espadrilles in silence. The Pathfinder was washing Sparrowhawk, who'd been rolling around in carrion, and the dog, miserable as the bowls of water were dumped over him, flared his teeth at whoever looked his way. Father Pedro was counting the threaded seeds of his rosary. I sensed, from all of them, a tacit solidarity with Rosario. Mouche was the cause of all the disturbances here, and everyone implicitly rejected her. It was plain to all of them that Rosario had been right to react violently in response to some untoward affront. The rubber tappers thought she was in love with Yannes and that my friend's insinuations were what drove her to frenzy. For several hours, the heat was suffocating, and each man turned inward. The deeper we penetrated the jungle, the more I found they tended to stay silent, which likely enhanced the grave, even biblical, tone of the reflections they expressed in few words. Each person spoke deliberately, and everyone listened and came to a conclusion before responding. As the shadows of the stones stretched outward, Dr. Montsalvatje emerged from his herbarium, surprising us with the news that Mouche was trembling with fever. After a deep sleep, she had stood, delirious, then fallen faint again, shaking all over. Father Pedro, who had traveled often through these parts, diagnosed her with malaria—an illness not thought particularly grave in these regions. They slipped quinine tablets between her lips, and I stayed grumbling with rage at her side. Two days from the end of my mission, on the border of the unknown, in a landscape that glowed with the prospect of marvels, Mouche just had to fall ill, the insect had to choose her, the person least equipped to cope with the illness. Nature—harsh, profound, and mighty—had taken her as its plaything, wearing her down, disarming her, degrading her, breaking her in a matter of days, and now it had dealt the coup de grâce. The speed of her decline astonished me, and resembled an exemplary punishment carried out on behalf of rigor and authenticity. Here Mouche cut an absurd figure, arrived from a future that had transformed the impenetrable forests into tree-lined avenues. For the people here, her time, her age, was foreign, and fidelity, respect for one's elders, straight dealing, kept promises, the obligations of honor and the honor of obligations, were ever present, timeless, inevitable values, not open to discussion. To ignore these laws was to lose the right to the respect of others, whereas killing a man, for instance, was no great fault. As in the theater, the characters on this real and present stage had stepped forth from engraved allegories of Good and Evil, the

Model Wife, the Faithful Lover, the Villain, the Loyal Friend, the Worthy or Unworthy Mother. River songs told in romantic verses the tragic tale of a violated wife who dies of shame, or the fidelity of a girl half black, half Indian, who waits ten years for her husband to return while everyone says he's been eaten by ants on the far end of the forest. On this stage, Mouche was an extra, and unless I wished to lose my dignity, I had to admit it, knowing as I did of her foray with the Greek to the island of Santa Prisca. But if she returned, sick with malaria, I, too, would have to return, renouncing my task, indebted, empty-handed, ashamed before the one person whose esteem was precious to me—and all that to play the absurd role of protector to a person I now detested. Guessing from my face the origins of my torment, Montsalvatje relieved me, saying he wouldn't in the least mind taking Mouche with him tomorrow. They would go to a place where she could wait for my return with all the comforts: weak as she'd be after that initial attack, there was no forcing her any further. She wasn't built for such rigors. "*Animula vagula blandula*," he concluded ironically. I responded by embracing him.

The moon has risen. At the foot of a large stone, the fire that brought the men together in early evening is dying. Mouche sighs more than respires, and narrates her fever dreams in words that sound like gasps and hacks. A hand rests on my shoulder: Rosario sits on the mat beside me without speaking. But I know an explanation is coming, and I wait for it in silence. A bird caws flying toward the river, awakening the cicadas on the roof, and this seems to make up her mind. In a voice so soft that I can hardly hear her, she begins to reveal something I suspected all too clearly. Bathing in the river, Mouche, never missing a chance to show off a body whose charms she was certain of, needled her about whether her flesh had started sagging, and dared her to strip off the underskirt that peasant morals deem compulsory. She wouldn't leave her in peace, and there was a defiance in her nudity, in her praises of the other woman's firm breasts and flat belly, an affectionate gesture, and then another one that exposed an intention contrary to Rosario's deepest instincts. Without knowing it, Mouche had com-

mitted an offense the women here consider worse than insulting
their mothers, worse than throwing them out, worse than heap-
ing curses on their parents or their offspring, worse than questioning their husband's faithfulness, worse than bitch, worse
than whore. Her eyes glimmer bright in the shadows remem-
bering that morning's fight, making me fear a new eruption of
violence. I grab her wrists to hold her still, so brusquely that
my foot upsets one of the Herbalist's baskets of plants drying
between layers of malanga leaves. Hay falls over us, thick and
crackling, in a veil of scents that bring to mind camphor, san-
dalwood, and saffron. A sudden feeling leaves me gasping in
suspense: this—almost—was the scent of the basket from my
magic voyages, the one where I embraced María del Carmen
when we were children, beside the flowerbed where her father
cultivated basil and mint. I look close at Rosario, feeling her
throbbing veins in my hands, and see something so anxious, so
determined, so impatient in her smile—less a smile than a
laugh deferred, a taut expectation—that my desire hurls me at
her with a will alien to all that is not possession. Our embrace
is quick and brutal, without tenderness, more a struggle to
break and to defeat with an ecstatic bond. But when we lie side
by side afterward, panting, and are aware of what we've done,
satisfaction suffuses us, as if our bodies have sealed a pact that
is the beginning of a new way of life. We lie on the scattered
herbs, mindful of nothing but our own delight. The bright
moon penetrating the open cabin door overtakes our legs: it
started at our ankles, and now it reaches the pits of Rosario's
knees, and she strokes me with an impatient hand. This time
she is the one who throws herself on me, her waist bucking
hungrily. We are looking for a more comfortable position when
a hoarse, cracking voice hisses insults into our ears, and we
separate. We've rolled under the hammock, forgetting who
was moaning above. And now Mouche peers down at us, rigid,
sardonic, mouth salivating, her locks falling over her forehead
a bit like the snakes on a Gorgon's head. "Pigs!" she shouts.
"Pigs!" Rosario kicks at the hammock to shut her up, and
Mouche's voice trails off in delirious divagations. The sundered
bodies are one again, and Rosario's thick hair comes between

my face and Mouche's pale face and arm hanging outside the
hammock, and my lover digs her elbows into the dirt to impose her rhythm. When we can hear what's around us again,
we don't care anymore about that woman above us rattling in
the darkness. She could die now, howling in pain, and her
agony wouldn't move us. We are two, in two different worlds.
I have sown my seed beneath that fleece that I stroke with a
master's hand, and with this gesture, the joyful commingling
of blood seals its encounter.

18

(Monday, June 18)

We've dispatched Mouche with the concerted cruelty of newfound lovers, insatiable, still unsure if the wonders they're ex-
periencing are real, ready to destroy whatever might oppose
their next coupling. We've set her, wrapped in a blanket, in
Montsalvatje's canoe; she weeps, she's barely conscious, and I
tell her I'm following behind in another boat. I've given the
Herbalist more money than he needs to care for her, to pay for
her tickets, her lodging, and her medicines, and all I have left
is a few filthy bills and coins—useless in the Jungle, where the
only commerce is bartering plain, practical objects, needles,
knives, and awls. My generosity is a secret ritual of etherizing
the last glimmers of conscience: anyway, Mouche is in no
condition to continue, and I've fulfilled my last duty to her in
monetary terms. Then again, Montsalvatje's willingness to accompany her surely harbored a malign hope of alleviating several months of chastity with a woman who could in no sense be
called unattractive. Not only do I not care, it even pains me that
the botanist's sorry aspect may doom him to a humiliating failure. The boat has vanished into a distant estuary, at the same
time drawing a stage of my existence to a close. Never have I
felt so light, so at home in my own body, as this morning. Seeing he looks forlorn, I clap Yannes scornfully on the back, and
he looks at me with a quizzical and rueful expression that only

vindicates my antipathy. Everyone knows Rosario is *engaged to* me, as they say around here. She tends to me, brings me food, milks the goats, dries my sweat with cool cloths, pays attention to my words, my thirst, my silence, or my repose, with a solicitude that makes me proud to be a man: here the female *serves* the man in the most noble sense of the word, her every gesture helping to create a home. Rosario and I may not have a roof of our own, but her hands are my table, and the cup of water she brings to my lips, pulling out a leaf that has fallen inside, is crockery marked with the initials of its owner, myself. "We'll see when you settle down with one woman," Father Pedro muses behind my back, to tell me he doesn't look kindly on puerile deceptions. I take the conversation elsewhere to avoid telling him I'm a committed heretic and married, then walk over toward the Greek, who's gathering his things to accompany us upriver. Sure that the mine here is exhausted, that fortune has defrauded him again, he's planning to go prospecting past the Caño Pintado in a little-explored mountainous zone. He reserves a place in his bundle for a book he carries with him everywhere: a cheap bilingual edition of the *Odyssey* with black oilcloth covers, its pages mottled with green from the humidity. Now that they must separate from the book, his brothers, who know long stretches of the text by heart, look at one of the Spanish pages, reading fragments in their hard, angular accents, pronouncing the *v*'s like *u*'s. In a little school in Kalamata, they had learned the names of the tragedians and the meanings of the myths, but they'd felt a deeper affinity with the adventurer Ulysses, visitor of marvelous countries, seeker of gold, who ignored the sirens to return to his home in Ithaca. A peccary had blinded the miners' dog in one eye, and they named him Polyphemus in memory of the cyclops whose baleful tale they'd read aloud a hundred times by the campfire. I ask Yannes why he left that country he was bound to by a bloodline that stretched back to the dawn of time. He sighs and describes the Mediterranean as a landscape in ruins, talking of all he left behind as he might of the walls of Mycenae, empty tombs, or peristyles inhabited by goats. The sea without fish, the useless murices, the confusion of the myths, the downfall

of hope. Then he speaks of the sea, home to his people for centuries, and of a vaster sea that led onward and away. He wept,
he tells me, when he saw the first mountain on this side of the
Ocean, because it was a hard red mountain and resembled
the hard mountains of nettles and thistles in his homeland.
Here he caught the fever for precious metals, the same call to
trade and make one's way that had impelled the oars of his ancestors. One day, when he finds the gem he's dreaming of, he'll
build himself a house with a colonnaded porch, like Poseidon's
temple, he says, on the sheer cliffs of the seashore. Again he
bemoans his people's fate, turns the book back to the beginning, and shouts: "Ah, how shameless—the way these mortals
blame the gods. From us alone, they say, come all their miseries, yes, but they themselves, with their reckless ways, com-
pound their pains beyond their proper share." Then he tells
me, "That's Zeus speaking," and puts the book aside, because
the rubber tappers come bearing a tree branch and, tied to it,
a strange hoofed animal they've just killed. For a moment, I
suppose it is a gigantic boar. "A tapir! A tapir!" Father Pedro
shouts, joining his hands in astonishment before running toward the hunters, with a relish that shows how tired he must
be of the manioc porridge that is the staple food in the jungle.
Festively, they light a bonfire, and the beast is scalded and
quartered; the hams, the offal, the loin are displayed, provoking in us a savage hunger. The miner with his bared torso, absorbed in his labors, looks to me tremendously archaic. When
he throws a few bristles from the animal's head on the flames,
the gesture's sacrificial air seems drawn from a verse of the
Odyssey. How he skewers the meat after rubbing it with lard,
how he serves it on a board after sprinkling it with brandy,
speaks to old Mediterranean traditions, and when Yannes offers me the best cut, for a second I see him transfigured into the
swineherd Eumaeus . . . When the feast is over, the Pathfinder
stands up and walks in long strides down to the river. Sparrowhawk follows him, barking noisily. Two rustic canoes—
two hollowed-out tree trunks—are coming downriver, rowed
by Indian oarsmen. It will soon be time to leave, and we set to
packing our things. I take Rosario to the cabin, and we em-

brace again on the dirt floor, which Montsalvatje has left covered after ordering his collections, in the same acrid and enervating dried plants whose perfumes we smelled yesterday. We remedy the inelegance and haste of our first encounters, mastering the syntax of our bodies. Our limbs are comfortable, our arms where they should be. We select, determine, in marveled experiments, the attitudes and postures that will mark the rhythm and the manner of our future couplings. We teach each other in the forge of lovemaking, giving birth to a secret language. Delight procreates an intimate language, off-limits to others, that will be the dialect of our nights. It is a two-part invention, with terms denoting possession, thanksgiving, sexual suffixes, vowels conceived by the skin, sobriquets unknown and unimaginable before yesterday, employed when others are out of earshot. Today, for the first time, Rosario has called me by my name, repeating it endlessly, as though its syllables must be constantly reshaped—and in her mouth, my name has a sound so singular, so bewildering, that this word that I know best sinks me in a kind of rapture, and I hear it as though it were only just created. We live the peerless elation of thirst shared and slaked, and when we look out at our surroundings, we seem to recall a country of unknown flavors. I jump in the water to wash off the dry herbs clinging to the sweat on my back, and I laugh when it occurs to me that what is happening now violates nature's rhythms—that I am in rut, and she in heat, in midsummer. My lover is now climbing into the boat. We take leave of the rubber tappers and depart. The Pathfinder, Rosario, and I huddle together in the first canoe. In the other are Father Pedro, Yannes, and the luggage. "We go with God!" says the Pathfinder when he sits down beside Sparrowhawk, who sniffs the air, his muzzle like a figurehead at the prow. Henceforth, we will no longer navigate by sail. Sun, moon, and bonfire—and occasionally, lightning—are the only lumination that will strike our faces.

CHAPTER FOUR

Will there be nothing more than silence, immobility at the feet of the trees, of the lianas?
It is well, then, that there are guardians.

POPOL VUH

19

(Monday afternoon)

After two hours' rowing between rocks, rock islands, rock
promontories, rock piles elaborating their geometries with
an inventiveness that no longer catches our eye, a very dense
vegetation—rigid grasses overshadowed by undulating and
dancing hills of bamboo—replaces the stone with an endless
monotony of deep green. I amuse myself recalling Montsalvatje's fireside sagas and pretending we are Conquistadors in
search of the Kingdom of Manoa. Father Pedro is our chaplain,
and we will beg him to take our confession if we are wounded
at the border. The Pathfinder might well be Philipp von Hutten. The Greek is Micer Codro, the astrologer. Sparrowhawk
stands in as Leoncico, Balboa's dog. And I dub myself the
trumpeter Juan de San Pedro, with my woman, stolen in the
siege of some village. The Indians are Indians, and, strange as
it seems, I have adopted that distinction of castes used by the
Pathfinder when he says blithely, without the least malice, recounting one of his adventures: "We were three *men* and
twenty *Indians*." I imagine this is a question of baptism, and it
gives a realist touch to the novel that I am composing in these
authentic surroundings. Where we skirt the left bank, the
bamboo has ceded to a low, colorless jungle whose roots sink
into the water, and the trees, standing erect, unbroken like a
palisade, form an impassible wall at the verge of the current,

with no visible inlets, chinks, or cracks. Beneath a sun raising a film of vapors from the damp leaves, this vegetal wall extends without cease, as though fashioned by men employing their theodolites and plummets. The canoe comes closer to the ragged shore, which the Pathfinder scrutinizes urgently. I cannot imagine there is anything to be found here, and yet the Indians row slowly, and the dog, its back arched, stares along with his owner. I close my eyes, bored from waiting and lulled by the swaying boat, and am awakened by the Pathfinder's shout: "There's the door . . . !" Six feet away from us stood a trunk like the others, neither wider nor scalier. But scratched into its bark were three V's, cradled together, in a design that might have gone on ad infinitum, but that here was only multiplied by its reflection in the waters. Beside it was a vaulted passage so low and narrow I couldn't imagine the boat steering through it. And yet, in we steered, with so little room to move that the sides of the boat scraped against the twisted roots on the banks. We pushed past obstacles and barriers with the oars and our hands to continue along that improbable course amid damp weeds. A sharp chip of wood fell on my shoulder with the violence of a club, and blood began to flow from my neck. A dreadful vegetal soot rained down from the branches, an airborne plankton, heavy at times like fistfuls of iron filings. From all sides dropped strands that chafed the skin, dead fruits, hairy seeds that made our eyes water, filth, fetid dust that turned our faces red. Lurching, the prow destroyed a nest of termites, which crumbled in an avalanche of brown sand. And yet the world below us was worse than the one that cast shadows from above. Punctured leaves swayed in the water, looking like masks of yellow velvet, decoys, cover for other creatures. Chains of filthy bubbles, caked with a varnish of red pollen, slipped off into backwaters hastened by the flapping of a fin, hesitant, uncertain, like holothurians. Elsewhere floated dense, opalescent gauzes stretched across the hollows of hidden stones. Hirsute claws waged war in the depths amid grotesque knots of serpents. Sudden clicks, undulations, lappings in the water revealed an exodus of invisible beings evinced in a wake of turbid rot—grayish whirlpools below black crust mottled with nits. An entire rampant fauna hinted at its presence, borne of timeless grime, of glaucous fermentation, under dark waters that smelled sour like mud kneaded with vinegar and carrion, and on its oily surface trod insects for which liquid was solid ground: translucent vermin, pale fleas, bandy-legged flies, tiny mosquitoes that were little more than a quiver in the green luminosity—for the scant rays of sun when they pierced the green fronds turned a moss-green color that took on swampy tones as they sought out the roots of plants. After floating awhile over that secret channel, we witnessed a phenomenon a bit like the one described by highlanders lost in the snow: disoriented, we lost all sense of the vertical, and our eyes were perplexed. I no longer knew what was tree and what reflection. It was no longer clear whether the glow came from above or below, whether the roof or the floor was of water, whether the openings in the dead leaves were not luminous wells drilled into the floodlands. The reflections of woods, sticks, vines in broad or narrow angles seduced us into seeing illusory passages, unreal detours, corridors, shores. The distortion of appearances, the succession of small mirages at arm's length, added to the angst of disorientation, of disconcertion. It was as if I'd been spun repeatedly around, dizzied and set on the threshold of a secret abode. I wondered if the rowers had any idea how far they'd gone. I was afraid, though nothing threatened me, and all around me, everything was tranquil; it was an indefinable fear, drawn from the hidden worlds of instinct, and I inhaled deeply, but the air remained thin. The damp clung unpleasantly to my clothing, skin, and hair; warm and sticky like an unguent, it penetrated everything, provoking swarms of long-legged insects, horseflies, unnamed pests that owned the air until the mosquitoes arrived at nightfall. After the initial surprise, I relished the spot of cool on my forehead where a toad had fallen. Had I not known what the slimy creature was, I would have trapped it in the hollow of my hand and rubbed it on my temples in search of relief. Tiny red spiders fell over the canoe from above. And thousands of spiderwebs opened just over the current between the low-hanging branches. As the canoe lurched forward, those gray rags draped its side, with dried wasps, the wisps of elytra, antennae, shells half sucked dry inside them. The men were dirty, grimy, their shirts ringed with sweat, with spatters of mud, resin, sap; their faces had the waxy, sallow, sunless look of faces in the jungle. When we reached a small pool that ended in a yellow slab of rock, I felt imprisoned, constricted. Near where we'd moored, the Pathfinder called me over to show me something horrendous: a dead caiman, flesh rotten, with hordes of green flies crawling beneath its skin. The humming was so loud it resembled a dirge, a woman weeping through the jaws of a saurian. I turned my back on this grotesque spectacle to seek my lover's warmth. I was scared. Night was falling early, the shadows closing in, and we had hardly set up a rough camp before dark. All of us took shelter in the isolation of our hammocks as the croaking of huge frogs filled the jungle. The darkness, slick and frightful, quivered. Someone—who knew where—seemed to be breathing into the mouthpiece of an oboe. A grotesque brass instrument cackled off in some tributary. A thousand flutes blew two notes in different octaves back and forth through the leaves. Metal combs, saws biting wood, harmonica reeds, quivering and scraping crickets seemed to cover the face of the earth. Peacocks squealed, stomachs gargled, whistles rose and fell, *things* crept beneath us on the ground; *things* dove, hammered, crackled, wailed like children, snorted in the crowns of the trees, shook bells in the bottom of a pit. I was stunned, frightened, feverish. The day's fatigues, the nervous expectation had worn me out. Sleep softened the fear of the threats around me just as I was about to give in—to shout in fear to hear the voices of men.

20

(Tuesday, June 19)

When the light returned, I realized I had passed the First Trial. The shadows' departure had swept away my fears from the night before. Washing my chest and my face in the still waters of a creek while Rosario rubbed the utensils with sand, getting them

ready for my breakfast, I felt I was sharing with the thousands of
inhabitants of the uncharted banks of the Great Rivers a primordial sensation of beauty, a beauty perceived physically, enjoyed
by body and mind alike, born with each sunrise—a beauty
whose possession in such distant regions is the pride of declaring
oneself master of the world, supreme usufructuary of creation.
The colors of the jungle at dawn are far less comely than at twilight. Where the soil exhales a millenary damp over the water
that divides the earth and vegetation enveloped in mist, dawn
seeps in with grisailles of rain, in indeterminate lights that refuse
to gather into a clear day. We must wait for hours before the sun,
up high, freed by the crowns of trees, can cast a beam of light
across the endless selva. Nonetheless, the jungle dawn renews
the atavistic vigor that coursed through the veins of ancestors
who saw for centuries in the sunrise the end of the evening's terrors, the retreat of roaring beasts, the dissipation of shadows,
the confusion of the specters, the boundary the malevolent could
not cross. At the start of day, I apologize to Rosario for what
little solitude this phase of the journey offers us. She laughs,
humming something I assume is from an old *romancero*: *I am
the woman newly wed / who wept without reprieve / to see myself so poorly wed / and ever doomed to grieve.* Her mischievous
verses, which alluded to the chastity our travels imposed, echoed
on as, back in the water, we reached a broad stretch of river that
plunged into what the Pathfinder told me was the heart of the
jungle. The water rose up, flooding huge stretches of terrain, and
the trees that sank into the clay tangled in lianas resembled anchored ships, while the golden red trunks of other trees stretched
out, giving an illusion of depth, and the long-dead forests, pale,
as though of marble rather than wood, soared like obelisks from
a sunken city. Behind the moriche palms, the bamboo, the
shoots along the banks, the fecund vegetation twisted through
snagging vines, underbrush, creepers, claws, stranglers, splin-
tered sometimes by the dun leather of a tapir seeking a water-
course to quench its maw. Hundreds of herons on tiptoe sank
their necks between their wings or stretched their beaks to the
edges of the lagoons, harassed now and then by an ill-humored
crane flying low. A steep branch gleamed where a croaking flock

of macaws scattered like violent brushstrokes over the rancid shadows beneath us, where species in a timeless struggle climbed one over the other, trying to reach the light, the sun. The verticality of the skeletal palms, the branches that birthed a single leaf after drinking the sap of trunks, were phases in a constant struggle ruled by larger trees I had never before laid eyes on. These abandoned like stragglers the vegetation grown thin in the shadows, and the clear sky spread wide above their cares and engendered aerial forests in their branches, unreal, as though levitating, with garlands of translucent mosses that resembled torn lace. After centuries, one of these trees would shed its leaves, its lichen, exterminate its orchids. Its body would gray, adopting the consistency of pink granite, remaining there nude and silent with its monumental branch work, a testament to the laws of an almost mineral architecture, with its symmetrical, rhythmic equilibria of crystals. Thrashed by the rains, immobile in the tempests, it would stand there through further centuries, until one fine day the lightning struck it and it descended to the hateful world below. Then, the colossus of prehistory would tumble, roaring in splinters, cloven, throwing slivers to the four winds, full of carbon and celestial fire to break and burn everything at its feet. As it fell, a hundred trees would perish, crushed, toppled, mutilated, hurling lianas that snapped and shot into the sky like bowstrings. Then it would lie over the jungle's ancient humus, drawing roots so intricate and vast from the soil that two creeks came together in an extraction of subsoils whose emergence from the shadows tore open nests of termites, and with honeyed tongue and brandished claws, the anteaters came running.

I was amazed by the interminable mimesis of virgin nature. Here everything seemed something else in a world of appearances that concealed reality, and there was no truth not open to question. The caimans that stalked the flooded jungle, immobile, with fauces in wait, looked like rotten logs covered in rose haws; the lianas resembled reptiles and the serpents resembled lianas, unless their skin possessed the nerving of precious woods, the eyes of phalaena wings, pineapple scales or coral rings; aquatic plants wove together in a dense carpet,

hiding the water flowing under them, false vegetation over
seemingly firm earth: fallen bark took on the consistency of laurel in brine, and the funguses looked copper-bleached or sulfur-
dusted beside chameleons too wooden, too stony like lapis,
too yellow like striations of lead, imitating the speckles of sun
struggling to penetrate a barrier of leaves. The jungle was mendacity, trap, masquerade; everything there was dissimulation,
stratagem, play of appearances, metamorphosis: world of the
lizard-gherkin, the sea urchin–chestnut, the chrysalis-centipede,
the larva with carrot flesh, and electric fish that shocked in the
waters flooding the stalks of flax. Near the banks, the shadows
of overhead vegetation breathed cool air over the canoes, but if
we stopped a few seconds, this relief transformed to an intolerable roil of insects. All around stood what seemed to be flowers,
but their colored petals were leaves in various stages of maturity
or decline. What seemed to be fruits, round and ripe, were
sweaty bulbs and stinking velvets; the vulvae of insectivore
plants looked like pansies sprayed with syrup; mottled cactuses
cast up, a palm's length from the soil, a tulip with saffron sperm.
When an orchid appeared up high, beyond the tops of the bam-
boos or the yopos, it was as unreal, as remote as the most se-
cluded alpine edelweiss. There were trees that weren't green but
stood like amaranth along the shore, or glowed yellow like the
burning bush. Even the sky would lie, inverting its stature in
the quicksilver of the lagoons and sinking in celestial abysses.
Only the birds were true, their plumage clearly identifiable.
The herons didn't lie when they arched their necks into inverted question marks, or when, frightened by the cry of the
vigilant crane, their white feathers took to the heights. The king-
fisher didn't lie with its carmine crest, small and fragile in that
terrible universe, a minor miracle like the powerful vibrations of
the hummingbird. Nor did the mirthful howler monkeys lie in
this constant shuffling of appearances and simulacra, this baroque proliferation of lianas, when they frolicked indecently in
the leaves, mugging and carousing like overgrown children
with five hands. And as if the wonders of below didn't suffice,
I discovered a new world of clouds: clouds unique, incomparable, forgotten by men, massing over immense, humid jungles,

rich in water as in the first chapters of Genesis; clouds of weath-
ered marble, flattened at the base, tremendously tall, immobile,
monumental, their shape like the amphora yet to be formed
when the potter's wheel has just begun to spin. Those clouds
rarely touched, and sat still in space, as though edified in the
sky, selfsame since the beginning of time, the separation of the
waters and the mystery of the first mergings of rivers.

21

(Tuesday afternoon)

When we stopped at midday in a wooded inlet so the rowers
could rest and the swelling in our legs would go down, Yannes
departed in search of a stream he said should harbor diamonds in its bed. But we've been calling him for the past two
hours, and the lone response has been the echoes of our voices
along the bends in the muddy river. Tired of waiting, Father
Pedro curses those who let the mania for stones and precious
metals blind them. His words perturb me, and I worry they
will offend the Pathfinder—who allegedly discovered a rich deposit once. But he smiles under matted eyebrows and asks the
missionary with contempt why it is that the Roman monstrances
twinkle with gold and gems. "It is proper," Father Pedro responds, "for the most beautiful materials in Creation to honor
their creator." He then inveighs against worldly priests, as
though to show he demanded pomp for the altar but humility
from the officiant, and he calls them modern-day indulgence
peddlers, nunciature-ruminants, and pulpit tenors. "The eternal rivalry between infantry and cavalry," the Pathfinder ex-
claims, laughing. An urban cleric must seem singularly idle, not
to say a fool, to a hermit who has spent forty years ministering
in the jungle, and I try to gratify him by seconding his words
with examples of unworthy priests and merchants in the temple. But Father Pedro cuts me short with an abrupt tone: "Do
not speak of the bad ones unless you know of the good ones."
And he talks to me of men I've never heard of; of fathers torn

to pieces by the Indians of Marañón; of a blessed Diego tortured horribly by the last of the Incas; of a Juan de Lizardi, pierced by the arrows of the Paraguayos; and of forty friars whose throats were slit by a heretic pirate—the Doctoress of Ávila saw them hurrying toward Heaven in an ecstatic vision, frightening the angels with their formidable saintly faces. He refers to all this as if it had happened yesterday; as if he had the power to travel forward and backward in time. Perhaps this is because his ministry is in a place without date, I tell myself. Father Pedro mentions that the sun is hiding behind the trees, and interrupts his hagiography to shout again to Yannes in a menacing tone, cursing like a mule driver looking for a lost beast. When the Greek reappears, the priest strikes his cane against the rocks so ferociously we take cover in the canoes. When we travel on, I realize why Father Pedro is so furious at the miner's delay. The waterway narrows between shores like black cliffs that announce an imminent change of terrain. Then the current hurls us into a wide yellow river that descends in torrents and eddies to the Río Mayor, which it had run alongside, joining the rapids falling from a slope of Grandes Mesetas. Today the waters swell dangerously with rains fallen somewhere. Father Pedro, with one foot on each edge of the vessel, guides the canoes with his cane. But the waters are rough and the night is coming quick and the hardest part of the struggle is not yet past. Something clusters in the sky: beneath a cold wind that raises immense waves, the trees shed whirlwinds of dead leaves, the air compresses to a funnel, and above the roaring forest, a storm breaks out. Everything is illuminated in green. Lightning bolts hammer down one after the other, the horizon still glowing from one strike when another plummets alongside it in claws that sink past the outlines of the mountains. The flickers of brightness from behind, ahead, from the sides, at times cloaked by the shadowy silhouette of islands whose tangled trees loom over the roiling waters—that cataclysmic light, that rain of aerolites, makes me suddenly afraid; I see hurdles, the furious currents, the multitude of dangers. No salvation is possible if we fall into that tumult that pounds, lifts, buffets our boat. All reason lost, unable to overcome my fear, I embrace

Rosario, seeking her body's warmth, with the gesture not of a lover but of a child hugging his mother's neck, and I lie on the floor of the canoe, burying my face in her hair to keep from seeing what is happening and escape in her the furor that surrounds us. But it is hard to forget, with half a span of warm water splashing from stem to stern in this same canoe. On the verge of overturning, we float from rapid to rapid, pushing the prow through whirlpools, dodging rocks, lurching ahead, our boat lathered with foam from the white water climbing its sides, tortured wood screeching across the keel. Worse still, it has started to rain. I glance at the Capuchin, and my horror grows; when the lightning flashes and reveals his black beard, I see he has given up guiding us and turned to prayer. Her teeth clenched, cradling my head like a mother cradling the skull of an infant after an agonizing birth, Rosario looks surprisingly composed. On his belly on the floor of the boat, the Pathfinder grabs the Indians' belts to keep the blasts of water from carrying them overboard, so they can continue rowing us to safety. My anguish makes endless this terrible struggle. But when Father Pedro returns to the prow, planting a foot on each of the gunwales, I realize the danger is past. The storm withdraws its lightning just as quickly as it deployed it, bringing to a close the tremendous symphony of rage with a very resonant and prolonged harmony of thunder, and the chanting of the frogs on every bank fills the night with croaking. The spine of the river slackens, making its way to the remote Ocean. Weary from nervous tension, I fall asleep on Rosario's chest. And soon the canoe comes to rest in a sand dock, and I find myself back on safe ground, and when Father Pedro leaps to the soil with a "Thanks be to God," I realize I've passed the Second Trial.

22

(Wednesday, June 20)

After long hours of sleep, I grabbed a water pitcher and took a long drink. When I replaced it and saw that it remained level with my face, I grasped, even in my torpor, that I was lying on the ground over a thin straw mat. There was a smell of woodsmoke, and a roof over my head. I remembered then how we'd disembarked in the cove, and the walk to the Indians' village, the feeling of exhaustion and the worry I'd caught a cold, and the Pathfinder making me take several swigs of strong liquor—*stomach fire*, as they call it here—that I would have refused had I not thought it might heal me. Behind me, several Indian women with bare breasts were kneading cassava, their sex barely hidden by a white breechcloth hanging from their waist, held fast by a cord that passed between their buttocks. From the walls of moriche palm leaves hung bows and arrows for fishing and hunting, blowguns, quivers of poisoned darts, calabash gourds of curare, and trowels shaped like hand mirrors used, I would discover later, to pulverize a seed whose intoxicating powders are inhaled through tubes made from the breastbones of birds. Between forking branches near the entry, three fat, reddish-violet fish were roasting over a bed of coals. Our hammocks were set out to dry; this, I remembered, was why we'd gone to sleep on the ground. Somewhat achy, I left the hut, stopping and staring in a daze, shouting exclamations that did nothing to exhaust my astonishment. Behind gigantic trees stood hills of black rock, enormous, solid, with vertical flanks, very present, very true, like fantastical monuments hurled down from above. I had to think back to the world of Bosch, the imaginary Babels of painters of marvels, the hallucinatory illustrators of temptations of the saints, to find anything that resembled the sight before me. And what analogies I hit upon I had to renounce as utterly alien to the proportions before me. What I was looking at was like a titanic city of multiple sparse edifications: cyclopic stairways, mausoleums in the clouds, huge esplanades loomed over by strange obsidian fortresses stripped of battlements and embrasures, defending the passage to some kingdom prohibited to man. And there, over a backdrop of cirrus clouds, stood the Capital of Forms: an improbable, mile-high Gothic cathedral, with two towers, a nave, an apse, and flying buttresses on a conical crag of strange material with shadowy, carbonaceous iridescences. Thick mists

swept the belfries, whirling when pierced by granite threads.
Such were the proportions of these Forms, their vertiginous terraces, their flanks of organ pipes, these dwellings of the gods,
thrones and tribunes arrayed as though in preparation for the
Last Judgment, that the soul was baffled, and sought no meaning behind their bewildering telluric architecture, simply accepting its vertical and inexorable beauty. The sun reflected like
mercury over that impossible temple rather suspended from the
sky than fixed upon the earth. In evanescent planes, defined in
greater or lesser densities of shadow, other Forms of the same
geological family were apparent, with edgings of cascades that
recoiled a hundred times and dispersed into rain over the
crowns of trees. Dazzled by such beauty, I resigned myself to
lowering my eyes to the things that lay before me: huts bordering black, almost stagnant water in inlets; a boy, standing on
hesitant legs, showing me a tiny bracelet of peonies; big black
birds with orange beaks passing by where Indians carried fish
hanging from a stick threaded through their gills. Farther off,
mothers were sewing with babies hanging off their nipples.
Surrounded by old women mashing milky tubers at the foot of
a tall tree, Rosario was washing my clothes. The way she knelt
by the water, her hair hanging loose, holding a bone to scrub
with, her profile took on an ancestral aspect that made her closer
to the women from here than those whose blood had lightened
her skin across generations. I saw why this idea of race and character had so beset me that day I watched her return from the
dead on the edge of a road in the mountains. She emanated the
mystery of a remote world whose light and time I knew nothing of. All around me were people devoted to their vocations in
the tranquil concert of the errands of a life subject to primordial rhythms. I had always seen the Indians through fantastical
stories, as beings on the margins of man's true existence, but
in their medium, their environment, they were absolute masters of their culture. Nothing was more alien to their reality
than the absurd concept of the *savage*. The fact that they were
unaware of things that for me were essential and necessary in
no way relegated them to the primitive. One's sovereign precision shooting fish in the inlet, another's able choreography

putting his mouth to the blowgun, one group's coordination covering the wood frame of their common dwelling with fibers, revealed a human being who had achieved excellence in the totality of professions the theater of his existence presented. Under the scrutiny of an old man so wrinkled that he no longer had any smooth flesh left, the boys exercised severe discipline in the handling of the bow. The males moved their potent dorsal muscles, sculpted by oars; the women's bellies were made for maternity, with strong hips framing a wide, bulging pubis. Many profiles were singularly ennobled by their aquiline noses and thick hair. Bodies evolved in line with their usage. Their fingers, meant for grasping, were powerful and rough; their legs, meant for walking, stood on solid ankles. Each carried his skeleton wrapped in capable flesh. Here there were no useless occupations, as mine had been for so many years. All this I thought of as I went back to see Rosario, but the Pathfinder appeared in the doorway of a hut and called me with loud jubilation. He had just found what I sought on this voyage: the object and purpose of my mission. There on the ground, beside a kind of clay oven, lay the instruments I was asked to collect at the beginning of the month. With the excitement of the pilgrim who hits upon the relic he has searched for on foot through twenty foreign lands, I touched the pyrographed cylinder, with its handle in the form of a cross, that marked the stage between the rhythm stick and the most primitive drums. I saw the ritual maraca, pierced by a feathered branch; the deer antler horns; the ornamented rattles; and the clay shell for calling to fishermen lost in the swamps. There were pan flutes, ancestors to the organ, and, with the hostile gravity of everything that touches death up close, a rude vase with a sinister sound, itself like an echo of the grave, with two tubes emerging from its sides, just as I had seen it represented in the book that gave the first description of it. After bartering for this assemblage of objects formed by man's most noble instinct, I felt I was entering a new cycle of existence. My mission was fulfilled. In just two weeks, I had done my duty in a laudable manner, and I was now proudly caressing the trophies of my diligence. The salvaging of the sounding vase—a truly magnificent piece—was the first exceptional act of my existence up to then, and it grew in my estimation, became tied to my destiny, abolishing the distance between myself and the man who had entrusted me with that task, and perhaps in that very moment he was thinking of me as he stood with some primitive instrument in his hand, feeling its weight with a gesture similar to my own. I fell silent for an interval my happiness made timeless. And when again I noticed time's passing, like a sleepy man opening his eyes to stretch, something inside me seemed to have matured enormously, revealing itself in a Palestrina counterpoint that echoed in my head in many majestic voices.

Leaving the hut to find vines to tie my bundles, I noticed a tumult had disrupted the rhythm of the goings-on in the village. Father Pedro entered and left the hut with the grace of a dancer, and Rosario followed him amid a chorus of trilling Indians. A table of joined branches stood before the door, laid with a cloth of torn lace mended with mismatched thread under two vases full of yellow flowers. In its center was the black wooden cross that hung around the priest's neck. He took from a brown leather suitcase rusted ornaments and liturgical utensils, some showing much wear, and rubbed them with his sleeve before placing them on the altar. I was astonished to see the Chalice and Host appear on the Altar stone; the Purificator was placed upon the Chalice, and the Corporal arranged between two ritual candles. Here, it all struck me as both dreadful and absurd. Knowing the Pathfinder saw himself as a man of character, I shot him an interrogating glance. He said, as if talking about something not pertaining to religion, that they had sworn during the previous night's storm to celebrate a Mass in thanksgiving. Rosario was standing before the altar, and now the Pathfinder approached. Yannes, a man of icons, surely, passed beside me mumbling something about how there was only one Christ. The Indians watched from a distance. The Village Chief, all wrinkled in the middle of his necklace of fangs, maintained a respectful posture from nearer by. Mothers hushed their children's squeals. Father Pedro turned to me: "Son, these Indians refuse the sacrament; I don't want them to see you indifferent. If you won't do it for God, do it for me."

And he added scornfully, appealing to the most universal doubt: "Remember, you were in the boat, and you, too, were afraid." There was a long silence. Then: *In nomine Patris et Filii et Spiritus Sancti. Amen.* My throat was painfully dry. Those words, unchanged through the centuries, had a portentous solemnity in the middle of the jungle—as though sprung from the subsoil of primitive Christianity, of the founding brotherhoods to find again, beneath these trees never felled, a heroic function anterior to hymns intoned in the naves of exultant cathedrals beneath spires rising in the light of day. *Sanctus, Sanctus, Sanctus, Dominus Deus Sabaoth* . . . Trees like columns cast shadows over us. Above our heads, the foliage weighed heavy with danger. Around us were gentiles, the adorers of idols, observing the mystery from their narthex of vines. Yesterday it had amused me to imagine us as Conquistadors searching for Manoa. But it baffles me now to recognize no difference exists between this Mass and the Masses heard in these climes by the Conquistadors of El Dorado. Time has stepped back four centuries. This is the Mass of Discoverers recently come to unnamed shores, who plant symbols of their solar migration to the West before the astonished eyes of the Men of Corn. The two men there kneeling at the two ends of the altar, haggard and bronzed—the Pathfinder with the face of an Extremaduran farmhand, Yannes with the profile of a bonesetter newly registered with the guild—are Conquistador-soldiers, nourished on dried beef and rotten tallow, hardened by fever, bitten by vermin, praying like donors with their helmets lying in the grasses with bitter sap. *Miserere nostri, Domine, miserere nostri. Fiat misericordia,* intones the chaplain of the Doorway in an accent that stops time. We are, perhaps, in the year 1540. A tempest lashed our ships, and now the monk is telling us in the language of Scripture how a great shifting of the seas battered the ship with waves; He was asleep, and when His disciples arrived they woke Him, saying: *Lord, save us, lest we perish,* and He said to them, *Why fear ye, ye of little faith?* and then He rose and restrained the wind and sea, and the weather turned clement and fine. It is, perhaps, the year 1540. But no. The years decrease, dilute, desist in the vertiginous process of time. We have not yet entered the sixteenth

century. We are living long before. We are in the Middle Ages.
For it is medieval man, not the man of the Renaissance, who
commences the Discovery and Conquest. Those drawn into the
great enterprise leave the Old World not through a door flanked
with Palladio's columns but through the Romanesque arch the
memory of which they carried and resurrected in the first
churches on this side of the Ocean, built over the blood-soaked
foundations of the teocalli. The Roman cross, garlanded with
pincers, nails, and lances, was chosen to wage battle on others
who used similar implements of holocaust in their sacrifices.
The devil costumes, parades of monsters, dances of the Peers
of France, and romances of Charlemagne that survive in the
towns we've recently passed through—these, too, are medieval.
And I admit the shocking truth: since that Corpus Christi afternoon in Santiago de los Aguinaldos, I have been living in
the early Middle Ages. The objects, garments, remedies may
pertain to a different calendar. But the rhythms of life, navigation, the oil lamp, and the cauldron, the stretching on of the
hours, the sublime duties of Horse and Dog, the reverence of
the Saints, are medieval—medieval like the prostitutes on feast
days, or the virile patriarchs who boasted of their forty children
from different mothers who beg for their blessing as they pass
through. I grasp that I have lived of late among besotted burghers ever ready to sample the flesh of some serving girl whose
mirthful life I dreamt about so often in museums; I have carved
suckling pigs with charred teats at their tables and shared the
intemperate craving for spices that made them seek new paths
to the Indies. In a hundred paintings I have seen their homes, of
rough red tiles, their huge kitchens, their studded doors. I was
acquainted with the custom of carrying money in one's belt, of
open-position dances, of plucked instruments, of cockfighting,
of drunken revels around animals on spits. I knew the blind and
crippled people of these streets; the poultices, sublimates, and
balms they used to relieve their pains. But I knew them from the
varnish of galleries, testimony to a dead past never to return.
And here that past is become present. I grasp it and inhale it. I
glimpse the perplexing possibility of traveling in time as others
travel through space . . . *Ite, missa est, Benedicamus Domino,*

Deo gratias. The Mass ended, and with it the Middle Ages. But
still, the days were undated. The years, unpassed, poured forth
in mad flight, turning the pages of calendars, raising and lowering moons, crossing from centuries with three numerals to a
century of single digits. The Grail lost its luster, the nails fell
from the cross, the merchants returned to the temple, the star of
the Nativity faded, and it was Year Zero, when the Angel of the
Annunciation returned to the sky. Dates emerged on the far side
of Year Zero—dates of two, three, five numbers—until we arrived at the time when man, weary of wandering the earth, invented agriculture, settling his first villages on riverbanks, and
needing other music, passed from the rhythm stick to the cylin-
drical drum of wood ornamented by pyrography, foresaw the
organ by blowing into a hollow reed, moaning for his dead in
the bellows of a clay amphora. We are in the Paleolithic Era.
Here, those who write the laws, who have the right of life and
death over us, who have the secret of comestibles and toxins,
the inventors of technics, are men who use stone knives and
stone scrapers, bone hooks and bone darts. We are intruders,
ignorant foreigners—latecomer metics—in a city born at History's dawn. If the fire the women are fanning now went out at
once, we could never relight it with the mere use of our hands.

23

(Thursday, June 21)

I know the Pathfinder's secret. He confessed it yesterday by the
fire, being careful that Yannes not hear us. They talk about his
discoveries of gold; they believe he's king of the former Maroons, they say he owns slaves; others imagine he has several
wives in a jungle gynaeceum, and that he travels alone so his
lovers won't see other men. The truth is much more beautiful. It
amazed me when, in a few words, he revealed to me a possibility I'm sure no man of my generation had ever glimpsed. At
night in the hut, before falling asleep, with the cords creaking
evenly as the hammocks sway softly, I speak through the fabric,

telling Rosario we will travel on a few more days. I fear she will be weary, discouraged, or childishly concerned with going back, but she responds with spirited consent. She doesn't care where we go, and is unbothered by the notion of countries near or far. Rosario has no notion of *being far* from some esteemed place that might fulfill her in any special, particular way. This woman who has traversed borders without ever changing tongues, who has never had the thought of crossing the ocean, takes the center of the world to be the place where the midday sun shines down on her from above. A woman of the earth, so long as she treads the earth and eats and has her health and has men she can serve as a mold and measure in exchange for that thing she calls *the pleasure of the body*, she is living out a destiny it's best not to analyze in depth, one determined by *great matters* whose mechanism is obscure but that certainly transcend human beings' capacity for interpretation. This is why she likes to say *it's bad to think about certain things*. She calls herself *Your woman*, referring to herself in the third person: *Your woman is sleeping; your woman was looking for you* . . . And in this constant re-iteration of the possessive I find a conceptual solidity, a strict definition of the situation at hand, that I could never find in the word *wife*. *Your woman* is an affirmation prior to all contracts and sacraments, possessed of that first truth of the *vulva* the Bible's prudish translators replaced with *matrix*, eradicating the passion of the cries of certain prophets. Such simplifications were habitual for Rosario. Alluding to intimate realities of which her lover oughtn't be ignorant, she resorts to expressions at once unequivocal and abashed that recall the *way of women* invoked by Rachel before Laban. All *Your woman* asks for to-night is to be taken with me wherever I go. She grabs her things and follows the man unquestioningly. I know little about her. I don't know whether she has no memories or doesn't want to talk about her past. She admits she's lived with other men. But she solemnly defends the secrecy of those parts of her life—or perhaps thinks it indelicate to allow me to believe that anything that happened to her before we met might possess some signifi-cance. It is remarkable to me, this life in the present, without possessions, without yesterday, without thinking of tomorrow.

But this spiritual disposition must lengthen the lapse of her hours from sun to sun. She talks of long and very brief days, as though they succeeded each other in different tempos—tempos in a telluric symphony with andantes and adagios, amid days performed in presto movements. And now that the hour no longer concerns me, I am surprised to sense in myself different sorts of duration, extended mornings, parsimoniously sculpted sundowns, and everything comes together hauntingly in the tempos of this symphony we read backward, from right to left, contrary to the key of G, returning to the measures of Genesis. At evening, we intrude upon the habitat of a culture predating by centuries that of the men we lived among yesterday. We have departed the paleolithic—era of craftsmanship like that of the Magdalenian and the Aurignacian, which had held me rapt before collections of lithic objects, thinking *it goes no further*, standing at the twilight hours of the night of the ages—to enter a place where human life is devolved to the midnight hours of the night of the ages. The people I see now, so similar to me with their legs and arms; those women with flaccid udders dangling over their swollen bellies; those children that stretch out and curl up like cats; those bodies still lacking in original shame and walking about with their genitals exposed, *nude without knowing it* like Adam and Eve before the Fall—all of them are, nonetheless, human. It hasn't occurred to them yet to exploit the energies of the seed; they are unsettled, and cannot imagine sowing; they walk aimlessly past themselves, eating hearts of palm, which they fight over with the apes hanging from the forest ceiling. When the flowing waters rise, isolating them between two rivers for months at a time, and they have peeled trees like termites, they eat wasp grubs, chew ants and nits, dig up the ground and swallow the worms and larvae that get stuck under their nails, and when they are done, they knead the dirt with their hands and eat the earth itself. They barely know the uses of fire. Their dogs, elusive, with the eyes of wolves and foxes, are the dogs that came before dogs. I contemplate these people's to-me impenetrable faces, realizing how useless it would be to speak, admitting we do not even share gestures that might make us understood. Grabbing my arm, the Pathfinder has me peek into a muddy hollow, a rank sty full of gnawed bones where I see the most horrible sight my eyes have beholden: two living fetuses with white beards, emitting moans from their thick-lipped mouths that resemble a newborn's cries; wrinkled midgets with swollen bellies, streaked with veins like the figures in an anatomical plate, smiling dumbly with gazes somehow timid and servile and slipping two fingers between their fangs. These beings so terrify me that I turn my back, driven by revulsion and fear. "Captives," the Pathfinder tells me sardonically. "Captives of others who think themselves the better race, the sole legitimate owners of the forest." Vertigo strikes me as I consider that other hierarchies of regression must exist, that these human larvae, an erectile sex like my own drooping from their loins, are not yet *the last stage*—that there might exist captives of these captives, so that they in turn would hold themselves up as the superior species, chosen, entitled, these creatures that rut at night, that howl in rut like beasts, that fight with vultures over rotten flesh, unable even to gnaw at the bones their dogs leave untouched. I have nothing in common with these creatures. Nothing. Not with them, not with their masters who surround me, swallowers of worms and lickers of the earth . . . And yet, in the midst of those hammocks that are barely hammocks, of those cradles of lianas where they lie and fornicate, stands sun-hardened clay given shape: a pitcher-like form without handles, with two twinned apertures near the upper edge, and a navel pressed into its convex body by a finger when the material was still soft. This is God. More than God: it is the Mother of God. The primordial Mother of all religions. The feminine principle, the generating matrix in the secret prologue of all theogonies. The Mother with her distended belly, a belly that is udders, vessel, and sex all at once, first figure modeled by man when from his hands the possibility of the Object was born. She stood before me, the Mother of the Child Gods, of the totems given to man so he would accustom himself to congress with divinities, preparing himself in this way for the coming of the Greater Gods. The Mother, *solitary, outside time and space*, whom Faust spoke of with the single word *Mother*, uttered twice in terror. Seeing how the old women with the wrinkled pubis, the tree climbers, the pregnant women are all looking at me, I bow clumsily before this holy vase. I am in these people's dwelling, and I must respect their Gods. But just now, they all take off running. To the rear, beneath the branches of bunched leaves that serve as a roof, they've just laid out the black, swollen body of a hunter bitten by a rattlesnake. Father Pedro says he's been dead for hours. Still, the Witch Doctor is shaking a gourd filled with gravel—the only instrument these people know—to frighten off the lords of Death. They prepare for the incantation in ritual silence, which raises the tension of the onlookers to the breaking point. Then the Word makes its appearance in a great jungle rife with nocturnal horrors. This word is more than word; it is a word that mimics the voice of the speaker but is equally attributed to the spirit that possesses the cadaver. One comes from the enchanter's throat, the other comes from his belly; the one is grave and unified like the subterranean roiling of lava, the other baritone and wrathful and discordant. They alternate, responding, one scolds while the other moans, the belly sarcastic, the windpipe hasty. There are guttural portamenti, stretched out into howls; syllables repeated so many times they turn rhythmic; sudden trills cut short by four notes that compose a melody in embryo. Between the lips, the tongue quivers; inside is a kind of snoring, off-beat panting that overlays the maraca's rattles. This is something that lies past language and yet remains very far from song; ignorant of vocalization and yet much more than words. It distends, turns horrible, bloodcurdling, this cry that echoes over the corpse surrounded by mute dogs. The Witch Doctor looks down at it, shrieks, pounds the dirt with his heels, in that awesome fury of imprecation that is the deep truth of all tragedy—the primordial struggle against the powers of annihilation that puncture the calculations of men. I try to remain aside from all of this, to keep my distance. And yet I cannot elude the horrendous fascination the ceremony inspires . . . When headstrong Death refuses to loose its prey, the Word turns soft and faint of heart. In the mouth of the Witch Doctor, the orphic enchanter, the *threnody* rattles and ceases—dazzling me with the understanding that I have just witnessed the Birth of Music.

24

(Saturday, June 23)

For two days we've walked over the planet's shell, oblivious to History and the obscure migrations of unchronicled eras. Always upward, navigating rapids rushing between waterfalls and streams between hills that oblige us to lift the boats and walk with them to the rhythm of shanties, we've reached the terrains of Grandes Mesetas. Stripped of their former vestments by millennia of rains, they are Forms of naked rock, reduced to the elemental grandeur of telluric geometry. They are the first monuments to rise from the earth's crust, before eyes existed to contemplate them, and their age, their incomparable lineage, confers upon them a severe majesty. Some resemble huge cylinders of bronze, squat pyramids, long quartz crystals motionless over the waters. Some, pitted with cavities, rise like gigantic madrepores from solid bases into splinters. Some are solemn and mysterious, *Gates to Somewhere*—a Somewhere unknown and terrible at the end of these tunnels that sink into their flanks a hundred spans overhead. Each plateau has its own morphology, of corners, hard edges, straight or jagged profiles. Where the basalt outcrop, the incarnadine obelisk is absent, there are hanging terraces or chamfers, sharp angles, bizarre milestones up high resembling pilgrims in a procession. And breaking with that artificial rigor, an arabesque of stone, a geological fantasia commingles with the water to instill this immobile country with a bit of movement. Above us, a mountain of reddish granite throws seven yellow cascades over its battlements. A river plunges into the void and disintegrates in rainbows over a hill thronged with petrified trees. The foam of a torrent bubbles under gigantic natural arches, thundering, echoing until it splits and falls into an interconnected succession of pools. In the heights, past the cusp of the last of the lunar planes, there must be lakes lying just under the clouds, guarding their virgin waters in a solitude never defiled by a human foot. There is hoarfrost at dawn, ice in the distance, shores glimmering like opal, depths filled with night before night falls; monoliths on the edges of summits, needles, signs, clefts expelling mists; rugose rocks like clots of lava—meteorites fallen from another planet, perhaps. These magnificent creations, these immense esplanades overwhelm us. Myriad are the forms, long are the shadows outstretched before us. We are intruders, ready to be cast from this forbidden realm. The world open before our eyes is anterior to man. In the great rivers below dwelled monstrous saurians, anacondas, fishes with breasts, lau laus with huge heads, freshwater sharks, electric eels and lungfish, prehistoric animals bequeathed by the dragon hordes of the Tertiary. Something flees beneath arborescent ferns, bees labor in the caverns, but nothing bespeaks any awareness of life. The waters have just parted, the Dry has appeared, the green grass is made, and the lights that will divide day from night shine for the first time. We are in the world of Genesis, at the end of the Fourth Day of Creation. A step further backward, and we would arrive at the origin of the Creator's terrible solitude—the sidereal sorrow of days before incense and praise, when the earth was disordered and empty and shadows lay over the face of the abyss.

CHAPTER FIVE

Thy statutes have been my songs.

PSALM 119

25

(Sunday, June 24)

The Pathfinder has raised his hand, pointing toward Gold, and Yannes leaves us to search for the earth's treasure. It must be lonely for a miner unwilling to share his discoveries: avaricious in his ways, deceitful in his words, hiding his footprints like a beast that sweeps its tracks away with its tail. We are briefly moved as we embrace this peasant with the Achaean profile, the aficionado of Homer we believe held us so dear. He is drawn away today by that craving for precious metal that made of Mycenae a city of gold, and he sets forth on the speculators' path. He wants to give us something, but has hardly anything apart from the clothes on his back. Finally, he hands Rosario and me his copy of the *Odyssey*. Ecstatic, *Your woman* grabs it. She thinks it's a Scripture that will bring us good luck. Before I can disappoint her, Yannes walks off toward his boat, looking like Ulysses with his oar on his shoulder. Father Pedro blesses him, and we proceed down the waters of a narrow canal that should take us to the City's port. Now that the Greek has left, we can speak the Secret aloud: the Pathfinder has founded a city. I haven't tired of repeating it to myself, since this rumor of *a city* was confided to me a few nights ago, and it shines brighter in my imagination than the most coveted of gems. To found a city. I found a city. He has founded a city. The verb exists, and you can conjugate it in this way. A man can be the Founder of a City, create and govern a city that doesn't appear on maps, free of the horrors of the Age, born from the will of man in this

world of Genesis. The first city. The city of Enoch, built before
the birth of Tubal-Cain, the blacksmith, and Jubal, player of
the harp and organ . . . I rest my head on Rosario's lap, thinking of the immense territories, unexplored sierras, countless
plateaus where cities might be founded on this continent of nature still untamed by man; the measured splashing of the oar
strokes lulls me into a happy sleep over those living waters
beside plants that now take on the fragrance of mountains,
breathing a thin air free of the forest's horrible insects. The
hours pass calmly as we skirt the plateaus, floating from channel to channel in mazes of calm waters, turning our backs to
the sun and then facing it again after circling a precipice
thronged with strange ivies. Afternoon falls as the boat moors,
letting me lay eyes on the wondrous Santa Mónica de los Venados. I pause, disconcerted. What I see in the heart of the
valley is a space some two hundred yards wide, cleared by machetes, with a large house on its edge with wattle-and-daub
walls, a door, and four windows. There are two smaller dwellings, built in a similar style, on either side of a storehouse or
stable. White smoke rises from the bonfires of the ten or so Indian huts. Pride makes the Pathfinder's voice quake as he tells
me: "Here is the main square . . . Here is the House of
Government . . . Here is where my son Marcos lives . . . My
three daughters live over there . . . We've got grain, tools, a few
animals in the storehouse . . . The Indian neighborhood is back
there . . ." And he adds, turning to Father Pedro: "In front of
the House of Government is where we'll build the Cathedral."
He shows me the garden, the cornfields, the pen where they've
raised a small herd of pigs and goats after the hardship of getting the animals here from Puerto Anunciación; while he talks,
the neighbors stream out, shouting words of welcome, the Indian wives and the mestiza daughters and the son, who is the
mayor, and all the Indian men, receive their Governor along
with the township's first Bishop. "Santa Mónica de los Venados," Father Pedro tells me. "We gave it that name because of
the *venado*, the local red deer, and because Mónica was the
name of the founder's mother: Mónica, same as the woman
who gave birth to Saint Augustine, a saintly lady herself, *wife*

of one man who raised her children on her own. I confess I'd imagined, when I heard the word *city*, something more imposing or impressive. "Manoa?" the friar asks scornfully. No. Not Manoa, not El Dorado. But I was thinking of something different. "It wasn't any different in the first years of the cities Francisco Pizarro, Diego de Losada, or Pedro de Mendoza built," Father Pedro observes. Despite my acquiescent silence, a series of new questions occurs to me, but the preparations for the feast—a pig roasted over a wood fire—prevent me from formulating them just now. It's inconceivable to me that the Pathfinder, with the unique opportunity to found a city free from the present Age, would burden himself with the church and its endless canons, interdictions, aspirations, and intransigences, especially as his faith is far from solid and he takes Mass mostly to give thanks for dangers overcome. For now, there are few opportunities to ask questions. I relish the joy of arriving somewhere. I help roast the meat, go for wood, observe the people's chanting, and loosen up with a kind of bubbly pulque tasting of earth and resin that they drink from gourds passed from mouth to mouth . . . Later, when everyone is full, the Indians are asleep, and the Founder's daughters are gathered in their gynaeceum, I sit by the fire at the House of Government and listen to a story about trails. "Well, sir," the Pathfinder says, throwing a log on the fire, "my name's Pablo, and my last name's no less common than Pablo is, and if that name, Pathfinder, sounds like I've accomplished something special, let me tell you, it's nothing more than a moniker the miners gave me when they saw how I always ran ahead of the rest to pan for gold in the sandy rivers . . ."

Beneath the emblem of the caduceus, a twenty-year-old man, chest rattling with a stubborn cough, looks out at the street through the crystal globes full of tinted water at an apothecary frequented by old people. His is the province of matins and rosaries, sweetmeats and pastries made by nuns; the priest passes in his *saturno*, and a sentry chants the Holy Mother's name along with the hour in the misty night. The Lands of the Horse are many days away; then there are roads rising upward, and the city with the big houses, where all the adolescent finds are

jobs in shadows, basements, coal cellars, sewers. Dejected and
ill, he agrees to work in the druggist's in exchange for medicine
and board. They teach him something about macerations and
entrust him with the recipes for remedies based on nux vom-
ica, mallow root, or tartar emetic. At the hour of the siesta,
when no one walks under the shadow of the eaves, the boy
finds himself alone in the laboratory, back turned to the street,
and his hands fall asleep in the flaxseed as he contemplates,
amid mortars and pestles, the slow flow of a wide river whose
waters descend from the lands of gold. At times men with a
worried gait come off the boats in the nearby wharf, boats so
old they seem an image of other times; with their canes, they
tap the rotten boards of the quay, as if in port they still doubted
the solidity of land. These malarial miners, mangy rubber tappers, lepers from abandoned missions, go to the pharmacy for
quinine, for chaulmoogra oil, for sulfur, and when they talk of
the lands where they contracted their plagues, the curtains to
an unknown world draw back before the apprentice's eyes.
Those who arrive there are defeated, but there are others, too,
who pulled a magnificent gem up from the mud and for eight
days had their fill of women and song. Those who've come up
empty have eyes feverish with surmises of possible treasures.
They neither rest nor ask where women can be found. They
lock themselves in their rooms, stare at the samples they carry
in jars, and as soon as their wounds are treated, their buboes
lanced, they leave by night, when the others are asleep, keeping
their destination secret. The boy doesn't envy the others his
age who don their Sunday best each Monday after listening to
the last Mass at the worm-eaten pulpit and go off to the distant
city. Amid flasks and pharmacopoeias, he learns to speak of
deposits; catches the name of the men who order demijohns of
attar to put in their Indian women's baths; studies the strange
names of rivers not written about in books; looks at maps and
dreams, gripped by the percussive sonority of the Cataniapó or
the Cunucunuma; stares voraciously at the zones colored in
green, bare patches where no towns or villages are named.
And one day, at dawn, he leaves through the window of his

laboratory, headed for the docks, where the miners are hoisting their ship's sails, and offers remedies to them if they let him go along. For ten years, he shares the prospectors' miseries, disappointments, bitterness, and the occasional fruits of their perseverance. Unlucky, he ventures farther and farther, accustomed to talking with his own shadow. One morning, he catches sight of Grandes Mesetas. He walks lost for ninety days among nameless mountains, eating grasshoppers and the larvae of stinging ants, as the Indians do in months of famine. When he enters the valley, the maggots in his wounded leg have eaten it down to the bone. The Indians there cure him with herbs. They are a settled group, their culture like that of the people who sculpted the funerary vase. They have seen only one white man before him, and like many in the jungle, they believe us to be the last vestiges of an industrious but weak species, once very numerous but now on the verge of extinction. Through his long convalescence, he comes to share in the penuries and labors of these people. He finds gold at the foot of an outcrop that glows in the moonlight like tin. After bartering it in Puerto Anunciación, he returns with seeds, shoots, and a few tools for farming or carpentry. Leaving a second time, he brings back two pigs, their feet tied, in the bottom of the boat. Later he acquires a pregnant goat and a weaned bull calf, and like Adam, the Indians must invent a name for this animal they've never seen. Life here begins to appeal to the Pathfinder. At night, when he washes at the bottom of the falls, Indian girls on the shore throw white pebbles from the shore to provoke him. One day he takes a wife, and there is a feast in the foothills. He realizes if he keeps traveling to Puerto Anunciación with gold dust in his pockets, the miners will soon follow him, invading his hidden valley and ruining it with their excesses, their hostility and greed. To deceive them, he pretends to deal in stuffed birds, orchids, turtle eggs. One day he realizes he's founded a city. He must feel as surprised as I do when he realizes the verb *to found* can be conjugated with reference to a city. But all cities are born this way, and in the future, Santa Mónica de los Venados may well boast monuments, bridges, and arcades.

The Pathfinder traces out the boundaries of the Town Square, builds the House of Government, signs a constitution, and buries it prominently under a stone. He designates a place for the cemetery, so even death will be subject to order. He knows where the gold is now. But gold doesn't speak to him. He's given up searching for Manoa, because this terrain is what interests him now, and the power of legislating here according to his will. He doesn't wish to replicate the old cartographers' Earthly Paradise. There are diseases here, scourges, poisonous reptiles, insects, wild beasts that devour the livestock; days of floods and hunger, and days of helplessness before a gangrenous arm. But man's atavism has made him to overcome such evils. And when he succumbs, he does so in the primordial struggle that is among the truest laws of the game of existence. "Gold," the Pathfinder says, "is for people who go back there." And this *back there* echoes with contempt—as if the preoccupations and commitments of the people from *back there* were a mark of inferiority. Nature here is implacable, terrible, despite its beauty. But for those who live among it, it is less horrible, easier to endure, than the anxieties and fears, the cold cruelties, the constant threats of the world *back there*. Insects, suffering, natural dangers are accepted here as a matter of course, part of an Order innately severe. Creation is not an entertainment, and they all know this instinctively, accepting the roles assigned them in the vast tragedy of generation. But it is a tragedy with unity of time, action, and place, with known aggressors as the instruments of death, sheathed in venom, scales, fire, miasmas, with thunder and lightning still employed here by the resident gods on their days of rage. By sunlight or the glow of the hearth, man lives out his destiny here, content with simple things, jubilant if the morning is warm or the catch abundant, or if rain falls after a drought, with collective bliss, singing and drumming—and even something as simple as our arrival is a cause for joy. *This is how life must have been in the city of Enoch*, I think, and a question that struck me when we disembarked rises again to my mind. We leave the House of Government to breathe the night air. The Pathfinder shows me then a

rock wall with signs traced out by unknown artisans up high—
artisans whose task must have demanded a scaffolding impossible for the material culture of the people here. In the moonlight,
I see scorpions, serpents, birds, and other signs without meaning for me, astral figures, perhaps. My bafflement is met by a
surprising explanation: one day, the Founder says, when he returned from a journey, his adolescent son Marcos shocked him
by recounting the story of the Great Flood. While the boy's
father was away, the Indians told him the petroglyphs we are
staring at now were drawn in the days of a tremendous deluge,
when the river swelled to the tops of the rocks, by a man who
gathered two of each animal in a large canoe when he saw the
water rising. It then rained for what might have been forty days
and forty nights, and when the sky cleared, and the man wished
to know whether the waters had subsided, he sent out a rat that
returned with an ear of corn in its claws. The Pathfinder had
avoided telling the story of Noah to his children—he didn't
want them hearing those kinds of fairy tales, he said—but
when he found they were already familiar with it, and that the
only detail that had changed was the substitution of a rat for a
dove and an ear of corn for an olive branch, he informed Father Pedro of the secret of this nascent city, trusting him as a
true man because he'd wandered alone through unmapped territories, was schooled in treating ailments, and knew the different plants. "Since they'll hear the same stories no matter
what, they may as well learn them the way I did," he said. Recalling the Noahs of so many religions, I consider objecting
that the Noah of the Indians and the ear of corn is closer to the
truth of these lands than the dove with the olive branch, since
no one in the jungle has ever seen an olive tree. But the friar
cuts me short in an aggressive tone, asking me if I've forgotten
the Resurrection: "A man died for those who were born here,
and they needed to hear the good word." Tying two branches
into a cross with a vine, he lays it scornfully where tomorrow
they will start work on the round hut that will be the first
church of the city of Enoch. "He's growing onions here, too,"
the Pathfinder says, by way of an excuse.

26

(June 27)

Dawn breaks over Grandes Mesetas. The night fog lingers between the shapes, throws up veils that glow and attenuate when the light reflects off a pink granite cliff and sinks to where long shadows lie across the ground. At the foot of the slopes—green, gray, and black—their summits diluted by the mist, the ferns shake off their thin glazing of frost. Peeking into a hollow barely big enough for a child, I contemplate the lichen, the silvery-tinted moss, the vegetal rusts that are a world as complex, in miniature scale, as the immensity of the jungle farther down. In a handbreadth, the damp ground teemed with vegetation just as species swarmed in narrow ambits of the trees. This terrestrial plankton is like a patina thickening at the foot of a cascade that plunges from a great height into turbulent foam digging puddles in the rock. We, the Couple, bathe nude here, in water that flows and churns, flourishing from sunlit summits, tumbling in green and white, and scattering over riverbeds turned ocher by tannic roots. Our limpid nudity is no flaunting, no Edenic charade, and yet it is unlike our zealous panting in the hut at night, and there is mirth in our indulgence here, an astonishment at the pleasure of feeling the light and breeze on parts of our bodies the people *back there* die without ever exposing to the open air. The sun browns that stretch from my hips to my thighs that remains white on the swimmers in my country, however much they swim through seas of sunlight. And the sun passes between my legs, warms my testicles, climbs my vertebrae, explodes in my pectorals, darkens my armpits, coats the nape of my neck in sweat, possesses me, invades me, and I feel its ardor consolidating in my seminal ducts to become again a tense throb searching for the opaque pulsations of the deepest depths of warm entrails, with a limitless desire to unite with another that is a longing for the womb. Here, again, is water, with icy springs gurgling below, and I seek them with my face, burying my hands in sand that is coarse like marble shavings. Later the Indians will come, and they will bathe naked, their lone concession to decorum a cupped hand over the penis. And Father Pedro, too, will come at midday, bony and gaunt like Saint John preaching in the desert, not even bothering to cover the gray hairs around his sex . . . Today I have made the momentous decision to not return *back there*. I will try to learn the honest trades practiced in Santa Mónica de los Venados, which are even now being taught to those observing the building of the church. I will elude the fate of Sisyphus that the world I've fled imposed on me, escaping sterile occupations that are like the endless hastening of a trapped squirrel in a wire drum, escaping time regulated and labor performed in the shadows. No longer will my Mondays be Ash Monday, nor will I need to know Monday is Monday, and the stone I once bore I shall cede to whatever man is willing to waste away beneath a useless burden. Setting it down, I will take up the saw and hoe and cease debasing music with a peddler's avarice. I tell all this to Rosario, who acquiesces meekly, happy as ever to obey the will of him she takes to be the man. *Your woman* hasn't grasped that for me, this decision is more serious than it appears, implying a renunciation of everything *back there*. Born on the edge of the jungle, her sisters married off to miners, she takes for granted that a man prefers vast hinterlands to overcrowded cities. Nor does it strike me that, in growing close to me, she has had to make the same sort of intellectual concessions as I. For her, I'm not so different from the other men she's known, whereas in order to love her—and I do believe I love her deeply—I've had to adopt an entirely new scale of values concerning the bonds between a man of my education and upbringing and a woman who is all woman and yet a woman and nothing more. I am completely aware of what I am doing. And when I tell myself again that I'm staying, that the sun and the bonfire will be my lights, that I will immerse myself each morning in the waters of this cascade, and that this consummate, supreme, untarnished woman will always be in my desire's reach, a sensation of great joy invades me. Lying on a rock while the bare-breasted Rosario washes her hair in the current, I take out the Greek's old copy of the *Odyssey* and open it to a paragraph that brings a smile to my face, in which Ulysses

sends his men to the land of the Lotus Eaters, who taste the
fruit they are given and forget any notion of returning home.
The hero says: *I brought them back by force, streaming tears,
and lashed them beneath the rower's seats in the bottom of
their ships.* The cruelty in this marvelous story has always vexed
me, the way Ulysses drags his companions away from their
newfound happiness with no recompense but serving him. I see
reflected in that myth society's constant exasperation at those
who through love, physical pleasure, an unexpected gift, find
respite from the ugliness, the limitations, the control others
must suffer through. I turn over on the warm stone, and find
several Indians sitting around the Pathfinder's firstborn son,
Marcos, weaving their baskets. My old theory about the origins
of music seems suddenly absurd, and I see the vanity of speculation for those who try to place themselves at the dawn of man's
arts or institutions with no awareness of the daily life or the
medicinal or religious practices of this prehistoric man who is
our contemporary. It was clever, that idea of mine to draw a
parallel between the magical intent of primitive plastic art—
representing the animal to gain power over the animal—and
the first manifestations of musical rhythm in an attempt to
imitate the gallop, the trot, the tread of beasts. But days ago, I
witnessed the birth of music. I saw beyond the dirge that resus-
citates the Persian Emperor in Aeschylus; beyond the ode of the
sons of Autolycus that stanches the black blood welling from
Ulysses's wounds; beyond the chant meant to protect Pharaoh
Unas from the bites of serpents on his journey to the under-
world. What I saw confirms the theses of those who claim a
magical origin for music. But they arrived at their conclusion
through books, psychological treatises, venturing uncertain hypotheses about remote magical practices that persisted in ancient tragedy, whereas I *saw* the word departing toward song,
which it didn't yet reach; saw the birth of a kind of rhythm in
the repetition of a monosyllable; saw the interplay of real and
feigned voices and the enchanter alternating between the two
tones; saw a musical theme develop from an extramusical rite.
How silly it seems that some maintain that prehistoric man
discovered music through his desire to imitate the beauty of

birds chirping—as if a bird's tweet possessed musico-aesthetic meaning for those who hear it constantly in the jungle in a concert of murmurs and snorts, splashes and flights, calls, tumblings, rising waters—a sonorous code the hunter interprets and that is essential for his vocation. I remember other flawed theories, and consider the controversy my ideas would generate among musical scholars devoted to theses from books. There would be profit in gathering some of the Indians' chants here, which are basic but very beautiful, with singular scales that give the lie to the notion that they can sing only in pentatonics . . . But my persistence in such thoughts exasperates me. I have decided to stay here—I must finally leave these vain intellectual speculations aside. To do so, I don what little clothing I wear here and go to visit those who are working on the church. It is a round, wide structure with a pointed roof like the other huts, of moriche leaves over struts of branches, crowned by a wooden cross. Father Pedro has established a Gothic outline with a broken arch for the windows, and this repetition of two curved lines on the wattle-and-daub walls is a premonition of plainsong. With no bell to hang from the gable, we use a hollowed trunk, a kind of makeshift *teponaztli*, which I thought of inspired by the rhythm-stick in the hut. I confess that the study of its resonances subjected me to a painful test. When, two days before, I untied the lianas around the protective matting, they flew open, swollen from the damp, and sent the funerary pitcher, the rattles, and the pan flutes flying across the ground. These objects lay around me like accusing creditors, and there was no point in putting them in the corner to try and forget them. I came to these jungles, set down my bundle, I found my woman, thanks to money I received for these instruments that do not belong to me. My evasion leaves my guarantor in a bind, as I am certain he will take responsibility for my defection, making sacrifices, commitments, maybe even taking out usurious loans to replace the funds lent me. I would have been happy, placid, not to see these museum pieces lying at the head of my hammock, clamoring without cease for their labels and display cases. I should take them away, shatter them, maybe, bury their shards at the foot of a cliff. But I can't, because my conscience has returned to this forgotten matter, and after long absence, it is exuding resentment and contempt. Rosario exhales into one of the tubes in the ritual vase, and it sounds like the wail of a horse, like an animal fallen into a dark pit. I push her away brusquely and she stands aside, wounded and uncomprehending. To soothe her, I tell her the reason for my irritation. She soon finds the simplest solution: I can send the instruments of Puerto Anunciación in a few months, when the Pathfinder returns there, as he does now and again, to buy medicines and repair those tools damaged from overuse. From there, his sister can send them to the post office downriver. My conscience ceases to torment me, because once the cargo is on its way, the keys for my escape will be paid for.

27

Father Pedro and I have climbed the hill with the petroglyphs and are now resting on a schist soil where black boulders stand with their edges to the wind or lie scattered like ruins, like rubble, amid a vegetation seemingly cut from gray felt. There is something remote, lunar, inhuman in this terrace to the clouds, cut by a stream of frozen water that comes not from a spring, but from the mist. I feel vaguely out of place—an intruder, or perhaps a profaner—when I realize that my presence here interrupts the arcana of a massively arid mineral teratology that over thousands of years has stripped the flesh from a skeleton of mountains wrought from what looks to be brimstone, lava, ground chalcedony, plutonian slag. The gravel reminds me of Byzantine mosaics knocked from the walls in an avalanche, then lifted by shovels and scattered here, a debris of quartz, gold, and carnelian. It took two days to get here, on paths where the reptiles grew ever sparser and the orchids and flowering trees more compact, crossing through the Lands of the Bird. Sumptuous macaws and pink parrots escort us from sun to sun, and the grave-faced toucan flaunts his breastplate of yellow-green enamel, his beak badly soldered to his head—

the theological bird that shouted to us *God sees you!* at twilight, when wicked thoughts tempt man unrelentingly. We see
hummingbirds that are more insects than birds, immobile in
their vertiginous phosphorescent suspension, over the parsimonious shadow of curassows dressed as night; looking up, we
observe the percussive diligence of the dark-striped woodpeck-
ers, the riotous disorder of the whistles and chirps on the forest's roof, startled creatures looking down on the gossiping
files of parakeets, and all the painted birds that have no proper
names, which Father Pedro tells me the men in their suits of
armor used to call *Indian sunflowers.* Just as other peoples' civilizations rose under the sign of the horse or the bull, the civilizations of the Indians with avian profiles thrived under the
protection of the bird. At the center of their mythologies is
the flying god, the bird god, the plumed serpent, and for them,
everything beautiful is adorned with feathers. The headdresses
of the emperors of Tenochtitlán were made of feathers; even
now the flutes and toys and festive and ritual vestments of the
people I have met here are all adorned with feathers. Astounded
that I, too, now dwell in the Lands of the Bird, I utter a facile
opinion about the difficulty of finding in these people's cosmog-
onies some myth that coincides with our own. Father Pedro
asks if I have read a book called the Popol Vuh. I've never
heard the name. "That ancient Ki'che' holy book already con-
tains a tragic vision of the robot, and I believe it is the only
cosmogony that foretells the threat the machine represents,
and the sad fate of the Sorcerer's Apprentice." And in the language of a scholar, which I suppose was his language before
the jungle hardened him, he surprises me with a story from the
early days of Creation when those objects man invented and
employed with the aid of fire rebelled against him and put him
to death: the pitchers, griddles, plates, pans, millstones, even
the houses fell upon him in a thunderous apocalypse seconded
by rabid, defiant dogs, and destroyed an entire generation of
humanity . . . He is still telling the story when I look up at a
wall of gray rock and see the drawings attributed to a demiurge who survived the Flood and repeopled the world, according to a tradition that has reached the ears of even the primitive

inhabitants of the lower forest. This is the Mount Ararat of this immense world, where the Ark arrived, running aground when the waters abated and the rat returned with an ear of corn between its claws, where the demiurge threw stones over his shoulder like Deucalion to give rise to a new human generation. But Deucalion and Noah and Utnapishtim and the Chinese and Egyptian Noahs never left a mark that endured for centuries where they struck land, whereas here there are huge images of insects, serpents, flying creatures, water beasts and land beasts, moons, suns, and stars, inexplicably carved by *someone* with a cyclopean chisel. Even today it would be impossible to raise the enormous scaffolding required to lift an army of stonecutters high enough to attack with their tools and leave behind such deep incisions . . . Father Pedro takes me to the opposite end of the row of Signs and shows me a kind of crater in a remote area with horrible vegetation growing in its core, membranous grasses with soft, round branches that resemble an arm or a tentacle. Their huge leaves open like hands, and the madrepore or algae textures remind me of underwater flora, with bulbous flowers like feathered lamps, birds strung from a vein, spindles of worms, bloody pistils, which flourish, tear, erupt from their edges with no trace of a delicate stem. Everything tangles, intermingles, knots in vast movements of possession, coupling, incest, monstrous and orgiastic—a supreme confusion of forms. "These are the plants that escaped man in the beginning," the friar tells me. "Rebel plants that refused to nourish him, that crossed rivers, scaled mountains, leapt over deserts for thousands and thousands of years to hide in the last valleys of Prehistory." I turn in mute stupor to observe things that elsewhere were fossils, petrified impressions, or remnants preserved in veins of coal, but that here remain alive in an endless spring that dawned long before the age of man, whose rhythms are not those of the solar year, scattering seeds that may germinate in hours or may wait a half century before growing into a tree. "These are the diabolical plants that surrounded Eden before the Fall." As I bend over the demonic cauldron, an abysmal vertigo invades me; if I let what I

look upon entrance me, this prenatal world, these things that
were here before there were eyes to see them, I will throw myself over the edge, into that density of leaves that will one day
vanish from the earth's face without being named, never to be
re-created in Words—the work, perhaps, of gods who antedate
our gods, of trial gods, unknown because never given a name,
never formed in the mouths of men . . . Father Pedro rouses me
from my hallucinatory contemplation, tapping me softly on the
shoulder with his cane. The shadows of the natural obelisks
grow shorter as midday approaches. We must start our descent
before evening surprises us on the summit, the clouds sink,
and we get lost in the frigid mists. Passing the demiurge's symbols again, we reach the edge of the fault where we will start
to walk downward. Father Pedro pauses, takes a deep breath,
and stares out at a horizon of trees. A range of broken peaks
emerges in slaty volumes, a hard, somber presence in the Valley's immense beauty. The friar holds out his knotty cane:
"Over there is where the only cruel, bloodthirsty Indians in the
region reside," he says. No missionary has ever returned from
there. I believe I permitted myself some waggish observation
about the foolishness of straying into such unwelcome terri-
tory. In response, two tremendously sad gray eyes transfixed
me in a strange manner, with an expression at once intense and
resigned, and I worried I might have angered him, though I
was unsure what might motivate such anger. I still see the Capuchin's wrinkled face, his long, tangled beard, his hairy ears,
his blue-veined temples, like something no longer his, that had
ceased to be flesh of his flesh: his entire self, just then, was en-
cased in those old pupils, reddish from chronic conjunctivitis,
gazing inward and outward, as though made of cloudy enamel.

28

Sitting in front of a board propped on two trestles, almost
nude on account of the ever-worsening heat, a student's notebook with the legend *Notebook of . . . Belonging to . . .* in

arm's reach, the Pathfinder is legislating in the presence of Father Pedro, the Indian Chief, and Marcos, the Tender of the Garden. Sparrowhawk is seated at his master's side, guarding a bone between his hind legs. They are attempting to draft a series of laws for the community. Informed that the residents have been hunting does in his absence, the Pathfinder forbids the killing of what he calls *female venison* and fawns except in case of famine, and even then, the prohibition can be lifted only by an emergency measure approved by all present. The measure is justified by the migration of some flocks, indiscrim- inate hunting, and the depredations of wild beasts, which have reduced the population of red deer in the region. The Law is marked as passed in the Book of the Council's Minutes once all have sworn to obey it and to demand that it be respected, and now they move on to a question of public works. The rainy season is approaching, and Marcos is dissatisfied with the ori- entation of Father Pedro's seed beds, which he says will chan- nel waters from a nearby slope and might easily flood the granary. With a severe expression, Pathfinder demands the friar explain himself. Father Pedro says he's been attempting to cul- tivate onions, and that the work requires a plot of land without standing water or excess humidity. This can be achieved only by tilling the beds in the direction of the slope. The danger the Tender of the Garden has pointed out can be avoided by build- ing a wall of earth one to three spans high between the garden and the granary. Those in attendance agree unanimously, and declare the work will commence tomorrow, and that the entire population of Santa Mónica de los Venados should help, be- cause the sky is cloudy and the midday heat hard to bear, with the humidity and the irritating invasions of flies that have come here from who knows where. Father Pedro reminds them that the church isn't yet built and demands an emergency measure be issued for its construction. In a cutting tone, the Pathfinder replies that the preservation of their grain stores is a more ur- gent question than benedictions and concludes the day's busi- ness with plans for the cutting and hauling of timbers for a fence and a few remarks on the need to post people to watch for the schools of fish, which are swimming upriver earlier this year than they have before. The town hall meeting has produced provisions for public works and a Law—a law the infraction of which *will be punished*, in the Pathfinder's words. I find this unsettling, and ask the diminutive man if he has already performed the terrible duty of enacting punishments in his City. "Before now," he replied, "the punishment for those guilty of misdemeanor was that for a time, no one would speak to them, and they would feel the community's disapproval; but a day will come when there will be too many of us, and harsher sentences will be necessary." Again, I am unsettled by the grave problems that arise in these terrains as unknown as the white *terra incognita* of the cartographers of old—places where the men from *back there* see only saurians, vampires, venomous serpents, and dancing Indians. In the time I've spent in this virgin world, I've seen very few serpents—a coral snake, a velvet snake, another time what might have been a rattler—and the only evidence of wild beasts I've encountered is their roars; though more than once, I've thrown stones at a cunning caiman disguised as a rotten log, treasonously serene in an inlet. I had little to tell as far as dangers braved—putting aside the storm in the rapids. And yet, all around, I've found fruit for the intellect, motives for meditation, art, poetry, myth, more instructive to the mind than hundreds of books in libraries written by men who boasted of their knowledge of Man. Not only has the Pathfinder founded a city—without realizing it, he is creating, one day at a time, a polis to be based on the code established solemnly in the *Notebook of . . . Belonging to . . .* A moment will come when he will have to chastise whoever kills the forbidden beast, and I am certain that when it comes, this small man who rarely speaks and who never raises his voice will not hesitate to condemn the guilty party to exile from the community and death by hunger in the forest—unless some other, more spectacular horror occurs to him, as among those people who doom parricides to be sewn in a leather sack with a dog and a viper and thrown into the river. I ask the Pathfinder what he would do if one of those gold prospectors who sully the lands with their avarice were to show up in Santa Mónica. "I'd give him a day to leave," he responds. "This is no place for

those people," Marcos continues in a bitter tone. They tell me
how the mestizo went *back there* some time ago against his father's will, but two years of ill treatment and humiliation from
the people he humbly approached drove him home full of hatred for all he'd seen in that newly discovered world. And without a word of explanation, he shows me the scars from the
shackles they riveted onto his body at some remote frontier
outpost. Now father and son fall quiet; but behind their silence, I see that both of them accept unhesitatingly the power
granted them by Reason of State: a power over the fate of the
Prospector set on making his way back to the Valley of the Mesetas, who will never return from his second voyage—*because
he got lost in the jungle,* as those who take an interest in his
fate will conclude. This reflection joined the many that kept
my spirit rapt at all hours. And after days of profound mental
torpor, days when I have been a physical man, alien to all that
is not sensation, burning beneath the sun, huddling with Rosario, learning to fish, getting used to flavors novel and unsettling to my palate, my brain has now begun working, after a
much-needed repose, at a rhythm both impatient and anxious.
One morning, I wish I were a naturalist, a geologist, an eth-
nographer, a botanist, a historian, to understand and note
down everything that can be explained. One afternoon I am
surprised to discover that the Indians here preserve an obscure
epic in their memory, and that Father Pedro is reconstructing
it from fragments: the tale of a Caribbean migration north-
ward that slays everything in its path and celebrates its victorious march with feats of grandeur. There are mountains raised
by the hands of heroes, rivers that change course, strange com-
bats in which the stars intervene. These tales reaffirm the unity
of all myths with their kidnapped princesses, ruses on the battlefield, timeless duels, alliances with animals. On the nights
when he sucks a powder through the bones of birds and is ritu-
ally intoxicated, the Indian Chief becomes a bard, and utters
snatches of a chanson de geste, saga, epic poem, that survives
dimly in the memory of the Jungle Notables, and the missionary writes them down . . . I shouldn't think too much. I'm not

here to think. My daily labors, my rustic existence, my scant diet of manioc, fish, and cassava have made me thin, and my flesh clings tightly to my skeleton; my body is slight, precise groupings of muscles clutching its structure. The odious fat I brought here, the white, flaccid flesh, the disappointments, the futile anguish, the foretaste of future misfortunes, the apprehensions, the thumping in the solar plexus—all that is gone. I feel good here in this setting that suits me. Approaching Rosario's flesh, I sense a surging tension, less the call of desire than the irrepressible craving of a beast in rut: the tension of a tautened bow that fires and returns to its repose. *Your woman* is near. I call her and she comes. I'm not here to think. I ought not think. Above all, I should feel and see. And when seeing becomes watching, strange lights emerge and everything unites in one voice. In a flash, this has revealed to me the existence of a Dance of the trees. Not all of them know the secret of dancing in the wind. But those endowed with the grace to do so celebrate balls of foliage, branches, and shoots around their swaying trunks. The rhythm is born in the leaves, ascendant and apprehensive, stiffening and waving, with empty pauses, exhalations, rising and sagging, jubilation in sudden whirlwinds of a prodigious singing of green. Nothing is more lovely than the dance of a bamboo stand in the breeze. No human choreography has the eurythmy of a branch drawn across the sky. I ask myself at times if the higher forms of aesthetic emotion might consist of nothing more than a supreme understanding of creation. One day, men will find an alphabet in the eyes of the chalcedony, in the dun velvet of the phalaena, and will realize in astonishment that every spotted snail was always already a poem.

29

For two days, it's been raining nonstop. Low thunder rolled long over the ground between the plateaus, tumbled into the bottoms, echoed in the caverns. Then the water came. The

palm thatch of the roof had withered in the heat, so we spent
the first night moving the hammocks from place to place, trying in vain to find a spot where it didn't leak. Soon there was a
muddy stream running across the ground beneath us, and to
salvage the instruments, I had to hang them from the support
beams. Dawn found us disconcerted, in soaked clothing, surrounded by grime. We struggled to light the fires, and when
they caught, they filled the huts with an acrid smoke that made
our eyes water. When the rain struck the badly set daub and
wattle of its walls, they buckled, and now the church is half
destroyed. His habit knotted around his waist, his genitals covered by a simple loincloth, Father Pedro is trying to shore up
what can be shored up with the help of a couple of Indians. In
a foul mood, he heaps invective on the Pathfinder, who refused
to issue an emergency measure to complete the construction.
Then the rain returns, and there is more rain and more rain
still until the afternoon, and when night falls, I am deprived of
the consolation of embracing Rosario, who *can't*, and at these
times when she *can't* she turns sullen and gruff as though every
show of affection were odious to her. I struggle to fall asleep in
this constant, ubiquitous roar of running water that effaces
every sound except the sound of running water, as if we were
in the midst of the forty days and forty nights . . . After sleeping awhile—dawn remained far off—I woke with the strange
feeling that my mind had just completed an immense labor, as
though formless, scattered elements, insignificant on their
own, had coalesced and taken on a very clear meaning. A work
has assembled itself in my spirit: it is a *thing* for my eyes,
whether open or closed, it is sound to my ears, it possesses a
remarkably logical order. A work is inscribed within me, and I
may bring it forth without difficulty, making it a text, a partitur, something to be touched, read, or understood by all.
Years ago, I indulged my curiosity by smoking opium, and I
remember that the fourth pipe provoked an intellectual euphoria that solved all of a sudden whatever creative problems had
tormented me until then. I saw everything clearly, everything
was thought, measured, consummated. When the drug wore

off, I would need only find a bit of manuscript paper, and in a few hours, painlessly, without hesitation, my pen would give birth to a Concerto I foresaw then without the arduous uncertainty of how to write it. But the next day, emerging from my lucid dream and ready to take up my pen, I realized, mortified, that nothing I had thought, imagined, solved under the effects of the Benares I'd smoked possessed any value at all: I'd fallen prey to vulgar formulas, inconsistent ideas, mindless inventions, impossible translations of principles from the aesthetics of the plastic arts or sounds that the bubbling of the smoke through water had sublimated by the heat of the fire. What is happening to me in the darkness tonight, surrounded by the noise from the leaks all around, is similar to the start of that delirious elucubration, but this time, I am conscious in the midst of euphoria, my ideas seek an order on their own, and in my mind, a hand is erasing, emending, delimiting, underlining. I have no need of the languor of intoxication to give my thoughts their due form: all I need is to wait for dawn, which will bring enough light to draft my *Threnody*. *Threnody*—this is the title that imposed itself on my thoughts as I slept.

Before yielding to the drudgery that had distracted me from composition—my former indolence, my weakness before every offer of pleasure, which was, at bottom, a fear of the creative mechanism operating in the absence of self-assurance—I had meditated a long while about the possibilities of pairing words with music. To focus more clearly on the problem, I had re-examined the long and striking history of the recitative in its liturgical and profane functions. But the study of the recitative—of ways of reciting while singing, of singing and saying, of seeking melody in the inflections of speech, of weaving word into accompaniment or freeing it from its harmonic frame—all those processes that plagued the modern composers, from Mussorgsky and Debussy to the exasperating, spasmodic achievements of the Viennese School—was not, in reality, what interested me. I was looking rather for the musical expression that arose from the naked word, the word prior to music and not the word *made* music through impressionistic, exaggerated, and stylized inflections—a word that would pass from spoken to sung almost undetectably, a poem making itself music, finding its music in prosody and scansion, as was likely the case of the marvel of the *Dies irae, dies illa* of plainsong, the music of which seems born of the natural accents of Latin. I imagined a sort of cantata in which a coryphaeus would step out before the public while the orchestra remained in silence, gesturing to the audience to pay attention and *mouthing* a simple poem of commonplace words, nouns like *man, woman, house, water, cloud, tree,* and others whose primordial eloquence demands no adjective. This would be tantamount to verbogenesis; and slowly, the repetition of words, their accents, would endow certain successions of vowels with a peculiar intonation that would return in precise, measured distances like a verbal refrain. This would affirm a melody suffused, according to my wishes, with linear simplicity, drawing out an Ambrosian hymn with a minimum of notes—*Aeterne rerum conditor*—and that, for me, is the state of music closest to the word: speaking transformed into melody, with instruments entering discreetly in the guise of sonic punctuation, delimiting the customary phrases of the recitative and affirming through these interventions the living matter each instrument was made of, the presence of wood, of brass, of string, of tense drumskins, as issuing a declaration about possible amalgams. Long ago, I had been deeply impressed by the discovery of a Compostelan trope—*Congaudeant catholici*—in which a second voice overlay the *cantus firmus* to adorn it, endue it with melisma, light, and shadow of a kind it would be indecent to add unmodified to a liturgical theme—and in this way, it safeguarded the sacred music's purity, like a garland hung from a stern column, adding a supple, ornamental, undulating element while in no way detracting from its dignity. I could see now the voices of the choir entering separately over the original chant of the coryphaeus, ordering themselves—masculine and feminine—according to the Compostelan trope. Here, novel accents would succeed one another, with their constants engendering an overarching rhythm that the orchestra would diversify and saturate with sonic colors. The melismatic element would then pass over to the instrumental domain, seeking planes of harmonic variation and oppositions of pure timbres while the chorus, now united, would turn to polyphonic inventions amid the increasingly rich contrapuntal movements. In this way, I intended to permute polyphonic and harmonic writing, which would combine and dovetail in line with the truest laws of music within an ode both vocal and symphonic, deriving an ever-growing expressive intensity from an elementary initial concept. The simple opening phrase would prepare the listener's perception for a simultaneity of planes that would have appeared recondite and confusing if presented all at once, enabling the audience to follow the ironbound logic of the process by which the cell-word developed through each of its possible musical implications. I had looked askance at the disordered styles such a reinvention of music might entail—in instrumental terms, it ran the risk of provocation. To defend myself from such a charge, I speculated with pure timbres, and quoted to myself those strange dialogues of piccolo and double bass or oboe and trombone that I'd found in the works of Albéric Magnard. I believed I could bring unity to the harmonic aspects of the piece with a deft employment of the ecclesiastic modes, which were an underexploited resource only recently returned to by some of the most intelligent musicians of the day . . . Rosario opens the door, and the daylight surprises me in blissful reflection. I still haven't emerged from my trance: the *Threnody* was inside me, but its seed was sown and began to grow on that Paleolithic night on the shores of the river populated with monsters, when the sorcerer had howled over a corpse left black by a rattler's venom two steps from that sty where the prisoners lay prostrate over their excrement and urine. That night I was taught a lesson by men I hadn't wished to consider men, men who compelled me to flaunt my superiority and who believed themselves superior to the two drooling old men gnawing on bones left behind by dogs. At the sight of this true threnody, the idea of the *Threnody* was reborn in me with its overture of the cellword, its verbal exorcism made music by the intonation of several voices, several notes, which gave it form—a form demanded by its magical function, whose alternating voices and grunts were already an embryo of the Sonata. A musician who had looked upon this scene, I was adding the final touches, intuiting darkly what future lay in it and what elements were still missing. I knew what in it was music and what was not yet music . . . Now I take off running to the Pathfinder's house under the rain to ask for one of the notebooks with the words *Notebook of . . . Belonging to . . .* on the cover, and he hands me one reluctantly, and I trace out staves in it, using the uneven spine of a machete as a ruler, to develop on them my musical ideas.

30

As a first attempt, faithful to an old project from my adolescence, I wanted to work on Shelley's *Prometheus Unbound*, which offers, in its first act—like the third act of *Faust II*—a marvelous subject for a cantata. The chained god's liberation, which I associate with my escape from *back there*, implies resurrection, return from the shadows, and responds to the original conception of the threnody, a magical chant intended to bring the dead back to life. The verses I recall now correspond admirably to my desire for a text of simple, direct words: *Ah me! alas, pain, pain ever, for ever! / No change, no pause, no hope! Yet I endure.* Then those choruses of mountains, springs, storms: the elements that surround me now, that I feel. That voice of the earth, that is mother, mud, and matrix, like the Mothers of the Gods that still live in the forest. And those *hounds of hell* that burst into the drama and howl more like Maenads than Furies: *Ha! I scent life! Let me but look into his eyes!* But no. There's no point in overheating my imagination like this, since I don't have Shelley's text and never will in this place where there are only three books: Rosario's *Geneviève de Brabant*, the *Liber usualis* with the texts of Father Pedro's sermons, and Yannes's *Odyssey*. Leafing through *Geneviève de Brabant*, it surprises me to find that the tale, if its execrable style is overlooked, is hardly worse than the greatest operas,

and indeed is quite similar to *Pelléas*. The Christian text, however, would mar the concept of the *Threnody*, saturating the
cantata with a biblical, versicular style. And so I remain with
the *Odyssey*, with its facing text in Spanish. It had never occurred to me to compose music for any poem in that language,
which, by its very nature, would pose an obstacle for choral
performances in any of the great artistic capitals. And immediately, it exasperates me, this evidence of an unconscious
desire *to see my work performed*. My *renunciation* would
never be true if such a vice could catch me unawares. I was the
poet on Rainer Maria Rilke's desert island, and I had to create
from profound necessity. And at any rate, what was my real
language? I had learned German from my Father. With Ruth I
spoke English, the language of my secondary studies; with
Mouche, most often French; with Rosario, the Spanish of my
Epitome of Grammar—Estos, Fabio . . . This last language
was also the language of that *Lives of the Saints* bound in purple velvet that my mother had read to me so many times: Saint
Rose of Lima, Rosario. In this matrix-coincidence, I see a propitiatory sign. Without further vacillation, I return to Yannes's
Odyssey. At first, its rhetorical qualities discourage me, for I
refuse to resort to invocations of the type: *Father, son of Kro-
nos, supreme majesty* or *Son of Laertes, Ulysses, descendant
of the gods, man of a thousand wiles.* Nothing is more contrary to the text my work demands. I read and reread certain
passages, impatient to begin writing. I keep stopping at the
episode of Polyphemus, but it's too busy, too full of adventure.
I leave the hut irritated and pace in the rain, to Rosario's dismay, and I barely respond to *Your woman*, who is alarmed to
see me so nervous; but soon she stops asking, admitting the
man has *bad days* and is in no way obliged to give an account
of what is furrowing his brow. To keep from bothering me, she
sits behind me in the corner and uses the tip of a bamboo shoot
to pry the many ticks from Sparrowhawk's ears. Soon my good
humor returns. The solution to the problem was simple: I
needed only thin out the dead leaves of the Homeric text to attain the wanted austerity. In the evocation of the dead, I find

the magical, elemental tone, solemn and precise at the same time: *I pour out three libations to all the dead. Libation of milk and honey. Libation of wine and libation of clear water. I sprinkle flour over it, and vow when I return to Ithaca I will slaughter the best of my cattle on the fire of the altar, and will offer to Tiresias a black ram, the finest from my herds . . . I have cut the beasts' throats, I have spilled their blood, and I see appear the shadows of those who sleep in death.* As the text achieves the desired texture, I grasp the structure of the musical discourse. The transition from word to music will occur when the voice of the coryphaeus turns almost imperceptibly tender over the stanza about virgins in mourning and warriors fallen beneath the bronze of the lances. The melismatic element that will overlie the first voice will come from Elpenor's plaint, when he weeps at not having *his grave on earth by the road-side.* The poem speaks of his long moan, which will be vocalized in my work as a prelude to his plea: *Do not abandon me without tears, or funerals; burn me with my weapons and raise my tomb on the seaside so all may know of my disgrace. Plant over my remains the oar I rowed among you.* Anticlea's appearance will be the contralto timbre in the vocal edifice that reveals itself to me more clearly by the day, entering as a sort of *faux bourdon* during Ulysses and Elpenor's descant. An open chord from the orchestra with the sonority of an organ pedal will announce the presence of Tiresias. I stop here. So imperious is the need to write in music that I start work on what I've already sketched out, witnessing long-forgotten notations reborn beneath the tip of my pencil. When I finish the first page, I stop, marveling at my crude staves, the lines more converging than parallel, with their notes detailing a homophonic overture that combines invocation and incantation, and it is a different kind of music from any I have ever written. This had nothing to do with the cleverness of my ill-fated *Prelude* to *Prometheus Unbound,* which had tried, like so many others, to invest what was in vogue at that time with the vigor and spontaneity of the craftsman's art—a work begun on Wednesday to be sung at Sunday's services—using the right formulas and contrapuntal techniques, the right rhetoric, but not recapturing its spirit. These dissonances, the notes ill placed above other notes, the shrill instruments played purposely in the crudest and most jarring registers, would not vouchsafe the continuance of this copied art, this cold fabrication, in which the only thing made new was the dead legacy—the forms and formulas of *evolution*—in works that too often neglected, and moreover clearly intended to forget, the shimmer of slow tempos, the sublimity of inspired airs, preferring the bewildering, hasty sleight of hand of rushed allegros. For years, a kind of locomotive ataxia had plagued the composers of concerti grossi, in which two movements in quavers and semiquavers—as if half and whole notes didn't exist—throbbed on both sides of a ricercare, disarrayed by a random placement of hammered accents that contradicted the *respiration* of music, with a poverty of ideas concealed under the shrillest counterpoint imaginable. Like many others, I had let myself be impressed by slogans about a *return to order*, the need for purity, geometry, asepsis, and had suppressed those songs struggling to rise up inside me. Now, far from the concert halls and manifestos and the inexhaustible tedium of artistic polemics, I am inventing music with astonishing ease, as if myriad ideas descended from my brain and emerged from my hand, stumbling over one another, zealous to emerge from the pencil's lead. I realize I should distrust such painless creation. But there will be time to erase, critique, constrain. Under the endlessly falling rain, I compose with joyous impatience, impelled by an inward burst of energy that obliges me to write in a shorthand only I can understand. Tonight, when I go to sleep, the first movements of my *Threnody* will fill the entire *Notebook of . . . Belonging to . . .*

31

There's been an unpleasant incident. I went to the Pathfinder for another notebook, and he asked me if I was eating them. I told him why I needed more paper. "This is the last one," he replied, irritable, saying the notebooks were for the sealing of accords, the transcription of laws, for essential business, and not to be wasted on music. To ease my disappointment, he offers me his son Marcos's guitar. He seems ignorant of the relationship between composition and writing. The only music he knows is that of harpists and mandolin players, medieval minstrels who strum their instruments like the entertainers on the first caravels, who don't need sheet music and don't know the meaning of partitur. I go to Father Pedro to complain. But the Capuchin tells me the Pathfinder is right, adding that he had forgotten to mention the Parish Books with their registers of Baptisms, Burials, and Weddings. He confronts me and asks me if I plan on living the rest of my life in sin. I didn't expect this, and sputter responses irrelevant to the question. Father Pedro begins to inveigh against self-styled persons of culture and knowledge, who make it hard for him to spread the gospel and set a bad example for the Indians. He tells me I must marry Rosario because the maintenance of order in Santa Mónica de los Venados demands legal unions blessed by God. My aplomb restored, I reply sarcastically that a person could live perfectly well here without his evangelizing. Every vein in the friar's face swells at once, and he shouts wrathfully that he will not stand for doubts about his ministry's legitimacy, and he justifies his presence there quoting Christ's words about the sheep not of his fold who must be brought near to hear his words. He strikes the ground with his staff, it seems as if he'll start cursing me, and I shrug and look elsewhere, keeping to myself what I intended to say: that this carping was the only thing the church was good for. Now the fetters beneath his Samaritan's robes are showing through. Two bodies can't even lie together taking pleasure in each other without a black-nailed finger tracing the sign of the cross over them. The mats they embrace on must be sprinkled with holy water on Sunday while we consent to playing the characters in an allegorical tableau. The nuptials he proposes are so absurd that I burst into cackles and depart from the church, where the rain drums over the cracks in the wall that have been temporarily sealed with broad malanga leaves. I return to the hut, and there I

must admit to myself that my scorn and my defiant laughter
were nothing more than the rash responses of a man hiding
behind notions of freedom derived from books to evade what
is painfully true: I am already married. This wouldn't matter if
I didn't love Rosario deeply, intimately. So far from my country and its courts, a charge of bigamy would be impossible to
prove. I could play along with the friar's moralistic farce, and
no one would be the wiser. But the time for deception is over.
Again, I feel like a man, and I forbid myself to resort to lying;
I treasure above all else Rosario's loyalty toward me and what
pertains to me, and the idea of misleading her enrages me—
particularly if I were to delude her with regard to that home a
woman instinctively seeks to harbor: the living home of a pregnancy that could arise at any moment. I could not tolerate the
grotesque spectacle of her tucking a document scrawled on
notebook paper declaring us *man and wife before God* in her
garments, smiling like a girl dolled up for Sunday service. I am
too aware of my conscience to permit such depravity. For this
same reason, I am afraid of what the friar might have in mind:
resolute, he will try to impress his will upon *Your woman's*
spirit until he pushes her over the edge. I will be forced to confess or lie. The truth—if I tell it—will bring me difficulties with
the missionary and make a lie of the placid, simple harmony of
my life with Rosario. The lie—if I acquiesce to it—will make
waste of that rectitude I have aimed to make a sacred law of
my new way of life. To escape the misery, the annoyance of
these cavillations, I try to concentrate on my composition, and
with great effort, I once again lose myself in it. I have reached
the delicate point when Anticlea appears, and Ulysses's voice
subsides, under the melismatic lament of Elpenor, into a simple
descant that produces the first lyrical episode of the cantata,
taken up by the orchestra after Tiresias appears, nourishing an
initial instrumental progression through the polyphony the vo-
cals have already established . . . At the day's end, despite my
extremely crabbed writing, the second notebook is one-third
full. I have got to solve this problem, and urgently. In the forest, so abundant in natural materials, jute, fiber, and bark,
there must be something a person can write on. But the rain will

not stop. Throughout the valleys of Grandes Mesetas, not a single thing is dry. Like a skilled amanuensis, I write even smaller, trying to make use of every millimeter of paper; but this thrifty, even avaricious preoccupation, so contrary to the generosity of my inspiration, inhibits me, and I begin to think in minuscule terms what I must visualize in grandeur. My hands tied, I feel diminished, manacled, ridiculous, and I give up shortly before nightfall, overcome with spite. I never thought something so stupid as a lack of paper could so thoroughly hobble the imagination. At the peak of my frustration, Rosario asks whom I'm writing to, since here there's no postman. Her confusion—this image of the letter kept from traveling, when travel is its only purpose—makes me see the vanity of all I've done these past two days. There's no purpose in a score that cannot be performed. Art is meant for others, particularly music, which can reach such vast audiences. To begin composing in earnest, I've waited until now, when I have arrived as far as possible from a place my work might be heard. It is absurd, senseless, risible. I may promise myself, swear softly to myself that the *Threnody* will end here, going no further than the first third of the second notebook, but I know at dawn tomorrow a force will possess me and I will take up my pencil, drafting Tiresias's appearance on the page, and already, I can hear it resounding with festive blasts like the piping of an organ: three oboes, three clarinets, a bassoon, two French horns, and a trombone. It doesn't matter that the *Threnody* will never be performed. I must write it and I will, even if just to show myself that I am not empty, thoroughly empty—just as I had tried to convince the Curator earlier this very year. Calmer now, I lie back on the hammock and think once more of the friar and his demand. Behind me, *Your woman* is grilling ears of corn on a fire she struggled to light because of the damp. She can't see my face in the shadows from where she sits, can't observe my expression as I speak to her. I ask her, finally, in a wavering voice, if she wants us to marry, if she thinks there's any point in it. I imagine she will grab this opportunity to make me a character in a Sunday school illustration, but she replies, as though dumbfounded, that matrimony is of absolutely no interest to her. Now my surprise transforms to vindictive jealousy. I turn, wounded, to ask her for explanations, and am outraged when she repeats to me an argument I presume she's heard from her sisters, who must have heard it from their mother in turn, and that is, perhaps, the source of that baffling pride of those women, who seem to fear nothing: that a legally binding marriage strips a woman of any opportunity to defend herself from her husband. That the one weapon a woman has against a man who strays is her ability to abandon him at any moment, to leave him bereft of any claim on her person. For Rosario, a lawfully wedded wife is a woman the police can track down when she escapes a home where adultery, enslavement, or drunkenness reign. To marry is to be crushed under the burden of laws created by men, not women. Whereas in a free union— Rosario affirms in a grave tone—"the man knows he must behave if he wishes to hold on to the woman who gives him pleasure and care." I confess, the peasant logic in this left me unable to reply. *Your woman's* notions, customs, and principles regarding life are evidently not my own. And I feel humiliated, vexingly inferior, because now I am trying to convince her to marry; I am the one who aspires to see myself in some sanctimonious nuptial charade, standing before the gathered Indians while Father Pedro utters the ritual words that unite us in matrimony. Still, whatever moral conviction I might have is sapped by the existence of a signed and notarized document *back there*, many miles away. *Back there*, on the paper in such short supply here . . . Just then, Rosario shrieks, and I hear a gasp of terror afterward. I look outside, and see leprosy appear in the window—the horrible, legendary leprosy of antiquity, the leprosy so many have forgotten, the leprosy of Leviticus, which still abides in backward pockets of the jungle. I see a pointed hat, and beneath it the residue, the wreckage of a face, a slag of flesh clinging to the edges of a black hole, the open shadow of a throat under expressionless eyes that are like a hardened plaint on the verge of dissolving, liquefying in the disintegration of that being that moves them while a rugged snore echoes from its trachea and it points with an ashen hand toward our corn. I am paralyzed before this nightmare, this body, this gesticulating cadaver, which shakes its stubs of fingers while Rosario kneels on the floor in mute dread. "Nicasio, go!" Marcos says, approaching impassively. "Nicasio, go, get out!" With a forked branch, he pushes him softly until he steps away from the window. Marcos laughs, comes inside, grabs an ear of corn, and tosses it to the wretch, who stuffs it into his satchel and wanders off toward the mountain, not so much walking as dragging his body along. I realize I have just seen Nicasio the gold digger. The Pathfinder met him when he first arrived here. Even then, he was quite ill, and he lives far off in a cavern, where he awaits a death that seems to have forgotten him. He is forbidden to come to our town. But Marcos leaves him be, since he hasn't tried in so long. Horrified that he might return, I invite the Pathfinder's son to share our dinner. He runs off beneath the rain to get his old four-string guitar—the same kind they played on the caravels—and strums a rhythm in which the blood of Negroes mingles with romantic melodies, singing:

> I am the son of King Mulatto
> And Queen Mulattina;
> Whoever's hand I take in marriage
> Will turn mulatto too.

32

Learning I had tried to write on palm leaves and bark, and on the deerskin lying in the corner of our hut, the Pathfinder has taken pity on me and given me another notebook, but he warns me he won't do so again. When the rain ends, he says, he will go for a few days to Puerto Anunciación, and then he can bring me all the notebooks I could ever want. But eight weeks must pass until the water subsides, and they'll have to finish building the church before leaving, apart from sowing the season's crops and repairing everything the water has damaged. I keep working, though I know that after filling the sixty-four small

pages my drafts will make little progress. I am almost afraid
that initial elation will revisit me, and with the eraser—to keep
from using more paper—I spend days erasing and amending
my first outlines. I haven't mentioned marriage to Rosario
again, but her refusal that afternoon stings me deep inside.
The days are interminable. It rains too much. The laggard sun,
which appears like a hazy disk at midday behind clouds that
turn from gray to white for a few hours, keeps in a state of nervous tension this nature that needs the sun to make its colors
sing and cast its mobile shadows over the soil. The rivers are
muddy, packed with trunks, rafts of rotten leaves, forest waste,
drowned animals. Dams appear, made of things uprooted and
torn, then break apart when a tree falls roots and all from the
top of a waterfall, sending forth an eruption of mud. Everything smells of water; everything sounds like water; my hands
find water everywhere they grasp. Looking for something to
write on, I've found myself caked with mud, sinking to my
knees in pits of mire half concealed by traitorous leaves. Whatever thrives on humidity is growing and rejoicing: the malanga
leaves were never thicker or greener; the mushrooms were never
so legion; the mosses have never climbed so high; the frogs have
never chanted so loud; the creatures in the rotten wood have
never been so abundant. The creeks run like black channels
over the outcrops on the plateaus; each crack, each furrow, each
fold in the rock is the bed of a miniature waterway, as though
the hills were tasked with the burdensome labor of watering
the land below, apportioning the copious rain across the expanses. Lift a log fallen to the ground, and you will find a mad
dash of gray insects below. The birds have vanished, and yesterday Sparrowhawk found a boa constrictor in the flooded
part of the garden. The men and women view this as a natural
disaster, unavoidable, and settle into their huts, sewing, twisting rope, immensely bored. Suffering through the rains is another rule of the game, like accepting the pain of childbirth or
that your right hand must cut off your left with a machete if a
venomous snake sinks its fangs into it. Life demands this, life
demands much that isn't pleasant. The days came when the

humus shifted, the rot began to ferment, the dead leaves macer-
ated in accordance with that law that all generation is generated
in proximity to excrement, the organs of generation mingled
with those of elimination, while what is born shall appear
glazed in spit, serum, and blood—just as manure yields the purity of asparagus and green mint. One night, we thought the
rain had stopped. There was a truce, the plunking against the
roofs went silent, and a sigh was heaved throughout the valley.
The distant river flowed audibly, and a thick, cold, white mist
gathered in all the interstices. Rosario and I looked for each
other's warmth in a long embrace. At the end of our delectation,
we became aware again of our surroundings, and once more, it
was raining. "The wet season is when women get pregnant,"
Your woman said into my ear. I put a hand on her belly in a
propitiatory gesture. For the first time, I am anxious to caress
a child born from my seed, to weigh it in my hand and watch
it bend its knees over my forearm and drip saliva on its
fingers . . . These fantasies surprise me while my pencil pauses
over a dialogue of horns. Then I hear a shout and run toward
the doorway. Something has happened in the Indians' dwelling, and they are screaming and waving their arms outside the
Chief's hut. Wrapped in her shawl, Rosario takes off running
under the downpour. There is an atrocious sight: a girl, some
eight years of age, who has just returned from the river, blood
running from her groin to her knees. When they make sense of
her horrified wails, they realize Nicasio, the leper, has tried to
rape her, clawing at her sex with his hands. Father Pedro presses
scraps of cloth over the hemorrhage while the men, armed with
clubs, go to search the surrounding area. "I already said that
cripple was wandering around here too much," the Pathfinder
tells the friar, and his words seem to conceal a long-suppressed
reproach. The Capuchin says nothing, drawing on his deep
knowledge of jungle remedies, wedging bundled spiderwebs between the girl's legs and scrubbing her pubis with a mercury
ointment. The incident has caused me unspeakable disgust and
indignation: it's as if I, as if all men were to blame for this re-
pugnant attack, because possession, even when consented to,
puts the male in an aggressive posture. I am clenching my fists

with fury when Marcos slides a rifle under my arm: one of those primitive Makiritare shotguns with the die stamp of the Demerara gunsmiths on its long barrel that are still found in this country. Placing an index finger over his lips so I will not speak and arouse Father Pedro's attention, he motions for me to follow him. We wrap the gun in rags and walk toward the river. The turbulent, muddy waters drag past the body of a buck, so swollen that its white abdomen looks like the belly of a manatee. We reached the scene of the crime, where the grass was tracked and dirty with blood. Footsteps sank into the ground. Marcos, bent over, followed the trail. We walked a long time. When it started to get dark, we were at the foot of the Ridge of the Petroglyphs, but we hadn't yet found the leper. We were about to go back when the mestizo pointed out a path newly cut through the damp weeds. We advanced a little farther, and suddenly the tracker stopped: Nicasio was there kneeling in the middle of a clearing, looking at us through horrible eyes. "Aim for his face," Marcos said. I raised the weapon and put the sight level with the hole in the middle of the miserable man's visage. But my finger refused to pull the trigger. A garbled word emerged from Nicasio's throat, something like *ofesseeo . . . ofesseeo . . . ofesseeo . . .* I lowered the gun: the blackguard was asking to confess before dying. I turned to Marcos. "Shoot," he insisted. "It's best if the priest doesn't get mixed up in this." I aimed again. But there were two eyes there: two eyes staring desperately without eyelids, almost without life. And my finger had been chosen to snuff them out. Two eyes. Two man's eyes. He was vile; he was guilty of a contemptible attack, he had corrupted a girl's flesh, maybe infecting her with his illness. He should be crushed, nullified, left as carrion for the birds. But inwardly, I resisted, as if once I pulled the trigger, *something would change forever.* There are acts that raise walls, milestones, boundaries in an existence. And I feared what time would be for me the second after I became Executioner. Furious, Marcos jerked the weapon from my hands. "You'll raze a city from the air, but you won't dare do this! You were in the war, weren't you . . . ?" The Makiritare had a slug in the left barrel and birdshot in the right. Two shots sounded, so close the reports nearly mingled, echoing from rock to rock, from valley to valley . . . The thunder hadn't died yet when I forced myself to look: Nicasio was still kneeling where he had been before, but his face was undrawn, smudged, lacking human contour. It was a meat-red stain that disintegrated into shreds and ran slowly down his chest, like molten wax. Eventually, the blood stopped streaming, and the torso fell forward on the wet grass. Then the rain picked up, and it was night. Marcos carried the shotgun home.

33

A long, percussive thunderbolt enters the Valley from the north and rumbles over us. I sit up so quickly in the swaying hammock that I almost overturn it. The Neolithic men flee in terror from the airplane turning in circles. The Pathfinder has emerged from the doorway of the House of Government, followed by Marcos, and both watch in a stupor as Father Pedro shouts to the Indian women howling in fear in their huts that this is a *white man's matter* and no danger to the people here. The airplane is perhaps five hundred feet from the ground, under a heavy ceiling of clouds ready to burst into rain again; but what separates the flying machine from the Indian Chief who looks at it defiant, hand clutching his bow, is not five hundred feet, but 150,000 years. For the first time in these parts, a combustion motor is rumbling; for the first time, a propellor stirs the air, and its two whirling blades where birds have their claws is as unprecedented as the invention of the wheel. There is something hesitant in its flight, and noticing the pilot is observing us as though looking for something or waiting for a sign, I run for the center of the esplanade, waving Rosario's shawl. My joy is so contagious the Indians emerge without fear, jumping and shouting, while Father Pedro pushes them aside with his cane to clear the field. The plane veers toward the river, descends a bit farther, and approaches us in a closed turn, wings quivering, lower and lower. It makes contact with the ground, rolls dangerously close to the curtain of trees, and turns at the right moment to come to a stop. Two men climb out: two men who call me by my name. It stupefies me to hear that several airplanes have been searching for me for over a week. Someone *back there*—I don't know who—has told them I'm lost in the jungle, possibly taken prisoner by bloodthirsty Indians. Legends have arisen around me, even grim hypotheses that I've been tortured. My case is a reenactment of Fawcett's, and the stories about me published in the press are a modern retelling of the saga of Livingstone. A major newspaper has offered a handsome reward for my rescue. The Curator had briefed the pilots on where to search for me, with indications of those regions where the instruments I came to gather could be found. They were close to giving up when they had to turn off-course this morning to avoid a squall. Passing over Grandes Mesetas, they were shocked to see a collection of dwellings where they expected nothing but terrain without a trace of man, and when they saw me waving the shawl, they assumed I was the fugitive they were seeking. It seems impossible that this city of Enoch, which doesn't yet have its own forge—this city where I am perhaps a stand-in for Jubal—lies three hours by plane, following the direct route, from the capital. This means that the fifty-eight centuries between the fourth book of Genesis and the current year *back there* are traversable in 180 minutes, and with that, one can return to the era some identify with the present—as if here, one weren't also in the *present*—traveling past cities from the Middle Ages, the Conquests, the Colonial and Romantic periods, that survive to this day. They bring out from the airplane a bundle wrapped in oilcloth that they had planned to parachute down if they couldn't land where they found me, taking out medicines, preserves, knives, and bandages and handing them to Marcos and the Capuchin. The pilot unscrews the cap from a large aluminum canteen and tells me to take a drink. I haven't tasted liquor since the night the storm caught us in the rapids. Here amid the damp, the alcohol induces a lucid drunkenness that fills my entrails with forgotten cravings. I want to keep drinking, and watch with jealous impatience as the Pathfinder and his son take nips from my brandy, and yearnings for a thousand other flavors crowd my mouth: an urge to drink tea and wine, to eat celery or shellfish, to taste vinegar or ice. I find myself with a cigarette reborn between my lips, with the aroma that of the blond tobacco I smoked as a teenager on my walks to the Conservatory away from my father's watchful eye. Another, who is also I, begins to tremble inside me, and the images of the two of them fail to coincide; he and I are badly interposed, one over the other, like slipped plates in a lithograph, the red figure straying slightly from the yellow, or like the vision of a healthy eye distorted by corrective lenses. This fiery liquid gliding down my throat weakens and unsettles me, a sensation of forlornness overcomes me, and I cower now under the mountains, under the clouds growing once more dense, under the trees, their canopies nourished by the rain, all of them closing in around me like curtains. Certain elements of the landscape grow strange, the planes subvert one another, the paths are no longer familiar, and the roar of the cascades is suddenly deafening. In the midst of this endlessly flowing water, I hear the pilot's voice, not as the language he employs, but as an inevitability, a summons not to be postponed, a call that had to reach me, no matter where I stood. He tells me to gather my things to depart immediately, because the rain will soon return, and he must start the motor as soon as the mist clears over the plateau. I gesture my refusal. But in that same instant, I hear within me the potent, joyous sonority of the first notes of an orchestra playing the *Threnody*. Again, the lack of writing paper distresses me. Again I recall the idea of books, the need for certain books. It won't be long before the desire to work on *Prometheus Unbound* grows tyrannical—*Ah, me! Alas, pain, pain, pain, ever, for ever!* The pilot is talking again, his back turned to me. And his words, never changing, awaken the memory of other verses from this same poem: *I hear a sound of voices; not the voice which I gave forth.* This morning, these airmen's language, my own language for many years, evicts from my mind the matrix language—my mother's language, Rosario's. The melodious vowels of the Spanish I had come to think in again fill my mind now with confusion. And yet I don't want to leave. The things I lack can be reduced to two words: *paper, ink*. I've managed to do without all that I once thought essential, casting aside like needless burdens objects, flavors, cloths, customs, making do with the utter simplicity of a hammock, ashes to clean my body, and grilled ears of corn gnawed at with relish. But paper and ink I cannot do without: the things expressed or begging to be expressed with paper and ink. Paper and ink are three hours from here, notebooks and reams of paper, tubes, bottles, and cartridges of ink. Three hours from here . . . I look at Rosario. Her face wears a cold and absent expression that shows neither disgust nor anguish nor pain. She must notice my grief, and her eyes avoid mine with the hard, haughty gaze of a person wishing to show she doesn't care what might happen. Marcos appears holding my suitcase, which is stained with green mildew. Again, I refuse, but my hand opens to accept the *Notebook of . . . Belonging to . . .* that is offered me. The pilot, surely tempted by the promise of a reward, hurries me along in an energetic tone. The mestizo loads the plane with the instruments that should already be in the Curator's possession. No, I say, then yes, imagining that once the rhythm stick, the castanets, and the funerary vase have departed in their fiber wrappings, I will at last be free of the troubled sleep their presence gave rise to each night. I drink the last drops from the aluminum canteen. My decision: I will buy what I need to live a life here as full as the lives of the others. All of them are living out a destiny with their hands, with their callings. The hunter hunts, the friar preaches, the Pathfinder governs. I must have a calling, a legitimate one, too, something more than the communal efforts that life here requires. I will soon return forever, once I've sent the Curator his instruments and spoken with Ruth, giving her an honest account of the situation and asking for a swift divorce. I see how I tried to adapt to this life too quickly; to end things with my past, I had a final duty to perform, breaking the legal tie that bound me to the world *back there*. Ruth wasn't a bad woman—she was the victim of her abortive vocation. She would take the blame once she realized there was no point in throwing up obstacles to our separation

or demanding things impossible for a man so skilled in evasion. In three or four weeks, I would return to Santa Mónica de
los Venados with all I needed for several years' labors. When
my work was done, the Pathfinder would take it to Puerto
Anunciación, leaving it in the care of the post boat that plied
the river. Sent to my musician and conductor friends, it would
be understood even if it was never performed. In this regard, I
felt I was cured of all vanity, however much I imagined myself
capable now of expressing ideas and inventing forms that would
cure the many perversions of the music of my era. Without
vaunting what I now knew—without seeking the hollow exaltation of applause—I ought not silence my insights. Somewhere, a young man might be waiting for a message from me,
and might find in himself, when he heard my voice, a world of
freedom. No deed was consummated until seen by another,
whereas a single glance sufficed to bring a thing into being, just
as a single word from one designated Adam sufficed to make of
that thing creation.

The pilot lays his hand resolutely on my shoulder. Rosario
seems indifferent to everything. In a few words, I tell her of my
decision. She shrugs wordlessly, face full of contempt. To prove
my loyalty, I hand her the notes to my *Threnody*. I tell her these
notebooks are the most valuable thing in the world to me after
her. "You can keep them," she says resentfully, staring elsewhere. I try to kiss her, but she quickly eludes my embrace, and
walks off without turning back, like an animal that refuses to
be petted. I call to her, go on talking, then the airplane's engines
start, and the Indians break out in an ecstatic cry. The pilot signals to me one last time from the cabin. A metal door closes behind me. I can't think over the racket of the motors. We roll to
one end of the esplanade, turn around, and stop still, shudder-
ing as the wheels seem to sink into the muddy soil. Now the
crowns of the trees are beneath us. We pass low over the Ridge
of the Petroglyphs, turning back over Santa Mónica de los Venados, where the villagers have amassed in the town square. I
see Father Pedro swing his cane in a circle. I see the Pathfinder,
arms akimbo, looking up next to Marcos, who waves his straw
hat. Rosario is walking alone on the path to our home, eyes

turned toward the ground, and I shudder when I notice that her black hair, parted down the middle—my nose delights as it recalls the animal odor of her scalp—covers her face like a widow's veil. In the distance, where Nicasio died, is a great whirling of vultures. Below us, the clouds thicken, and in search of better weather, we ascend into an opalescent mist that effaces everything around us. Told we will be flying blind for some time, I lie on the floor of the aircraft and sleep, dazed by the liquor and the extreme altitude.

CHAPTER SIX

What you call dying is the conclusion of your death,
And what you call birth is your death's beginning,
And what you call living is death in life.

QUEVEDO, *Dreams*

34

(July 18)

We've just crossed a soft cluster of clouds still bright with day-light, pierced by broken arches, rotten obelisks, titans with smoke-streaked faces—and down below lies a crepuscular city where the lights are beginning to turn on. Various passengers amuse themselves pointing out a stadium, a park, a main street in the luminous geography, dragging an index finger over the window. The others are relieved to arrive, while I am apprehensive as I approach a world I left a month and a half ago, according to calculations based on conventional calendars, though in truth what I lived in the distension of those six weeks transcends the chronologies of these climes. My wife has quit the theater and is now playing a new role, the role of wife. That is the terrible disclosure that's forced me to fly over these hazy suburbs I thought I'd never see again, instead of preparing for my return to Santa Mónica de los Venados, where *Your woman* is waiting with the notes for the *Threnody*, which can now be fleshed out on reams and reams of paper. More absurdly still, it appears I am an object of envy of those around me, and the star attraction of their trip: everyone's shown me cutouts from newspapers and magazines of Ruth in our home surrounded by journalists, cutting a tragic pose in front of the Organo-graphical Museum's collections, or staring dramatically at a

map in the Curator's apartment. One night onstage, she allegedly had a strange feeling. Mid-line, she burst into tears, and
soon after the opening of her dialogue with Booth, she ran
straight to the newsroom of one of the major papers, telling
them I was supposed to be home at the beginning of the month,
that she had no idea where I'd gone, and that my teacher, who
had visited her that very afternoon, was deeply distressed that
he hadn't heard from me. The journalists' imaginations grew
heated, and they evoked explorers, wisemen, captives of bloodthirsty tribes—Fawcett, obviously, took pride of place here—
and Ruth went to pieces and begged for the newspaper to
demand my rescue, offering a reward for whoever found me on
that great green unexplored blotch where the Curator surmised
that destiny had taken me. By the next morning, Ruth was cutting a pathetic figure in the news, and my disappearance, unknown the night before, had become a matter of national
significance. Every known photograph of me was published,
even one from my First Communion—a First Communion my
father had agreed to with clenched teeth—in front of the Church
of Jesus of the Mount, and two others of me in uniform, one by
the ruins of Monte Cassino and the other with a group of black
soldiers with our backs to Villa Wahnfried. To the press, the
Curator sang the praises of my theory of *magical-rhythmical
mimetism*—how ridiculous it strikes me today!—while my
spouse painted a pretty picture of our placid conjugal bliss. But
there is another thing that irritates me to no end: the newspaper that paid the aviators so generously has decided to cod-
dle its home-and-family readership by presenting me as some
sort of exemplary figure. The prose of the articles about me
hums with the obstinate notion of me as a martyr to scientific
research, now returned to the lap of his doting wife, as though
to say that marital virtue exists even in the world of theater
and art, and so talent is no excuse for infringing upon society's
norms—just look at *The Little Chronicle of Magdalena Bach*,
consider the tranquility of the Mendelssohn household, and so
on. When I hear all that was done to extract me from the jungle, I feel at once ashamed and irate. I've cost the country a
fortune: more than enough to secure a comfortable existence

for several families for a lifetime. Like Fawcett, I am overwhelmed by the absurdity of a society that can look coldly on
at the spectacle of its fringes—like the people we are flying
over now, whose children cower under sheet metal—while its
heart melts with pity at the thought of an explorer, ethnogra-
pher, or hunter gone astray or captured by savages in the exercise of a freely chosen profession that by its nature implies such
risks—same as the bullfighter, whom fate may impale at any
moment on the horns of the beast. For a brief moment, millions of people have forgotten the wars that mar the face of the
world and turned instead to fretting over me. And now they
are applauding me, unaware that they are applauding a swindler. Because everything about this flight, which is now approaching the landing strip, is a swindle. I was in the hotel bar
where they held the Kapellmeister's vigil when I heard Ruth's
voice on the line from the shore of the other hemisphere. She
was crying and laughing, and there were so many people around
I could hardly understand what she was trying to say. She expressed her love, and told me she had left the theater and would
always remain by my side. She would take the first plane to join
me there. Horrified at the thought of her coming to my land, to
the anteroom of my escape, in a place where the Spanish influ-
ence on the law—which even demanded appeals be sent to the
Apostolic Tribunal of the Roman Rota—made divorce a long
and arduous process, I shouted to her to stay home, saying I
would fly out that very night. Interrupted by parasitic noises, I
thought I heard her say amid confused goodbyes that she
wanted to be a mother. But later, going over the intelligible
parts of the conversation in my mind, my pulse froze, and I
couldn't be sure whether she'd said she wanted to be a mother
or *was going to be a mother.* The latter was a real possibility;
I was not an especially cautious man, and had slept with her
for the last time—our last Sunday ritual—around six weeks
ago. I then accepted the considerable sum the newspaper covering my rescue offered for exclusive access to my numberless
lies—fifty quarto pages of deception I will now sell. I cannot
reveal the most marvelous parts of my journey, as that would
mean putting the worst sort of adventurers on the road to

Santa Mónica and the Valle de las Mesetas. Fortunately, in their reports, the pilots who found me made mention only of a *mission*, a word they used for any far-flung place where some friar has stuck a cross. And since missions don't hold much interest for the public, I can leave many details out. What I will sell is a charade I've been cobbling together during the journey back: prisoner of a tribe more wary than cruel, I escaped, crossing hundreds of miles of jungle alone; lost and hungry, I happened upon the *mission* where I was eventually found. In my suitcase, I have a famous novel by a South American author full of names of animals and·trees and indigenous legends and ancient events, everything needed to give my tale the veneer of truth. They will pay me for my prose, and with a sum that will assure Ruth thirty years of peaceful living, I won't feel so bad about the divorce. That she might be pregnant has certainly hurt my case, in moral terms—and if she is, that explains her sudden desertion of the stage and her urge to have me close. I sense I must gird myself to repel the worst of all tyrannies: the tyranny of the lover over one who cares not to be loved, with that weight of tenderness and humility that defuse violence and stifle words of reproach. In a battle like the one I am on the verge of inciting, there is no worse adversary than the person who takes all the blame and begs for forgiveness before being shown the door.

I've barely left the plane when Ruth comes to meet me, her lips seeking me out, her body struggling to find intimacy between our open coats, whose edges join on either side of us. I recognize her belly and breasts beneath the light fabric that covers them, and she bursts into sobs over my shoulder. A thousand flashes blind me like broken mirrors this afternoon at the aerodrome. Here comes the Curator, and he embraces me with feeling; a delegation from the University arrives soon afterward, led by the Rector and several Deans from the various Departments; then a number of ranking civil servants from the state and municipal government, the newspaper chief— perhaps Extyaich, too, with the painter of ceramics and the ballerina?—and last, my studio staff with the company president and the PR department, all of them dead drunk. Faces long

forgotten rise up amid the surrounding confusion, faces of those
many people who lived alongside us for years, people from the
profession, people who went to work in the same places, who
disappeared along with their names and the sound of their
voices after a brief while without seeing them. I walk among
these spectral escorts to a reception at City Hall. And now I see
Ruth beneath the chandeliers of the portrait gallery, as though
she were playing the role of a lifetime: turning and returning in
an unending arabesque, she makes herself gradually the center
of events, their gravitational axis, upstaging all the women and
adopting the role of housewife with the grace of a ballerina.
She's everywhere, slipping past columns, vanishing and reappearing, ubiquitous, ungraspable, changing her expression
for a persistent photographer, relieving a bad headache with a
pill from her purse; she brings me a drink or a treat, gazes at
me enthralled for a second, rubs her body against mine in a
way that each onlooker thinks he and he alone has noticed,
comes, goes, gives a witty reply when someone quotes Shake-
speare, makes a brief statement to the press, says next time, she
will go with me into the jungle; she straightens up sveltely before the news cameraman, and so subtle, so protean, so sug-
gestive is her performance, rousing the admiration of others
while attending only to me, drawing on a thousand sly artifices
to paint a picture of the happy couple, that I am tempted to ap-
plaud. Ruth's trembling joy at the reception is that of a wife
preparing for her second wedding night, but this time, without
the pain of being deflowered: she is Geneviève de Brabant returned to her castle; Penelope listening to Ulysses speak of
their marriage bed; Griselda inflamed by faith and hope. When
she senses her resources are growing thin, that a reprise might
steal some dazzle from her starring role, she says earnestly that
I'm exhausted, that I need rest and privacy after my cruel tribu-
lations, and we are allowed to leave, and the men wink know-
ingly as they watch my wife descend the great staircase hanging
on my arm, her dress hugging her body. I have the sense, as we
depart City Hall, that nothing remains but for the curtain to
fall and the lights to go down. All this is alien to me. I remain
far away. A moment ago, when the company president told me,

"Take a few days to rest," I gave him a strange look, as though indignant that he might presume to possess some power over my time. And now, as I discover what once was my home, it feels I am entering another's abode. Nothing here means what it did before, and I no longer want to possess any of it. Hundreds of books lined up on the shelves on the wall are dead to me. An entire literature I had taken to be the wisest and subtlest of my day now appears to me rampant with artifice. Even the apartment's peculiar scent returns to me a life I don't care to live again . . . When she came in, Ruth bent over to pick up a newspaper clipping someone—a neighbor, maybe—had slipped under the door. She looks increasingly startled as she reads. I am pleased at the sight of this mental distraction, which will delay the dreaded shows of affection, giving me time to think of what to say; but then she comes at me violently, eyes full of wrath. She hands me the clipping, and I tremble when I see a photo of Mouche chatting with a known scandal monger. The headline of the article from this disreputable tabloid promises *revelations* about my journey. Its author relates the contents of a conversation with my former lover. According to her declarations, she was my collaborator in the jungle: while I was studying primitive instruments from the organographical perspective, she was examining their connection to astrology—as everyone knew, many ancient people composed their musical scales in relation to the hierarchies of planets. With frightful audacity, Mouche mentions the *rain dance* of the Zuni Indians, with its elementary symphony in seven movements, cites the Hindustani ragas, invokes Pythagoras, drawing, one supposes, on bits of knowledge acquired in the course of her friendship with *Extyaich*. Despite everything, she's crafty, as this display of false erudition is meant to justify to the public her presence on my journey, so they won't dwell on the true nature of our relationship. She presents herself as a scholar of astrology, taking advantage of her friend's mission to acquaint herself with the cosmogonic notions of primitive Indians. She rounds off this tale with the admission that she abandoned the enterprise early, after falling sick with malaria, and returned in Dr. Montsalvatje's canoe. She offers nothing more, fully aware

that her words suffice for interested parties to understand what
she wants them to understand: in reality, she is taking ven-
geance on me for running off with Rosario and for the starring
role public opinion has conferred on my wife in this vast im-
posture. And what she leaves out, the journalist hints at with
malicious irony: Ruth committed the entire nation to the rescue of a man who actually snuck off to the jungle with his
lover. The story was shaken, that was evident now that this
spiteful opportunist had emerged from the shadows to break
her silence. My wife's sublime conjugal theater turned suddenly ridiculous. At that instant, she looked at me with a fury
beyond words, her face seemed made from the plaster of the
tragedian's mask, and her mouth, frozen in a sardonic gri-
mace, revealed the eerie arch of her unsightly teeth—a defect
she usually kept hidden. She sank her stiff hands in her hair, as
though looking for something to clutch and break. I realized I
needed to anticipate the outburst of a no longer repressible
rage, and forestalled the crisis by telling her all I had planned
to say several days later, aided by the abject but irrefutable
force of money. I cast blame on the theater, on her profession,
which she placed above all else, on our physical separation, on
the absurdity of a married life reduced to copulation every seventh day. With the vindictive need for a precise detail to wound
her, I told her how, one fine day, her flesh had grown strange to
me, her person the mere avatar of a duty performed to avoid the
temporary unpleasantness that would arise if I were to leave
her without apparent justification. I spoke of Mouche, our first
encounters, the studio with the signs of the Zodiac, where at
least I'd found a bit of blithe shamelessness, juvenile disorder,
a taste of that animality that for me is inseparable from physical love. Ruth collapsed on the carpet, panting, and green
veins emerged in her face; in a rattling moan, she managed
to get out, as though wishing to make it through a painful
operation: "Keep going . . . Keep going . . . Keep going . . ."
But already I was telling her how I'd split from Mouche, how
her failings and lies disgusted me, how I hated her deceptions
and everything that came with them, her mendacity and her
flighty friends eternally fooled by the foolish notions of other

fools—and it had been like that ever since I'd come to contemplate things with new eyes, as if returning, my sight restored, from a long journey through the houses of truth. Ruth got on her knees to listen better, and I saw in her gaze the birth of a facile compassion, a generous indulgence that I absolutely refused to accept. Her face turned kind, with humane comprehension for a weakness that has already been punished, and soon enough a hand would stretch out to the fallen one, followed by a sobbing, magnanimous pardon. Through an open door, I saw her bed looking too neat, laid with the best sheets, and the flowers on the nightstand, my slippers set out beside hers in anticipation of an embrace to be followed consolingly by a delicate dinner already prepared elsewhere in the apartment, to be served with white wine on ice. With forgiveness so near, the moment to deal the coup de grâce had come, and I brought up Rosario, presenting this unimagined, hitherto secret person to Ruth's stupefaction as a remote, singular being incomprehensible for people from here, because to understand her required a grasp of certain enigmas. I depicted her as a being who transcended our codes, unreachable by common roads, arcana made human, whose noble essences had marked me after trials I could no more describe than a knight could tell of the secrets of his order. In the midst of this dramalette framed by our familiar dwelling, I took malign pleasure in multiplying my wife's heartaches, adding notes of Kundry to Rosario's character, arranging her in a Garden of Eden where the boa Sparrowhawk had caught stood in for the serpent. Carried away by this verbal inventiveness, my voice turned so sensible and resolute that Ruth, sensing danger, leaned in to listen attentively. I let fall the word *divorce*, and since she didn't seem to understand, I repeated it coolly several times in the resolved, unaffected tone of a person issuing a final verdict. This was the great tragedienne's cue. I don't remember what she said for that half hour when the room was her stage. What impressed me most were her gestures: the movements of her slender arms, which traveled from her immobile body to her plaster face, freighting her words with pathetic precision. I suspect now that all of Ruth's theatrical humiliations, her confinement

to the same role for years on end, her eternally deferred desire
to be wounded on the stage, to experience Medea's wrath and
sorrow, were channeled into that monologue that erupted from
her . . . But then her arms sank, her voice grew graver, and my
wife became the Law. Her language was the language of tribu-
nals, lawyers, prosecutors. Frozen, fixed in an accusatory posture, stiff in the black dress that was now sagging, she warned
me that she had ways of keeping me tied down indefinitely,
that she would drag our divorce on down the most winding
and sinuous paths, confuse me with perfidious legal niceties
and recondite proceedings to keep me from returning to the
home of that woman she now denominated, preposterously,
Your Atala. She looked like a majestic statue, almost stripped
of femininity, rooted to the green carpet like an obdurate
Power, like the very incarnation of Justice. I asked her if it was
true that she was pregnant. And then, Themis became mother,
patted her belly desolately, bent over the life gestating in her
entrails as though to defend it from my vileness, and burst into
humble, almost childlike tears, turning her eyes from me,
wounded and sobbing from deep within, so softly I could
hardly hear her moan. When she was calmer, she stared
straight at the wall, seeming to contemplate some remote object; then she struggled to her feet and walked to her bedroom,
closing the door behind her. Exhausted from this crisis, in need
of fresh air, I went downstairs. At the end of the steps was the
street.

35

(Later)

I am accustomed to walking in time with my own breath, and
it never ceases to amaze me that those around me come and go,
crisscrossing on the broad sidewalk, at a rhythm foreign to their
organic will. They choose this pace rather than another because
their stride responds to the fixed idea of reaching a corner in
time to see the green bulb light up that will allow them to cross

the avenue. At times, I note a greater-than-average haste in the multitude that emerges every few minutes from the subway, constant as a pulse; but soon the ordinary, agitated tempo between the traffic lights returns. No longer able to conform to the laws of this collective movement, I go slowly, close to the shop windows, along which exists a sort of zone of indulgence for the old, the invalid, and the idle. In the narrow, sheltered spaces between one window and another, or in the alley between two homes, I find the occasional resting being, stunned, like a stationary mummy. In a kind of niche is a waxen-faced woman in an advanced stage of pregnancy; a black man in a ratty overcoat tries out his just-purchased ocarina in a redbrick sentry box; a dog in a pothole shivers between the shoes of a drunk who has fallen asleep standing up. I reach a church, where the notes of a Gradual played on the organ invite me into the penumbras of incense smoke. Liturgical Latin resounds in deep echoes beneath the vaults of the ambulatory. I look at the faces turned to the officiant, reflecting the yellow of the candles: none of the congregation this stifling evening service has brought in understands a word of what the priest is saying. They are oblivious to the beauty of his words. Since the schools have cast Latin aside, deeming it useless, what I am witnessing now is the performance, the theater, of cumulative incomprehension, a pit of dead words growing deeper by the year between the altar and the faithful. The Gregorian chant soars: *Justus ut palma florebit: Sicut cedrus Libani multiplicabitur: plantatus in domo Domini in atriis domus Dei nostri.* The text, unintelligible to those present, is accompanied by music that for the majority has ceased to be music: a chant heard but not listened to, dead like the language itself. Seeing the foreignness, the alienation of the men and women gathered here before words spoken and chanted to them in an unknown language, I realize the unconscious state in which they apprehend this mystery is common to almost everything they do. When people marry here, exchange rings, hand over wedding coins, and the guests throw rice at their heads, they know nothing of the millenary symbolism of their gestures. They look for the fève in the king cake, take almonds to a baptism, cover a fir tree with lights and garlands, but they know not what a fève is or the reason behind the almond or the name of the tree they are bejeweling. Men here take pride in preserving traditions whose origins are lost, traditions that are generally reduced to the automatism of collective reflex—bearing objects of unknown purpose covered in inscriptions that ceased to speak forty centuries ago. Whereas in the world I will now return to, there is no gesture whose significance is unknown: the dinner over the tomb, the purification of the dwelling, the masked dance, the herb bath, the dowry, the challenge dance, the veiled mirror, the propitiatory drumming, the devils' dance on Corpus Christi, all are practices whose implications are fully understood. I look up at the frieze of the public library standing in the square like an ancient temple: in its triglyphs is carved a bucranium sketched by some diligent architect who likely didn't realize this ornament, come down from the night of the ages, is an emblem of the hunter's trophy sticky with congealed blood that the head of the family used to hang over the door of his dwelling. Back in the city, I find it replete with ruins that are more ruins than ruins proper. Wherever I look, I see sick columns and agonizing buildings, with the last classical entablatures carved in this century and the last of the desiccated Renaissance acanthus leaves in orders that new architecture has abandoned without substituting new orders or any grand style at all. Palladio's beautiful inspirations, Borromini's ingenious rigor, have lost all meaning in these facades made with trimmings of dead cultures soon to be drowned in the surrounding cement. And over these roads of concrete emerge extenuated men and women who have sold another day's worth of their time to the companies that feed them. They have lived another day without living it, and will now gather their strength to live another tomorrow that will not be lived either, unless they run away—as I used to do at this very hour—into the din of the dancehalls and the bewilderment of liquor, finding themselves still more dismayed, more forlorn, more fatigued at sunrise. I have reached the door to the *Venusberg*, the place Mouche and I came to drink so many times, with its neon sign in Gothic letters. I follow the diversion seekers down into the basement, with its walls painted with scenes of arid, airless plains, with skeletons, crumbling arches, bicycles without riders, crutches sustaining what look like phalluses of stone, and in the foreground, as though writhing in the pit of despair, old, half-flayed men seemingly ignorant of the bloodless Gorgon whose ribs are torn open over a stomach devoured by green ants. Farther off, a metronome, an hourglass, and a seashell rest on the cornice of a Greek temple with columns of female legs sheathed in black leggings with red garters for astragals. The bandstand rises over a wood-and-stucco structure with bits of metal lined with small, illuminated grottoes featuring plaster heads, hippocamps, anatomical plates, and a mobile of two wax breasts on a spinning disk, their nipples repeatedly grazed each time they pass under the middle finger of a marble hand. In a larger niche are blown-up photos of Ludwig of Bavaria, the equerry Hornig, and the actor Josef Kainz playing Romeo over panoramic views of the rococo Wagnerian castles—in the Munich style, essentially— of that king made famous by assorted paeans to madness that had long grown stale, even if Mouche had been loyal to them until recently in opposition to all she disparaged beneath the name *the bourgeois spirit*. The smooth ceiling is like the dome of a cavern, with irregular green spots from fungi and leaks. Refamiliarized with the setting, I observe the people around me. On the dance floor, a tangle of bodies, disjointed arms and legs malaxate one another like the elements of magma, of a lava moved by an inner force, edging in and out to a blues song reduced to simple rhythms. The lights go down, and the darkness stimulates embraces, pointless intimacy, contacts stymied by silk or wool, bringing a new sorrow to this collective movement that recalls a buried rite, a dance to level the soil—but there is no soil to level. I go back outside, dreaming of monuments to these people, rutting bulls mounting heifers over plinths adorned with dung in the center of public squares. I stop at the window of an art gallery displaying dead idols stripped of meaning by the absence of worshippers, their enigmatic, sometimes terrible faces scrutinized by many of today's painters who search for the secrets of lost eloquence the way composers of my own generation batter percussion instruments in hopes of recovering the elemental power of primitive rituals. For more than twenty years, an exhausted culture has tried to rejuvenate itself, seeking vitality in incitements to fervor divorced from reason. How risible these people looked, waving around masks from Bandiagara, African Ibejis, and nail-studded fetishes in cities inspired by the *Discourse on Method*, wholly blind to the true significance of the objects they held in their hands. They sought barbarism in things that had never been *barbarous* when they fulfilled their ritual functions in their proper domain—and when a person did dub them *barbarous*, this banished him to the terrain of the *cogito* and Descartes, the very contrary of whatever truth he hoped to find. They thought they could renew occidental music imitating rhythms that had never possessed a *musical* function for their primitive creators. These reflections suggested to me that the jungle, with its resolute men, its chance encounters, its time that had not yet lapsed, had taught me much more about the essence of my art, the deep meaning of certain texts, the unhailed grandeur of certain paths, than the reading of all those books lying dead forever on my shelves. The Pathfinder made me realize the supreme labor a human being can carry out is that of forging a destiny. Because here, in the surrounding multitude that prowls wild and tame all at once, I see many faces but few destinies. And in these faces, every profound yearning, every rebellion, every impulse is inevitably cut short by fear. Fear of some reprimand, fear of the hour, fear of the news, fear of the collective that makes one a servant a hundred times over; fear of one's own body before the interpellations and tensed index fingers of advertising; fear of the womb that accepts the seed, fear of fruit and water; fear of dates, of laws, of slogans, of error, fear of the sealed envelope, fear of what might happen. This street has returned me to the world of Revelation where everyone seems to be waiting for the opening of the Sixth Seal—when the moon became as blood, the stars fell like figs, and the islands were moved out of their places. Everything foretells it: the covers of the magazines in the shop windows, the titles, the letters over the cornices, the phrases shot up into space. It's as if time in this labyrinth and in other, similar labyrinths were already weighed, counted, divvied up. And then I recall with relief the tavern in Puerto Anunciación where the jungle came to meet me in the person of the Pathfinder. Again I taste the flavor of the rustic hazelnut liquor with lime and salt, and the letters with their ornaments of shadow and garlands spelling out the bar's name compose themselves in my brain: *Memories of the Future.* My life here is a transit amid remembrances of the future, of the vast country of licit Utopias, possible Ikarias. My journey has shuffled the notions of preterit, present, and future. What will be yesterday before man has managed to live and contemplate it cannot be the present; this cold, insipid geometry where everything tires and ages a few hours after its birth cannot be the present. The only present I believe in now is the present of that which is intact; the future of that which is created with our face turned toward the glow Genesis. I refuse to be a Wasp-Man, a Nobody-Man, and the rhythm of my existence shall not be marked by a galley master's mallet.

36

(October 20)

Three months ago, the quarto pages of my report were returned to me without explanation, and my legs buckled and I shook all over. I'd fallen into the trap of publicizing the news of my divorce. The newspaper didn't forgive me for all the money it had spent on my rescue or the shame of mounting an edifying spectacle around me for a public whose Reverends now saw me as a lawbreaker and a person worthy of contempt. I wound up selling my story for pennies to a fourth-rate rag, and soon enough, international events made my novelty fade. Here began my struggle with Ruth in her black dress, her lips free of makeup, determined to play the part of a wife wounded in heart and womb before the judges of the nation. Her pregnancy was a false alarm, but instead of simplifying my case, this made matters worse, as her lawyer craftily explained that she had chosen to end her career as soon as the least hint of pregnancy appeared. This made of me a scoundrel who, *pace* the Good Book, builds a house and doesn't inhabit it, plants a vineyard but does not eat of its fruit. The stage, with its War of Secession, that had provided Ruth with endless torments, being mere work, humdrum, an automatic performance, has been reborn as the sanctuary of art, the royal road of her career, which she did not hesitate to step away from, sacrificing glory and fame, to give herself fully to the sublime labor of creating a life—a life my amoral doings have now denied her. I have everything to lose in this imbroglio, which my wife is stretching out indefinitely to put time on her side and force me to return, to forget my escape, my other existence. She is the leading lady in this vast comedy, and Mouche has been booted from the stage. And so, for the past three months, from one afternoon to the next, I turn the same corners, travel between floors, open doors, wait, ask questions of secretaries, sign whatever they want me to sign, then land again on sidewalks tinted red from neon signs. My lawyer's had it with my impatience, and receives me in a foul mood, warning me with an expert's eye that I don't have much left to manage the expenses of my divorce. I've moved from a good hotel to a rooming house for students, and from there to a pension on Fourteenth Street, where the carpets smell like margarine and molten lard. The public relations firm has not forgiven me for my reluctance to return, and Hugo, my former assistant, is now the head of the studio. In vain have I sought some job in this city where each post draws a hundred applicants. Divorced or not, I am running away from here. But I need money to reach Puerto Anunciación; as time passes I need more of it and it grows more important, and all I can find are small orchestration jobs that I carry out half-heartedly, knowing as soon as I'm paid that I'll be penniless again within the week. The city won't let me go. Its streets weave around me like the strings of a net thrown down on me from above. With every week I come closer to being one of those who wash their one shirt at night, cross the snow with holes in their shoes, smoke cast-off butts of cast-off butts, cook in closets. I still haven't fallen that far, but already my room is furnished with the alcohol stove, the aluminum pot, and the packet of oatmeal that speak of something which I contemplate in horror. I spend whole days in bed, trying to forget what looms over me, lost in my readings of the Popol Vuh, Inca Garcilaso, or the travels of Fray Servando de Castillejos. Sometimes I open the *Lives of the Saints*, bound in purple velvet with my mother's initials stamped in gold, and search for the story of Saint Rose, which opened by chance before my eyes the day of Ruth's departure—that day when a stunning convergence of events silently altered so many routes. And whenever I do, I feel bitter when I see those tender little letters that appear heavy with dolorous allusions:

> Oh me! My beloved,
> What delays him?
> He tarries, the sun is falling
> And still he doesn't come.

When the memory of Rosario eats unbearably into my flesh, I take endless walks that always lead me to Central Park, where the scent of the trees with autumn rust dozing in the mist brings me some satisfaction. When I touch the rain-damp bark, it reminds me of the wet logs of our last bonfires, with that acrid smoke that made *Your woman* tear up and laugh by the window she opened to catch her breath. I contemplate the Dance of the Firs, searching in its needles' movement for some propitiatory sign. And it is so impossible to think of anything but my return to her who awaits me that every morning I see prophecies in whatever I come across: a spider is a bad sign, as is a snakeskin exposed in a display case; but when a dog approaches and lets me pet him, it is auspicious. I read horoscopes in the papers. I look in everything for portents. Last night I dreamed I was in a prison with walls as high as a cathedral nave, and between its pillars swayed ropes intended for the strappado; there were thick vaults that multiplied off into the distance, shifting slightly upward, like an object seen in two facing mirrors. There were subterranean shadows that resounded with a horse's dull gallop. When I opened my eyes, the aquatint shades of the scene led me to believe some memory from a museum had imprisoned me briefly in Piranesi's *Carceri d'invenzione*. I didn't think any more about it for the rest of the day. But now, as night falls, I go into a bookstore to leaf through a treatise on the interpretation of dreams: "PRISON. *Egypt*: a position is affirmed. *Occult sciences*: possibility of love from a person from whom no affection is expected or desired. *Psychoanalysis*: linked to circumstances, things, and persons from which one must free oneself." I smell a familiar perfume, and a woman appears next to me in a mirror close by. Mouche is there, looking scornfully at the book. And then she says: "If you want a consultation, I'll give you the friends and family rate." The street is near. Seven, eight, nine steps and I'm out. I don't want to talk to her. I don't want to hear her. I don't want to argue. All my present torments are her fault. But at the same time, a well-known feeling returns to my thighs and groin, and heat seems to rise up the back of my knees. It isn't lust or even excitement, exactly, but muscular acquiescence, weakness in the face of provocation, the same kind that led me to the brothel many times in my adolescence even as my soul struggled to impede my body. Back then I used to feel myself give in, and the memory of it was atrociously painful: terrified, my mind would try to cling to God, to my mother's memory, to the threat of illness, and I would pray the Our Father, but all the while, my feet would guide me slowly, firmly to that room with the bedspread with the red ribbon trim, and I knew that when I caught a whiff of certain oils stirred on the marble of a dressing table, my sex would overcome my will, and my soul would be left unsheltered in the shadows. It would remain there, furious with my body, turned against it till night came, and the obligation to sleep as one brought us together in prayer, and I prepared for the coming days of penitence, anticipating the appearance of those humors and scabs that punish the sins of the flesh. Once more, I was immersed in that adolescent combat as I strolled beside Mouche past the reddish wall of Saint Nicholas's Church. She spoke at great speed, as though to quiet her conscience with words, declaring she was innocent of the scandals in the press, that the journalist in question had abused her trust, et

cetera. Naturally, she hadn't lost the power of looking straight
at you and lying without her eyes clouding over. She didn't reproach me for how I'd treated her when she came down with
malaria; magnanimously, she attributed my behavior to my
promise to find the real instruments. Since she was feverish the
first time Rosario and I embraced in the Greeks' cabin, I wasn't
sure she had seen us. Dejectedly, I accepted her company that
night, to talk to someone, to keep from returning to my badly
lit room, pacing between the walls over the stench of margarine; and, firm in my resolution to thwart her attempts at se-
duction, I let her take me to the *Venusberg*, where I still had
credit on my tab. This saved me from having to confess my
penury, so long as I drank in moderation. But liquor is treacherous, and it undermined my resolve, and I found myself, before it had even gotten very late, in the astrologer's consultation
room with its now finished decor. Several times, Mouche filled
my glass, then asked if she could step into something more
comfortable, and when she returned, she treated me like a fool
for depriving myself of a pleasure that would hurt no one;
whatever I did, she told me, wouldn't compromise me in the
least, and her wiles were so adept that I gave in to her desires
easily, owing in large part to several weeks of far-from-
customary abstinence. Within minutes, I knew the disappointment and despair of those who return to a flesh that no longer
harbors any secrets after what might have been a definitive separation, when nothing is there to unite one with the being that
flesh enfolds. I was sad, angry with myself, lonelier than ever, as
I lay beside her body, gazing at it with renewed contempt. Any
prostitute picked up in a bar, paid for, and possessed would
have been preferable to this. I looked through the open door
and saw the paintings in her consulting room. The night before
she and I left, Mouche had told me, "This journey was already
written on the wall," and that had endued with an air of foreboding these illustrations of Sagittarius, the Argo Navis, and
the Coma Berenices, in which she saw a reflection of herself.
Now, the nature of this foreboding—if indeed it were to be
trusted—became painfully clear in my mind: the Coma Berenices was Rosario, with her uncut virgin hair, while Ruth was

the Hydra that completed the image, lurking behind the piano, which might be taken to be a symbol of my profession. Mouche sensed that my silence, my lack of interest in what I'd retaken were far from favorable to her cause, and to pull me from my thoughts, she grabbed a magazine from the nightstand, a small religious publication a black nun had tried to sign her up for when they were sharing a seat for a few hours on her return flight. Mouche laughed and said she'd agreed to subscribe, thinking perhaps Jehovah was the one true god, when they were flying through bad weather. She opened the modest missionary bulletin printed on cheap paper and placed it in my hands. "I think there's something in it about the Capuchin we met. It has a picture of him." And indeed, in a frame of thick black edging was a portrait of Father Pedro de Henestrosa, most likely taken many years before, showing a face still youthful despite his graying beard. I was moved to read that the friar had decided to travel to the rugged Indian territories he had pointed out to me once from the Ridge of the Petroglyphs. According to the article, a gold prospector newly arrived in Puerto Anunciación declared that Father Pedro de Henestrosa's body had been found mutilated in a canoe that his killers had thrown in the river so this grisly warning would reach the land of the whites. Without answering Mouche's questions, I dressed quickly and fled, certain I would never set foot in her home again. I walked till dawn among the deserted shops, banks, sleepy hospitals, and silent funeral homes. Restless, I took the ferry at dawn, crossed the river, and strolled between the warehouses and customs offices of Hoboken. I think how the butchers must have stripped Father Pedro naked after piercing him with arrows, cracking his thin ribs with a flint knife and tearing out his heart in accordance with ancient rituals. Perhaps they'd castrated him; perhaps they'd skinned him, quartered him, chopped him to pieces like a cow. I imagine his old body mangled, dismembered, torn apart. And yet his wretched death fails to horrify me like the deaths of other men who never knew what they had died for, who cried for their mothers or held up their hands to try and protect a face from which nose and cheeks had already been cut away. Father Pedro de Henestrosa had known the supreme mercy a man can attain: that of going to meet his death, of staring it down, of falling in a struggle that remains, for the vanquished, a victory akin to that of Saint Sebastian pierced by arrows—the confusion, the final vanquishment of death.

37

(December 8)

When the boy guiding me pointed to the house and said there was the new inn, I stopped, startled and sad: it was there, behind those thick walls, beneath a roof covered in windswept grasses, that we had kept vigil over Rosario's father one night. It was there, in the enormous kitchen, that *Your woman* had first approached me, obscurely aware of her significance for my future. A Don Melisio comes out to meet us with his Doña, a black dwarf, who takes three suitcases from the hands of the porters behind me, piles them on her head as though their filling of papers and books, which is nearly bursting the straps, weighed nothing, and takes off toward the courtyard, eyes bulging from their sockets. The rooms are unchanged, but the innocent old prints that adorned them have been taken down. In the courtyard are the same shrubs, and the kitchen still has that bulbous cauldron that echoes like the nave of a cathedral. The vast salon is now a dining room and general store, with large coils of rope in the corners and shelves with canisters of black gunpowder, balms, oils, and medicines in old, obsolete-looking bottles, seemingly destined to cure ailments from a century before. Don Melisio tells me he bought the house from Rosario's mother, and that she and her unmarried daughters have gone to stay with a sister who lives beyond the Andes, eleven or twelve days' journey from here. Again, I marvel at how naturally the gaze of the people from these lands encompasses the wide world, how they roll up their hammocks, throw them over their shoulders, and set off for weeks over road or river, undaunted, as a cultivated man would be, before the dis-

tances made immense by their precarious means of transport.
Pitching a tent, traveling from the estuary to the headwaters of
a river, moving their home to the opposite edge of the plain,
several days away, is all part of the inborn sense of liberty of
these people who see the world without boundaries, fences,
borders. Here, the land is for him who takes it: clear the river's
banks with fire and a machete, place a roof over four forking
branches, and a place becomes a *homestead*, named for whoever proclaims himself its owner, like the ancient Conquistadors who prayed an Our Father before throwing their oars
against the wind. A man becomes no richer thereby, but in
Puerto Anunciación, whoever doesn't believe he knows of a secret vein of gold is pleased to boast of his own estate. The
house is filled with the scent of tonka bean and vanilla, which
puts me in a good mood. Again, there is a fire in the fireplace,
and a tapir ham is roasting, its crackling fat exuding a scent of
unfamiliar acorns. I am back with the fire, the light, the dancing flame, the spark that leaps and in the wisdom of the ember
lives its resplendent old age beneath the grayish wrinkles of
ashes. I ask Doña Casilda, the black dwarf, for a bottle and
glasses, and welcome to my table whoever may remember my
presence here seven months ago—and soon enough, companions surround me. They bring me news from the highlands and
lowlands, the Tuna Fisher, the man of the manatees, the Carpenter who measured coffins with an expert eye, and a slow
boy they call Simón, with Indian traits, who tired of working
as a cobbler in Santiago de los Aguinaldos and stopped here
before traveling farther upriver with a canoe full of merchandise for barter. As soon as I ask, they confirm that Father Pedro
is dead: one of Yannes's brothers found his body, riddled with
arrows and with his chest cavity torn open. As a warning to
those who would tread on their domains, the fierce Indians laid
his disfigured body in a canoe, and it floated over the water to
the shore of a tributary, where the Greek found it swarming
with vultures. "He's the second one to die that way," the Carpenter says, remarking that more than a few of those bearded
clergymen had guts. To my dismay, I hear that the Pathfinder
was in Puerto Anunciación two weeks back. They repeat the

rumors about what he might possess or what he's looking for in the jungle. Simón says he discovered people in the unexplored regions near the headwaters who weren't gold hunters, but had settled and were building houses and working the land. Someone else mentions a man who's founded three cities named Santa Inés, Santa Clara, and Santa Cecilia, after his three elder daughters' patron saints. By the time the dwarf, Doña Casilda, has brought us the third bottle of hazelnut brandy, Simón is offering to take me in his canoe to the place where I found the Curator's instruments. To avoid telling him the purpose of my trip, I say I'm looking to collect more drums and flutes. When he leaves me, I will travel on with the same Indian rowers from before, who know the route to my destination. Simón hasn't been through those parts, and only once, from far away, did he see the first counterforts of Grandes Mesetas. I tell him I'll guide him past the Greeks' old mine. After three hours' rowing upriver, we will have to look for that rampart of trees—that wall of trunks, seemingly planted in a straight line—where the tributary opens up. I will keep an eye out for the sign carved in the bark that marks the passage of branches that hang down like a vault. From there, using the compass to be sure we are still heading eastward, we will seek the river where I got caught in the storm on that memorable afternoon. When we reach the place where I found the instruments, I will have to dispense with my companion and travel on with the people from the village. Knowing I will leave tomorrow, I go to bed feeling delighted and relieved. No longer are the spiders weaving webs between the roof beams a bad omen. Just when everything seemed lost *back there*—and how distant everything *back there* now seems!—I sidestepped the legal quagmire, and an opportune bit of inspiration for a mock Romantic concerto for cinema opened a door that allowed me to emerge from the maze. Now I am on the threshold of my chosen homeland, with everything I need for a long spell of work. Out of caution, in obedience to a vague superstition that compels me to admit the worst in order to avoid it, I imagine myself growing tired of what I've come here in search of, and my work making me yearn to go *back there* to see it published. Even knowing that this acceptance of the unacceptable is nothing more than a mental exercise, I am waylaid by fear: fear of all I've seen and suffered, all that has burdened my existence. Fear of pincers, fear of the circles of hell. I don't want to go back to creating bad music, fully aware that bad music is what I am making. I am running away from pointless professions, from talking as anesthesia, from meaningless gestures, from the Apocalypse raining down over everything. I want to feel again the breeze blowing between my thighs, to sink into the cold streams of Grandes Mesetas and turn somersaults underwater to see the live crystal enveloping me tinted bright green in the light of dawn. Most of all, I want to hold Rosario with the whole of my body, feel her warmth over my throbbing flesh, and when my hands recall her knee pits, her shoulders, the soft profundity beneath her short, stiff fur, desire's thrusting is almost painful in its urgency. I smile, recalling that I have escaped the Hydra and rowed aboard the Argo Navis, and now that the rain has passed, she of the Coma Berenices dwells in the foothills of the Rubrics of the Flood, gathering herbs she used to soak in jars to brew effervescent potions, ennobled by the tranquil moonlight or the clear north wind at dawn. I return to her more aware than ever of my love for her after all the recent Trials I have passed through: the theater, the fakery of elsewhere. Here, a more pressing question arises as regards my wanderings through the Kingdom of this World—the only question, in the end, that admits no dilemmas: whether I or others will be the master of my time, whether I am prepared to live rather than row alongside the galley slaves. So long as my eyes are open, my hours are mine in Santa Mónica de los Venados. My steps are mine, and I shall leave them where I choose.

38

(December 9)

The sun has just emerged over the trees as we dock at the Greeks' former mine. Their house is abandoned. Just seven months have

passed since I was here, and the jungle has taken over everything. The hut where Rosario and I embraced for the first time
has burst from the pressure of plants growing inside it, which
have lifted the roof and split the walls, turning the dwelling
into a mass of dead leaves and rotting timbers. The rapids tore
through here, and the lands were flooded. With the unseason-
able rains, the waters never sank, and a fringe of damp land
still borders the banks covered with branches and saplings
from the forest. Over them twirl myriad yellow butterflies in
hosts so dense that if you struck them with a stick, it would
come away as yellow as sulfur. Now I understand where those
migrations come from like the one I saw in Puerto Anunciación,
when an interminable cloud of wings darkened the sky. The
water stirs and a school of fish leap, bump, tumble, soar over
our boat, piercing the current with leaden fins and tails that
buffet with a sound like applause. A flock of herons passes in a
dense triangle, and all the birds call out in concert, as though
responding to an order. This omnipresence of birds, placing the
frights of the jungle under the sign of the wing, calls to mind for
me the importance of the many roles the Bird plays in mythologies of the New World. From the Spirit-Bird of the Eskimos
that gives its first squawk at the Pole on the uppermost point of
the continent to the flying heads with wings for ears of the
Tierra del Fuego, all along the coasts are ornaments of wooden
birds, birds painted on stone, birds drawn on the soil—so big,
they can be seen only from the mountaintops—in an iridescent
parade of majesties of the air: Thunder-Bird, Dew-Eagle, Sun-
Bird, Messenger-Condor, Meteor-Parrots hurtling over the vast
Orinoco, zentzontles and quetzals and their lords, the great
triad of plumed serpents: Quetzalcoatl, Gucumatz, and Culcán.
We are already floating onward, and as the midday swelter
turns unbearable over those yellow, bubbling waters, I point to
Simón's left at the wall of trees closing the riverbank for as far
as the eye can see. We approach slowly, looking for the sign that
marks the entrance to our route. Eyes fixed on the tree trunks,
I watch out for the incision of the three Vs in a vertical row—a
sign that could stretch on into infinity—at the height of a man's
chest if he were standing on the surface of the water. Simón

rows slowly, asking me questions now and again. We drift on. So attentively do I stare, do I force myself to keep staring, that my eyes soon weary of seeing identical trunks pass. Doubts assail me: Have I *seen* it without realizing? Might I have gotten distracted for a few seconds? I demand we go back, but find nothing beyond a pale blotch or a streak of sunlight on a stretch of bark. Ever calm, Simón follows my orders with no complaint. The canoe scrapes the trees, and at times I push it back from the bank, pressing the blade of my machete into a tree. The search for the sign in this endless succession of vegetation leads to a sort of vertigo. And yet I tell myself I am not searching in vain. None of the trees have anything on them resembling a row of three Vs. And these exist, and what is carved on a tree trunk cannot be erased, so we will find them. We row for another half hour. Then I see a black spur that emerges from the jungle, so singular and irregular in form that I would have remembered it had I ever been here before. The entrance must lie behind us. I motion to Simón to turn back, and we retrace our path. I imagine he's giving me an ironic look, and the thought of this irritates me no less than my own impatience. I turn my back to him and go on examining the trees. If I've overlooked some sign, I will certainly see it now, when we are floating alongside this wall of green for the second time. There were two trunks, like the two jambs of an open door with a lintel of leaves. On the left one, halfway up, was the symbol. When we left, the sun struck us head-on. Now, as we travel in the opposite direction, the shadows stretch longer and longer. I am anguished at the thought that night may fall before I've found what I'm looking for, that we'll have to stop and return tomorrow. In itself, the delay wouldn't be so bad, but it strikes me as an inauspicious sign. Everything has gone right of late, and I refuse to accept any obstacles. Simón goes on staring at me, ironic and impassive. At last, just to say something, he points at a stand of trees and asks if the entrance lies over there. "It's possible," I respond, knowing it isn't. "Possible doesn't sound like a verdict," he responds sententiously, and just then, I fall overboard, because the boat has struck a tangle of lianas head-on. Simón stands, grabs the punt pole, and sinks it in the water, looking for solid ground to push the canoe backward. In that instant, just long enough for the rod to get wet, I grasp why we haven't found the symbol and why we never will: the punt pole, nine feet in length, can't find ground to push off of, and my companion has to chop the lianas away with a machete. When we are moving again and he looks at me, he sees the consternation on my face and comes over, thinking something's happened. I remember when we came here with the Pathfinder, *the oars touched bottom the whole time.* This means the river is still flooding, and *the mark we're looking for is underwater.* I tell Simón what I've just realized. He laughs and says he'd already guessed as much, but didn't say anything *out of respect*, thinking I must have taken the level of the water into account. Afraid of his response, stretching out my words, I ask if he thinks the waters will soon subside enough that the symbol will be visible. "In April or May," he responds, placing me face-to-face with an implacable reality. Until April or May, the narrow gate to the jungle will be closed. After emerging victorious from the trial of nocturnal terrors, of the tempest, I've confronted the decisive trial of the temptation to return. From the other end of the world, Ruth had dispatched Mandatories who had come down one morning from the sky, with eyes of yellow glass and headphones around their necks, to tell me that everything I needed to express myself was only three hours away by plane. And I had climbed into the clouds, to the Neolithic men's astonishment, all for a few reams of paper, never suspecting I was being kidnapped by a woman mysteriously aware that only the most extreme means would give her a last chance to have me on her terrain. Over the past few days, I felt Rosario's presence. Sometimes at night, I thought I could hear her soft breathing as she slept. Now, with the symbol covered, the gate closed, this presage seems to be vanishing. Seeking the bitter truth in words that my companion listens to without understanding, I tell myself that you dwell in ignorance as you embark upon new roads, and do not recognize marvels as you live them: stepping out past the familiar, beyond what man has cordoned off, you grow vain in the privilege of discovery, and think yourself the owner of unknown paths, and you tell yourself you can repeat this feat whenever you wish. And one day, you are foolish enough to retrace your steps, thinking that the exceptional can be exceptional again, but when you return, you find the landscape changed, the reference points erased, the informants' faces different . . . The slapping of the oars startles me from my despair. Night fills the forest, the plagues of insects thicken and hum at the bottom of the trees. Simón has stopped listening to me and floats toward the center of the current, hoping to return quickly to the Greeks' former mine.

39

(December 30)

I'm working on Shelley's text, easing certain passages to give them the feel proper to a cantata. I've shortened Prometheus's long lament at the magnificent opening of the poem, and busy myself now framing the scene of the Voices with its irregular stanzas and the dialogue between Titan and the Earth. In doing so, I am merely attempting to forget my impatience, to distract myself from the single idea, the single purpose that has held me here in Puerto Anunciación for three weeks now. Word has it a local guide is soon to return from the Río Negro, a man expert in the pass I need to take or other waterways that can get me to my destiny. But men here are masters of their time, and a wait of fifteen days is no cause for impatience. "He'll be back . . . He'll be back," the dwarf Doña Casilda responds as I have my morning coffee and ask if there's any news about my guide. I keep hoping the Pathfinder will need remedies or seeds and will show up unexpectedly, and for that same reason, I remain in the village, ignoring Simón's tempting offer to take a boat through the northern waterways. The slow passage of days would delight me in Santa Mónica de los Venados, but here it is tedious, as my mind eschews all serious labor. Moreover, what I wish to work on is my *Threnody*, and I left my notes for it behind with Rosario. I could try to begin the composition afresh, but I was so pleased with my work there, with the spontaneity of accent, that I shrink at the thought of starting cold, with a critical eye, struggling from memory, harried all the time by my desire to journey onward. Each afternoon I walk to the rapids and lie on the stones shaken by the waters rushing through the creeks, shoals, and sinkholes, and its thundering relieves my irritation here where the sculptures of foam insulate me from everything around, bubbling into forms that buckle and dissipate in the intermittent currents but maintain a volume, a consistency whose constant, vertiginous mutation remains fresh and alive, something you can stroke like the spine of a dog or place your lips against like the swell of an apple. Noise hammers the underbrush, the island of Santa Prisca unites with its inverted reflection, and the sky drowns in the bottom of the river. To the staccato rhythm of a dog that always barks with the same high-pitched diapason, all the dogs in the neighborhood intone a canticle of howls, which I listen to with rapt attention, walking back on the rocky path, and from one afternoon to the next I have realized its duration never changes, and that it inevitably ends as it begins, with two barks—never more—from the mysterious dog shaman leading the pack. After discovering the dances of monkeys and certain birds, I consider how a recording of the calls of domesticated animals might reveal an obscure musical meaning not so far from the chant of the witch doctor that awed me one afternoon in the Selva del Sur. For five days, the dogs of Puerto Anunciación have been howling in this way: their uniform baying responds to some order, and at an unmistakable signal, they go silent. Then they return home, lie down under the chairs, listen to the people talking, or lick their bowls, calm until the paroxysm comes, the females go into heat, and men wait with resignation for the animals of the Alliance to bring their reproductive rites to an end. This is what I am thinking of as I reach the first street in the village, where two strong hands land on my back, turning me around so brutally that I shout in pain. I writhe away from this ill-advised jostling, ready to throw a punch. But then a cackle erupts, I recognize it, and my anger turns to joy. Yannes hugs me, pressing into me with his sweaty shirt. I grab his arm, as though fearing he might escape, and take him to my hotel, where Doña Casilda serves us a bottle of hazelnut brandy. I feign to flatter him with interest in his doings to stoke the fire of friendship, and taking an affectionate tone, turn as soon as possible to the one thing that interests me: Yannes must know the flooded tributary; he was with us when we rowed through it; and he knows the forest well, and will surely find the Gate without needing to look for the triple incision. At any rate, the water likely subsided these past few weeks. But something in the Greek's demeanor has changed: his eyes, so penetrating and self-assured, seem unquiet, mistrustful, and never rest long in one place. He seems nervous, impatient, and it's hard to converse with him logically. When he says something, he stumbles or hesitates, and never lingers on a single idea the way he always did before. Finally, with a conspiratorial air, he begs me to take him to my room. He locks the door, makes sure the windows are closed, and in the lamplight shows me an empty chloroquine bottle containing crystals that look like smoked glass. He tells me softly that these quartzes are sentinels of diamonds: if you find them, there is always treasure nearby. And somewhere, he had sunk his pick and struck a spectacular deposit. "Fourteen-carat diamonds," he tells me in a muffled voice. "Some of them must be even bigger." Surely he's dreaming already of a recently discovered hundred-carat diamond that has addled the brains of all those seekers of El Dorado who go on roaming this continent and have not yet relinquished the quest for those same treasures sought by Philipp von Hutten. Yannes's find has unnerved him, and he is going now to the capital to stake a legal claim to the mine, terrified that someone will discover the remote vein in his absence. Apparently there have been cases of two prospectors hitting upon the same small stretch of riches on this country's immense map. None of this means anything to me, and I raise my voice to distract him and mention the one thing that matters to me. "Sure, when I'm back," he responds. "When I'm back . . ." I beg him to delay the journey, to take me out this very night, before sunup. But the Greek tells me the *Manatee* has just reached port and he must ship out tomorrow at midday. No discussion is possible.

He can think of nothing but his diamonds, and when he falls quiet, it is to avoid speaking of them, because he's afraid Don Melisio or the dwarf is listening. Bitter, I resign myself to another delay: I will wait for him to return, and he will soon, spurred on by greed. To be certain he won't forget me here, I offer to help him open the mine. He embraces me boisterously, calls me his brother, and takes me to the same tavern where I first met the Pathfinder; he orders another bottle of hazelnut brandy, and to make his discovery seem more alluring, he offers me supposedly secret details about where he found the quartz that pointed to his treasure. In this way, I learn something I hadn't expected, that *he found the vein while returning from Santa Mónica de los Venados*, a city previously unknown to him, which he happened upon by accident and stayed in for two days. "Idiot people," he says. "Stupid people, they got gold close and don't dig it; I wanted to work; they said kill me with rifle." I grab Yannes by the shoulders and shout questions at him about Rosario, anything, her health, what she looks like, what she's doing. "Wife of Marcos," the Greek responds. "Pathfinder happy, she pregnant now . . ." I can no longer hear him. Cold needles rise up on my skin, emerging from within me. I struggle to bring my hands to the bottle, clutch it, and it seems to burn me. I fill my glass slowly and spill liquor down a throat that doesn't know how to swallow and coughs until its fibers tear. When I catch my breath, I look at myself in the mirror in the back of the room blackened by flies and see a body sitting next to the table that may as well be empty. If I order it to move, to walk away, I am not certain it will obey me. But eventually, the being inside me moaning, lacerated, flayed, rubbed with salt, pushes an attempt at a babbled protest up my raw gullet. I say something to Yannes, but I don't know what. I hear the voice of another man talking about his right to *Your woman*, saying external factors forced him to delay his return, trying to justify himself, appealing his case, as though standing before a tribunal determined to destroy him. Distracted from his diamonds by this broken timbre, by the implorations of a voice determined to turn back time and undo what's been done, the Greek looks at me with an astonishment that soon turns to compassion: "She no Penelope. Young, strong woman, beautiful, need husband. She no Penelope. Nature woman here need man . . ." The truth, the agonizing truth—I understand now—is that the people of these climes never once believed in me. I was provisional, and nothing more. Even Rosario must have seen me as a Visitor, incapable of remaining indefinitely in the Valley of Stopped Time. I remember now the strange look she used to give me when I spent days writing feverishly in a place where all writing was superfluous. New worlds must be lived rather than explained. Those who live here do so not from intellectual conviction, but because they believe the easy life is this one and none other. They prefer this present to the present of the makers of the Apocalypse. He who tries to understand too much, who suffers the anguish of conversion, who cloaks renunciation in an embrace of the customs of people who forge their destinies over this primordial silt, fighting tooth and nail against the mountains and trees, remains vulnerable to the sway of the world he has left behind. I have traveled through the ages; I passed through bodies, through the times of bodies, never knowing I had wedged myself in the narrow confines of the widest door. A life among marvels, the founding of cities, the freedom that thrived in the Land of Enoch among these Inventors of Trades, were realities of a grandeur ill-suited to my slight person as a counterpointist ever on the lookout for repose that would permit me to triumph over death in the ordering of neumes. I have tried to straighten the destiny made crooked by my weakness, and what emerged from me was a song—a song now cut short—that took me down my former roads with a body covered in ash, incapable of being someone other than who I was. Yannes hands me a ticket to leave with him tomorrow aboard the *Manatee*. I will sail, then, toward the task that awaits me. I raise my burning eyes to the florid sign of *Memories of the Future*. In two days, the century will have finished another year, and none of the people around me now will care. Here you can get along fine without knowing the year you live in, and those who say a man can't escape his era are wrong. The Stone Age, like the Middle Ages, is here in the present day. The spectral manses of Romanticism full of amorous strife remain open. But none of this is destined for me, because the only race that may not flee the clutches of chronology is the race of artists, who must hurry past the tangible testimonies of the day before and anticipate the songs and forms of those still to come, leaving new tangible testimonies in full awareness of what has been done up to the present day. Marcos and Rosario know nothing of history. The Pathfinder is in its first chapter, and I might have remained beside him if my profession had been any other than composer—a profession suited to the last of the race. All that remains to be seen now is whether I will go deaf and lose my voice amid the hammer blows of the Galley Master who already is waiting for me somewhere. Today, the vacation of Sisyphus has ended.

Behind me, someone says the river has fallen notably in recent days. The submerged stones are reappearing, and the rapids are dotted now with rocky crags coated in soft algae that perish in the light. The trees on the shores seem taller now that their roots sense the heat of the sun. On a scaly trunk of ocher streaked with bright green, some three handbreadths below the water now that the rapids are settling, a Sign carved in the Bark with the point of a knife is starting to appear.

Note

If the setting of the first chapters of the present book need not be specified, if I have chosen not to situate in any precise location the Latin American capital and the provincial cities that appear later, since they are mere prototypes composed of elements common to many countries, still, the author feels a need to clarify, in response to legitimate curiosity, that beginning with Puerto Anunciación, the landscape described corresponds very precisely to places little known and hardly ever photographed—if they have been photographed at all.

The river, which in the earlier sections might be any large river in the Americas, is afterward very clearly the headwaters of the Orinoco. The Greeks' mine could be situated not far from its confluence with the Vichada. The fork marked by the triple incision in the form of a V that signals the entrance to the hidden tributary exists, and with this very Sign, at the mouth of the Caño de la Guacharaca, two hours upriver by boat along the Vichada: it winds beneath vaults of vegetation, leading to a village of Guahibo Indians who dock their boats in a hidden cove.

The storm occurs in an area that might be the Raudal de la Muerte. The Capital of Forms is Monte Autana, with its profile like a Gothic cathedral. From there, the landscape of the Upper Orinoco and the Autana transforms into the Gran Sabana, a view of which appears in various passages in chapters 3 and 4. Santa Mónica de los Venados could be Santa Elena de Uairén in the first years of its founding, when the easiest way to reach the newly founded city was upriver from Brazil, a seven-day journey through turbulent rapids. Since that time, many similar villages and towns have been born—still without geographical coordinates—throughout the American jungle. Not long ago, two famous French explorers discovered one otherwise unknown that was remarkably similar to Santa Mónica de los Venados, and a man lived there whose story was like that of Marcos.

The chapter of the Conquistadors' Mass takes place in a real Piaroa village near the Cerro Autana. The Indians described on day twenty-three are Chirichanos from the Upper Caura. An explorer made phonograph recordings—the record exists in Venezuela's folklore archives—of the Witch Doctor's Threnody.

The Pathfinder, Montsalvatje, Marcos, and Father Pedro are characters every traveler comes across in the great theater of the jungle. All correspond to a reality—just as the myth of El Dorado, fed by deposits of gold and precious stones, corresponds to a certain reality. As for Yannes, the Greek miner who traveled with nothing but his copy of the *Odyssey*, suffice it to say the author has changed nothing, not even his name. I must add simply that, along with the *Odyssey*, he admired above all else Xenophon's *Anabasis*.

A.C.

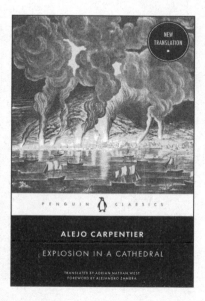